EDGE OF LIGHT

JAY ANTANI

Edge of Light by Jay Antani published by Bandwagon Press

ISBN-978-0-9884193-1-5
Cover design and interior design by Rafael Andres

For Pappa and for Nicolas
the past and the future.

CHAPTER ONE

October 23, 2030

We're on our way to the game when Abby gives me and Conner the news. She'll be moving east with her family after the fall semester, probably in January. With her father out of work and the California fires making her younger brother's breathing worse, it all makes sense. Conner says he's sorry to hear, maybe it's for the best, but I stay quiet. Hard to speak when you feel like you just got sucker punched in the chest.

All through the game, I keep it together, telling myself it won't be so bad, Abby being gone. Maybe she won't leave, maybe there's another way. There's an ache in my chest. I'm thinking ahead to next semester and life without Abby when the field begins to glow and shadows form and shift. I look up, shielding my eyes, and see this *thing*, this blinding object tearing out of the north.

People scream and gasp. Cries of awe go up around me in the bleachers. I can't utter a sound. It's like a dragon just invaded our skies, racing southward, a ragged arc trailing behind it. Dread surges into my chest. It's the difference between watching someone dying in a movie and knowing for sure that you're about to die—for real.

It streaks death-ray-white over Oberon Heights and goes on for what seems like miles and miles. We stare, astonished, and murmurs run through the crowd. A few are aiming their phones at it when, trailing away to the edge of sight, the glowing thing blows open, and the whole world turns inside-out. Violet evening becomes bright-white afternoon, and everyone's ducking for cover! Abby leans into me. I reach out for Conner, and, huddled together, we all brace for radiation. Are we about to be burnt to a crisp?

Seconds pass. The glow fades. We're here! I'm alive!

I collect my breath, hearing howls and claps and nervous laughter.

"What the—?" are my only words when the blast wave hits: a sound so loud you're sure it's the last thing you're ever going to hear. Glass shatters near and far. The field goes half-dark. Car alarms go off all over the place. And a warm gust blows through us, above the noise. Out of the corner of my eye, I catch birds scattering.

Dozens of smaller explosions, like artillery fire—*pop! pop-pop! pop! pop-pop-pop! pop!*—sound from the far southern distance. The booms settle and, eventually, all I hear are dogs barking, a child crying somewhere. On the field, in the bleachers, stunned, heavy silence. It's much darker now, and in the light of their phone screens, a terrified man talks to a woman, nervously laughing, below us.

Conner looks back at me. "Had to be a comet or some shit, right?" He's got a slightly crazy look like he's giddy *and* freaked out. Abby is sure it was a missile. But I feel like we just saw and heard the gates of hell open.

As the wind and the noise die down, people start climbing up the bleachers to get a better look southward. From the bottom of my heart, a fear starts to rise and fill my being: Is this World War III? Are we all about to die?

"Check it out!" Conner's on his feet now and staring south. There's a red-orange aura, a fingerprint stamped on the horizon, which flares for a few more seconds and gets fainter and fainter. Once it's gone, we're aware of the dark: only a couple of lights over the field didn't get blown out.

The stands fill with more shouts and the glow of phone screens. I can feel bodies. Elbows and feet crushing down the stands. "Move," somebody in the stands yells. "Out of the way!" The players on the field, the cheerleaders, everyone on the sidelines is making for the far side of the field where people are scaling the high chain-link fence and over into the parking lot.

I check on Abby, crouched down, her hands in her hair, covering her ears.

"You okay?" are the first words out of my mouth.

But she only looks at me, unsure what to say.

"Let's get up above this crowd," Conner says. "Get a better look around."

I get up, point to the top of the stands. "How about the announcer's booth?"

Police and ambulance sirens cut the air from all directions. We push our way up the ten or twelve rows to the announcer's booth. We peer through the blown-out windows. It's a cave, darkness in the greater dark. Glass and debris cover the bleachers below the booth. The vice principal and gym teacher, who were just announcing the game a couple of minutes ago, are gone.

Abby and I try to make calls. She's trying to reach her parents. I'm calling my mom in the ER. Her shift started at 2 p.m. today. CALL FAILED.

"Anything?" I ask her. She shakes her head. And there's this dread in my heart like we're trapped and cut off from our worlds. From the look on her face, I can tell she's feeling it too.

After Conner and I brush off shards from the window ledge, I scramble up onto it, hoisting myself onto the roof. I reach down and help the others up.

Whole neighborhoods are in pitch dark—black, bottomless wells around rims and patches of light. The horizon is a monstrous ink-blackness behind clouds of smoke and dust. Above us, we can still see the vapor trail, dissipating now, twisty and bulbous. I've seen barium x-rays of intestines that look like that.

The flashlights from phones bob and dance like manic fireflies at the bottom of the bleachers where a restless bottleneck is trickling through the gate. People are hollering and crying to get through, and what seems like a fight between two guys—maybe they're high or drunk—is brewing while a third tries to pull them apart, laughing. "I don't like the look of that," I say to Abby, and we turn our attention directly below us to the scaffolding behind the bleachers. Anyone who doesn't want to deal with the pileup at the gate is taking their chances by climbing down.

We lower ourselves off the booth, right up against the railing and take a look. More and more people—mostly kids I've seen around at school—are on the scaffold, a colony of panicked ants crawling thirty feet to the ground. Two lose their grip and fall, grunting as they land in the hard dirt.

We lean out over the railing and consider the scaffold when we hear, "Here goes nothing," and watch Conner swing one leg over the railing, then the other.

"Dude!" I grab at his shoulder. The guy gets queasy at the mere *thought* of heights.

He pushes out a breath. "First rule of life: don't look down," he says.

As he begins lowering himself, Abby tells me her phone's going off.

She presses a hand to one ear, answers her phone. "Dad? Yeah, I'm here!"

As Abby listens to her call, Conner, who's been frozen in place on the scaffold while people are scrambling down all around him, says he'll meet us down on the ground. I give him a thumbs up. "Right behind you!"

Abby begins to explain into her phone where we are when she stops and holds the phone away, brings it to her ear again. "Hello?" Again, staring at her phone: "Shit!"

Her family's okay, she tells me, and her parents are on their way to pick up her brother at a friend's house—

We hear a clang, like a bolt popping, a short metallic groan. Screams follow: in the lights of phones and cars, we see one of the wide struts of the scaffolding broken loose—maybe from the weight of everybody—and it's dangling, half-bent and sticking out like a mangled arm. People drop like dominoes all the way down.

"Conner!" I shout. Abby and I train the lights of our phones, searching the bodies moaning and stumbling back onto their feet. "Conner!"

People, shouting over and at each other, begin limping toward the sidewalk. We call down for Conner again but can't see or hear any sign of him.

We consider scaling down the scaffolding too, chance the broken strut.

"That way," Abby tells me, pointing down the bleachers to the front gate where the vice principal and gym teacher are directing crowds toward the exit.

Once we're out on the street, we scan for Conner: still nothing. I check my phone again. Signal's still weak. I try the hospital: CALL FAILED. Abby tries her parents: CALL FAILED. I imagine all the injured on their way to ERs all over the city. I want to see my mom right now. Need to know she's okay.

I'm doing all I can to stay calm. Beneath all this is the feeling nothing will ever be the same.

Crowds and police are everywhere. A police chopper circles a mile south. Down below, cars are on a crawl all the way to Skyland Boulevard where the traffic light is blinking red, out of service. We can hear the shrill staccato of a traffic cop's whistle somewhere beyond the cars.

We cross the street behind the stands and look for Conner. No sign of him anywhere. We yell for him, cross from one side of the block to the other.

"You think we left him back by the stands?" I ask and picture him lying there, injured in a bush somewhere.

"But there was no sign of anybody. It was pretty much cleared out."

We walk east toward Skyland and cross it toward our neighborhoods. I try to reach him on my phone but no luck.

Half the streetlights are blown out. Lot of the houses are dark too. Streets are dotted with flashlights of people's phones. There's a smell in the air that's part burning tire and part electrical short.

Even with the sirens coming from all directions and the garbled commands of a police officer on a loudspeaker, the crowds here—pedestrians, neighbors, people from the game—are all weirdly quiet like they're in a panicky daze, like everyone's holding their breath; edgy, waiting for something—like an aftershock, another explosion. That's when I feel Abby's hand slip into mine. Even with all that's going on, the feel of her hand, slender and firm and as cold with fear as mine, is a charge that goes through my heart. Neither of us says anything. We hold on to each other, side by side, weaving through knots of pedestrians for a couple more blocks before we find an opening in the crowds and pick up our pace.

"It's going to be all right, Ab," I say. But the words do nothing; the sight and sound of that explosion's got me too freaked out. Did a bioweapon just go off and poison the whole city? Will we find Conner?

Hundreds of people are on the move out here. As we pass Carlton Park on our right, we see the flashlights of neighbors who've gathered here in the dark.

"Abigail!" A block ahead, from the park side, Abby's mom is running toward us.

Abby lets go of my hand, and we break into a run. "Oh my God," she says, giving her mom a hug. "How're you guys? How's Danny?"

"He's in the car," her mom says. "We're fine. Let's get you home." Her mom, tears in her eyes, presses her hands to her daughter's face and hugs her again. "Are you all right?"

Across the street, in the haze and headlights, we see her father waving to us from their car.

"Dev, hop in," her mom offers. "We'll get you home."

"It's okay. I'm only a couple of blocks from here. I'll be okay."

Abby's mom looks unsure, but then her eyes soften, and her mouth forms a tight smile. "You be careful. Got it?"

"I do. I want to keep a lookout for Conner." We explain about what happened.

"You need us, you know where to find us," she tells me. "Don't hesitate, do you hear?"

I nod. "Of course, Ms. Mendes."

"Any time. You need a place tonight? Is your mom home?"

"I can't get ahold of her. She's working tonight. I want to be home in case she shows up."

Abby looks off across the street at her dad and brother in the car for a second then gives me one last hug. I want to tell her goodbye, but as they're getting ready to cross the street, Abby turns, grabs my face, and kisses me. And not on the cheek.

My heart gives a kick against the front of my chest, my breath stops. I feel her mouth for all of two seconds, but already I know it will blaze for eons in my mind.

She steps away, doesn't say a word, and I watch them move across the street. "Uhh," I hear myself saying, "bye!" but all I'm thinking about are her lips. We wave to each other, Abby and I, before she gets into the car and the whole family is waving at me as the car merges in with the slow-moving caravan along the street. And just as suddenly as the kiss, she is gone.

I walk up the block, trying to puzzle out where Conner could be. He figures shit out. He's not the lost-in-a-crowd type. Maybe he's trying to reach his dad. He and his stepmom are on location in Thailand for a film shoot. They're screenwriters. His dad also makes commercials. This is his first big project. They're supposed to be in Thailand for a month, but now, who knows.

My phone goes off. Mom!

"Dev?" Her voice is spotty from the weak signal. "How . . . doing okay? Where . . . you?"

I tell her I'm on my way home and how we saw everything. "It was insane, Mom! The whole world just lit up for a second and then this blast of heat. And all this glass exploded and frickin' sirens and shit. We found our way out, but we lost Conner!" I realize I'm breathing fast and try to slow it down. The line's scratchy and her voice comes through in spots.

"Didn't catch all that, D," I hear her say. "We . . . slammed here . . . will be home as soon as I can." I hear a lot of background noise. People yelling. A voice booming over a P.A. Then she's back on the line: "Listen, I've got to go, sweethea— I will be in touch."

"Sure, Mom. I should be home in a few. Take care of yourself, all right?"

No answer. "Mom, you there?" The line's dead.

I hurry the rest of way, anxious to reach home, which is about halfway down Hamilton. I can still hear the police sirens and, from farther south, the faint chop of helicopters. Otherwise, the street's quiet, and except for a few people around a fender-bender near the top of the street, it's empty. There are signs of damage, windowpanes smashed or blown in, but nothing too bad.

I walk through the gate and up the path to our door. It all looks intact. I step inside, flip the switches. The lights work! And apart from a few picture frames and a broken vase on the floor, things are in one piece. I walk the house, turning on lights and sniffing for signs of a gas leak. My nose detects nothing. The water in the tap is running too.

Now I realize how hungry and parched I am, so I gulp down a couple of glasses of water, devour two bananas and a handful of almonds. There's a signal on my phone, so I text Conner: *You good? What happened?*

Sorry, he texts back after a minute, *after things got crazy, the cops pushed us all back.* Next text: *I waited around but never saw you guys.* We text back and forth like that, both of us surprised that we never spotted each other.

I check my laptop for more news. The internet is choppy, but I'm able to pull up dashcam and smartphone clips from Mexico City: bustling neon streets then, *bam!*, the meteor flashes open like an evil eye and the airburst turns night . . . not into day exactly, but a creepy and phantom version of day—an atomic-bomb version of day—before the light folds into dark again. I keep watching as seconds later, a boom erupts from the phone speaker along with screams from onlookers and the shattering of glass as the camera shakes and goes dark. A Google search confirms So Cal got hit with a blast wave from "a large meteorite that exploded in the lower atmosphere." Not only that. It was one in a *series* of hits, all in the Western Hemisphere. A weather blogger reports that meteor sightings out in the desert have been way up lately. I click to read more, but the signal jams up again.

Feeling a bit survivalist, I find the earthquake kits. From the hall closet, I dig out a flashlight, fresh batteries, and a palm-sized shortwave radio from a plastic bin jammed full of random junk.

In my room, I pop the batteries into the flashlight and the radio. The radio used to belong to my dad—well, *his* dad, in fact—and hasn't been used in years. Not since camping trips up to Yosemite and Tahoe when I was six, seven years old.

I switch on the radio, hear paper-thin voices on waves of garble and fuzz. Searching the dial, I can't find anything but religion and Latin jazz . . . then I hear a newscaster with a British accent: "The unprecedented events occurred between 6:20 and 7:45 p.m. Pacific Standard Time. Witnesses in Los Angeles, Mexico City, Havana, and La Paz in Bolivia reported seeing fireballs, which exploded in the lower atmosphere and sent shockwaves in all directions, shattering glass, triggering minor quakes and knocking out power in many areas. The American disaster-management agency, FEMA, predicts billions of dollars in damage and casualties in the hundreds across the Western Hemisphere. Authorities in the affected countries have mobilized local and federal operations to assess damage." A buzzing drowns out the broadcast, and I click off the radio.

I wonder how Mom is holding up. I hope Conner's okay and wonder if his parents will cut their schedule short and come home early. And Abby: even with all the confusion of tonight, I think of her lips, the feel of her hand in mine.

CHAPTER TWO

When I was seven, I woke in the middle of the night to the sounds of my life being gutted. It took me a few seconds to realize there were strangers in the house. Low voices asking questions. Then came the hard *snap* of the hallway light outlining my closed door. I could hear my mother, hushed and tense.

After sliding out of bed, I cracked open the door. People in jumpsuits were walking in and out of my father's office, their arms loaded with my father's things, followed by two black suits. The first was a normal-sized, dark-haired woman with a dark complexion. Behind her, ducking under the doorway, was the tallest man I'd ever seen, pale, bald, and wide-shouldered. For a brief moment, he turned his head in my direction and his heavy-lidded eyes found me. I shrank back behind the door. Steeling up my courage, I leaned out in the hall to glimpse my mom chatting with the black suits, both their backs to me.

Eventually, Mom noticed me and excused herself. I asked her what was going on, but she ushered me back to bed, said everything was okay, and she would tell me later. Of course, I didn't go to bed. I crept right back to the door and opened it a crack.

From my father's office came the sounds of folders being dumped into boxes, the rummaging of hands, fingers typing on my dad's computer. Why were they here—taking away all his things? Why was our home being invaded?

The agents stood side by side in the living room, folders in their hands and shoulder holsters visible through the front of their suits. I could see them more clearly now through the hallway. Now and then, they'd move aside for the jumpsuited men as they filed out of the office with their loot. Of my mother, I could only see a sliver.

"Did your husband talk at all about his research? What he was working on?" the woman asked.

"Energy research of some kind."

"Anything else?"

"He never really talked about his work. Said it was classified. Can't you just look all that stuff up?"

The woman looked down at the floor. The bald giant just stared at my mom with a bland expression.

"Earlier this evening, there was an accident at a research facility," the woman said. "We believe your husband may have been involved. He was seen entering the facility several hours before it happened. We know that one security guard was killed."

Mom covered her face with her hands. "Where is he?"

Silence.

"We're trying to determine that," the woman said.

"Dev." My mother's voice startled me, and she was staring back at me through the hallway. "Door shut, please. Go to bed."

The news that week said my father died in the explosion, that he'd been wanted in an FBI investigation of a "sensitive military nature." Two other people died that night—a security guard and somebody on the cleaning staff. It wasn't long before the rumors started circulating at school and on social media: "Hey, wasn't your dad like a suicide bomber?" or "Before you friend this dude, heads up—his dad was a terrorist." They made al-Qaeda jokes (low-hanging fruit when you've already got dark hair and brown skin). Bullying and taunts followed. Seventh grade was the hardest. By ninth grade, I knew enough to keep a low profile.

Mom tried her best. She'd meet with the principal and my teachers, tell them what was going on. Mostly, though, she lost herself in her job as a doctor in the ER department at West LA Memorial . . . the way adults lose themselves in things when their lives aren't right.

But Dad's vanishing—the suddenness of it and no explanations or goodbyes—made me obsessed with what had happened to him, to keep him in my life somehow. When I was old enough to comprehend things like the multiverse, quantum physics, and string theory, I'd spend my free hours in seventh and eighth grade in the computer lab looking that stuff up. I also dug out Dad's old astronomy books from the garage and piled them in my room. His handwriting was still scrawled in their margins, a bunch of equations and Greek symbols that I couldn't decipher, but they briefly brought him back to life for me.

In the last year before he vanished, Dad was hardly around. One of the last times I saw him, I asked what he was doing all those days in his lab. Laying his fork down, he turned in his chair and shook his head, as if in disbelief. His eyes shone. "Do you remember when I told you about atoms?"

I nodded and, scrunching one eye closed, I pressed my forefinger and thumb together. "They're reeeaaally small."

He raised his forefinger and turned it upside down. "Pretend the tip of my finger . . . is an atom," and he began whipping the finger around in a circle, like he was whisking eggs with it. "Now you're the other atom," he said and told me to do the same thing but with my finger right-side up. He brought our spinning fingers closer till they tangled together. "Ka*pow*!" he boomed and smashed his hands into mine, both of us laughing. I was glad because we were rarely together and laughing anymore. Then Dad became still, the smile lingering on his face, and gave me a look of wonderment. "We've been smashing these very special atoms we found over and over and over again."

"Why do you do that?"

"To see where we came from."

"Did you find out?"

He looked at me, drawing back and considering me for a couple of seconds. "You know what?" He leaned forward and held both my hands in his. "I think we might've."

A week later, he was gone, and the FBI was taking away his things.

Dad's disappearance that December night in 2020 was the start of the long drop. The California drought bore down like a beast. The eastern ridges of the state turned into wind tunnels, open flues in a blast furnace, channeling desert gusts for months on end into the valleys and the LA basin. Winters got out of whack. When it rained now, it was random unpredictable rampages that broke apart the hills, unleashing a mud-washed hell on the coast. More and more torrential storms began thrashing Louisiana, Florida, and other low-lying parts of the world like Holland and Bangladesh.

War became this all-consuming wildfire, its first sparks being lit in 2022 when China crushed a protest movement in Hong Kong, imposing martial law there, and then invaded Taiwan to repossess the island in 2024. Resistance in the streets of Hong Kong and Taipei hadn't let up since. With China in control of the South China Sea, India began a massive blockade of Chinese shipping lanes in the Indian Ocean. The Chinese navy responded by sinking a bunch of Indian ships and crippling one of their carriers. And just as the blockade was about to fall apart, Japan and Australia rolled in, offering backup. The standoff got the whole world freaked out. Talks started.

In school there are rules. But in the world there are no rules. Not when it comes to oil, water, power, all the shit that the big players want to control. Just a big-ass turf war out there. And no two players have been more ferocious and cunning in my lifetime than the Chinese and the Americans—not in that order. While America bombed and pillaged everything in sight from Venezuela to Libya to Iran, the Chinese cashed in on massive military and oil deals in Africa. "If you're one of the elites," Conner once said me, "war is Vegas."

Since before I was born, Syria was a hellhole, a decade-long proxy war that finally ended when the leader there stepped down and the country got broken up into smaller bits under US and Russian control. From North Africa to Afghanistan, it's all just a vast turf war as the US, China, and Russia all vie for more oil, more territory, more whatever. They don't rumble, though. They let their proxy gangs—terror groups and private armies—do it for them.

Here in America, southern and Midwest states started going broke around 2026. California took up the slack, but with the drought, the lower crop yields, higher food prices, housing shortages and whatever, we were on fumes. On TV and social feeds, right in our own neighborhoods, we'd see protests, strikes over jobs, wages, water, especially water. Shit was getting deep, first for the people who *worked* in your neighborhood, then the people who *lived* in your neighborhood.

For me, life went on more or less like always with classes, clubs, friends, plans for college, but little by little, the shadow of what was happening across the state, in the lives of our neighbors, crept into our homes, our minds. Kids started quitting school to start working or moving out of state with their families. Teachers left, programs got cut, classes looked more and more like those underfunded refugee detention centers.

Then something huge dropped.

In 2027, a massive Chinese-American conglomerate called Triton Corp announced plans to build an epic-size network of "economic zones" from Colorado to Ohio, Wisconsin to north Texas, a utopia rising from the ashes of the American wasteland. If Congress chipped in a bit of money—say, half—Triton would build out the zones, hiring Chinese and American labor. The zones would guarantee manufacturing and tech jobs, education, housing, healthcare, the works. To make it work, though, its residents would have to give up their US citizenship and get paid in digital credits that had zero value outside the zones.

For months, the corporate mouthpieces online and on cable all warned against it, calling it a potential hostile takeover of our country and constitution. But once all the top CEOs, the biggest bankers, and the wealthiest politicians were promised kickbacks by Triton lobbyists, all the talking heads on CNN, MSNBC, FOX, etc., etc. started singing Triton's praises, crowing about how the zones would be "job creation engines" and "prosperity hubs" for the "long-lost middle class." The zones were going to save the country. The same politicians who were railing against the deal a year ago were now blubbering on and on about how America couldn't afford *not* to take up Triton on its "patriotic" offer. And after decades of doing uphill battle against companies and politicians over shitty jobs, the parasitic war spending, the starved schools, and the homeless dead in the streets, we the people by and large gave in. Jobs? Sure, where do we sign? And like a cartoon wolf rubbing its paws and licking its chops, Congress gave the Triton deal the go-ahead.

The long drop also meant less money for fire and police. That meant more crime and accidents, making ER departments the most popular hangout spots in the city. Mom started pulling extra shifts every week. This past year, I'd seen less and less of her. But, weirdly, three months ago, I started seeing more and more of Dad again—for the first time since he disappeared.

The dreams started in July. Once or twice a week at first. In the beginning, they were the same, simple, on a loop:

I'm in a forest, on a hiking trail up a steep hill. It's sunup, the weather's blustery, snowflakes swirling everywhere. Weak sunlight reaches the tops of the pines. Then I see him. It's Dad, his face turning to look at me over his shoulder like he's holding a camera. I'm just behind him, climbing the trail.

I try to quicken my pace, to get alongside him. But I'm not walking at all. I have no legs, no body. I'm just a consciousness. I know that I'm seeing a recorded image like I'm wearing a VR headset.

We reach a peak high above the lake. Flurries scatter and dance. A flagpole sticking out of a mound of rocks marks the proper peak, and I can see a flag blowing in the high wind. It bears an image of a redwood tree inside a large "S." The Stanford flag, where Dad went to school.

Now I know exactly what I'm seeing: it's the peak above the cabin where my dad took us every summer. Eagle Lake, near Tahoe. I see my dad crouch next to the mound. He looks back at me, pointing to a rock on the side of the mound. I see him pull the rock, revealing a hole there. That's when the images get scrambled and merge into bands of light flowing past me, pulsing all different shades of red, and I wake up.

After I'd had this dream three times, I went into my mom's closet and dug out some old photos of Dad. The photos had all been pried from their frames and stashed in a box. Under these photos and a bunch of med-school textbooks, I found a thumb drive. I had a hunch the drive held more photos, and I was right. Hundreds of them.

Most I'd never seen before: pictures of my dad growing up in Palo Alto, when he was a grad student in Arizona, wearing a scruffy beard and long hair that fell below his eyes. The photos that really hurt were the ones with both my parents—when they first met in England, then in Wisconsin where my dad got his first teaching gig and my mom was doing her medical residency. They seemed so happy.

Then one photograph hit me like punch in the jaw: standing on a peak was my father, in T-shirt, shorts and hiking boots, the beard and hair trimmer now, his eyes hidden by wraparound shades. It was *that* peak. His hand gripped the flagpole, and there was no mistaking the Stanford flag fluttering from it.

I took the laptop into the kitchen. "Mom, do you remember this?"

She looked up from the cutting board and did a double take when she saw the picture. "Sure," she said, turning her attention back to the vegetables on the cutting board. "It's from our last summer up at the cabin. You were . . . four." She turned to me. "What're you digging up old pictures for?"

"I had this dream about this place," I began, but stopped, held back by something. "It's nothing. Just felt like looking at old photos, I guess."

Mom grasped the handle of the cutting board and, with the side of her knife, pushed the cauliflower and potatoes into a wok heating on the stove. The food sizzled, filling the kitchen with Indian spices.

"We haven't been up there in, like, forever, right? It's funny 'cause I have no memory of it."

"It's not surprising," she said, stirring the vegetables around with a wooden spoon. "We have suppressed memories, and a lot of times, when you go through something difficult as a child, like you did, your mind tries to process it for years and years after. And memories of things you don't even remember can surface."

I looked at her quizzically. "You for real?"

"Please, Dev." She tapped the rim of the pan with her spoon and pointed to herself with it. "You're talking to a doctor."

"Ha!"

"Put the rice on. Set the table."

We said nothing more till dinner when she suddenly looked up from her plate. "The subconscious can do that to a person, Dev. You miss him, I know you do." She spooned dal onto her rice, still mulling over her thoughts. "Have you been looking at a lot of old pictures lately?"

I shake my head. "Just curious, Mom. I'm fine."

She nodded, considering my answer. "Good," she said, smiling, and her mood seemed to lift as she closed the book on the subject.

The dreams stopped, and I began to accept Mom's explanation that it was just a tripped-out figment of my subconscious. But a month after that conversation, it happened again. And again. Three consecutive nights, every detail the same right down to the rock revealing a hole on the side of the mound. Except this time, the dream continued:

Now, he reaches into the hole and produces a gray metal box, the size of a shoebox, only flatter. On front of this box is a clasp with a small padlock. Two words are scribbled on top of the box in marker: "Find Bollinger"

The day following the third night was a recovery day for Mom—or "pajama day" as she liked to call it. I found her at her laptop on the recliner, in a T-shirt and pajama pants, when I got home from school. She had her glasses on, and her eyes were fixed on the screen.

"How was school?" she asked absently.

"Fine." I stepped behind the sofa so I could look over her shoulder at the screen.

It was a clinical video of a doctor examining a patient, narrating observations to the camera. But something about his tone and the fact that restraints held the patient down as he moaned and struggled made the whole thing super disturbing.

"What's this?"

"I'm not sure," Mom said. "A link a colleague in Atlanta sent me about a case he's investigating. He thought it was rabies or . . ." She shook her head. "Maybe it's a new strain." She shut the laptop, tossed it aside. "That'd be something."

I set my things down and followed Mom into the kitchen where she was grabbing a soda from the fridge.

"Remember that weird dream I told you about, like, a month ago," I began, "the one about Dad, the cabin, the hiking trail?"

She popped open the can, took a gulp. "Yeah, sure. You have it again?"

"I think it's way more than a dream."

"Of course, it is, Dev. You two were close, you and Dad."

"That's not what I mean."

She moved past me, down the hall and, walking into her bedroom, shut the door behind her. "Keep talking," she yelled. "I just have to put on normal-people clothes."

I leaned up against the wall of the hallway. "Who, or what, was Bollinger?" From behind the door came only the sounds of dresser drawers, the clatter of clothes hangers.

"Mom?"

A few seconds later and dressed in "normal-people clothes," Mom stood in the doorway, staring at me curiously. "What did you say?"

"Bollinger."

"Give me your phone," she ordered.

"My phone?"

She made a "give it here" gesture. I turned my phone over, and she immediately began checking my phone calls and emails. "Anyone been calling you?"

"Who? No, nobody."

She handed the phone back to me. "What'd you see in this . . . dream?"

"A box with the name 'Bollinger' on it."

She glared at me for a few seconds then slowly shook her head and walked away. I followed her into the living room and onto the back patio. She sat down at one of the deck chairs, perched on the edge.

"What's going on?" I asked.

"Sit."

I did, confused and curious, at the chair next to hers.

I was almost sure she'd next tell me to see a therapist. Instead, she began, "Bollinger was someone your dad worked for, a guy who ran this private tech company called Breakthrough. Your dad worked for him on some classified project for five years, right up until he died."

"Disappeared."

Mom waved a hand. "Fine." She took off her glasses and began chewing nervously on the tip of the earpiece. "But why his name is turning up in your dreams is . . ."

"Weird."

We sat there in silence. I couldn't escape the feeling that this was a top secret conversation we were having, with only the bougainvillea to muffle our words.

"When the FBI came here that night," Mom went on, "Bollinger's name came up. I'd only met him once, back when your father was having a tough time making a go of it. And he offered your dad a job. Right after, he took your dad and me out for dinner. He seemed like your typical driven, smart CEO. A bit brash, arrogant. He thought highly of your father. But after that, his name never came up much. They were neck-deep in their research, and whenever your dad would mention his name, it was always about funding or meetings or your standard office shoptalk. Honestly, that final year, the name Bollinger never came up. I thought nothing of it." She looked off into the far corner of the yard. "In fact, I didn't give it a second thought . . . until the night the Feds showed up. On top of everything, they said this man—Bollinger—had gone missing. And they were looking for him."

"Was he at the lab that same night?"

She shook her head. "No record of him being there. And I still don't know what happened to him."

"So why does his name come up? I mean, in my dream?"

She drew a breath and shrugged. "Maybe I brought his name up once, and it stuck. And it's been locked away in your mind from childhood. You miss your father, Dev, probably more than you realize."

From somewhere in the living room, her phone rang. I hated that phone. It was always her job calling, and her job always won.

Two minutes later, she was back on the patio saying goodbye with her handbag at her shoulder and her sunglasses on. There was an emergency conference call that folks from the CDC wanted her in on. Atlanta was seeing more cases of that bizarre strain. She gave me a quick kiss on the cheek and was out the door without another word about Dad, the dream, or Bollinger.

CHAPTER THREE

October 24, 2030

A low-flying helicopter wakes me out of a restless sleep. I sit up in bed, startled for some reason, and I recall the dream I was pulled out of, the sensation of watching images unfolding . . . everything just as before, down to the name Bollinger on the box.

I turn on my phone. It's 7:45 a.m. A fire engine blares its horn on some faraway street.

Mom isn't home yet. I try to call the ER and (miraculously) get through. The receptionist connects me to Mom's voicemail. I debate whether I should sit tight and wait for her, but . . . no. Since the insanity of last night, I want to make sure she's holding up. I leave the message that I'm heading over.

I consider driving to the hospital. It's not too far. We still have my dad's beat-up Outback draped in the garage. Mom keeps it that way. I took it out a few times last spring and summer while practicing for my driver's license. But Mom made me garage it right afterward. It might still run. But then I remember the crazy streets last night and decide I'll walk.

I shoot texts to Conner and Abby about everything I'd heard on the radio about the airbursts. Conner texts back with more info: all schools are declared closed next week for repairs. He also thinks the event is going to intensify the traffic out of Southern California and out to states where Triton's new zones are going up.

The phone vibrates. My heart jumps: it's Abby.

"What up?" I answer, trying to sound casual.

"Hi. Um . . ." She sounds uncertain—a surprise. There's never anything uncertain about Abby.

"You hear about the schools being closed? Repairs."

"Yeah," she tells me. "I heard."

"Man, this city's going to be a mess for a while." Pause. Awkward silence. "Hey, uh, so, how're your parents? Glad your house didn't get damaged. Or did it? Things are pretty intact here. What about Danny? He good?"

I hear a laugh. "Everyone's fine."

"It's nuts, right? Helicopters, police cars all night. Could you sleep through that? Probably a mess for miles around." I have a bad feeling about this call, and I want to keep from—

"My parents just moved up our moving date. Like, to five days from now."

A punch to the gut. "Oh shit." My throat tightens. "Okay."

Though she sounds muffled over the phone, I get the feeling she's trying not to cry. I've never seen her cry. "My parents already have movers coming in a few days, they made all these arrangements. There's nothing I could do."

"Abby. I'm sorry."

I'm sorry. A feeble expression for when we can't change a damn thing.

"I'm sorry too."

Conner's words enter my mind, about how the disaster will only drive more people out. I wish it didn't have to drive Abby out. "Like, so"—I make a mental count—"Thursday, then."

"I just wanted to tell you. My parents sat us down and told us. First thing I thought of . . . was I'm really going to miss you."

"Thanks," I say, unthinking. But that's not right. "What I mean is . . . thanks for . . . being a friend. You didn't have to, but you did."

"Didn't have to?" Abby laughs lightly. "What's that mean?"

"We weren't exactly, you know, running in the same circles way back when. You had all your friends. I had Conner."

"Well, you may as well know, Dev. I needed a charity case for school credit. You were it."

"Happy to help."

Unlike myself, Abby is a high school darling. She's a star soccer player, absolutely crushes her piano recitals, and owned that lead in the school play last year. She runs charity races for her brother, gets straight As and routinely kicks my ass in video games—and Conner's too. Everybody falls for her, so it's no surprise that I did too. Secretly, of course. I'd never risk embarrassing her—and losing her—by telling her how I feel. But then last night happened.

Abby goes on: "Things aren't getting better here. Dad's been out of work for a year. No need for builders when LA isn't building anything. And Danny's asthma . . ."

"I know."

"So . . . we'll be staying with my mom's sister in Evanston. From there, Dad talked about moving into one of those zones. Plenty of work, we hear. Could be a fresh start for him."

"Yeah."

As she's speaking, all I can think of is the moment between us last night. She must've guessed what was on my mind because then she says, "And I'm sorry if I made you, you know, feel weird holding your hand and, well, kissing you."

"It's okay. Things got a little scary. I would've kissed me too."

A quick laugh on the other end. "I just didn't want there to be any weirdness between us with only a few days left, you know?"

"No worries. I mean, of course." I'm suddenly overwhelmed by the desire to get off the phone. "I wouldn't want things to get weird between us either. We'll be going our separate ways soon." Where in my mind is this coming from? "There's enough in your life to deal with right now."

"I'll miss you," she says again.

A helicopter whirs distantly and, from two doors down, the German Shepherd begins barking insanely. I tell her I'll catch up with her later and hang up.

Here's the thing: Abby was going to leave no matter what. Everyone leaves. People leave. *I'll miss you too. So much that it scares me.*

Once Mom said to me, "We lost someone. He died. And I moved on."

"But how?" I asked, crying.

"At work," she said, "it's part of the job. But for you, it's going to take a little while longer."

That was the day she packed away all the pictures.

The ER is packed. Ambulances jam the front area. Medics are rushing through with patients in wheelchairs and gurneys. A police officer stands by at the entrance and blocks my way as soon as he sees me approaching.

"Can I help you?"

"I'm here to see my mom," I tell him. "She's an attending physician."

"If you aren't sick or injured, can't let you through. Triage is overloaded."

"But can I get a message through? I just want her to know I'm okay."

The officer is shaking his head even before I finish talking. "I'm not letting anybody through unless they're sick or injured. Give me your name and number, and I'll see—"

"Dev!"

I look past the officer and see a familiar face—I can't place his name, though. He's a nurse on the ER staff, tall, black, dressed in scrubs, looking bleary-eyed. On the badge clipped to the front pocket of his top, it reads "Michael Something-or-other."

"It's okay, officer, he's with me. I'll vouch for him."

Reluctantly, the officer lets me by, and Michael leads me through a jammed registration area, full of crying children and tense words in Spanish and English.

"Thanks," I tell Michael. "I see you've been busy."

"Madness, man. Your mom will be happy to see you."

"How's she been?"

"You know her," he says. "It's like watching an NBA all-star rallying for a game seven win."

I laugh. He's got that right: Mom's in her element here.

We take an elevator up one floor where there are offices, a break room and critical-care rooms. Like the registration area downstairs, the floor is bustling.

"Wait right there," Michael says, pointing to a chair next to an IV stand behind reception.

A clerk at the desk, worn-out and red-eyed, smiles at me. "Who're you waiting on?"

"My mom. Seema Godrej."

Then I see her, in her white coat, her black hair disheveled and tied back. She gives me a tired smile and, with tired arms, gives me a hug.

She says she's got a patient to look in on, so I wait in her office with the sandwich, snacks, and soda I got from the vending machine. A text comes through from Conner telling me that we need to talk later. I'm about to text him back when Mom walks in, a coffee cup in one hand and a clipboard in the other.

Without a word to me, she edges up to her desk and pulls up her email on her computer screen. She opens a digital file, and I notice it's a brain CT. She presses keys to zoom in on portions of the scan.

"Everything all right?"

"Oh, this guy came in last night. Ran some tests, everything looked fine, discharged him with a few meds. He comes back again this morning looking worse. Ran a bunch more tests. Nothing. Damnedest thing." She studies the screen for a few more seconds then exhales deeply, and I can sense both exhaustion and defeat in it. She pulls up a chair in front of me.

Mom asks if I have details on what happened last night. I tell her everything I know.

"You're saying there were four of these giant meteorites?"

"Yeah, at least four. Each like sixty or eighty feet across."

She takes a sip from her coffee cup. "Great. So we're going the way of the dinosaurs."

"They weren't that big," I say, laughing. "But big enough to break a lot of shit." I tell her about the videos I saw of the explosions over Mexico and Havana and how the world lit up in a flash like it was the middle of the day before the explosions went off.

A text from Conner arrives: *Shit just went down.*

I start to tap out a reply when Mom says, "I wanted a better life for you."

She leans back in her chair, staring into her coffee cup. I follow her gaze out through the half-drawn vertical blinds, at the Santa Monica Mountains, the tops of office buildings, billboards, palms, everything blanched in the heat.

"I spoke with a friend of mine," Mom says and turns to look at me. "We went to med school together. He runs a practice near London."

I know where this is going. "I hate London."

"Might be a place for me out there. We'll be close to your grandparents, won't we? We've got to do something, Dev." She shakes her head. "Way things are going in the state, the water levels and the economy are both about to bottom out. It's looking like asteroids aren't too crazy about us either. We need a fresh start."

When she says those words, I feel the first stirrings of anger inside me. I don't know why. Her words make total sense—it's getting bleaker here every day—but, all the same, leaving California means leaving my father.

"Not going to do it."

"Dev. We need to make a future. We'll be lucky if we make any money on the house as it is. I'd like to leave California with something." Her voice is like flint, enunciating each word as if I were a child.

I stare at the food on my lap. I don't know what more to say because I know she's right.

"He's not coming back."

I'm so pissed right now. At her. At everything. Sometimes the most obvious facts can be unbearable to hear.

Just then, we hear a crash and shouts from the hallway. Mom opens her door in time to see a security guard run past. She steps out, watching something.

I rush to the door to see two staff members—Michael is one of them—and a guard trying to restrain a patient in a gurney as another RN is getting back on his feet. Office files, IV stands, a metal tray, ampules, needles, rolls of gauze are scattered all over. Of the patient, all I can see are wiry hair and thin arms thrashing wildly.

A woman in scrubs shouts that she needs room as she hurries in with a syringe and injects the patient while the others force him down. The patient relaxes and, in the relative calm, my mom approaches the gurney, extending an arm back at me, telling me to stay put. Meanwhile, every nurse and PA within hearing distance has come running but keep several feet away, cautious. I watch as my mom consults with another doctor, and all together they wheel the patient into a room.

Gradually, people ease up and clear the floor. The staff at the front desk laugh nervously, the receptionist continues a hushed conversation on the phone.

Two or three minutes later, Mom walks back out, tucking her stethoscope into the front pocket of her white coat. "You okay?" she asks me, guiding me back to the office.

"What the hell was that?"

"In fifteen years, I've never seen that."

I try to sum up what just happened. "That was . . . that was."

Mom pulls a medical reference book from a low shelf and pauses dramatically and fixes her eyes on me. "Something."

I nod, and she dumps the book on the desk and opens the email file again.

"Rabies?" she mumbles to herself, shaking her head and peering at the brain scan. "Why would we suddenly get three cases?" She snaps out of her thoughts, remembering I'm there. "Sweetheart, I'll catch up with you in a few, okay?"

I swig down the last of the soda and gather the sandwich and bag of potato chips. As Mom is walking me out of the office, we become aware of raised voices again.

Staff are converging on the patient's room. The door to the room flies open and a nurse—spattered with blood and clutching her face—rushes out and a security guard rushes in, shutting the door.

I hear the sounds of crashing equipment, cries of pain, and human growling from inside the room. Seconds later, we hear gunshots—three *bangs*, loud and final—leaving screams of shock in their wake before a doctor throws open the door. Now, every staffer—anyone who isn't tending to the blood-covered nurse slumped in a chair behind reception—is rushing into the room.

Mom spins, takes me by the arm and leads me down the hall to the stairwell. "You can't be here right now," is all she says. I only have time to tell her to be safe before we say our goodbyes, and she leaves me at the door.

—✶—

Two more guards run past me and up the stairwell. It isn't the first time guns have gone off at West LA Memorial—last year, security shot a man who'd smuggled his handgun into the ER and taken a nurse hostage.

The TVs in the lobby, all set to mute, display shiny CNN faces alternating with images of a crippled Chinese container ship in the Indian Ocean, of clashes between police and demonstrators in city after city protesting poisoned water, and, finally, the fireball, seen from a dashcam, blazing over a southbound freeway before the world flashes daylight-bright.

I offer the food in my hands to a tired-looking woman sitting with a sleeping girl, her hand bandaged, and hurry out.

Sixteen hours since the event, the city's beginning to dust itself off. People are sweeping up glass and plaster in front of their businesses and on their porches. The heat, though, is the same as ever, pressing its weight on everything. The trees look like torture victims.

—✶—

As grateful as I am for having Abby in my life, I'm almost as thankful for Conner. One day in fourth grade, he tripped me up during a PE soccer game. I shoved him and then we were both on the ground punching each other until the coach pulled us apart and sent us to the principal's office. We've been best friends ever since.

Exhausted, still messed up by what's happened, I decide to stop by his house. Gulping down a refill of water, I join Conner in the living room, cool in the air conditioning, where he broods over a laptop, occasionally scratching at the coarse mat of hair, his version of a beard, that clings to his face.

Shirtless and still, he's sitting there like a sandy-haired Buddha, cross-legged on the sofa. The TV on the far wall, thankfully set on mute, shows the same parade of disasters I'd seen in the hospital lobby.

I sit in the quiet coolness of the room and close my eyes. Conner hasn't said much, and I get the distinct feeling I shouldn't be here right now.

I debate whether to get up and leave, but decide instead to tell him about the ER, the insanity, the gunshots, the maniac patient. "The place was a war zone." But he barely looks at me.

"It's a war zone everywhere," he says, not turning his eyes from the TV, "if you haven't noticed."

I tell him about the nurse, her face bloodied, about patients bursting out of their restraints. Conner taps absently at keys on his laptop. "Doctors don't know what it is. I'm worried about her. My mom, I mean."

"A bomb scare shut down the airport in Bangkok," he says, not even looking at me. "So my dad and stepmom can't get out. Now they're telling me I'm moving to Florida to live with my mom." He curses under his breath. "Sorry, man. I need a minute right now." He turns up the volume on the TV and says something snarky about a commercial that's playing. I don't think he's heard one word I said.

Fuck this. "Good luck," I say. "Thanks for the water." As I slam the door shut behind me, Conner mumbles something, but I'm done here.

I make my way to the park. That Conner can be a real prick, you know. Self-involved smart-ass. Probably good he's leaving.

I'm still seething about it as I reach Carlton Park—the same park that was filled last night with neighbors with flashlights.

I find a patch of grass in the shade where I can sit back and catch a little breeze. Only a trace of smoke. Two people are walking their dogs around the park. Across the street, neighbors are fixing a window. City workers are in the front yard of a house; I can hear the whining of their chainsaw. Everything is muted and stifled as if there's another dimension between us: the heat.

I smile at that. Dimensions remind me of my dad, of the time we were at the beach when I was seven. He told me there were more stars than all the grains of sand on every beach on Earth. "But," he said, "there's much more, so much more than we can actually see. There are *dimensions*."

"Where are they?" I asked.

"Everywhere. We just can't see them," he said.

I held out my hand before my eyes and turned my palms back and forth, hoping to catch a glimpse of these dimensions, as if they were cobwebs. "How do you know?" I asked. "You can't see them."

"No? Maybe I have," my father said. He tapped me on the tip of my nose. "Come on." He got up and waved for me to follow him to the water. That is the last summer day I can remember with him.

Lying back on the grass, hands behind my head, I stare up at the branches.

Memories run through my mind like movies on a loop, taking me back to the first thing Abby ever said to me, early in eighth grade, biology class: "I had this weird dream last night, and this was it. We were sitting right here, and I was telling you I had a dream about you."

"Well," I replied. "Congratulations. Sounds like your dreams just came true."

"Ha," she said. "But check this out: What if *this* is a dream, and I wake up, come to class and tell you I had a dream where I told you I had a dream about you?" At that point, I was trying to figure out if she was messing with me or if this beautiful girl was being seriously profound. "Like that illusion with the mirrors in the funhouse. Two mirrors reflecting each other, looking at each other. You ever notice how the reflections get tinier and tinier . . . all the way to, like, infinity? It's like that, don't you think?"

I sat there thinking it was the most romantic gibberish any human had ever said to me.

And I think back to how stoked I was at the start of freshman year when she showed up at my birthday cookout. And she stayed way past midnight with me and Conner, watching horror movies and playing video games. What made her stay? I wondered it then and wonder about it now. She didn't have to. It wasn't like she was into me or Conner or anything. Just genuinely liked hanging with us. Even now, I'm still kind of flattered by it.

Under the eucalyptus, the breeze lifting, I feel my eyes getting heavy. A minute later, I feel myself giving in to sleep.

And when the dream begins again, I'm already holding the box lifted out from under the rock: "Find Bollinger." Now it goes one step further: the view swings, pans across the slopes of granite, scrub, and pine that lead out to a turquoise sheet—Eagle Lake—and pans past a glimpse of sunrise, and there he is in close-up: my father.

The dream goes dark, like a movie screen, as I become aware of an approaching noise. I wake to seeing Conner on his skateboard. He's got on his shades and his backward-worn Lakers cap.

I sit up, panicky. "Something weird is going on," I say to myself in a daze as Conner hops off the board and walks over.

He drops to the grass beside me, turning his cap around forward. "Look, uh, sorry for being a dick back there. Frickin' Florida—"

Against every instinct I have, I tell him about the dream. Down to the instructions on the box: "Find Bollinger."

Conner's silent for a few seconds, then: "You're losing your mind."

"Thanks."

"Seriously, what do you want me to say? It's a stressful time, right? Everyone's leaving, you had a disaster scenario here last night. You loved your dad. Maybe you never actually grieved, you know, and this is all suppressed shit coming out now."

I decide to change the subject. "When do you leave?"

Conner takes a deep breath, shuts his eyes. "Flight's next week. Thursday. Parents talked and agreed it was best I get out, stay with my mom. No future here, they say. Can't freakin' believe it."

"Maybe there *is* no future here."

"Not that." He sits up, sighing heavily. "I can't believe they actually agreed about something,"

I tell him I'm sorry about the news. I'm genuinely hurt by it. But right now, I need to get home. The dream's giving me ideas.

CHAPTER FOUR

The key to the Outback hangs on a rack beneath a kitchen cabinet. I grab it, go to the garage, and remove the tarp from the Outback. In the passenger door's storage pocket are several road maps. Crumpled, dog-eared and faded, these are the maps my parents would use on cross-country drives and camping trips. I pull out a map and, unfolding it, I bring it inside to the dining table. The paper's frail now, like parchment, the seams along the folds torn in many places.

It's less than 500 miles from LA to Eagle Lake. Take the 5 to Sacramento then the 50 all the way into Lake Tahoe. Most of the traffic would be moving east these days, out of the state. Not so much north or south. With luck, I could make it to the cabin in seven hours.

But you're crazy. What're you thinking? And how're you going to make it up there, Dev?

I need to know if these really are messages. And the Outback runs, doesn't it?

I go back to the garage, fit the key in the ignition. The engine turns, and roars to life. Half a tank of fuel. It does run! I switch off the engine, palm the key. This car feels like my ally right now. My only ally.

From beyond the closed garage door, I can hear a car pull up in the drive: Mom's home. I smooth the tarp back on the Outback. Mom's inside the house now; the front door shuts, keys drop onto the credenza, and now I remember the map lying open on the dining table.

She dumps her handbag on one of the dining chairs, glances at the maps on the table as she passes. "What's all this? You planning a trip?"

I laugh, real casual. "Just wanted to see what a paper map looked like. Never seen one before, you know."

Ugh. Shut up, Dev.

Luckily, Mom ignores me and drops onto the sofa, her face in her hands. It's the first time she's been home since last night's craziness She's worked twenty-four hours straight.

"Get me a scotch."

"It's four o'clock."

"It's not every day that a patient almost kills two people on your staff. And he has to be, what's the polite term, *put down*?"

I make the drink, adding water and three ice cubes, and hand it to her. She sips, sighs and rolls the glass across her forehead. "Damn headache." She sets the glass down and swivels her head around her neck. As I grab a bottle of Advil for her, I remember the hospital, the madness. It all comes rushing back to me.

I hand her the Advil with a glass of water. "Any idea what happened in there today?"

She gulps down three tablets with the water and sets down the glass. "Nobody can figure out what that was," she says and sips the scotch. "I talked to someone at County, and they had a case there too. Just as bad. Six in LA today. All of them died after things took the kind of turn you saw today."

"What the hell is going on?"

"Waiting on results from the CDC, but we're leading with encephalitis or something parasitic."

"How'd they catch it?"

She sips again, shaking her head. "Don't know. We're in contact with the health people in San Bernardino and OC."

"And you? Are you all right?"

"It's not contagious." She smiles. She must've picked up on the worry in my voice. "Otherwise, there'd be dozens or hundreds of cases by now."

I sit down and throw my arms around her. "Tell me you've got at least a day off."

"Not yet. We're just slammed over there, and everyone's putting in extra shifts."

"You want to get some sleep? I can fix you something."

She closes her eyes and makes a sound like she's giving my question some thought. She gulps a bit more of her drink then tilts over on the sofa, stretching out her legs as I get up. "Sandwich sounds good. Let me lie here and think about it." But maybe ten seconds later, she turns over, breathing soundly.

I place her drink next to the water on the table, spread an afghan over her and turn back to the map on the table. I find Eagle Lake, the size of a rice grain, a figment of blue just south of Tahoe. The instructions in the dream were clear enough: recover this box and deliver it to Bollinger.

But where do I find this guy?

Back in my room, I flip open my laptop and Google the name "Javier Bollinger." The search results come back with three matches, one in Texas, one in Oklahoma, one in New York. The first is a fifty-seven-year-old owner of a tire store in Lubbock, the second a high school student on a track team in Albany, and the third's been dead since 2008.

Next, I Google my dad's name, Gavin Harrison. Articles pop up about the explosion at the lab, his death, his research, and motives. Every word written about him invites in me the same feelings of outrage and violation as when the FBI invaded our home that night. By now, I've learned to ignore a lot of what the world says about my father.

I find an article on a science blog about a particle physics conference my father attended in Shanghai in 2016. I scroll through the article for mention of my father: "Dr. Gavin Harrison of Breakthrough Concepts led a symposium on the quantum field theory." The picture next to the article is of four men and two women together on the conference stage. Two names in the caption below stand out: Gavin Harrison and Javier Bollinger. The other man is shorter than my father and wears stylish, square-framed glasses and a neat, salt-and-pepper goatee (at least he did fourteen years ago). His eyes and smile are polite, cheerful, mild-mannered. So that's him. He's real! Somewhere out in the world, this man exists!

I'm knocking these thoughts around in my head when Conner texts: *Ppl sayin the meteor strikes wr really chinese military tests. That's some b.s.* Next text: *Think about it. We've got a massive corp blding econ zones in the midwest, trying to coax millions of people to move into them.* Next text: *What better way than to scare the shit outta everybody first?*

As I'm deciding that Conner's probably right, another text from him arrives: *Conspiracies make me hungry Af.*

Pizza Fix? I message back.

Let's go.

I text Abby: *Fix. Wanna meet us?*

OFC. Five mins.

Pizza Fix is where we always hang out, after school, after parties, during summers, whatever. Always open and always good. But now the thought of seeing Abby makes me nervous. What am I nervous for? She did kiss me, didn't she? Held my hand.

Ugh, doofus. She's leaving! Play it cool. Keep it chill.

Five minutes later, as I'm shutting the front gate, I see the white van. It's parked two houses down and across the street, its windows tinted so I can't make out who's behind the wheel. I'm staring at it when the van pulls away and rolls past me.

I've seen this van before, right here, on this street, but I can't be sure. And as I'm wondering about it, it cruises up the block like it's any other day, takes a left, and disappears.

Abby's already in front of the pizza place, head down, texting somebody, when I get there. Her hair is tied back today—she wears it like that after a workout or practice, and I secretly like it because it brings out her eyes. She looks up. Now I'm nervous again. Get a grip, dude.

"What's good?" I call out.

"Check it out," she says, pointing her chin at a sign on the door as she pockets her phone.

The sign says Pizza Fix will be closing in a week, and thanks to all the loyal customers. Shit.

"First you," I grumble, "then Conner, now this."

"What about Conner?"

I pass on what Conner's told me: the situation with his dad and stepmom in Thailand, and how they're sending him to live with his mother in Florida. "And speak of the devil."

Conner rolls in on his skateboard just then. "Hope you don't mind," I tell him. "I filled Abby in. On Jacksonville and everything."

"No worries." Conner takes off his shades, hooks them into the neck of his T-shirt.

The place is scattered with a few students and families and a couple of homeless-looking types, and under the heavy aroma of cheese and garlic, there's a dazed, tense vibe in here, everybody is quiet, mumbling to each other or watching stone-faced out at the street. The plate glass window has a fresh crack that seams from corner to corner.

Richie, the owner, rings up our orders as his two cooks scurry around, opening and closing the pizza ovens, and mopping the back of the kitchen.

"Glad you could make it in before we shut our doors," Richie tells us, looking tired, the gray eyes puffy in his wide face. He smiles under his red visor.

We ask him why he's doing it, and he blows exhausted air out through his walrus mustache and says the overhead in a drought economy finally got too high to keep a small joint like his going. Then he clucks his tongue and says he expects he'll go out of business at this rate anyway. Cashing out now while he's still ahead is probably the smart move. "So it's off to Fresno to live with my kid."

We're about to pay him for the slices when he shakes his head, cancels out the register, and says it's on him. "For old times' sake."

We tell him thanks and wish him luck. But the vibe in here is too grim to stick around, so we decide to grab our slices and walk around town. Abby gives Richie a hug and Conner and I shake his hand again, wish him the best, and we walk a few minutes to the plaza between the movie theater and the Oberon Hotel, a hundred-year-old triangle-shaped hulk that used to be the proud centerpiece of town. It's still the centerpiece, but without the pride.

Dipping halfway below the rooftops, the sun isn't stabbing at our eyes now. We find a bench to finish our food, and the hot wind picks up, carrying with it that faint smell of wildfire. Conner and Abby bring up memories: a teacher we all liked, a weird girl that Conner dated, a freshman-year Yosemite trip where half of Abby's class got sick.

My eyes track the way we've just walked: what used to be a lit-up stretch of all kinds of restaurants is a line of dark storefronts all the way to the movie theater behind me. The theater used to be a shiny multiplex. But now its walls are tagged with graffiti. The plaza fountain is lifeless so all you hear is the churn of traffic and the random shouts of kids or some crazy person with a shopping cart.

Across the plaza, the Oberon Hotel is a looming skull. It closed a year ago. Rising above the low downtown buildings, it's like some ancient, ornate ruin. I did a charcoal sketch of it once for art class.

"We're all just ghosts now," I think out loud.

"What's good, Dev?" says Conner.

"We live in a ghost town."

I finish up my pizza and toss the box into a trash bin.

"What happened to all our plans," Abby wonders. "Everything we were going to do?" The three of us have talked so much about how we'd finish high school here, then go on to the same college or to colleges that were close to each other's. Conner and I talked about taking a gap year to work on something together—a movie, a startup business, we were never sure—and to travel (to Europe or Japan, we hadn't decided).

"War, drought, and banks stealing all our money," Conner says with a smirk. "I think that's what happened."

Abby leans her head down and rubs at her eyes. "Count on you to lay it out there."

"Sorry," Conner smiles and pats Abby's back. "Don't mean to be a downer. Look, I was as stoked about our plans as you all were."

I sit back down next to Abby. She's giving out cold vibes. If there's a precipice to our friendship, dropping off from a place of togetherness to a place where you don't even know each other anymore, she and I are at the edge of it now.

"You'll like Evanston," I say. "Fresh air, clean water. And it's near Chicago, isn't it? That'll be fun." I feel nauseated by every word I just said.

Abby doesn't answer.

"Gonna be weird living with my mom," Conner says from his end of the bench. "Haven't seen her in over a year." He shakes his head slowly. "I got a bad feeling."

"Why's that?" asks Abby.

"She's made it very clear that I was 'part of the wreckage of her past,' to use her words."

Conner's parents divorced the year he and I met—in fourth grade. He's told me about fights (physical), affairs, a lot of drama. After the divorce, his mom unraveled and, five years ago, went into rehab. Drugs of some kind (Conner won't say). She moved to Jacksonville when he was thirteen, saying she needed time to steady out on her own. She writes self-help books and teaches writing at a small college out there.

"Things are better between you two guys now, aren't they?" Abby asks.

"I guess." Conner and his mom only see each other when she comes out to visit, once or twice a year. And even then, it's only a dinner or something. Like she's checking in with her agent or an accountant, not her son. "Some people aren't cut out to be parents," he says at last. "Mine, for example."

He's right. His mom's no winner. And his stepmom? She's more like his dad's live-in girlfriend, as far as Conner goes. As for his dad, he's never really "shown up" in his life. I can't tell you how many times we've been at Conner's and overheard a fight between the two of them, or how many times his father flaked out on a camping trip or movie or attending one of his baseball games. Sometimes, I think his parents think of him as an expensive piece of furniture or a rare breed of dog to be looked after.

My father was around less and less as I grew up—the week-long vacations turned into a day at the park or the planetarium, which turned into twenty minutes of stories before bedtime, which turned into quick phone calls to say good night—but, unlike Conner's dad, I always felt like we stayed connected. Farther from each other, but always in each other's orbits.

The howl from an unseen police car screams in from out of the east and fades away. We spend another minute in the plaza before Abby gets up and turns to both of us. "Let's walk. This place is a downer."

We leave through the south end of the plaza, past the movie theater, and make our way down Dickerson Avenue to where the bridge crosses over Machado Creek. The sky is flushed purple after the sunset, and the world a far cry from the chaos of twenty-four hours ago.

We lean against the railing overlooking a bone-dry concrete channel, pocked with weeds, receding into the distance. The searchlight of a police chopper on patrol finds children and dogs along the slope of the channel before it roars away. Farther west, bonfires and lanterns, tiny signs of a homeless encampment, pierce the shadows beneath a footbridge.

Ever since last night, my adrenaline has kept me buzzing. And it's been a long day. My body just wants to crash. But I don't want to leave, not while Abby is still here. So I decide to make conversation. "Conner says the airburst last night was a military test to scare people away to the zones. Says Triton is behind it all. But don't tell anybody."

Abby emits either a laugh or a snort.

"Follow the money is all I'm saying," says Conner. "Let's check Triton's share price right now."

As he's checking his phone, I'm noticing other groups of kids across the road, like us, looking out over this sad waterway. I wonder if their families will flee to the zones or if they'll scrape by here.

I scan from them, across the road, over to Abby, and our eyes meet. I'm caught in her gaze for what seems like forever, but it's probably only two seconds. Then her eyes fall away, letting me go.

"How're you going to get by without us?" she asks me.

I can't come up with an answer, not without getting emotional. "I don't know."

Conner displays his phone screen at us. "What'd I tell you? They ended the day up, five percent."

We begin our walk back up Dickerson, beneath the streetlights, not saying much. I'm aware only of the sound of Conner's skateboard somewhere ahead of us. We're walking, and every step brings us closer to what feels like the edge . . . the end.

I wish I could stop time, freeze-frame the universe, hold everything still, except for me and Abby. Then I would tell her not to go. I would tell her to go away with me. Anywhere. While the universe stops in place, I would tell Abby here's our chance. *Because if you leave, I will never see you again, and I don't want that to happen.*

Time and the universe move so fast, you know. It's overwhelming.

"Abby," I begin. She looks at me. *Don't say anything. It might be weird.* "I'm going away." Did I just say that?

"Going where?" She sounds intrigued, a little wary.

And no sooner are the words forming in my mind than they're leaving my mouth: "Up to my parents' cabin up near Tahoe. Haven't been up there in a while, but I can find it, I think."

"Really? But . . . what for?"

"Something I want to check out." And for the first time, I tell Abby about the dreams. Every single detail. She asks me why this is the first time I'm mentioning this to her.

"Because I didn't want you to think I was losing my mind," I reply. "My mom and Conner have tried to tell me it's all part of some repressed trauma or whatever."

"Hmm. What do *you* think?"

"I think they're more than dreams. They're like transmissions, like I'm looking at a recorded message beamed straight into my mind."

She gives me a worried look.

"Weird, I know," I say, feeling a touch embarrassed.

"So you want to drive up to Tahoe to see if there's a box hidden under a rock on a mountain . . .?"

Maybe this is when I should just say I'm kidding about the whole thing. Instead, I say: "Yes."

Abby nods coolly. "When're you leaving?"

"Not sure yet." But I do know, just can't bring myself to say it.

"I wish I could go with you," I hear her say. "Sounds fun."

"Really?"

"Go where?" Conner's off his skateboard and waiting for us.

"Dev told me about the dreams he's been having for like the last three months."

"Ha! You mean the one where he's up on a mountain with his dad?"

"He's going to find out if there's anything to it."

I cringe when she says that. Because the next thing out of Conner's mouth will be about how I should get checked into the nearest psych ward. Here it comes. One, two—

"We need to check you into the nearest psych ward."

"Screw you." I'm suddenly so annoyed. Also, I'm embarrassed because Abby is here. She probably agrees with Conner. I don't dare look at her. Switching tacks, I say, "It's not a big deal, really. It'll take half a day to get up there. I'll check it out. Drive back down right after."

Long silences follow as we pass under the glow of weak streetlights.

"Fine," Conner says finally. "I'm game. Let's go."

I smile, ignoring what could be another joke.

"Come on, man," Conner pleads. He hops on his board and begins rolling away. "Road trip. Our last hoorah."

"Conner, why would I want you on this trip? You already think I'm crazy."

He spins around on the heel of the board, raises two fingers of one hand. "Scout's honor, I'll be good. Plus, you're going to need at least one sane person with you."

"Sorry." And I walk on past him.

But there's another reason I don't want Conner and Abby along, a much heavier one. "And I don't want a last hoorah. I don't want a road trip to remind me how it's the last time we'll all be together. That's not cool. Let's just please drop the subject."

Conner looks at me, mouth in a frown. "Okay." He gets back on his board and pushes on, nonchalant.

We get to the corner where we have to part ways with Abby. Conner and I tell her goodbye and give her hugs. There is some murmuring from Abby and Conner about when would be a good time for us to see each other again. Is there time for a movie or a run to Starbucks or a last trip to the beach over the next four days? Abby mentions all the packing she has to do. "But whatever," she says. "Let's make something happen. We need a last hoorah." She pokes her tongue out at me.

"That's what I'm sayin'." Conner laughs, holding out his fist. Abby bumps it with her own, a playful sneer on her face.

I tolerate the next few minutes, feeling more and more disgusted by the small talk. Am I the only one here feeling an ache in the core of his chest?

Eventually, Abby turns and leaves, crossing the street toward the shadows on the far side. I wonder if it's the last time I'll see her. And as we make the three-block walk before Conner turns off onto his street, it's like there's a buffer between us now. Because there are things I have to do and things he has to do, and the two aren't the same anymore.

When we get to his street, Conner does something he's never done. He leans in and gives me a hug. "Catch up later," he says. "Don't do anything funny, all right?"

I don't know what to say. Nothing feels right. "See ya."

When I get home, Mom's still asleep on the sofa, the remote in her hand. The TV is on mute, showing a bunch of media clowns in a shiny studio as graphics and screens show Chinese troops tear-gassing rioters in Africa. I turn off the TV, the lights, and snatching up the map from the dining table, I head back to my room.

At the end of the road, at the edge of Eagle Lake, is where I would leave the car. I locate the point on the map. There is already a tiny circle drawn there in ballpoint pen. From videos, pictures, and conversations over the years, I know that the cabin is at the foot of the peak. Find the cabin, the trail that passes above it, and the rest is a cinch.

Abby and Conner don't leave till Thursday. But in a lot of ways, they're already gone.

CHAPTER FIVE

I'm following my father again up the trail, to the rock . . . now holding out the box with the words, "Find Bollinger," before the whole thing resets and starts all over again.

I do something different this time: I take a step through the "wall" of the dream, feeling an electric shock, like I've just passed through pure energy.

On the other side, I'm in a tunnel. Like being inside one of those walk-through tubes in aquariums where the fish swim all around you, but instead of fish, the walls are filled with dream-images. Like being on the other side of a movie screen. And the only light is the twilight of the dream.

I'm floating. There's no above, no below. Weightless.

Behind me, the tunnel recedes to a dark point, I can't tell how far. Ahead, the tunnel ends in a point of bright light.

My ears are filled with radio static: harsh, roaring, high and low. I cover my ears and now the feeling of claustrophobia builds and swallows my mind. I'm trapped inside this tunnel. Terror. This storm of noise. My hands and feet flail, useless.

I feel in place, but the shapes along the walls are rushing by, slow at first then faster and faster, the light at the far end is brighter, closer. Falling into the sun. Either the tunnel is moving, or I am.

Wake up! My brain hears the command but can't respond. Wake up! It's like raising myself from the grave, from underground. My mouth makes a noise, no more than a hollow moan. Climb! Climb out! My arm rises—like a weight on pulleys—drops, and my head shakes clumsily. Am I paralyzed? What. Is. Happening?

And I'm up, nerves tense, breathing hard. I clutch my chest, feel sweat across my forehead. My room light is on.

I check my phone: 3:30 a.m. The map is open on the bed. I sit up, catch my breath. Walking through the screen was a mistake. "Don't do that again," I say to myself. "Don't ever do that again."

"You still up?" Mom is squinting at me from the doorway, a glass of water in her hand.

I rub my eyes and feign a soft laugh. "Fell asleep. You too, huh?"

"Must've been more tired than I thought. Okay, bud, lights out, hmm?"

"'Night, Mom."

She switches off my room light. A moment later, she switches on the light in her room and shuts the door. The hallway goes dark, all is quiet.

I try to sleep but think of my mom, alone, waking up on the sofa, dragging herself through the dark of the house to her room. It makes me sad.

My phone buzzes, a text from Conner: *Shit just went down with the power grid.* Below the text, a link to a CNN article. I tap the link, and the headline reads: "EAST COAST GOES DARK." I skim the article:

Authorities from Delaware to Ohio, Georgia to Arkansas are baffled over why huge swaths of the eastern power grid collapsed early Sunday morning. The outages occurred across nine states in a cascading pattern and could affect as many as thirty million people. NOAA has reported no significant solar activity that could've caused the mass blackout and, while Department of Energy officials can attribute no definite cause, they suspect that foreign hackers may have infiltrated the grid . . .

I text back: *Shit, man, what you think went down?* I need to know Conner's take.

He texts back: *It's like the strike last night. Same deal. Scaring people shitless. Pointing fingers at "foreign actors" aka Chinese or Russians or whoever. Srsly who wins here?*

Let's hope WE don't get hit, I reply.

We got hit last night, remember? That was our scare. Don't think we'll get the blackout. That'd be way too cruel.

I've been studying the California map, tracing the route I'm going to take with a marker. I want to stay close to bigger cities and towns in case I run into car trouble—especially because I'll be driving at night. I should be able to get to Eagle Lake in one go. Then I need a way to get to the cabin. It can't be more than a three- or four-mile hike from the boat launch on the southeast side of the lake. And the peak is due east of the cabin, which sits right at its base.

I peek through the blinds and right away the light's not right: a soot-spotted gold. Wildfires. Throwing open the blinds, I see the sun is a perfect disc behind a veil of ashen grain all across the sky. Like the apocalypse quietly stealing over Earth.

Mom's out in the living room in the recliner, eyes peering through her glasses on her laptop screen. "They're saying the meteor is what triggered it." We stare out at the surreal sky. "Hills were a tinderbox to begin with. And the extra heat was just enough to spark another fire."

"They close any of the freeways?"

"Parts of the 210." She looks up now and takes off her glasses. "There's coffee if you want some."

As I pour myself a cup, I check to make sure the key to the Outback is still on the rack. Shit. It isn't. I walk over to that corner of the kitchen and pretend to be checking if the bananas are ripe.

"How was last night?" Mom asks from the recliner. "Did you see your friends?"

Friends? What does she care if I saw my friends? I bet she couldn't even name them if I asked her. "I guess."

"You guess?" She steps into the kitchen with her coffee cup and opens the dishwasher to put it away. "You either did or you didn't."

"They're leaving anyway."

She seems unfazed as she takes a cleaning cloth from the sink and starts wiping the counter. "Who's leaving?"

"Both moving out in a few days."

"You mean Conner and, um . . ."

"Abby! Their names are Conner and Abby."

Calm down.

Why is she irritating me right now? I wish she'd left for work already so I could get on with what I need do.

"Take it easy," she says, turning toward me. "What's gotten into you?"

"Sorry," I say. "Upset about it."

She runs the faucet, starts rinsing plates. "Smart idea, if you ask me. I'm trying to get us out of here too."

"Let me know," is all I can think to say that won't make me feel like I've surrendered. My thoughts are still on the key. I make my way back to my room. I hear her getting on the phone now, checking in with the hospital.

The key's not under the bed or in my desk or in the pockets of the clothes I wore yesterday. I step out in the hallway—she's still on the phone—and sneak into the garage. The doors to the Outback are locked. I lift the driver side corner of the cover, enough so I can get a peek through the window—no sign of the key on the seats or on the floor. I check the garage floor, underneath the car—nothing.

Could I have brought it out with me last night? Could it have dropped out of my pocket somewhere along our walk? That key could be anywhere. Relax! I go inside again, shutting the door as noiselessly as I can. Now she's finishing up on the phone.

"They want me in earlier. ER's still slammed."

"Would you mind if I used the other car?" I'm scrambling for a reason, but she heads me off.

"Can't let you do that."

"What? Why not?"

"Look, I know what you're doing. And the answer is no."

"Going to the mall?"

"You're going a bit farther than the mall. And I'm telling you no."

"What're you talking about? I'm only going to the mall—"

Now she's shaking her head, walking—very slowly—back into the living room. A second later, she's back, again with slow, sure steps and a faint, intimidating smile on her face. She produces the map—Dad's map—in her hands, unfolds it, and lays it face up on the kitchen counter so I can see the path in black marker all the way up to Tahoe. "Like I said, you're going a bit further than the mall. You have any idea what's out there?"

"Mom, please, I'm not going anywhere. And, even if I did, I'd be careful."

"You don't know what careful is." Her eyes are fixed on me, punishing. "You're not the one on the phone with the CDC, seeing patients coming in out of the desert. There is something out there we still can't get a handle on."

Shit. I need to contain this before Mom goes even more ballistic. But she's not done yet. "You haven't driven up past Encino by yourself, Dev, and now you want to drive hundreds of miles— Do you have any idea what things are like out there? This isn't the California your dad took you out on camping trips in." She straightens up, taking the map in her hands and folding it back up. "Look, I've got another monster of a shift in a little while. When I get back, we'll talk it over."

"No. We won't. 'Cause you won't listen to what I have to say."

"I can't have you risking your life over silliness."

"Like I said. There's no talking this over."

"Fine. I'll make a deal with you." She begins pacing, weighing her words. "Wait a couple of weeks. I'll take a few days off. And we can drive up to the cabin together."

"So you can humor me and my silliness? No, thanks. If I go up there, Mom, I'm going up there alone. This isn't about you. This is about me, and . . . and it's about Dad." My voice shakes. "In a few days, my two best friends will be moving on, like, *forever*. Parting of ways, you know? Well . . . this is *my* way."

Mom draws a chair at the dining table and sits down. She looks tired. She motions for me to sit down next to her. But I don't move.

"They're only dreams, Dev."

"And that's why you can't come. Because to you, they're only dreams."

Mom sits, her forehead pressed to her folded hands.

"Look, this is the last thing I need to do."

"Last thing before what?" she says, her eyes closed.

"Before I put all of this behind me . . . before I put him behind me, before I put everything that's ever happened behind me."

"And I suppose you'll be sleeping in the car? It's not exactly a trip to the mall and back."

"I've got it all figured out," I say, not lying, not exactly. Sensing a drop in her resistance, I keep talking. "I'll drive only in the day, and there's a Sheraton outside of Sacramento I can stay at. I've got a bit of money saved up." Not a lie, not really.

She scrunches her eyebrows, and, for a second, I'm afraid she's going to make me produce the money as evidence, so I keep talking. "Really, Mom. Please. Don't worry."

She takes a deep breath. What feels like a minute passes, but it's probably ten seconds. "You go up there, do what you need to do, and I don't want to hear any more about it, got it?" She raises her face to me. "Not another word about the dreams. I want you back in forty-eight hours. Call, text, stay in touch with me. If you don't, you will never get behind the wheel of a car again as long as I live."

Mom stands now and goes over to her handbag, still on the coffee table from last night. Her back is to me, but I can tell she's digging around in it. She finds what she's looking for and, turning around, shows me a key in her hand. She was paying attention all along. All that talk of dreams, seeing the map on the table, the car running in the garage the other day. I can sense the defeat and agony wrestling inside her. The key is a capitulation. "Forty-eight hours."

I can't take the key. It feels wrong. She puts it down on the table.

Outside, a huge bang goes off and crackling noises like firecrackers, followed by another bang a little farther away. My first thought is that it's a shotgun, some madman firing off rounds.

Mom throws open the door and hurries out to the gate, her eyes scanning the north end of the street. Cars rush by, and a woman pushing a stroller jogs past, nervously glancing behind her.

I try the light switch: nothing. Check the TV: nothing. The ceiling fan's spin is starting to slow. In the kitchen, the fridge is dark, the clock on the microwave is out. Mom's at the gate, talking to the neighbor from across the street.

A minute later, she's back in the house.

"Transformers blew," she says.

From the sounds of it, getting the power back on won't be easy. Could mean crews working for hours, maybe days. I wonder about all the patients at the hospital. Clearly, Mom's thinking the same thing: "Generators at the clinic must've kicked in," she says from the living room. From her bag, she takes out her phone and begins tapping numbers.

I wonder about Abby and Conner and reach for my phone to text them. But there's no signal. Mom sets her phone aside, saying, "I'm not getting anything."

"Looks like the towers got zapped too," I say.

Mom mutters something under her breath as she tucks her phone back into her bag.

I check the faucet. "At least we've got water."

"We'll lose that too if the power isn't back. Let's make a run for some water."

Everyone else is thinking the same thing: The market up the street is already raided, swarming with cars, parked bumper to bumper on the curb in front. I weave through the aisles, a basket in hand, and grab canned soups, canned beans, bread, peanut butter, bananas, apples, potato chips, chocolates, whatever I see that isn't perishable, and pick up the last packs of D and AA batteries on the rack.

I can feel the panic in the air like it's a virus that we're all breathing. Mom takes the basket from my hands and takes her place in the checkout. The register's down, and the cashier's struggling with one of those manual credit-card swipers.

I make a beeline for the refrigerated shelves in the back, picked over and half empty now. The lighting in the shelving is dark. People are hauling off cases of sodas, gallons of water. Voices are yelling about how "it's down everywhere" and "it could be a week before the power's back on." I grab a 2.5-gallon dispenser of water and right away someone tries to rip it out of my hand. A punch is thrown behind me, and a fight breaks out between a gangbanger type—bald, tattooed, wearing a wife-beater—and a heavy, baby-faced kid in black who I recognize from history class. As the shouts and shoving build behind me, I use the opportunity to weave through the tangle of humans at the deli counter and rejoin Mom at the checkout. The scuffle in the shop is starting to rage like a flashfire.

"You go ahead," I tell Mom. "I'll take care of this. You shouldn't be here."

Mom smiles and tosses my hair in her fingers. "I do this every day, remember?"

There's screaming now in the store—a female voice: "Boy just got stabbed!" A couple of people break free from the crowd and run out of the store. The cashier slams the phone back down just as a police car pulls up in front.

"Miss!" It's the cashier, terror in his eyes. He pushes through and comes over to my mom. "Miss Seema, can you come help this man?"

Mom shoves plastic bags loaded with food and the water at me. "Take these back to the house. I will meet you in a few."

"Mom, forget it. Some dude's got a knife," I tell her harshly, blocking her way. "The medics will be here in like—"

She presses a hand at my cheek. "It's okay. I'll see you back at the house." And she turns, shouting for people to clear out, make a path, so she can get through. In Spanish, the cashier yells for people to make way.

"Go!" she urges. I do as she says. And as I'm leaving, an ambulance pulls up, its siren wailing. Medics emerge and file through the door with their field cases and portable equipment, and I'm relieved to know that Mom's "backup" is here.

I'm sweating, stumbling, and out of breath by the time I get to our front porch, hauling the water container and what feels like thirty pounds of supplies. Inside, it's only as I'm passing the dining table on my way to the kitchen that I see the note and a shiny object beside it. Dropping the supplies on the floor, I investigate: It's the size of my pinky nail, flat, with three tiny holes on one side. In a hasty scrawl, the note reads: "They're listening. Be careful."

I turn it over in my hands. There's a tiny window above the holes, like an indicator of some kind. It's not lit up right now; maybe it's not listening? And who wrote that note? I look at it again: "They're listening." Who's "they"? I check around, behind the TV and sofas and chairs, under the tables, inside lampshades, the lighting fixtures above the dining table. I make a sweep of the bathroom in the hallway. I do the same with my mom's room and my room. I find nothing. Now I'm thinking, *Am I crazy? Is Conner clowning with me?* I wouldn't put it past him. He knows I've been worked up. That's it. Yeah, he's probably laughing his ass off right now—

But what if someone *is* listening? Who is it? Why? A thought flashes through my mind like a giant, blinking neon sign: *Get your ass out of here.* I pocket the bug and the note and hurry into the kitchen.

Into a grocery bag, I pack a two-day ration of foodstuffs, off the kitchen shelf and from the supplies we got at the market: peanut butter, bread, snacks, bananas, etc. From the pantry, I pull out a small, soft-sided cooler bag, dump in some ice, a couple of sodas, a few water bottles. There are plenty more bottles and a backup water dispenser in the fridge for Mom should the water get cut. Next, I take the key from the table, take the bag and cooler into the garage and throw it all into the back seat of the Outback along with its tarp.

Shit. The power's out. The garage won't open.

I grab hold of the handle on the garage door and yank upward a bunch of times. The door won't budge. I follow the metal arm that leads up along a track from the door toward the opener, and my eyes stop at the cord hanging from the track attached to the door. I yank down on the cord and feel the arm detaching from the track with a clank. The garage door rises freely now. I slide through, lock up the house and start hauling ass back up to the market.

But I'm only a few steps up the block when I see Mom heading back down. "Thank God, you're okay," I shout.

As she gets closer, I see the blood on her T-shirt, on her hands. Seeing my mouth fall open, she gives me a taut smile. "Too much blood loss." Her words are quiet, almost lost in the rustling of trees in the warm breeze. "They'll do their best." I wonder if it's the kid from my school and as the shock of that is still sinking in, I remember about the note, the bug.

For a second, I debate whether to tell her. Do I really want to let her in on something I'm having a hard enough time believing myself? It would only add fuel to her fire.

After we get into the house, Mom tells me she has to shower, get ready for her shift. "And Dev," she adds, stopped at the doorway to her room, "about what we talked about, don't do anything while I'm gone. With the power down, I don't want you out on the road."

I say nothing. All I can think of is the possibility that we're being heard. A minute later comes the gush of water running in the bathroom.

I leave a note on the table: "Going over to Conner's. Talk to you later and be safe. Dev."

If there's anyone I need to talk to right now, it's Conner. Plus, I need to find out if he's pranking me.

His first words, as he's looking over the note and the bug, are: "You can't go back to your house. Obviously."

"Cut the shit, Conner. Did you write this, and put that fake-ass-looking bug in our house? That'd be low, man, even for you."

"Dev"—he's looking me dead in the eye—"I don't know anything about this." He's about to say more when he stops himself and glances toward the back of the house. His fingers close around the bug in his palm. I'm right behind him as he goes through a hallway to the back door, opens it and chucks the bug and the note in the garbage bin. He gestures for me to follow as he goes to the side gate, unlatches it, and we walk out onto the street.

When Conner speaks next, it's almost in a whisper. "If you're being bugged, there's no reason to think that I'm not."

"Who would want to bug us?" I say out loud.

"Shh! Is there anyone you can think of who'd have any motive to bug you or make you *think* you were being bugged?"

"No," I reply. "Well . . . except you."

"Wasn't me, I swear."

Conner's denial has made things much worse. "This is crazy. Someone is bugging my house and maybe yours."

"And, from that note, someone *else* is trying to warn you about it."

We breathe in the faint whiff of wildfire and notice the aperture of sun through the soot and the yellowy orange of the light. We walk up to the corner where there's steady traffic rolling east along the boulevard. With the lights out, traffic all over the city must've slowed to a crawl.

"Have you noticed anything or anyone weird . . . lately?" Conner asks, scanning the neighborhood, the line of cars.

"Lately"—here goes—"I've been seeing a van on my street. Like, off and on. Saw it again last night when I was leaving to meet you guys."

Conner's eyes narrow, and I half-expect him to brush it all off as nothing. Instead he nods. "You see that van around right now?" His voice is low and even.

"No."

"Any idea what it's about? Like, did you say or do anything weird? Threaten the president on the internet or try to hack the government or something?"

"What're you, crazy? The only thing I can think of is . . . they're still looking for something my dad was working on and never found it."

"That was ten years ago about your dad, Dev."

"But they haven't given up. So, now, they're staking me out and my mom, listening, watching, waiting for info."

"What info? Hell was he working on that was so important?"

"Mom says he never talked about it. But it was big enough that the FBI—or whoever this is—won't quit looking."

"So . . . you got no ideas? No hunch?"

"Only one."

"This about the dreams?" I don't answer. He exhales heavily, and it's not till we've gone another block that Conner stops and asks, "Were you even going to say goodbye before you left? We might never even have seen each other again."

I shrug, betraying no emotion, if only to keep from feeling guilty. "Leaving was my goodbye," I say. "I don't think I could've dealt with it any other way."

"You leave without your friends, and I swear I'll hunt you down wherever you are and beat the living crap out of you again."

"What do you mean 'again'?"

"Fourth grade?" He brandishes a fist. "Or did I give you amnesia too?"

"Ha! I got in some good punches. Did you see your face?"

"I'm not the one who needed to be carried to the nurse's office."

He had me there. In the principal's office, I was sobbing, not from pain so much as the shame and terror in seeing my mom show up, glaring at me.

"I'm leaving right now," I say. "My mom's probably left for her shift. It's safer for her if I get away asap."

Conner nods, absorbing the full meaning of what we're planning. "Let's meet at your place in fifteen minutes." He turns and starts walking back the way we came. The deal is done. I'm closer than ever now. But there's an ache: Abby. If we leave now, then I'll never . . .

First things first. I reach home in a few minutes. No sign of any weird vans. Good. And Mom's car isn't there either. I step up to the garage door and lift it back up. It slides with a groan that I'm afraid will attract attention.

And there's the Outback. My stuff's still inside where I'd left it. In the house, there's no sign of Mom, but the note I'd set on the table about going to Conner's is now on the kitchen counter.

I shove a change of clothes into a backpack along with the map from the table, the shortwave radio, and a flashlight. My phone has enough battery life to last through today, but, if we stay dark for much longer, we're all screwed.

Leaving through the door that leads into the garage, I see a bundle of dirty clothes on top of the washing machine in the laundry nook. In the bundle is the T-shirt, rumpled and bloodied, that Mom was wearing when I last saw her.

I slide into the driver's seat of the Outback. A thought hits me, and I climb back out. From my pack, I grab the flashlight. Dropping onto my back, I peer under the car, angling the light here and there, looking for anything that looks remotely like a tracking device or another bug. I run my fingers behind the wheel wells. Nothing.

"Good idea." Conner has appeared in the driveway, his backpack around his shoulders. "Check under the hood too?"

"Not yet."

We both look the car over as thoroughly as we can—which isn't saying much when you're a couple of seventeen-year-olds with no intelligence training aside from stuff we've picked up from movies and TV—and, again, find nothing. The street looks clear too.

I back the car out of the driveway, step out to close the garage and feel anxious, afraid that Mom will show up any minute. I get back into the car, press the gas pedal, and now we're moving, moving,

moving up the street. No one's stopping us. At the end, where we're supposed to turn left to the freeway, I go right.

Conner doesn't say anything till we're stopped at the next intersection where a traffic cop's blowing his whistle and jerking his arms.

"Abby, right?"

I nod. "Can't leave. Not both of us, not like this."

"I know."

As we pull up to Abby's house a couple of minutes later, we find her father in the garage, sorting through shelves and tossing things into a plastic garbage can. Her mother comes out of the front door, arms full of boxes. Conner and I get out of the Outback and, before we even reach the driveway, Abby's parents meet us like a greeting party. Her mom's beaming at us. "What're you boys up to? Trouble, I hope." She sets the boxes down at the curb and gives us both a hug, apologizing for being covered in house dust. She's been packing all day, and, with the power down, the job's gotten more miserable.

We tell them we're out picking up supplies in case the power stays down and ask if Abby's around. Usually, her parents would wave us into the house and tell us to look for her inside. But this time, there's a pause. "You know," her mother says hesitantly, "I think she's out running errands, dropping bags off at the thrift store, like that." There's a cheerfulness about her that feels, I don't know, forced. "Why don't you check back in later?"

"We'll be busy today," her father interrupts. "Tomorrow might be better."

Conner and I awkwardly say our goodbyes as we shuffle back to the car. Abby's dad goes back in the garage but keeps his eye on us, like he wants to make sure we're on our way. "Something's not right," I say, starting the car.

At the north end of her street, I cross over and turn down the street one block west. Conner's already thinking what I'm thinking; there's a back way into their house, beyond a cement wall. "Be right back," I tell Conner and hurry along the narrow space between houses to the alleyway separating this row of houses from the one over. The wall isn't high, only about six feet, but there's a lattice frame along the top of it and, beyond that, a row of cypresses. In one corner is a lime tree. If I can make it to the lime tree, I can probably scramble over the lattice, through the branches and down the other side. But I see somebody's already beaten me to it: a blue pack comes punching through the tree branches and drops to the asphalt at my feet. I stare up and see the branches wriggling, then a hand and hair and a body struggle up, and scooch along the narrow ledge between the lattice and wall for a couple of seconds before dropping down nearly on top of me.

"What took you so long?" Abby says, brushing herself off. "Come on." And she takes off across the alleyway.

I'm dazed, stumbling, and hurrying to catch up to her. "What're you—? How'd you—?" is all I can blurt out.

She doesn't say anything, just keeps on for the street, back the way I've just come, emerging out the other side where Conner now waits outside the car with the passenger door open. "Come on, let's go, let's go!" Abby jumps into the front seat. And, as Conner is sliding into the back, I'm wondering if they're both in on something.

After we're out of the neighborhood, I make straight for the 405. The sky is now a mix of ashen purple, tinged with gold, out of the northeast, and the reddish-gray marine layer creeping in off the coast. Either way, it's a beautiful chemistry that softens the hated sun and brings in puffs of ocean breeze. The cars all along the boulevard are crawling. The lights are all down, traffic cops are everywhere. I file into a line of on-ramping cars and turn the corner toward the freeway.

CHAPTER SIX

I glance at Abby. "You knew? How?"

"Wasn't hard to figure out."

"But . . . how?"

"You got into one of your really quiet moods last night," Abby says. "It was right after you told me about your plan to drive up to Tahoe, as we were saying goodbye."

"I wasn't quiet."

"You're an open book, Harrison. I knew you'd pull something like this. And today, Conner told me about the bug you found in your house and that note. He came over after you guys talked." I stare through the rearview mirror at Conner. Our eyes meet, and he just shrugs. "He told me to pack a bag and be ready in fifteen minutes if I wanted to go along."

"But . . . what made you want to?"

Abby reaches into the front pocket of her shorts. "Check this out." She opens her palm to reveal the same circular device I'd found in my house. She drops it into my palm. "My dad found that while we were packing this morning. On top of one of the kitchen cabinets."

"Oh, shit," I say under my breath. I can't have this in the car. I check the rearview for any signs of police then chuck the device out my window. "It's like we've all been infected."

"None of us could've known," Conner says.

"I'm sorry," is all I can say, all I can think to say.

"What is it they think you have? Or know?" Abby asks. "Is this all still about your dad?"

"It was secret," I say, trying to puzzle this out. "I know it was classified."

"It's got to be weapons-related," Abby says. "He was a physicist. It's got to be about weapons."

"Or aliens," Conner says and, knowing him, it's not a joke.

We're crawling along—the northbound 405 as sluggish as ever—when an explosion goes up, about ten blocks east of us, the blast as loud as thunder. All three of us cry out. I slam on the brakes and avoid the truck in front of me by inches. Screeches sound from every lane and twice we hear the crunch of vehicles colliding. At that explosion site, smoke and fire roll up into a ball and rise. We're too shocked to speak. A gas station must've exploded, or maybe it was an overloaded generator.

At Pico, I pull off the freeway and take a left, driving several blocks into Santa Monica. I need to think, get away from all this traffic. I turn north on Barrington, feeling easier here because the roads clear up.

Two blocks north of Exposition, I turn into a mini-mall parking lot with a 7-Eleven. I park between a pizza place and a dry cleaner's. Why are so many men out here right now? Some of them are our age, but most of them look in their twenties, white, black, Hispanic, all kinds. Groups are shouting to each other; I hear a bottle smash on the sidewalk behind us.

"What're you doing?" Abby asks as I turn off the engine.

"Guys," I begin, "this is a bad idea. You do realize that you're both at risk, right, as long as you're around me?"

Abby and Conner exchange looks.

"If we don't go, then you don't go," says Abby.

"We're in it now," Conner says. "Somebody bugged the both of you. And me too, for all I know. Sticking together might be better than taking our chances at home, where we know we're being listened to—or watched."

"And you can't tell me about those dreams and leave me hanging," Abby adds. "That's just rude."

"Your parents are going to be looking for you," I say to her.

"It's all right." She looks straight ahead, at ease. "I left them a note." There's always been a defiant streak about Abby. It's awesome.

I turn to Conner. "And what about your parents—"

"We're on a need-to-know basis."

That's true: His parents are checked out anyway. They'll be none the wiser.

But my mom is going to go ballistic. Right now, she's at the hospital, the phones are down. She can't call me. But she'll be home eventually, and then she'll find the car still gone and know what's up. I'll be up shit's creek. But then I steel myself, remind myself of the whole reason I'm out here. I'm living my life now, doing what I need to do.

"Dev, we're already on our way," says Abby. "Let's do this."

I look at her. She's beautiful.

The glass doors of the 7-Eleven thrust open, and three guys in black hoodies tumble out. One has his arms loaded up with bags of food, bottles of water, soda. The second guy's stuffing cash into his pockets, whooping it up, a pistol in his hand, and the third has cases of beer in both arms. People are suddenly streaming in and out of the 7-Eleven, screaming and laughing, hauling off inventory, as much as their hands can carry. Somebody in a mask tosses a chunk of brick through the storefront.

All this is happening so rapidly that it's hard to register how things went from weird to dangerous. I hear the thump of hands against the back window as I start the car, push the stick in reverse, and back out, hoping to God I don't crush anybody. In first gear now, I hit the gas, turning to get out of the lot; second gear, and now there's a thumping of fists, hands on the window glass. I turn to my left to see a huge face, a swastika tattooed on one side of it, telling me to get out of the car, displaying his pistol at me. I lurch the car into third, floor it, hoping the car doesn't give out, and peel out of the lot. One gunshot goes off behind us. Flooring the gas, I roar through a stoplight back onto Barrington. Another gunshot.

"Stay down!" I yell, trying to shield Abby, crouched low in the passenger seat.

As we're tearing through the next intersection, I know it's only by sheer luck that we didn't get shot or smash into another car or get carjacked. There are people on the streets out there roving in gangs, people dashing out of stores, loaded with car seats, lamps, toilet paper. Abby and I look at each other, puzzled, freaked out. Police sirens sound from far off behind us. I drive west a couple more blocks.

"What're you thinking?" I ask no one in particular. "Surface streets, Sepulveda Pass, all the way to Mulholland?"

But they're still shaken, scanning for more signs of trouble.

"Yeah," Conner says, shaking his head, still catching his breath. "Sounds good."

"I saw your text from last night," I say to Conner, looking at him through the rearview, "about the blackout on the East Coast. Looks like the whole country got it."

"Yeah, that blackout was a bit weird," Conner says. "And schizo, too. I was talking to my mom, and she says power in Florida was out last night and came back on this morning. Then our power went out, like, twenty minutes after I talked to her." He plugs his phone into a portable charger and starts checking for a signal.

We're back on the 405, but farther north now. Taking surface streets saved us some time, but it was still a slog to get this far. What should've taken twenty minutes took us two hours with gridlock at every intersection, emergency vehicles and traffic cops everywhere. Conner gets out a bag of trail mix, munches down a handful and passes it up to Abby.

"Was there a hurricane out there or something?" I ask, holding out my palm. Abby shakes trail mix into it.

"Nope, nothing." He shakes his head, eyes on the phone screen. "Clear skies all up and down the East Coast. What I don't get is why *our* power went out, and Florida's is back on."

Abby slugs from her water bottle. "And didn't Texas go on and off twice last night too?"

"Could be hackers," Conner suggests. "Maybe they hacked into security codes to different power plants. And they're just, you know, controlling the voltage, starving out cities of power then dialing the power back up."

I know what's coming next. "Triton conspiracy in three . . . two . . ."

"Nah," Conner says, smiling. "This could've been anybody. We've got enough enemies out in the world. Plus, our grid's been fubar for decades. Not that hard to hack into. Surprised it took till 2030 to do it."

"You're pretty sure it's a hack, then," I say.

Conner's nodding. "I think so, yeah," when Abby cuts in sharply—

"Who cares what it is or who it is?"

Conner and I are stunned into silence. "Abby," Conner says with mock sternness, "you are really messing with my conspiracy mojo here."

"Two days ago," she says, "a humongous freakin' rock blew up over So Cal. But what it really was, none of us have a clue. Now the country's power is shutting down. And we'll never know the real reason for that either." She takes a deep breath, shaking her head, "At this point, I'm like, does it even matter? Because whoever's involved, whoever they all are, they'll just get whatever they want, and the rest of us will have to deal with it. Our parents tried, every previous generation tried, to change shit, but it's worse than ever."

"Can't argue with that, Mendes," Conner replies.

Abby's on a roll now. "Look, our enemy is either some corporation or the Russians, the CIA, or the Chinese. No matter the players, we're still gonna be the ones being screwed over. The best use of our energy right now is to make sure that we—you, me, you, our families, every common citizen—figures out a way to either escape this craziness or survive it. More and more, it's every man for himself."

After a long pause, Conner observes, "You got a real anarcho-nihilism thing going. I can dig it."

Abby shakes her head, knocks back a handful of the mix into her mouth and passes the bag to me.

"We've been at war, one kind or another, for, like, eighty years. You don't hear about the chess game, who's moving the pieces and why, unless you're paying attention," Conner says, a smile playing across his face. "We Americans used to play this game better than anybody, messing with everybody in the schoolyard before other players got better and smoother at the game than we were. And then the internet happened. Now our enemies can wipe us out with one hack. One well-executed hack like a kick to the balls. Just a matter of time before hackers zeroed in on the grid."

"I pray we get the lights back on . . . we're clearly losing our shit out here." She's right. If the pandemonium we saw back in LA is possible after only a couple of hours being in the dark . . . what kind of city are we going to come back to tomorrow?

As we merge from the 405 to the 5, driving north now, I feel on edge. It's like the African savannah out here, and we're herds in some starved landscape, past loops of highways closed off to traffic like they're long-abandoned migratory tracks. Semi trucks rage and bellow in the right lanes, but the gangbangers in their souped-up race cars aren't intimidated. They're the hyenas out here, ruthless, wedging in between and one-upping each other, firing through lanes, threading needles between the rest of us who just want to live to see another day.

I watch the weary faces of parents with their children and belongings loaded up in SUVs and more desperate-looking brown faces side by side in overloaded pickup trucks. The families: where are they going on the 5? Sacramento? Fresno? Arid cities where water is as prized as hope. California is shriveling in the dust, under all that smoke pouring out of the tinderbox we call the Angeles National Forest.

"We're all just animals," I say, gesturing out to the choked traffic, "fleeing to wherever." Abby nods. Her eyes are on ash clouds and the brown-backed hills, everything steeped in the gold sunset. "It's funny how beautiful it still looks," she says. "I've always thought wildfires were beautiful in their own way. Making everything look surreal. Nothing could be further, I guess."

"True," I say. "The smoke cover cools us off a bit, but you're still breathing ash."

"Sad it's come to this." Abby keeps her eyes on the hills.

With the 210 closed off because of the wildfires, the 14 is the only way open to people going east. And, from the looks of it, almost everybody wants to go east. They line up for miles before the 14 exit, and, for an hour, we're just sitting in traffic, crawling along a few feet of road at a time. We've been on the road for three hours, and we're barely out of the city.

I can't stay trapped here. Checking the side mirror, I see there's maybe enough room to get a rumbling truck's attention by signaling and lurching the car over, so I take the gamble and hit the gas. Abby lets out a stifled scream and Conner grumbles, "Shit," under his breath as we make our move. There's a shuddering bump as the truck makes contact, not terrible, but enough to get everybody's attention. I'm not stopping, though, and yank left on the wheel again, squeezing into the carpool and gunning it. It's only seconds later that I'm aware of the honking behind us. I remember the thud and guess that the back bumper got crunched, nothing serious, and keep moving. It's a relief to cruise past the 14 off-ramp, but a part of my soul cries out for the thousands trying to squeeze into that exit.

We're eating up road now, doing about sixty; any faster and the steering wheel starts to shake. The flats on either side of the freeway are flushed with deep shades of purple and amber lighting up the stucco shopping malls and terracotta rooftops of Santa Clarita.

"There's something we still have to figure out," I say.

Conner takes out his ear buds. "You say something?"

"There's something we still need to figure out. Where we gonna sleep? 'Cause it's gonna be dark when we get up there. No rangers, no police. No one's staffing the boathouse, and the trail's technically closed. So . . . not a place we want to be in the middle of the night, you know?"

We decide on going as far as Sacramento. Abby says she has friends at a college up there, and we can crash with them tonight. Or we could scrounge together enough cash to pay for a hotel room.

"Hey, Abs," I ask, "can you get my water out of my backpack?" She reaches behind my seat, and I inhale the scent of her hair—just for one second. Its fragrance is exactly what it's been this whole year, an intensely sweet, flowery something. It calms me. I take the steel bottle, unscrew it, and take a swig. We trade quick smiles. I take another gulp and check the rearview and immediately cough out half the contents through my mouth and nose.

"Careful! Gross!" Abby chuckles.

Like the symptom of a disease you prayed you didn't have, I see it again—in the far-right lane, sixty feet behind us: the van. Plain white. Tinted windows. It could've been behind us the whole time as we were leaving the city, camouflaged by traffic jams. "Keep your eyes on that one." I point the van out to the others.

"Why?" Abby asks. "What's going on?"

"Dev says he's been seeing a van lately, like, following him around."

"Are you kidding me? There's like a million white vans in LA."

"We went over this," Conner explains. "I think he's being legit."

I feel validated by Conner's endorsement—a far cry from his attitude yesterday.

"After finding that bug in our house," Abby says, "I'm finding it hard to doubt anything you say."

"Never doubt me," I joke.

"Get off at the exit," Conner suggests, pointing to an approaching sign for Magic Mountain Parkway. It's three lanes over, one over from the van. But before I even signal, I notice the van's turn lights blinking. "Hang on," I say, and watch with confusion and relief as the van shifts into the exit lane. It's a long, agonizingly long exit lane. Thankfully, it stays in the exit, finally descending a slope toward an intersection and, just like that, it's gone, like a wasp that's lost its scent.

"Slow up," Conner instructs, his attention still on the van. But it's obscured now by the railing of the overpass we're on. "Shit. I lost him."

"Just so long as he isn't behind me, I don't care." I slow down enough to steady out the wheel.

Conner unzips the cooler bag I stowed in the back seat and cracks open a soda. "You sure that was him?"

"Looked like him, but,"—I shrug—"Abby's right. There're tons of white vans in the world. Coulda been the same one. Coulda not."

We cruise past Valencia and Castaic Junction. On either side, it's all just scrub, power lines, and broken hills visible between the caravans of semi-trailers hauling northward. I can see the interstate stretching far, curving up the Grapevine—the long, endurance test up and over the Tehachapi Mountains. I haven't been out this way in a couple of years. Now, whenever I go with Mom to SF, she insists we fly up. She says she doesn't want to deal with the ugliness of the land and the traffic anymore. But I don't find this land that ugly: the hills run gently and low, like a ridge of backbone riffled by a coarse brown blanket of wool, studded with pompoms of mesquite and chaparral.

Minutes later, with no sign of the van anywhere, we begin the ascent. I keep a steady foot on the gas, careful not to strain the engine too much. And I get the sense that everyone in every truck, van and car around me is as desperate as I am to get over this pass before sundown. Everyone's staring straight ahead, white-knuckling the wheel. The sun drills into our eyes and brains, still about an hour away from sinking behind the hills to our northwest. I wonder what time it'll be when we reach Sacramento. It's already six now. At least four more hours of driving if the traffic cooperates—let alone the car. The wheel shudders; the speedometer is up past seventy. I ease up on the gas.

"Have you had any of those dreams lately?" Abby asks. She's got her shades on and her seat tilted back.

"Yeah," I confess and tell her about the one last night, about the tunnel, the intense light, the feeling of terror and weightlessness, how all I wanted was to break out and wake up.

Conner's listening too. "You never told me about the tunnel."

"I never saw it till last night. It was like I stepped through something, like a screen or hologram."

"Like you've been looking at VR this whole time. But then you kinda broke the fourth wall."

That clicks: the dreams have never felt like true dreams, more like VR. And stepping through it was breaking the wall of that illusion.

"What do you think this dream is trying to tell you?" Abby asks. "What do you think we'll find?"

My mind comes up blank, and I shake my head. "Don't know."

The traffic ahead begins to slow down and bunch up. I drop down to third, then second. A police car, lights flashing, speeds by in the service lane. I'm in second gear for the next half hour and starting to get really pissed off. All three of us are getting anxious. That's when we see the ambulance, fire truck, and police cars on the far right, next to a water truck. The truck is on the shoulder in front of two rear-ended cars.

There's a body, covered by a sheet, next to one of the cars, its crumpled hood smoking. Boxes, broken pottery, pieces of furniture, a tricycle are piled hastily behind the car, as if they'd all been thrown off its roof by the impact.

"Oh my God," Abby half-whispers.

Several distressed-looking people, including a sobbing woman and child, are next to the truck, talking to police officers. One of them, probably the truck driver, is just shaking his head. He bends down to pick up an empty five-gallon water bottle and stands it up in a row of several spilled bottles at his feet.

There's a massive patch of wet asphalt as what looks like gallons of water have spilled all over that side of the road. As bad as I feel about the tragedy to life here, I can't help but feel terrible about the wasted water. I think of the homeless in LA dying from lack of water, the schools in South and East LA that depend on water tanker deliveries just so the kids can keep their bottles filled.

The twilight's deepening in the hills, the traffic's sparser up here along the higher ridge. It's making the driving easier, but we still have the whole stretch of the Central Valley to get through before Sacramento.

"Tank's only got a quarter left," I say, sighing deeply. "Only if it hadn't taken so effing long to get out of the city."

"No worries," says Conner. "We'll be up in Sacramento by eleven tonight, I bet. Tahoe in the morning. Then we'll chill and ride back."

Abby surveys the road. "Any sign of that van since he dropped off?"

I shake my head. "Let's hope it stays that way."

Things are silent for the next several minutes. My thoughts settle, and I focus my mind on the road. We round a big curve and cruise past rural outposts called Lebec and Fort Tejon. Conner's got his earphones on, grooving out to whatever beats are filling his head. With his phone's flashlight, he's studying the California map. Abby's staring out at the road, at the passing blur.

As the mountains get swallowed up by the dark and the lights of passing cars become the only signs of civilization, I'm reminded of road trips with my folks, when I'd be sitting in the back pretending that our car was our spaceship in a frightening universe. And I'd peer out at the reach of our headlights, how the edge of the light would cut across the dark, protecting us like a forcefield.

"Dad, what is light?" I asked him on one of these trips.

From the driver's seat, he told me that light was made up of tiny things called photons. "They're scouts," he told me. "Little scouts sent out into the world, lighting up the universe for us."

"Photons are brave."

Dad laughed. "I guess they are."

I say that again now to myself: "Photons are brave."

Abby yawns and twists her body in a stretch. "Hmm?"

"It's a game I used to play in my head when I was a kid," I say. "Whenever we'd go on road trips, I used to stare out and pretend—*holy shit!*"

In that instant, my life becomes about two things: one, hitting the brakes without skidding out of control . . . because, two, I want to keep from hitting . . . *whatever the hell just ran out in front of me.*

As I slam on the brakes, I hear Abby screaming. Out of the corner of my eye, I see her planting both hands against the dash.

Conner braces his arm against the front seat. "Whoa-whoa-whoa!"

As I slow down to a crawl in the middle of the road, and it's confirmed that we're all still in one piece, he says, "You goin' loco? What is up?" He pops his earphones out. A car speeds past us on the left, and I maneuver onto the shoulder carefully.

I steady my thoughts, pull to a stop. Collect my breath. I saw it for only a split second in the headlights: a naked, hairy human-looking thing crouched on all fours, carrying an animal in its mouth. It charged—sort of *galloped*—into my lane, full speed. I get out of the car, into the cold dry wind of the high pass, and take a look around. The highway is all but black except for the few-and-far-between headlights of passing cars. The slopes to the east are craggy and otherwise featureless in this dark.

"Hang on," I say, grabbing my flashlight out of my backpack.

"What happened?" Conner asks.

"You hit something?"

I tell them everything I just saw and walk back maybe fifty feet to confirm it. There, in the section of road where I'd slammed on the brakes, is a headless possum.

I keep the flashlight trained on it then I see prints: human-like hand- and footprints, muddy and smeared in dark red.

"Shit." Conner's next to me now.

"It was human," I say. "It looked human."

"Prints look it."

With the flashlight, we follow the prints to the shoulder of the road. The prints disappear a few yards up the slope, which is just a black bulk, dotted with tiny clumps of shrub. It rises to a stony ridge about fifty feet up.

A few steps up the slope, it levels to a service road that rises north to a transmission tower, looming like a grim skeletal overlord, deeper black than the sky. The flashlight shows the prints on the service road, crossing the road and continuing up the slope, beyond the reach of my flashlight. Whatever it was, it wasn't human. But it looked human. I feel compelled to follow the tracks.

I point toward the transmission tower. "Went up that way," I say and, almost in a trance, I keep going up the incline of the service road.

"Dev, forget this, man. We should go back."

"*Psst*!" Abby's standing below us, on the edge of the service road. "Guys!" she whisper-screams, pointing manically at something on the slope above us. We look, and what we see makes my stomach clench: there are four shapes, all human-like and upright, all staring up at the inky sky. They're perfectly still. Like they're sculptures placed up on the ridge.

"That. Is. Weird."

"Yeah, let's go, Dev."

"Move!" comes Abby's whisper.

Maybe it was our voices or likely the flashlights, but the figures on the ridge, one by one, look down at us, four glittering pairs of eyes, like red-hot coals. Conner and I are rooted in place. We see one figure crouch down and begin crawling down the slope. I can make out its eyes, melting out of the darkness, bobbing and shifting, like wolves' eyes. On the wind come faint sounds of sniffing.

Abby all-out yells, "Move!"

My legs come unstuck, and I find myself running hard, back down the slope toward the car idling, its lights still on. Abby's got the passenger door open, one foot in the car, and waving us to run faster. I know Conner is right behind me as we haul ass. I hear nothing, no pursuing feet, no noises at all, and, seconds later, I see the driver's side door opening; Abby's inside now, and she's pushed the door open. Conner and I climb in, slam the doors shut.

We sit there, catching our breath, expecting that something is going to jump in front or on top of the car. Nothing happens. We hear only our breathing, steadying out, and we look at each other, eyes wide.

I can't speak until I'm back on the road and up to highway speed. "WTF. You saw it. You saw it?"

"Saw all four of them," Conner gasps. "Up on that hill."

"Kinda animal?"

"Not an animal."

"Had to be. You saw how fast it ran."

"The footprints," Conner gasps again. "How about the footprints?"

"Shit. Coulda been like a chimp. You know, a primate? They can look a lot like humans."

"What?" Abby pipes up. "They all escape from a zoo? There are no zoos here!"

"No, dude," Conner objects, "you saw its face!"

We shout and argue and talk over each other for long enough that we've dropped down the north end of the Grapevine and entered the flatlands of the San Joaquin before we can each think straight. The light's all but leaked out of the sky now. It's almost eight.

I can see a sliver of moon to the west, a few stars. Endless rows of what used to be lettuce and tomato fields skitter by in the moonlight. A low range of hills follows along to the west. To the east, I can't make out anything except for power lines and sagebrush blocking our view of, well . . . blackness.

Less than a quarter-tank of fuel now. We pass a sign for a gas-food-hotel stop, an exit called Buttonwillow.

"Hey, guys?" I ask. "If the power's down, will the gas stations be open? Don't the pumps run on power?"

Conner says to take things one step at a time. "Maybe they have a generator there," he says. "Let's keep our fingers crossed."

About ten minutes later, we roll into Buttonwillow. We round the turn at the bottom of the off-ramp. The main road takes us past fast-food restaurants and gas stations. The stations are all dark, but there's a bunch of fast-food places, a Denny's, a Subway, a Starbucks, that are all lit up, apparently open.

Just past the Starbucks, there's a Motel 6 and, opposite that, a sign that reads Travel Center. The Travel Center is a massive paved lot containing a convenience store and gas station. The sign, the gas station, and the windows of the convenience store are all dark, though, and overshadow any hope of getting refueled.

"So much for generators," Abby says.

We pull into the Travel Center complex anyway. A semi-truck, its engine idling, sits on the right side of the lot. Its headlights and side lights are torches in the darkness. As we pull closer to the truck, we see the driver side is open.

Before I'm even fully stopped, Abby grabs a flashlight and gets out of the car. She walks up to the driver side of the truck and shines the light into the cab, roving the light, exploring the ground and the front area of the truck.

Something on the ground catches her attention. She stoops down, training the light to the ground at her feet, and picks up a hat. She peers inside the cab again. By now, Conner and I are too intrigued to stay put, so I cut the engine, and we join her.

"What's going on?"

The cab's abandoned. Conner runs back, gets another flashlight, and searches the cab and the grounds nearby. On the pavement, there's a shoe and a handprint. The print looks like it could be oil or blood. We don't touch it. The lights show clods of dirt kicked up along the fringe of grass leading to a field.

Our first thought is to call the police. We grab our phones. Nothing. No power, no signal. Conner climbs into the cab with his light and turns off the ignition. With the growl of the engine silenced and the truck's lights off, the night is eerie and all-enveloping. We grab our packs and run across the street toward the light of the Starbucks.

It feels like a sanctuary in here, a reminder of civilization, even though the two baristas—both about our age—are wearing face masks. They talk to each other in clipped, nervous tones and don't acknowledge us. We don't mind: the lights and coffee machines work. We don't want to freak them out, so we simply ask if we can use the phone to call the police.

"Phone isn't working. What's wrong?"

"The truck outside," I venture. "It was running, lights on, but no driver."

"It's like he bailed," Conner adds.

The barista, freckly and pale, cranes his head to look out the front doors, makes a clucking noise and shakes his head. "Sorry, I wish I could help. Like I said, no phones here."

"No worries," Conner says, wanting to push the matter away. "Those masks help?"

The barista shrugs. "Our manager wanted us to wear them after what happened down in LA. Precaution, you know." He picks up a rag and starts wiping down the counter.

We get juice, coffee, whatever pickings of food are left on display, and huddle at a table in the corner, dumping our packs at our feet.

"That was no animal," Conner says in a hushed voice. "That wasn't dogs, coyotes . . . or chimpanzees."

"Whatever they were," Abby responds, "I just want to get through tonight and not be a meal for one of them."

"Shh," I interject, noticing there's a family at a small table near us. Two young kids, one practically an infant, are getting restless. The parents begin to gather up their things, push their chair back.

"Excuse me," Abby asks the couple, "are you staying at one of the motels around here?"

The father, worn-out and worried-looking, shakes his head. "There aren't any rooms here." He tosses a balled-up napkin onto his plate. "They're either full up or not checking in guests because of the outage."

The mom lifts the baby out of the high seat and the other child, a boy of about five, stands up, nibbling on a muffin.

"So," the father adds, "it's back in the car and on the road till we find something."

"Which direction?" I ask.

"Del Mar," the father says. I notice the woman, his wife, is nervous and edgy. "Her sister is there."

We say we're headed up to Fresno to see friends. The man tells us to be careful, that the 5 above the Central Valley is dicey around the cities with people packing up and heading east.

We wish them good luck. They wish us the same, but, before leaving, the mom, rocking the fussing baby in her arms, recommends that we turn around and go back. "Safer near your homes. That's where we'd be if it hadn't burned down."

After they're gone, the Starbucks is empty except for us and the two baristas.

It strikes me that all I did today was take my friends from a bad situation to a worse one. "Shit. I'm sorry, you guys shouldn't have to deal with this."

Conner shrugs. "You saw what things are like in LA. We'd be no better off there."

"But you'd be home, with a roof over your head."

"Why don't we all sleep on it?" Abby suggests. "See how we feel in the morning. Maybe going back isn't the worst idea?"

"Subaru Outback Motel?" Conner jokes.

Abby cracks a smile. "We can hit the road at sunup."

The flashlights from our phones punch holes in the night, and the only sign the world is still alive is the occasional sweep of the warm desert winds. There's still no Wi-Fi or phone signal. All day with no contact with families or the outside world. The only sound above the wind is the clacking of a distant train. It's so easy, I think, to wipe out any traces of the twenty-first century.

CHAPTER SEVEN

Conner's snoring from the front passenger seat. His earphones are on, his arms folded, and his legs stretched out as far as the car will allow. I'm on the opposite side, behind the wheel, in the same position. The only difference is I'm not sleeping.

Because we're gracious gentlemen, we gave Abby the whole back seat. She's got her eyes closed, her head resting in the corner of the seat and the window frame. Her body curls along the length of the back seat. I doubt she's sleeping, though.

From my backpack, I fish out the shortwave radio. I click it on and search the band, the volume on low. I dial the needle back and forth, across the fuzz and crackle and land on a voice, an Australian accent, a news broadcast: Iran bombed Tel Aviv because Israel lobbed missiles at the Islamic regime in Tehran; the US, UK and EU are urging calm after the Indian Army commandeered Pakistan's northeastern nuclear sites where jihadists were holed up; meanwhile, the US joined Japan and Australia in a naval blockade of Chinese container ships and Taiwan is under Chinese martial law. More meteors have exploded over Russia, Turkey and the Black Sea.

"Did he say something about meteors?" Conner asks in a low voice.

I nod, turning down the volume. "Yeah. Over Russia, Turkey."

Conner yawns, turns over and closes his eyes again. I think he's gone back to sleep when he says, "Not surprised."

"About what?"

All I hear in response is a faint snore.

I know Conner suspects that the meteors aren't really meteors but weapons tests doubling as scare tactics. But whose, though? China, Russia, the US on its own people? It could be anybody. There are so many forces making and shaping the world, no one knows where to look till the damage is already done. Conner would say that there's a shadow committee, an inner circle made up of the world's richest and most powerful—like a half-dozen people, maybe—wheeling and dealing, shifting billions—*trillions*—in oil, money, weapons, assets of every kind in backroom deals to make sure everybody in the circle is flush and happy. Meanwhile, the rest of us—the *proles*—we're living inside an illusion of nations, governments, elections, all meant to keep us hypnotized and under control. The hypnosis, that's what the media's for. It's his story, he likes to say, and he's sticking to it.

I listen to the news a little longer and learn that our entire power grid is still switching on and off, and officials are stumped. The Department of Energy and the CIA are both pointing fingers at the Russians and in a cable interview, the president blamed the Chinese. I click the radio off.

"Can't sleep, huh?" Even in this near-dark, I can see Abby in the far corner of the back seat. "I heard you listening to the radio," she adds in a hushed tone. "Find out anything?"

"More of the same. A lot more, actually."

"A mess, in other words." She straightens and sits up. "Where'd you find that little radio?"

"Dug it out of a closet." I turn it over in my hands. "We'd take this with us on camping trips when I was little. My dad would always have this on at night. He'd point up at the stars, tell me about them. We'd listen to stations from all these weird little places around the world. Languages he didn't even understand."

She laughs a little. "What for?"

"He'd say the voices made the world feel smaller. Like it was all within reach, you know? He'd hold up the radio like it was some miraculous thing and talk to me about radio waves."

Abby closes her eyes, pondering. "It *is* . . . kind of miraculous." She picks up her phone and places it in her palm. "You want the world? Here it is."

"Yeah, until the power goes out, and the world goes dark."

She turns her phone on. Her face glows in the screen's eerie light. She frowns, shaking her head. "No signal."

"It'll be better tomorrow," I say, trying to sound upbeat.

I tell her goodnight, but what I really want to tell her is that I think she's beautiful. But in the quiet of that car, with Conner asleep only feet away, I don't say a word.

It's not exactly the Four Seasons in here. We've got packs, water bottles, and bags of food everywhere so there isn't much space to stretch out. Once, Conner and I get out of the car to stretch. All the lights are out and not a sound. It's like we're in some forgotten corner of the world or exiled in some faraway corner of the universe.

At around 3 a.m., on the outer edges of sleep I hear what sounds like glass breaking. It's very faint. I sit up and, rubbing my eyes, squint toward the mini-mart. All's quiet now except for the drifting brush, the rasp of trees nearby in the wind.

A tapping at the window wakes us. Bleary and achy, I check the window to see a man in black glasses, salt-and-pepper beard, and baseball cap waving me over in the direction of the convenience store. I rub my eyes, force myself to wake up.

Hints of sunlight on the cold, gray ridge to the east, tints the pale air. My phone says 6 a.m. On the far side of the lot, the truck is a cold, decomposing corpse.

The bearded man's halfway to the store now, and I realize Conner's gone. In the back, Abby's asleep, her face turned toward the back rest.

"Abby," I call in a hushed voice. "*Psst.*"

She opens her eyes, her face scrunched against the light, and a second later straightens up. "What time's it?"

"Early. Some guy just tapped the window, woke me up. He waved us up to that store. Looks open. You know where Conner went?"

She points toward the mini-mart. There's Conner, stepping out from behind the building, zipping himself up.

"You could've used the bathroom inside," I call out to him. "Guy just opened it."

He stops, looks toward the mart for a second, shrugs.

The lot is empty, the gas pumps vacant. But we see something that gives us hope: The neon signs advertising sodas and beers on the store's windows are lit up.

"Power on?" I say, half to myself, as I turn over the engine and drive up to one of the pumps. The digital displays on the pump are on!

"Best fill up now," the bearded man hollers, loping out of the store toward me. He's stoop-shouldered, thin, and wearing a greasy brown jacket with his name on the tag. It reads Earl. "Power came back a few minutes ago. Hurry up before it decides to cut out again." He gives me a pleasant smile from behind that scruffy beard.

"Will do," I say, pulling out cash from my pocket. I give him forty.

He pockets the cash and eyes us both over. "Whereabouts you kids going?"

"Sacramento," Abby says.

Earl scratches at his beard. "Hmm," he mutters, taking off his glasses and wiping the lenses with the hem of the shirt under his jacket. "Be careful, then. Road closures all up the 5 on account of the fires. Lotsa traffic having a hell of a time."

I recall the family from last night warning us about the road north. "What route do you recommend?"

The man gazes out at the freeway, beyond the restaurants and motels to the west. "I recommend a magic carpet." He snickers and snorts. "Come on inside," he says, "after you fill up, and we'll get you figured out."

While I fill up the gas tank, Abby goes inside to use the ladies' room, and Conner paces the front of the mini-mart, a water bottle in one hand, brushing his teeth. The air out here is brisk in the way of desert mornings. I draw in a deep cold breath, appreciating it.

Conner spits into a garbage bin. "We better enjoy it. In a couple of hours, we'll be baking." He swigs from the bottle and says he's going back to the car to change.

It's like the power outage was some kind of nightmare, and we've woken up to civilization again. As I'm filling up the gas tank, I check my phone: oh my God. Four bars! My excitement mixes with dread, though, because I fully expect a conversation with my mother at any minute. I check my messages, expecting a backlog of furious and/or confused texts.

But there's nothing. Not one text. No voicemails. She should've been home by now from her shift and found me gone. Any minute now, I reason, this phone will start buzzing. But the phone is quiet—for now.

I grab my pack from the car and head into the store. Earl's got the TV on behind the counter showing news footage about the power outage. And there's something else too.

Even with the volume turned off, I can tell the world's fallen apart overnight. I recognize the streets even before I read the caption, "Los Angeles." The streets, seen in helicopter shots, are berserk with riots, fires, looters. Then I see pictures of a hospital emergency entrance: it's Mom's hospital. Ambulances, lights whirling, are backed up at the entrance. Not just ambulances but also armored trucks, like SWAT vehicles. People in scrubs push gurneys in and out; others in black jumpsuits pace the entrance, rifles in hand.

"Hey, my mom works there."

Earl turns to look at the TV screen. He reaches for the remote on a shelf behind him and turns up the volume: ". . . from San Diego to Los Angeles, a mysterious and potentially fatal infection of unknown cause has sent more than six hundred people to local emergency rooms. Doctors report that the initial symptoms resemble the flu before the victim turns violent. Several deaths have already been confirmed. The National Guard has been deployed to Los Angeles to quell the spike in looting and riots sparked by yesterday's citywide power outage, as well as to assist public health officials and doctors as they seek to contain the disease spread. The city is under quarantine until the severity and extent of the illness can be determined."

"Hell's going on?" Conner mumbles, strolling in through the front doors.

Earl turns down the volume again. "Sounds like the three of you got out in the nick of time."

"That's the last time I sleep in a car. My hair is ridic," Abby says, stepping up behind us and sees the stricken looks on our faces. "What happened?" Her pack droops low from her fingers, her hair's tied back and, like Conner, she's changed her clothes.

I'm too stunned to explain anything to her so Conner does the talking. She looks in vain at her phone. It's probably the millionth time she's checked it since waking. "Nothing. Still nothing."

"Servers might be overloaded," Conner suggests. "I'm sure they're all okay."

Abby and I both try texting our moms. Neither of us can send anything out. DELIVERY FAILED both times.

Conner recommends we chill, that they're probably repairing the towers after the transformers failed, and in a few hours, we'll probably be connected. While Conner and Abby check out the snack aisles, I hoist up my pack and head through the aisles to the men's room.

"Want anything?" Abby asks me. "I'm going to grab a juice or something."

"Juice would be good."

As I'm about to enter the hallway to the restroom, she calls, "Hey."

We look at each other and give each other as comforting a smile as we can.

"She's fine," she tells me.

I nod. "Yours too."

It's a small bathroom, just space enough for two stalls, a couple of urinals and a sink. The frosted glass fixture above the mirror gives off a dull, flickering white light. There's a smell, a sickly combo of disinfectant and faint sewage—about what I'd expect in a gas station bathroom. And there isn't any noise above the soft hum of the exhaust fan. I do my business, wash my hands, change clothes, and I'm collecting my thoughts, standing there at the bathroom sink, when I see it through the mirror—up on the ceiling.

It's attached by its palms and feet to the corner of the ceiling, there above the door. It's definitely human—or human-*like*. The size of maybe a ten- or twelve-year-old. I can confirm it's not a chimp, but its face has features like one. The nostrils are upturned, widened, flared, the brow ridged. The mouth hangs open to bare yellow and reddish teeth, the canines longer, sharper. The skin is milky pale, mapped all over with blue and black veins. Scant bristles of black hair cover its body, not the face. And there's a thicker crop of bristles on its top and back, like a mane. It's wearing torn, mud-smeared jeans. And worst of all, it's looking at me.

Through the mirror, I see its eyes, bloodshot, unblinking, locked on me, and a face that seems to register surprise—like when a cat spots unexpected prey.

What creeps me out most is that it was up there the whole time I've been in here.

I turn off the faucet carefully. The thing is above the door, blocking my exit. *Oh, shit.*

I scooch back, alongside the sink, then slowly walk into one of the stalls. What I'm hoping for happens: the thing follows me with its eyes. I lift my foot to the flush on the side of the tank and press down on the handle. The immediate *whoosh* attracts the thing's attention, and I hear the thump of its palms and feet as it scrabbles across the top of the wall and positions itself directly above me. The toilet stops filling, the room goes silent, so I raise my foot and push down on the handle again. The *whoosh* erupts and, this time, the thing begins to lower itself toward the toilet, its focus on the noise, not on me. And that's when I back out of the stall and make backward for door. As I smack into the door, I can hear it jostling the flush and emitting a few shrieks.

In a flash, I'm out of there and screaming my head off. "Run! It's in there! We've got to get out of here!" It's like I'm looking at a freeze-frame of a movie: Abby, juice bottles in hand; Conner at the entrance of the store, halfway through the door; Earl at the register, craning his head toward me, astonished.

"What're you yelling about?" shouts Earl.

From the hallway comes the slamming noise of the restroom door, and we see the thing burst out of the hallway a second later. I'm staring at it now as it crouches fifteen feet away. Standing in the aisle,

I feel Abby next to me, the brush of her hand on my elbow, pulling at me to back up. The thing's not moving, just sizing us up. It grunts and rubs the bristles of its head against its shoulder—scratching an itch, maybe. From behind me, at the register, I hear the clink of metal objects dropping to the floor: shells scattering as Earl fumbles to load a fistful of shells, one by one, into a pump-action shotgun he's produced from behind the counter. "Out of the way," he yells at us.

"Dev, Abby," Conner's voice, coming from far behind us, is nervous but steady. "Back . . . the . . . F . . . up."

We trade stares with this thing for what seems like a long minute, then the thing begins to crawl in our direction with a knuckle-dragging gait. Its eyes—black and dilated—fix on us, and I can see the gaping, almost grinning mouth. Looking at it now, I can see I was right: it's got the body of an older child. But beneath the hairs, the arms, torso and legs have the muscle definition of a much stronger creature. As it nears, we hear it sniffing, and behind that sniffing sound is a snarl, like a low flame.

That's when I feel a hand grip my shoulder and shove me aside. A muzzle of a shotgun comes into view off to my side. Earl's already leveled his aim at the thing as he steps between me and Abby. Under his breath, he drawls, "What in God's name?"

I can think of nothing to say, no way to help him.

"Get behind me," he says, low and calm.

Abby and I retreat several steps, and as we do, see the thing leap and hear the shotgun go off—a massive sound that makes us crouch down. From the floor, I see the thing grab onto Earl's collar—the blast must've missed—pull him to the ground and start dragging his body back and forth, slamming it against both sides of the aisle. I'm shocked by this thing's strength.

Earl is screaming, his arms trying to grab onto something. His hat's on the floor, his shotgun flung onto a bottom shelf, a few feet away.

Abby is screaming, back on her feet, clutching the shelves.

I scramble to my own feet.

Meanwhile, Earl's gone quiet, unconscious. The thing grabs hold of the man's head and, before we can blink, it's plunged its jaws into his throat and ripped out the windpipe.

My mind can't process what I'm seeing yet: a stump of bone and flesh where the larynx used to be and an opened fountain of blood spraying all over the tile, the shelving.

Abby, grunting, snatches up the shotgun. The ratcheting noise of her sliding back the pump-action attracts the thing's attention. My ears register the clatter of a shell on the floor but my eyes are on the thing as it looks up, mouth and chin dripping, and fixes its dilated eyes on her. It raises itself up on Earl's body, its arms cocked back like it's about to spring. Then it hisses at Abby, mouth wide open, and hisses again when I hear the gun go off. The top half of the thing's head explodes like a pumpkin, and its body drops.

"Shit," Abby says under her breath, lowering the shotgun. "Shit, shit, shit." I take it from her and lay it on the floor. She's got her hands over her face. She's trembling. "It's okay, it's okay," I whisper, freaked out, knowing nothing's okay. I put my arm around her.

"Guys." Conner rushes up to us, puts his arms around our shoulders. I'm aware of the three of us standing there, asking questions of each other out of disbelief. *What just happened? What is that thing? What do we do? Do we call the police? Medics?* Still something holds us back. Maybe it was the sight of the armored vehicles and the men in jumpsuits with carbines in front of my mom's hospital.

We agree it's best to clear out of here before more people show up. If they want us, they can find us. Right now, we agree, we're on a mission and, clearly, shit is going down everywhere we look—as if the world is conspiring to scare us, freak us out, trip us up.

A minute later, with the sun over the eastern range, the three of us are climbing back in the car. My hands are shaking, but I manage to turn over the ignition. The car running, I floor it. The tires whine, and I jerk the wheel toward the parking lot exit. There are cars now starting to pull into the Travel Center lot. Well, they're about to walk into a massacre. I floor it all the way down the strip.

"Don't take the on-ramp north, don't do it," Conner says anxiously from the back seat.

"Not going back," I say. "We can't go back."

"Not going back, but we can't go north. Remember all that about the roads and the fires?"

I pass the on-ramp for the northbound 5, feeling rattled, terrified. I don't like this feeling of speeding around aimlessly like a bunch of fugitives. Who or what did we just kill? It wasn't human, I know that. But it wasn't an animal or like any animal I've ever seen.

I stop in a parking lot and fumble around in my pack, fish out my dad's worn-out old map. *Try to focus.* I find where we are: Buttonwillow, just off the interstate. I see the small-print word, a squiggle of black in a plane of gray, numbers and names, veins of road— *Focus!* The north is a snare of closed roads and burning hills and the south—home—is under quarantine.

Out of the corner of my eye, I notice that Abby, crouched in the passenger seat, has her hand over her mouth. She throws opens the door, leans out and hurls up everything in her stomach onto a strip of dirt. I feel horrible for her, upset; she wouldn't be sick if she weren't here— *Focus!*

"How about the 58?" I mumble.

"I'm seeing the 99 as the best way," Conner says, checking the mapping app on his phone. "The 99 to Fresno and on through—"

"No." I turn to him. "No towns, no cities. I wanna stay away from all the crazy."

Conner thinks, his eyes half-shut, the way he always does when he's giving my words serious consideration. Finally, he nods his head. "Fine. Maybe that's better."

Abby heaves again. She's got one hand bunching together the back of her hair. After few more coughs, she straightens up, and shuts the door. She picks up a water bottle at her feet. "Whose is this?"

Conner starts, "That's mi—" but Abby's already swigging from the bottle. "Yours now."

I find a Texaco near the on-ramp where I grab more water, a can of Sprite and crackers for Abby, and breakfast-type grub—a muffin, bananas, a juice—for myself. I feel no appetite but know I'll need to eat as the day goes.

It's past 7 a.m. now, the road's getting busier; people are on the move again. We hear police sirens and the roar of trucks seconds before we see the military caravan.

As I'm putting the Outback in gear, they appear, rolling down the off-ramp in single file: a pair of police cars, several unmarked four-doors and an armored vehicle with "FBI" on its side, bullying their way around traffic, heading south.

We watch as the caravan turns into the Travel Center parking lot. There are about a dozen other cars in the lot and several people gathered around the store entrance.

"Whole place is going to be taped off in five minutes," I observe as we drive past the scene, continuing south toward the 58 junction, where we'll turn east.

"It's going to be all over the news now."

Conner's staring out the window behind me. "I don't think so. I think the Feds are here to make sure it *isn't* all over the news."

We're cruising now, and all's quiet. I'm checking the rearview mirror at least once a minute, each time expecting the police, the Feds or ...

the white van right behind me. Things out here are quiet, the traffic is sparse and local. I'm sharing the lane with an SUV hauling a horse trailer and a pickup loaded with what looks like bags of feed.

Westbound, heading toward the interstate, is a little heavier with U-Haul trucks and loaded minivans. Finding the local news on the radio, we realize that the miles-long shelf of ashen clouds, shaped like a battleship and filling the southern horizon, are from wildfires cutting off routes to Barstow and the California border.

"They don't know the 5 is a no-go," Conner says, a note of pity in his voice. "Gotta feel sorry for them."

Next to me, Abby is nibbling at crackers, sipping from the Sprite. I can't get a deep breath. My head hurts, and the muscles in my arms and legs feel stiff, every nerve's on edge. I keep swigging from my water bottle.

We stare out the window at acre after acre of almond orchards flickering by. Half of the orchards looked withered, the branches either pruned or rotted away. Pickers with burlap sacks make their way among the healthier trees. Barren fields and power lines take up most of the right-side view, interrupted by run-down ranch homes and abandoned stables. There are no other signs of life here.

Conner cuts the silence. "Abby?" She sips from her soda and turns in her seat. "That was a sick headshot, gotta say."

First I chuckle then Abby cracks a smile, and we both burst into uncomfortable—cathartic—laughter.

"How is it . . ." I grip the wheel tighter, trying not to be repulsed by the thought of that thing up on the bathroom wall. "How is it able to crawl on walls, up and down, like that? It was up near the ceiling in the bathroom when I first saw it."

"Can't begin to guess," Conner replies. "And it's strong as hell too. Flung that guy around like a ragdoll . . ." His eyes glaze over, and he groans, placing his hand on his chest. "I'm gonna see that in my mind forever."

Abby groans, "Don't talk about this or I'm going to be sick again." She presses her hand over her mouth for a second to collect herself. "And you just know that . . . crawler is what killed the driver of that truck last night."

We all agree that, yes, that mystery was hereby solved.

And there was another mystery that I was struggling with. I look through the rearview mirror at Conner. "Something in the desert is doing this to people."

"But what about the people *not* in the desert? There's two hundred new cases in So Cal since Friday. And what about this?" He hands his phone up to Abby.

She's silent as she scans what I'm guessing is an article. "Dev, didn't you say more of those meteors fell in Russia and other places?"

"Meteoroids," I correct her, and we stick our tongues out at each other. "Yeah, last night. Heard it on the shortwave."

"Hundreds more cases in Moscow, the Crimea and"—she scrolls the article—"eastern Turkey."

"So it's not just the desert," Conner says, leaning back in his seat.

Abby starts as her phone goes off—the funky beat of a song I know she loves (and the memory of a high-school party it brings to mind is so out of place right now)—and reaches down to her feet to pick it up. She looks at the display, takes a deep breath and turns to me. "It's my parents."

In a way, I'm glad they were able to reach her. But before I can respond, she's answered the phone and begun speaking. Her first words are garbled, barely audible above the sound of the engine. I can hear, "I'm sorry, Dad, but I already knew how you'd feel about it." Pause, then, "We're fine. No, I'm not hurt." Pause. "Because you wouldn't hear my side or any other side." Now she sounds angry, defiant, and Conner and I, glancing uncomfortably at each other through the rearview, are feeling like eavesdroppers. "No," she says, "maybe I needed us to talk about it. Maybe we don't have to move, have you thought about that?" Another pause; this is a long one.

Something is being revealed to her. She wipes at her eyes and says, "Oh no." She motions for me to pull over to the side of the road.

Before I'm even fully stopped, Abby's got her door open, and she's out of the car. She walks into the field, the phone to her ear, and stands with her arm pushing her hair away from her face. Conner and I say nothing; we don't have to. Something's definitely up.

For the next ten minutes, Abby paces in the dirt. I use the time to check my phone: still no messages. Okay, I can't go longer without contacting my mom; I've been delaying this ever since I saw those images on TV back at the gas station. I begin with typing out a text: *Hi, Mom. I want you to know I'm OK. We are near Bakersfield. Are you OK?*

I hit send, wait a minute, then text again: *I heard on the news about disease cases in LA. I saw West LA Mem on the TV. Can you pls confirm you're OK?* Another minute goes by. Abby's wandering back toward the car, apparently winding up her conversation. *Please tell me how you're doing,* I text. *Love you.*

"What's going on?" I ask Abby.

"It's Danny," she says, closing her eyes and letting out a deep breath to calm herself down. "He had a pretty bad attack yesterday. A couple of hours after we left."

"Where is he?"

Abby shakes her head. "At the hospital. But the doctors are saying to evacuate him because of the fires and all the new medical cases. They got him under control, but he's on oxygen. My dad got in touch with a specialist in Chicago, and they're leaving tonight. They said he needs to be, like, *out* with everything happening and all. Or his health won't—" She presses both hands to her face. "I told them to get him out asap. Said I'd see them there."

I feel like all the air's gotten knocked out of me.

"They must've loved that," I say to her. "I'm sorry, Ab." Conner sinks back in his seat. "We could . . . we could try to turn back."

Abby drops her hands away. Her eyes look straight ahead, a resolve in them. "There's no going back."

"We could . . . we could get to Fresno," Conner suggests. "We could see about getting you on a plane from there . . .?"

"No," Abby says. "Fresno's a bad idea. Airports are jammed. I wouldn't get to Chicago till tomorrow at the least. And by then—" It takes her a few seconds before she can take a deep breath. "Look, I can't change what's happening with Danny right now. My being in Chicago won't change a thing. All I know is we need to get where we're going."

Conner and I trade shocked, confused stares. "You want us to keep going?"

"Everything's going to shit. We need to see this through. Or else . . ." She turns to look at us, her eyes hard as steel. It's more dead-serious than I've ever seen her look.

"It's more important than anything," I say to her, and Abby nods like I'm reciting words already swirling in her mind. "I've had that same feeling. Like something's driving me on, you know? I don't know why or what it is. But everything's at stake. I thought it was all in my head."

"Well," she says, "it's in mine too. So maybe it's rubbing off."

We laugh uneasily together. At least she's smiling again. We both turn to Conner, like we need his vote to make it unanimous. He looks from Abby to me, back to Abby. "Okay, you two are mind-melding now, and it's weirding me out. Whatever, hit the gas. Let's go."

We follow a half-filled apple truck all the way into Bakersfield. The town feels half-awake, like everyone's been drugged. Conner mentions how the desert towns have been dying a slow death for decades. We just haven't noticed it because the cities are still on their feet.

There are crowds of people of every color hanging out at burger and taco stalls, outside a car wash, on street corners, parking lots, or leering at us from pickups piled up with TVs, mattresses, lawnmowers. Up on side streets, we see campers everywhere, awnings pitched outside them where rough-looking families sit around in lawn chairs, moms and dads smoking while kids toddle around in kiddie pools.

We take a detour around police cars blocking the road and catch sight of gangbangers handcuffed and sitting in a row on the curb. Going south then east, we glimpse marchers, hundreds of them, a block to our south. From their signs, in English and Spanish, they're farmers striking against the bottling companies that've dried up all the groundwater here. Driving eastward, we glance past the barricade of police cars and roadblocks and hear the marchers scream and chant slogans like tribal warriors getting ready to confront an army. This is how LA felt as we were leaving the city yesterday—on the verge of battle and the seams of the city bursting.

We rejoin the main road after a few blocks. The farther we get into the outskirts, despair replaces the unrest: the strip malls are half-empty, the dealerships are closed and the pool at the E-Z8 Motel drained. Abandoned homes look back at us like skulls in a graveyard, behind chain-link fences and jungles of yucca and chaparral.

My dad said the universe will die off trillions of years from now in a cold death. Colder than anything you can imagine. After all the stars are long gone and the black holes have all extinguished themselves. "Colder than the freezer?" I would ask. "Colder than the Arctic?" "So cold," he'd smile back at me, "it won't be able to get any colder." But down here in Bakersfield, 2030, it's a heat death: death by boiling sun. Death by drought and by every other kind of rage and loss.

We continue east. The traffic thins. And I think of how one day only the stubborn oaks will be left after all these people have left, been killed, or been jailed. The oaks and the eucalyptus stand tall along the road, and their drooping limbs remind me of Dark Age monks performing rites for the dead.

CHAPTER EIGHT

Los Angeles

June 2015

Gavin Harrison was slumped in his office at Breakthrough Concepts, eyes glazed as he went over the results of some computer modeling of solar-cell designs. He was in mid-yawn when his cell went off. Normally, he didn't answer calls unless it was his wife or his son's school. This time, it was Megan Chen, an out-of-the-blue surprise and worth answering the phone for.

"Sorry to bother you at work, Gavin."

"Couldn't be happier for the interruption." He sat up in his chair. "What's new?"

The two caught up briefly—it had been months since they'd spoken last—before she got around to the gist of her call. "I'm looking at this meteorite sample—"

Gavin gasped. "You're kidding!"

Megan gave a short laugh. "Seriously, though, this one's pretty out there. You might want to look. The notes aren't very helpful. I don't think it's Martian. But . . . well, just come on down."

Gavin made a show of huffing and fussing.

"Whenever you can," she said, "this week or next. I'd appreciate your—"

"Give me an hour."

Minutes later, Gavin was throwing his Outback into fourth as he sped away from the campus of Breakthrough Concepts in Pasadena and made his way across the city toward UCLA. He wondered what made this particular find so interesting. It couldn't be anything trivial, he knew that. Not with Megan.

Halfway through his four years on the faculty of astrophysics at UCLA, Gavin agreed to be Megan's advisor for her thesis (titled "Evolutionary Convergence and Divergence in the Cosmos: Evidence-Based Extrapolations on Extraterrestrial Life"). But then the chair of the department criticized the direction that Gavin was taking his own research, and Gavin told him to "stick it where the sun don't shine." He packed up and left campus that afternoon.

That was two years ago. He hadn't been back on the UCLA campus—till today. From time to time, Megan would still contact him, asking for bits of advice because she knew that her old mentor had her back. For Gavin, astrobiology was one of cosmology's next great frontiers.

What the hell was so mysterious about a meteorite? he thought as he pulled into the parking garage. *It's just a meteorite.*

Through the eyepiece, the quarter-size meteorite fragment was beautiful. Nothing extraordinary at first glance. Gavin turned from the microscope for another look at the field notes describing the find, turning the pages with a gloved hand. The notes in the binder said the meteorite fragments were found in the Mojave Desert in 1981. The piece now under the microscope was one of three recovered in a rancher's field. "Possibly of Martian origin," the notes said, "but this is inconclusive due to anomalies in the morphology and in determining its precise age."

"Anomalies?" he said, closing the binder. It didn't *look* anomalous: igneous rock with speckles of zircon was his best guess.

He sighed, somewhat disappointed. Gavin didn't care about Mars. Mars bored him. Even if life had once existed there, it was dead. The solar system itself bored him. Its most mysterious corners—the ice fields of Europa and Enceladus, the hydrocarbon lakes of Titan—had already been staked out by NASA, the Chinese, and the Europeans. Those worlds would remain devoid of potential until the sun began its red-giant expansion phase and caused these frozen netherworlds to thaw out, releasing rivers and oceans of liquid water, and to become laboratories for new life. But that was billions of years away. He wanted to find his own corner of the undiscovered—now.

As a PhD student at Cambridge, Gavin had become captivated by origins. The origin of life, the origin of stars, of solar systems. These questions dazzled him. But most dazzling of all, the mother of all questions, was the one surrounding the origin of the universe: the whole enchilada.

One day, he was sure, we would glimpse it: a force particle no one had ever seen before. For Gavin, the search for what he called the universe's First and Last Secret—whatever it was, anti-gravity or dark matter—had to end in a very simple discovery. A discovery of a binding agent that glued not only time and space together but also consciousness. It was more than asking why there was something rather than nothing; it was asking why exactly this and not something else?

Gavin had looked up at the stars all his life. The answers were all there, right in front of him. Only they were hidden—either behind dimensions or beyond sight. Then, in 2007, as he was about to start his final year at Cambridge, NASA released the first image of the cosmic microwave background—a kind of map that showed the distribution of the most ancient light detectable in the universe. With its speckles of blues and reds, yellows and greens, the picture was a pixilated view of Earth. But these weren't oceans, continents and clouds. These colors in the image marked minute temperature fluctuations in that first burst of light as photons galloped away into the newly pastured fields of space and time.

Gavin was not a religious person, but the moment of seeing the CMB, projected on a screen in a lecture room when he was a third-year dissertator at Cambridge, was as close to a religious experience as he'd ever had; if there was a God, this was His fingerprint.

The other religious experience he had that year was meeting Seema Godrej. She was in London visiting her parents that Christmas, and he walked right up to her at the bar, feeling emboldened by the Guinness. Once they got to talking, they didn't go back to the music set in the main room—neither cared for the DJ—so they walked around Piccadilly well past midnight comparing the finer points of growing up in Palo Alto versus London. The hours flew, and as he was preparing himself to seduce her with a visual tour of the constellations—you know, like lovers did in the movies—Seema abruptly said she had to get back to her parents' place in Hampstead. She said it was going to be a long day tomorrow, capped off by a flight late the next night . . . back to the States. Gavin's heart fell several stories in his chest. She had to get back to her medical residency at the university hospital in Madison, Wisconsin, but, she said, it had been lovely to meet him. He didn't let her go without getting her number and the next day, his heart beating, he called her, interrupting her kindly, perplexed Punjabi family's teatime, and took her to his favorite pub.

Over pints, she told him her residency was going to take up all her time and a relationship wasn't what she was looking for. He told her he totally understood, but outside the pub, he took a risk and kissed her and, for one epiphany-like flash, the cosmic microwave came in a distant second. By the time he dropped her back home, she'd softened enough to tell him to "keep in touch." Emails followed as well as phone calls, flowers on her birthday, even a stopover in Madison to see her the following Christmas. It was thrilling at first and soon it was love. His Cambridge studies hit a detour, funding was threatened, but, in the end, he defended his thesis about the search for the missing fifth force and, the same time next day, he was with Seema Godrej in her one-bedroom off-campus apartment with everything he owned inside a suitcase he wouldn't open for two days.

As a PhD trying to decide which field of astrophysics to pursue, Gavin plunged into string theory, the multiverse, the frontier theories. But those avenues all dead-ended in problems: there was too much speculation, the multidimensional math was working too hard, he thought, and if it was that hard to find coherence between the mathematical and the observable, it was a twisty and treacherous path to trouble. You needed numbers and nature to be in sync, without too much finagling. If you could achieve that—find a formula that worked on both galactic and quantum scales—you could break down nature's first and final wall, and its first and final secret would be revealed.

Once, Seema walked out of their bedroom at 4 a.m. to find him alone in the living room, equations spread out all over the coffee table, eyes shut, fingers pressed against the bridge of his nose. "What are you?" he was muttering. "Where you hiding?"

"Who're you talking to?"

"Oh," he answered, eyes still shut, "just a pesky particle billions of times smaller than a proton."

"That all? What's it saying?"

"It's not talking."

Path-breaking physicists had already wound the clock back to roughly ten-million-trillion-trillion-trillionths of a second after the singularity. Anything before that and the math fell apart, the numbers collapsing like tinker toys.

During a 2010 fellowship at Brookhaven, he felt like a kid on Christmas morning each day he reported to the laboratory's ion collider facility. But after a year—as thrilling as it was to re-create the universe's infant moments in miniature—his frustrations returned. Physics was tantalizingly close to big discoveries, but it was still light years away from what, on paper anyway, felt achingly within reach. But to get the conditions he'd need to see beyond the instant of creation, he realized he'd need a collider the size of the . . . well, the solar system.

Gavin left Brookhaven for his brief stint at UCLA, dreams deferred yet undimmed.

Now, all these years later, Gavin sharpened the image under the microscope. He marveled at the rock's illuminated patterns, then turned the ring around for a look through a longer lens. He refocused, and that's when he saw what made Megan pick up the phone and call him: the anomaly. Or rather, anomal*ies*. Scores of them. Magnified a thousand times, rust-colored globules crystallized into the rock. Gavin turned a knob that raised the stage of the microscope, refocused, for a closer look. Inside the globules, tinier dark shapes were discernible, curled in on themselves.

"See what I'm talking about?" Megan asked.

"Hell is that?" Gavin said, still peering through the eyepiece, his words muffled by the mask he had to wear. "What am I looking at?" He turned from the microscope to face Megan, her arms folded, sitting beside him in the required garb of hooded coverall, face mask and latex gloves. Gavin too was in the same garb and loved it; for him, the gadgetry and anti-contamination outfit were the coolest things about being inside a microbiology lab.

"There's no mention in the notes."

"Chemical assay?"

Megan riffled through the papers in the folder on her lap and read out loud: "Iron-nickel core, silicate crust, zircon, hints of uranium, mostly olivine."

Gavin once again stared into the eyepiece, shaking his head. "And those round shapes?"

"Notes say magnetite formation inside olivine crystals."

Gavin turned to Megan and made a scrunched-up face. "I suppose they'd know."

"The thing is," Megan began, taking off her glasses and dropping her hands in her lap, "I had it assayed again." Suddenly, they became aware of others in the lab: there were two other students in their corners, tending to their own work. A teacher poked her head into the room and began muttering with one of the students. Megan turned back to Gavin and continued, "There are hints of carbon in it. Like, *organic* carbon."

"Why don't the notes mention anything?"

"But it's like 0.00001 percent."

"Could be a Martian rock then, from back when there was organic activity on Mars?"

"That's the other thing," Megan's voice was strained, almost hushed. "The rock's older than Mars. It's older than the solar system. We ran the isotope numbers on the uranium."

Reaching for the folder on the counter, Gavin froze, waiting for Megan's next words. The teacher at the lab door said goodbye and went away.

Megan went on. "It's, like, *twice* the age of the solar system."

Gavin was aware of a fluttering in his chest, excitement competing with every instinct for skepticism he'd ever honed as a scientist. He let out a deep breath and began flipping through the notes in the folder. Nowhere was there any mention of dating or origin. It was as if this tiny, ordinary-seeming piece of space rock, one of thousands around the world, either didn't warrant the additional analysis or the follow-up. A forgotten jewel of the most mysterious sort.

"There's something else weird about this rock," Megan said, her tone lower now. The confidentiality in their conversation had Gavin thinking of spy movies. "The specific gravity of this rock doesn't match the spectrometry I did on it." She pulled out her phone and, with a couple of swipes, presented a screenshot of a report: a specific gravity analysis, but, on closer look, it couldn't be right.

The rock was "heavier" than it should be, just by a fraction but enough that any biologist, chemist or physicist would begin doubting the lab or their math or their own sanity if the results were true.

"Your thoughts?"

Megan tightened her lips. "Maybe my analysis is wrong. Has to be, right?"

"Has to be? Why?" Gavin was feeling every bit like the teacher again.

Megan turned the phone toward her. "Because it's not making sense."

Gavin smiled. "That's when things are the most fun."

Gavin replaced the folder again on the table. He leaned back on the opposite table and stared at the flecked patterns on the floor tiles, thinking. Finally, he said, "Still . . . this is . . ." They shared astonished looks, eyes wide in wonderment. "Weird."

They laughed.

"Yeah, it's weird."

"But if these numbers are right," Gavin said, "your career just took off. Tie a bow around it and send it up."

"I've already got paper ideas lined up. The *centerpiece* of my dissertation, right? It's gonna blow up the field—"

"Wait." Gavin waved off her words. "Wait." For a stomach-turning instant, he could see the future. Something, an inner distrust of the system—committees champing at the bit to ridicule and disprove one's work, the media latching on the story like dogs, eager to praise then discredit in one go. He'd seen this happen to too many others. He wanted to shield not only Megan but also the rock itself, sitting there innocently on the stage of the microscope.

He got Megan to agree to say nothing about her analysis to anyone. Let the excitement cool, he told her. There was likely a simple explanation: dating and chemical analyses have been known to give false results.

Megan frowned. She put her glasses back on and stood up. "It would fit in perfectly with my research, though."

"Keep going on your research," he urged her, "only, let's keep this"—he pointed to the rock—"between you and me. Until we know what's going on."

She nodded as an obedient child might, and, to be fair, she respected Gavin, twelve years her senior and by far the most encouraging and out-of-the-box teacher she'd ever had. He was the only one in the UCLA faculty before his dismissal who expressed total enthusiasm in her work. For that, she was willing to concede to his request.

"And there's one other thing," he said and pointed to the rock, as if he were identifying a suspect in a lineup. "Can I hold on to that? Only for a couple of days. Just to run a few tests."

Megan's eyes narrowed. She looked from the rock back to Gavin. "You know you're not supposed to—"

"I know. But I'll be *really* careful." He took a step toward her. "Trust me."

Gavin's "couple of days" stretched to a week and longer as he re-ran the dating, chemical and specific gravity analyses. What he found was that all of Megan's findings were correct: the rock was very ancient. And with every new confirmation, a gnawing grew in his stomach, telling him that Megan had better be prepared for the flood of skepticism, scrutiny and ridicule that would soon follow anything she published. As to the globules and the tiny structures inside them, he was still mystified.

Thus far, Gavin hadn't said a word about the rock to his boss, Dr. Javier Bollinger. He did feel pangs of guilt about it. It was Bollinger, after all, who'd hired Gavin and rescued his flailing career after his less-than-cordial departure from UCLA.

The two went back a ways. They'd known each other as undergrads at Stanford where they'd both excelled. Both asked the same questions, shared an ambition to dismantle the Standard Model on which the entire musty institution of physics had built its theoretical house of cards. So it was no surprise that the two were friends and competitors, though not in that order.

They'd parted ways after Stanford, Gavin leaving for England and Bollinger for Arizona, where he made a name for himself as a bold, imaginative mind in the particle research game. Bollinger graduated with his PhD two years earlier than Gavin. He was a whiz-kid who'd written a dissertation that posited genuinely workable solutions for the storage and production of antimatter. It caught the attention not only of NASA but also of top thinkers in the worlds of cosmology and particle physics.

After graduating, Bollinger turned down lucrative teaching offers to jump at the chance at leading cutting-edge projects at CERN, then at the Johnson Space Center. Colleagues found him undeniably brilliant, but equally undeniably a pain in the ass: a man whose intellect almost, *almost* made up for his childish stubbornness and tendency to get hostile whenever he felt others weren't up to his standards.

In 2013, his second year at Johnson, Bollinger received a phone call from someone in the Breakthrough Concepts division of Triton Corp asking if he would direct a fully funded off-site skunkworks devoted to energy research for future space travel.

Would he? He asked the caller to "hang on for just one moment," put the phone on the table so he could pump his fist multiple times and do a manic dance. Bollinger picked the phone back up and answered calmly, "I'd be open to talking about it."

Near Pasadena, east of Los Angeles, the facility was to be entirely funded by Triton, an 800-pound gorilla in the worlds of banking, pharmaceuticals, petrochemicals, agribusiness, aerospace and defense. After signing an NDA, Bollinger went on to learn that Triton had constructed a next-generation compact ion collider at the base of the San Gabriel Mountains near a vast complex that also housed the various divisions for engineering, software and systems development, and clean rooms for assembly and analysis. Why they'd decided to keep this awe-inspiring development a secret from the public mystified Bollinger, when CERN's Large Hadron Collider (which had opened a year earlier) had become such a darling in the press. When Bollinger met with a high-level Triton executive, he was assured that Triton's collider was superior to CERN's. It was smaller but equipped with drive beams that boosted the collider power by several orders of magnitude above and beyond the LHC.

"Why keep this all a secret?" Bollinger asked. With Triton's reputation blackened by years of profiteering from war, pharmaceuticals, pipelines and pollution, wouldn't the company stand to gain by advertising its ambitions in learning and science? Don't people love companies that invest in that kind of shit? Bollinger never did get a good answer. All the Triton executive told him was that they didn't want their discoveries and developments leaked, not a word—and that was the best he got.

Still, Bollinger had to admit: Triton was serious. As icing on the cake, as operations director, he would have total independence. He would have to answer only to himself—well, himself and the CEO of Triton.

Like Gavin, Bollinger was driven to pushing past the limits of the math and toward what he called "spitball" experimentation. That meant failures, lots of them, but he was sure that, eventually, he'd hit upon a result that made up for all of them. This recklessness as well as his lashing out at colleagues who couldn't "keep up" drove his team crazy. At the end of the first year, three members of his five-member team left. Who the hell could he work with? He sat at his desk, scrambling through his mental Rolodex for the names of past colleagues or mentors. None was up to snuff. Then he drew up his laptop and Googled the name "Gavin Harrison." He hadn't seen or heard from Gavin in eight years. He was good. He was sharp. A guy like that would be at some prestigious institution now, he imagined. Maybe he was still in England. These thoughts flashed through his mind as the search results came up.

At the top was an entry for a Gavin Harrison, physics teacher, Oberon High School, Oberon Heights, California. He clicked on the name. No mistaking it, there he was. That was Gavin in the photo, on the faculty page of Oberon High School. It was hard to believe. Last he'd heard, Gavin was at Brookhaven on fellowship. Before punching in the number on his phone, he considered the situation. Was this a good idea? Maybe Gavin had lost his spark, settled for the high school job. Feel things out, he told himself, tell him you're calling to say hello, old time's sake, and all that. If he's clearly burnt out, hang up. No harm done.

The phone rang at the other end. Once, twice . . .

"Hello. I'm looking for Gavin Harrison," he spoke into the phone. "Gavin! This is Javier Bollinger. Yup, that's the one. Glad you remembered me!"

Their chat was cordial, both playing their hands close. Maybe out of regret or out of shame, Gavin didn't say a word about his exit from UCLA or that he was on suspension from Oberon High School for calling his students "punk-ass losers" last week. And for his part, Bollinger didn't say a word about Breakthrough. Instead, he said he was "between jobs" and "writing a book."

They revealed none of these things until they met face-to-face the next day over coffee. They shook hands after an hour, one of them exhilarated by the idea of Breakthrough Concepts and the other convinced he'd found the right man for his team.

Gavin couldn't make heads or tails of Bizarro, his nickname for the rock. He ran tests a second time around and got the same results; the tests couldn't account for the whole of the rock's mass. There was something there—hidden mass—that the tests couldn't see or measure, and he had a hunch that those wiggly shapes in the hundreds of little globules in the rock were the culprits.

Two weeks after borrowing the rock from Megan, Gavin decided to take a page from Bollinger's "spitball" playbook. What if he isolated a globule sample, ionized it, and smashed the protons together in the collider? At worst, nothing would happen. But at best, it could point him toward solving the mystery.

It would take a few days to prep the experiment and get time on the collider, but he could bluff his way into the lab late at night and run the experiment himself. He was still iffy about letting Bollinger or any other team member in on what he was analyzing. Until he had solid evidence of a genuine anomaly, he didn't want to disrupt the day-to-day here.

As soon as the last of the team had cleared out one evening, Gavin went to a workstation. Isolating two samples of grain from the rock didn't take long. In the fugitive quiet of the lab, he could feel the exhilaration climb up through his chest as he took the samples down three floors, through an empty hallway toward the collider annex. He could hear his heart hammering. "Calm down," he told himself, "you're just running a test. This is probably nothing. Nothing. Don't get excited. You're a scientist."

A half-hour later, he was in the control room. Electric currents inside the collider's source chamber were heating the samples up to a thousand degrees Fahrenheit, vaporizing out bits of electrons. Soon, ionized protons would take off through the drift tubes at near-light speed until he pressed a few keys, giving the command for the protons to smash into each other, a traffic accident with the energy equivalent to the first glorious microseconds after the Big Bang.

The ionization complete, Gavin conducted a safety check and began to input the commands for the protons, grouped into grape-like bunches, to be launched from their pressurized chambers into the first pair of booster rings.

And they were off! Gavin kept a close eye on the screens as the rings' superconducting pods, arranged like gems along a necklace, accelerated the protons first around a smaller, then a larger pair of rings. Within minutes, the particles were bounding around the rings at thousands of times per second, boosted by the superconductors and guided through each turn by super-cooled magnets.

He observed, minute by minute, making minor adjustments to the electromagnetic field, till the protons were within a hair's breadth of the speed of light. After twenty minutes of calibrating the ions to their optimum speed, all that remained was the collision itself. If there was anything truly bizarre about Bizarro, this is when it would show itself.

Gavin input the commands that would guide the protons into collision inside the largest ring where the detectors would register the aftermath. "Boom," he said softy to himself, pressing ENTER. At that instant, inside the vacuum tubing three hundred feet below, hundreds of millions of ions smashed together in a head-on pile-up. For a microsecond, he was within shouting distance of quark-gluon plasma, the blistering soup out of which all matter had once come into being. At times like this, in the presence of something so much greater than himself, Gavin felt deeply humbled, unworthy of the privilege.

The screens suddenly blazed with information as detectors and calorimeters began relaying data sets from beyond the realm of human perception. His breath caught in his chest as he turned from screen to screen checking readings on momentum, charge, and, in one display on the screen above him, an animation of the collision, a star-like pattern showing paths shooting off the center in every direction, some straight as arrows, others looped and curved.

As subatomic traffic accidents went, this one looked pretty ordinary. And that's when screens around the control room went black.

The system rebooted. Error messages popped up everywhere. A readout said there had been a power surge and everything had powered off. But the overhead bank of screens, displaying the graphical relays from the rings' collision points, stayed on and showed thousands of collisions overlapping in rapid succession. But these electrical pathways weren't shooting off in lines or curves. They were rapidly expanding split-second spheres, popping in and out existence, one after another. These were— *What were they?* The screens went black again. The lights too. This time, the backup lights in the control room snapped on. Everything felt very quiet, very still.

Gavin sat there in the half-dark. He spun around in the chair to face the empty room. *That was an energy field he'd just seen.* The creation and annihilation of an energy field, thousands of times over. Had he just solved the mystery of the missing mass? Had Bizarro given up its secret? Whatever the answer, this was something no one had seen before.

Three hours later, after filing reports for the maintenance personnel, Gavin drove home, unnerved and exhilarated. It was too early, too early to speculate. *Look at the data,* he thought. *The error will be easy to spot.* Something had malfunctioned: the magnets or the superconductors might've shorted. Maybe the ion load was corrupted.

He was sure he'd be fired for this. Not right away. But once word got out that he'd breached protocol and singlehandedly broken a freaking particle collider, he'd be through. No one, not even a high-school principal, would ever hire him. And yet . . .

As he rolled into the garage and entered his home, he went through the entire procedure again. Everything had gone normally. He knew his way around a particle experiment. Nothing was amiss. Until the electrical surge, the weird energy readings, and the power outage. It would be in the data. If he was going to be vindicated, it would be in the data.

He walked into his and Seema's bedroom. The TV was on mute, the channel set to a detective show. He switched it off and sat at the edge of the bed to take off his shoes. The clock read 2 a.m. He remembered calling the nanny around dinnertime to let her know he was running late. Seema must've relieved the nanny at 8 or 9, put Dev to bed. He was always home in time to put Dev to bed. He gazed at his sleeping wife and wondered if she'd taken anything to help her fall asleep tonight. ERs could be stressful places, and he knew that, lately, she'd been having a tough time with the chief of the department. A flicker of guilt went through his mind like a hopped-up electric current.

He went into Dev's room and slid in next to his sleeping son, whose soft breathing and peaceful face helped soothe him. He stared at the glow-in-the-dark solar system and stars on the ceiling. Sometimes, Gavin would lie here next to his two-year-old and stare up at the plastic-and-putty heavens above. It stirred his imagination. He hoped one day, it would do the same for his son.

At that moment, he knew in his heart that what he'd seen was no accident. Sometimes it was easier to dismiss something just because you couldn't understand or explain it. But that didn't make it any less real. This was real.

CHAPTER NINE

East of Bakersfield

October 26, 2030

Dry fields and abandoned ranch homes mark the last traces of Bakersfield. The road cuts through orchards on both sides. They look dusty and desolate. Low brown hills run along behind the fields. The sun's bleaching the sky, roasting out the blue and turning it white. I'd really like to get us to the 395 and heading north into higher terrain. I look at the speedometer, a steady seventy. A couple of more hours of this, assuming the traffic stays light, I can get us there.

"Look," Conner says, pointing toward the south. "See it?"

Maybe five hundred feet up, there's an object. It's hard to get a sense of scale since there's nothing up there to compare it with, but it looks smallish and makes a slow circle to the north, passing just above us. It could be anywhere in size from a minifridge to a small car. It does a wide turn and disappears from sight.

"Where'd it—? Anyone see it?" I ask, trying to keep my eyes on the road.

Abby searches the outline of hills. "How could it just—?"

"It must've landed on a ledge or gone behind the hills," I say. "Hard to tell with all those trees up there."

"Drone," says Conner. "Had to be."

"What? Like a farmer's drone?"

"Farms? See any?"

"Wait. Isn't there like an air force base around here?" Abby says. She unfolds the map and scans it. "Edwards. But"—she pauses, looking at it more closely—"it's, like, forty miles from here."

We're silent for a while. The drone's gotten me nervous; I'm still not over the whole white van thing from the other day. I'm starting to breathe easier, and it's all good except—the drone appears again, like some punk at school who isn't done messing with you. It whirs along across our line of sight but much lower now—and descending.

It turns in from the south and skims the air about a hundred feet above us, passing directly in front so I can almost see a small window—like a camera—on the underside of the drone. Conner turns to look out the back window, tracking the drone's path westward.

"What do you think?" Abby turns to ask Conner. "The cops or the military?"

"Hard to say," he replies. "I didn't see any markings." He takes another look through the back window. "Disappeared over the ridge."

"It's the military," I say. "It's got to be. Probably about that shit back at the gas station, I bet. They know we killed one of 'em. Now they're tracking us."

No one speaks. Conner sits in the center of the backseat, his posture tense as he stares out the windshield. "Let's get out of here."

In a single bend in the road, the whole look of the land changes. Walls of granite lean into us like giants frowning down at trespassers. Abby and Conner crane their necks, peering above the ridges for more signs of the drone.

We instantly remember this landscape from when we were kids and talk about the family drives we took through here on our way to

Yosemite or Mammoth. But it's not the same anymore. The shape of the terrain matches our memory of it, but it's more arid now, browner, smokier.

The passageway of looming rock opens out to a wider view of grassy plains and stony, tree-dotted ridges. There is no sign of anyone following us, on the ground or in the sky. Our spirits start to ramp up again. We'll be at the cabin by evening.

The traffic's been steady, mostly horse trailers, campers, and pickups transporting farmers and fruit pickers. And I'm in third or fourth, doing between thirty-five and sixty.

We begin to see groups of people—migrants and Mexican families—along the side of the road, carrying signs in Spanish, urging ranchers not to vote for a bill that would deport migrant farmers, legal or not. Families squat or stand along the edge of the highway with signs that say "Yendo al este" or "montar favor." Older men, women, and children huddle a few feet from the shoulder, under canopies of tattered fabric. Boys fly kites in the blazing afternoon.

A line of young men, in straw cowboy hats or ball caps or shirts wrapped around their heads, look like they're taking their chances on foot—some to the east, some to the west, each with a pack on his back.

Above the northern and southern horizons are anvil-shaped formations of ash and smoke reminding us that, beyond the edge of sight, there are walls of fire keeping everyone here hemmed in. We drive through a landscape of conical peaks and flat stretches peppered with brush, prickly-pear and Joshua trees before hitting a wide, empty stretch pocked with flimsy-looking power lines and signposts.

The road arrows dead ahead toward a T-junction where this highway meets the 395, the road that'll take us to Tahoe. I slow to a stop at the T and wait for a line of half-loaded fruit trucks to pass. It's the edge of the Mojave. Death Valley.

"That's death out there," Conner says, his eyes beyond the T, on the miles of waterless scrub that ends at a range of foothills.

I remember my mother's words about the emergency patients who'd been out in the desert. The thought freaks me out just as trucks roar across the T, the last fully loaded, not with fruit but with people hunched behind the wood slats. I can't see how many. We take a left, heading north now, chewing up road. We're still five or six hours away.

I check my phone. No reply from Mom yet. This is too weird. Is she so upset with me that she's ignoring my texts? Ghosting me? This is not like her. But then again, taking off like this without telling her isn't like me either. Time to bite the bullet. I swipe the phone to wake it up, bring up her contact info and call. The phone doesn't even bother ringing; it goes straight to voicemail. "Hi Mom," I begin, "it's Dev, obviously. I tried texting you a bit ago but got no answer. I don't know if you're at home or at work. I want you to know I'm safe. I'm with Abby and Conner. We're going up to the cabin, planning on getting there tonight. Drive's been really smooth. Took it easy and stayed at a hotel in Buttonwillow last night. We're all doing great, so don't worry about us. I'll be back before you know it." I tell her I love her and hang up, feeling relieved that I avoided a conversation but also lame and guilty for putting on a front.

"Can't get through, huh?" Abby looks at me, unscrewing a water bottle.

"She's probably held up at the hospital," Conner says. "You saw how nuts it was on the TV."

Conner's trying, but I know he's thinking what I'm thinking. The scene on TV didn't look good. Two hundred more cases of some gnarly disease no one's understood yet. How many of those cases showed up last night at Mom's hospital? I exhale loudly and thump my hand against my chest, over and over, to center myself.

"You okay?" It's Abby's voice. It comforts me. I feel her hand on my hand.

"Worried."

"I know," she says. "Me too." She rubs the side of my arm. The touch of her hand brings me back. I'm glad she said that: sometimes, it helps to be reminded you're not alone. I know she's got her family on her mind, that she's freaked out too.

Grasslands stretch out on both sides, empty except for the occasional horse fencing and the clustered aspens and oaks. The hills to the east have a confidence about them. Their bulging brown arms cast steep, dramatic shadows in the sun. About a mile west, beyond pylons of high-voltage lines, are the soft, furled shoulders of the foothills of the powerful, proud Sierras far beyond. While the rest of our state is roasting, choked, drought-stricken, the Sierras are the holdout, a last line of defiance. I point to them. "Look at them. It's like they're flipping off the rest of the world."

"With fingers of granite," Abby says, mimicking them by sneering and giving the world the bird. She pops open the glove compartment. "Got any tunes?"

I tell her I haven't checked this car for music when she comes up with a CD from the compartment. Even from here, I can tell it's a mix and that's Dad's handwriting on the track list.

"That is insane," I say to her. "Blasts from the past."

She turns the case over in her hands. "I guess the Feds wanted nothing to do with your dad's music, huh?"

"Damn," says Conner, "I haven't seen one of those things in years."

We laugh over this round metallic relic. Abby reads off the track list on the back of the case. As she does, I can remember being five, six, seven, and Dad playing all these tunes at home and on drives north.

Abby puts the CD in, and soon, we're howling and singing at the top of our lungs to Bowie and Prince and Eminem. It's like Dad sent this music to us to keep up our spirits. It's maybe the reason I don't fail right now.

We're holding a steady sixty for a half-hour when I notice a warning light on the dashboard: It's the oil light. "We're leaking."

The others stop singing and go quiet. I explain about the light. We agree to pull over at the next town and get it checked out.

A few miles later, we close in on what looks like a roadblock. Three small barricades are set up across the 395. There weren't any warnings of a closure either on our phones or on the road south of here, so this doesn't feel right. We come to a stop in front of the barricades, each of us remarking on how weird this is. There's no one around and nothing but open land interrupted by clumps of aspen, lots of scrub and a few housing tracts and warehouses. To the far left, the Sierras run alongside us like the Earth's backbone toward the north as far as the eye can see.

We get out of the car and move the roadblocks to the side of the road. Up ahead about thirty feet and on the shoulder, there's a billboard with the words "Welcome to" but under that, there's a sheet of cloth with the word "Freetown" spray-painted on it in black.

I point to it. "What's that about?"

"Some kinda prank?" Conner says vaguely. "The roadblocks are probably a prank too."

"Cute prank," Abby agrees. "This is supposed to be Independence on the map."

When we get seated again and I'm about to turn the ignition is when I see three people appear from behind the billboard and run toward us: two men and a chunky-looking boy of about eight or nine, dressed in a soiled T-shirt and camo pants. Of the two grown-ups, one is a thin, dark-haired man with wispy facial hair in a frayed baseball cap and jeans, with tattoos on his arms and bare torso. And closer up, I see the other man isn't a man at all, but a woman in a cowboy hat and plaid shirt buttoned to the top of a pregnant belly. Sweating, his mouth slack and panting, the boy's clearly having trouble keeping up with the grown-ups.

It's the grown-ups who're making me nervous. Because they're carrying semiautomatic rifles.

Baseball Cap shouts and waves for me to lower my windows, keeping the rifle trained at my head. I do as he says.

"Moving roadblocks is an ordinance violation, boy," Baseball Cap says with the kind of authority you hear from cops. "Where you from?"

"LA," I say, feeling stupid and confused. "Why is the road closed?"

"Shit. LA, you say?" He backs up a step, his eyes wide, suddenly feral. "I oughta shoot all three of you right now."

"We're okay," interjects Conner. "We got out before the quarantine. We're not sick."

Baseball Cap glances over at Pregnant Lady as if he's looking to her to make the call. She's calm, though, and waves for him to lower his weapon and chill.

"What's your business in Freetown?" Baseball Cap and Pregnant Lady look only a couple of years older than us.

"No business at all," I stammer. "Just driving through. Didn't realize the road was supposed to be blocked."

"Freetown?" Abby speaks, checking the map in her hands. "I don't see a Freetown."

"We're Freetown," Baseball Cap says.

"Sir," Conner says, his elbow braced against the back of Abby's seat. "We're sorry, we didn't know about the roadblock. We're happy to turn—"

"Shut your hole and you, drive on over to the other side of that billboard. And don't even think of hittin' the gas because we'll plug your car full of holes if you do."

For a second, I'm paralyzed, freaked out by the distinct possibility that our road trip just ended at the barrel of a gun.

Baseball Cap shouts, "Move!"

I do as he says, following in the direction of Pregnant Lady's arm-waving, pulling to a stop, rolling over the shoulder and onto the scrub and dust behind the billboard. Not far to my left is a dusty green Dodge Charger sitting at a distance, still obscured by the billboard.

"Everybody chill," Conner says in a low, steady tone.

"Man," I mutter, "I've seen way too many movies, and this does not end well."

"Shh," Abby says. "Maybe they just want money."

Meanwhile, Baseball Cap, Pregnant Belly, and the kid have surrounded the car.

"Pop open the trunk and get out of the car," Baseball Cap says in the same businesslike tone. This time, he backs up a step and levels his weapon at me. My nerves jump, and my hands go up.

"Pop open the trunk and—"

"Okay, okay," I interrupt, anxious to let him know I'm complying. I press the switch that unlocks the trunk, open the car door, and slowly step out. The man shoves me against the side of the car and shouts, "Keep your hands on the car. Daniel, go to it."

The boy starts patting me down, checking my pockets. He finds my wallet, my phone, removes them. Out of the corner of my eye, I see the woman lift the hatch and start sorting through the contents. She orders Abby and Conner out of the car. Baseball Cap orders the boy, Daniel, to search our packs.

Baseball Cap tells me to face him as he studies my driver's license, a scowl across his mouth. "Dev Ra-*bin*-der Harrison." His eyes glare up at me as he tucks the license back into my wallet. There is a crumb of food in his beard. "You Arab or Paki or what?"

"Not at all," I say, feeling shame for some reason.

"You radicalized? Lotta half-breeds and sympathizers go over and get radicalized."

"No."

"What's your business here?" Now I see a smile play across his lips, and the smile makes me both angry and even more freaked out because that's when I know this is all an act meant to scare us. All fun and games to these pricks before they . . . . I don't even want to think about what they have in mind.

"Like I said, just passing through on our way to Yosemite."

"Yosemite?" He and Pregnant Lady share amused looks and start laughing.

"Place went up like a tinderbox days ago," the woman snickers. "This just isn't your day."

Conner and Abby, their arms behind their heads, line up beside me. Pregnant Lady, rifle aimed at us, steps up next to Baseball Cap. She hands over Abby's and Conner's wallets along with their phones to Baseball Cap. The fat boy, Daniel, dumps our packs at the grownups' feet.

"Great, we'll take all this shit over," Baseball Cap says.

A pickup truck approaches along the highway and motors past us, heading east. There's nothing I can do, and in seconds, it's receded to a hopeless mote far down the road. It's a sick feeling, seeing him drive off. But no one out on the road can see us here behind this billboard. We're cornered in.

"What'd you find?" Baseball Cap asks.

"Lawn chair, wiper fluid, tarp."

"Keep the wiper fluid. Might come in handy. What about their packs?"

Daniel's voice is solemn, like a schoolboy who wants to recite his lesson right: "Flashlights, water bottles, some food, a radio." The boy's face is pink, the cheeks glistening.

"Radio? Lemme see it."

Daniel hands over the tiny shortwave. Baseball Cap turns it over in his hand, clicks it on, and presses it to his ear. He makes a cackling noise. "This is like some real survival shit." He laughs and pockets the radio. A memory of my father, tied to that radio, floods my mind, and I instantly feel violated like when the Feds showed up.

"Hey, stop messin' around," Pregnant Lady says irritably. "What do you want to do?"

"Look, you're welcome to take whatever," Conner says. "We've got money."

Baseball Cap runs his fingers through his beard and finally says, "Let's take 'em in. They're a nice enough catch. You take my car and follow me while I drive 'em over to the sheriff. Daniel, got a weapon on you?"

"No, sir."

Baseball Cap reaches behind him and pulls a pistol from his waistband. "Take this. Now you sit in the back with the girl and her boyfriend. You, boy"—he snaps his fingers at me—"ride up with me. Get in."

Toting her rifle, the woman takes short, waddling steps up the road to the Charger and fires it up, waiting for us to clear past her.

As we make our drive into Freetown, we pass bold-yellow flags tacked up on porches and the sides of trailers. The flags show a coiled rattlesnake above the words: DON'T TREAD ON ME. I've seen that flag before, in stories about militias and separatists. I look back at Abby and Conner, but they're both more concerned about the Glock pointed at them by a nine-year-old boy.

We drive up the 395, the main strip through "Freetown." The streets are deserted, not so surprising at this blinding-hot hour. Of the four people I do see, three are toting semiautos. We pass a couple of run-down motels, a couple of gas stations (one of them boarded up), and a salvage yard.

Off the main street, the homes are in all kinds of ruin. Garbage bags cover the windows of a few, and the shells of cars can be seen propped up on cinder blocks in weedy front yards where dogs sleep.

We drive a couple of more minutes, the highway now a two-lane main drag, and turn off onto a side street where the car pulls over in front of a gray-blue stucco building. A sun-faded circular sign attached to the building says: Corner Market & Deli. Baseball Cap tells us to get out of the car.

With his rifle, he points us in the direction of the market's front doors. Daniel yells at Abby and Conner: "Move! Get inside!" He's definitely feeling more comfortable with that pistol in his hand.

I open the door into a stifling, noisy room where the air's laced with cigarette smoke. First thing I hear is the smack of a cue ball and find three guys at a pool table on my left, laughing and smoking. Past the pool table are a few small plastic tables and a larger wooden table where a group of men sit, smoking, playing cards, drinking beer. A thick-set man, baggy-eyed, maybe sixty, wearing a cowboy hat, sits at the head of this big table where the ashtrays are full and greasy plates and empty beer bottles are everywhere. A ceiling fan spins furiously above the room, swirling its odors of beer, sweat, and cigarettes.

On the far side of the room is a counter and a kitchen and a couple of rows of what look like shelves stocked with random groceries and household items. There are two fifty-ish women behind the counter: one wears a pale cotton housedress, her hair in a bun, and a startled look in her eyes. The other's lean, tough-looking, in a gray-and-black jersey and jeans. She steps around the counter and leans against it, her arms crossed.

A flat-screen TV mounted on the far wall plays what looks like a Mexican action movie on low volume: bad guys firing machine guns from a Pinto chase after a guy and girl who return fire as they peel around alleys and squares crazy with pigeons.

Pregnant Lady, her gun on us, orders us to stay put and keep our hands up. Baseball Cap goes over to the man at the head of the big table, the one with the cowboy hat. Judging from the tan regulation shirt with the badge above the breast pocket and the patch on his short sleeves, he seems to be the law around here. Baseball Cap whispers a few words to him, pointing at us. The man sneaks a sliding glance at us, utters a few hushed words in reply. Baseball Cap marches back with that rifle on us, shouting, "Okay, back up, have a seat right there against the wall."

The barrels of their guns have a force of their own, pushing us all back and into folding chairs set up along the wall opposite the big table. Daniel stands off to one side, his pistol pointing at us. I get the feeling he's really relishing the role he's getting to play. It makes me want to punch him in the head—*hard*.

The murmuring among the men at the table is suddenly cut short with an "All right" from the man in the cowboy hat. He pushes his chair back. "We seem to have guests," he announces in this raspy, haughty voice. The man straightens up, bulges out his chest, but I get the sense it's a sad attempt to hide the roundness of his gut. His whole face puckers—his mouth, his eyes—as he sizes us up, staying a bit longer on Abby than I'm comfortable with.

Sitting beside me, she says nothing, just glares at him.

The sheriff narrows his eyes at me, a crooked smile on his face, and hoists himself to his feet. "Name's Tod Bunting. I'm the sheriff here. Ben tells me you're up from LA," he says stepping toward me, adjusting his hat. "Been a lot of trouble there lately. Not a pretty scene." He pivots on his heel and leers down at me. "You believe all that about the meteor and all these victims turning into maniacs?"

"We saw it all," I reply. "We even saw these horrible things. They're out there."

The sheriff briefly laughs. "Oh, I've no doubt you saw what you think you saw, no doubt you saw what's out there. But I know what it *wasn't*, and it was no space rocks. The Chinese, Russians, the Arabs, they've all been planning this for decades. Bioweapons delivered using hypersonics. People have been warning about it for a long time. Start of a new day. That strike on Friday, that was a declaration of war."

Others in the room call out with "Damn right" and "Amen."

The sheriff starts waving his hands. "Now you've got a city shut down. Half the Western Hemisphere on alert. Our government got caught with its shorts down. I can tell you it has no plan nor intention of defending us. And now that it's run out of our money, it's sold all of us out to some international conglomerate and the whole country is on a forced march to these so-called Triton zones, am I right? Stalinist gulags is what they seem like to me. Forced labor and mind control."

As he's speaking (and I get the impression he's delivered this lecture before), my eyes go to the shelves in the kitchen area. Opened and unopened bags of snack bars, cheese puffs, and potato chips are stacked there. I see suitcases, backpacks, jewelry, purses, wallets, a camping tent, a car vac. None of these things look new, nothing is in its packaging. Pregnant Lady and Daniel drag the lawn chair, tarp, and wiper fluid from the Outback, along with our packs, to the shelves and start placing the things there one by one. There's something very creepy about it.

In this hot room with the guns on us, I feel terror rising in my chest, and below it is the thudding of my heart beneath my ribs. I can't look at Conner or Abby because I know we're all freaked out, and I couldn't handle looking into their eyes and what it would do to me. We just have to stay together and keep it together.

Another voice cuts in, interrupting the sheriff—it's the take-no-shit woman at the kitchen counter: "They don't need the whole spiel, Tod. Why don't you take what you want and let them go. Thought we were having a meeting here. Are we going to shake down every damn person driving through town?" She waves a hand at us like we're three feral cats dragged in off the street. "Didn't you say we've got bigger priorities here?"

The sheriff appears unfazed. Smiling, he takes off his hat and places it on the table. He says, "It's hardly every person, June. Now I understand we got big priorities. But without security, how safe are we, really? God knows who the government's sending up and down that road to spy on us. I'm trying to protect us. And that means keeping the checkpoints open and doing these, uh, random inspections."

So is that it? He thinks we're spies? Abby and Conner and I trade quick, puzzled glances.

"A bit more than inspections," the woman, June, cuts in with a sneer.

"All borders have customs, don't they, that can seize whatever goods and items deemed worth the taking? You drive through here, you deal with *our* customs and inspection. And we made a pledge: what we confiscate is collected for our own survival. Fair and square." The sheriff studies us, his boots shuffling to a stop, only his eyes moving from one to the other. "We need to be on the alert, June. Country's going to hell in case you haven't noticed." He turns to the others at the table. "First, the government comes in and clears out our jobs. Damn near ruins me and my ranch. And now we've got the illegals getting high and mighty down there in Bakersfield, protesting and whatnot."

He goes to the table and, as he puts his hat back on, we hear sounds of struggle. From a doorway behind the counter, a plump, fiftysomething man in boxers and an undershirt stained by sweat and blood comes stumbling out, pushed forward by two large men in sunglasses and deputy uniforms.

The man's arms are bound behind his back and his mouth is gagged by a wad of cloth. A frantic howl sounds from his throat. In the kitchen, the woman in the housedress moans, backs up toward the stove while, at the counter, June steps aside, pressing a hand to her mouth. The deputies shove the half-naked man toward the door, passing the sheriff, who's been ignoring the whole spectacle.

The men at the table avert their eyes as the parade moves through. Not the three men at the pool table though: they're whooping and joking and there's a wave of laughter that goes up as the bound and gagged man is herded out the front door.

The sheriff clicks his tongue, shakes his head. "Gotten so you can't trust anybody. Not even our last sheriff." The sheriff puffs out his chest again. "Besides, I think I look better in this uniform than he ever did."

"Fits you like a glove, Sheriff," Ben chuckles.

"Sir," Conner speaks up, his voice calm and pleading, "I swear we mean no harm and no one sent us. We were just passing through. You can take anything we have. We just want to be on our way."

But it's like the sheriff didn't even hear him. He just keeps pacing; his boots tap on the tiles as the ceiling fan jostles warm, stifling drafts around the room.

"I'll make a deal with you," the sheriff says. "I'm gonna believe you that you're just passing through and in exchange—" He interrupts himself to turn back to a man in suspenders and reading glasses, hunched over a newspaper. "Fowler, how many workers we got recruited back at the ranch?"

Fowler looks up from his paper and takes off his glasses. "Including the pickers and them illegals last week, maybe fifteen, twenty."

"Add two more hands to this season's outbuilding crew." The sheriff takes a few slow steps toward us, stopping in front of Abby. "And we need good God-fearing women in Freetown too. Help us build up our nation."

"We do need more women," comes a small voice, which I see belongs to the anxious woman in the kitchen. "I would be pleased to have the help. Thank you, Sheriff."

"Hell, let's put it to a vote right now," the sheriff says. "How many here think we should induct these three into our Freetown family?"

The sheriff raises his hand. Everyone's hands go up around the room. Only June, standing against the counter, doesn't. She scoffs, shakes her head.

This is all either mind games or something much worse. Whatever it is, we need to think fast. The sheriff beams at us. "Ayes have it. Welcome to Freetown."

He bangs the palm of his hand on the table several times. Others clap.

"You'll stay with the crew out in the camp," the sheriff says, "and we'll put you to work. I even pay wages." He touches my shoulder, feeling there and my upper arm. It's sickening. "You'll get big and strong by the end of the season, you'll see." He steps over to Abby. "But I got even bigger plans for you, young lady. You're welcome to stay at my ranch along with all the VIPs of Freetown. What you think of that?"

One of the Pool Table Boys blows smoke and croaks out, "Can I be VIP, Sheriff?"

I hold out my hand. "Sir"—my voice sounds so tiny, like nothing—"we can't stay. We all of us have families back in LA. They'll be looking for us."

"They're expecting us back tomorrow," Conner backs me up. "They'll sound the alarm. I don't think you want that."

"Oh, I'm sure I don't, but I'm not too worried," the sheriff says, laughing under his breath. "LA is shut down with riots and mutants tearing the place apart. I doubt anyone's going to fret over a few missing kids." He cocks his head toward Ben and Pregnant Lady. "Ben, Carla, take this young lady back to the ranch so she can have a look around, get washed up and changed. Set her up in the big house." He leans toward Abby. "You'll be living like a five-star princess here in

Freetown. And you'll be with gals your own age. We're up to some big things here, pretty lady. What's your name?"

The three of us don't budge or speak. Suddenly, I hear her voice: "Go Fuck Yourself. That's my name."

Somebody laughs, snorts. "Ha! Hold on to that one."

The sheriff turns his back to us, takes a few steps to the table. When he spins around again, he's got a flat, unamused smile on his face.

My mind comes unstuck. "She's not going anywhere. With any of you."

The sheriff drops the smile, nods. "You all need a lesson in courtesy and how to cooperate. If only for the good of your health. Go on. Have a look."

Conner and I are shoved up by our armpits by Ben and Pregnant Lady and pushed toward a tall window along the front wall of the room. Ben throws aside a pair of black curtains that cover the lower half of the window on a thin rod. Our faces are shoved against the glass.

It takes a while for our eyes to adjust to the glare. I squint and gradually become aware of a scene directly across the road, playing out under an oak on the edge of a parking lot.

People are there, dogs and kids, and two of the three deputies from before—who'd rushed the half-naked man out of the room a minute ago—are hauling back on a rope, bracing. The taut rope extends up to a tree branch, loops around it and ends at the bloated neck of the half-naked man, his hands still bound, his legs tottering on the trunk of a sedan. The third deputy gets into the driver's seat of the sedan.

He fires up the car. The sedan pulls forward, the man's legs sway loose, and the two deputies haul back mightily on the rope to haul up the man in mid-air.

I can hear some whoops and claps from the assembled crowd. The man twitches for a few seconds then goes limp, turning like an ornament from the branch as the third deputy gets out of the sedan and unlocks the trunk, popping it wide open. He backs up the sedan so that the opened trunk rolls up directly under the hanged man.

The other deputies loosen their grip on the rope, lowering the corpse squarely into the trunk. The rope is cut, the trunk is shut, and the three deputies drive off in the sedan, leaving the crowd to disperse. All I hear is the barking of a dog.

That all was too efficient. These guys have done this before.

I'm thinking how, just a few minutes ago, that man was alive and now he is dead, stashed in the trunk of a car. I wonder where they'll dump his body, and if they'll be coming back for three more.

The sheriff has the slightest crook of a smile. His eyelids droop, becoming slits as he considers Abby for a few seconds. With a cue from the sheriff, Ben and Pregnant Lady—Carla—step up and order Abby to her feet. But she doesn't budge. Another cue from the sheriff, and two of the guys from the pool table chuck their cigarettes, set their cue sticks on the felt, and advance on Abby, ready to haul her up. The instant they touch her is when things get blurry.

CHAPTER TEN

I jolt awake. Heart pounding. *What time is it?* I'm thinking. *What day? Where am I? Where's Abby?* There's a throbbing ache above and behind my left ear that's radiating across my skull. I'm on my back. A smell, like grease, hits my nostrils. It's hard to breathe, the air is hot. And for a second, I think I've lost my eyesight and start to freak out. I sit up with a grunt onto my butt and realize I'm in a different room, nearly pitch-black.

The urge to throw up wells up in my throat, and I push it down with deep breaths. It takes a while, but slowly, I start to feel more composed. No broken bones. My brain seems to be functioning. That's good. But the ache behind my ear, that's not going away. I feel a lump there, like an egg embedded under the skin, and touching it sets off waves of dull pain. And that gets me remembering:

As soon as Ben and one of the Pool Table Boys started getting rough with Abby, trying to get her to her feet, it was like a switch tripped in my brain—and in Conner's. I didn't care about the guns anymore, didn't care what happened.

I reached for a cue stick lying on the table, grabbed it by its middle so the thick, blunt side of it could land heavy on somebody's skull or ribs. I rushed up to Ben and swung, landing the hilt across his bare torso, saw him stagger, heard him yell, "Son of a bitch!" while letting go of Abby and arching his back. Out of the corner of my eye, I saw Conner pile-drive into another Pool Table Boy. Conner's a big dude, so his weight and momentum alone were enough to plow him into the big table, sending chairs toppling as the men at the table jumped to their feet. Abby twisted out of her other captor's grip, and both of us rushed him into the wall.

Any second, I was sure gunshots would go off, killing one or all of us—as the room filled with grunts, whoops, screams. I was swinging the cue stick back and forth like a torch to fend off attacking wolves when I felt a hand close around my throat; I spun out of it, swinging, and saw Conner bring a chair down on somebody. "Conner!" I shouted. "Ab—!"

That's when the gunshot went off: the sheriff, standing there enjoying this scene, had fired into the ceiling. From June, crouched under the counter, we heard, "What the hell! You goddamn fools all insane?!"

The room went silent. And breaking that silence was the sheriff: "Put 'em in storage." Then something thudded against my skull and my body slumped to the floor and, through half-closed eyes and brain-fog, I saw the ceiling fan whirling crazily. That's all . . . till now.

I look around, wait for my eyes to adjust. There are slivers of daylight leaking in along the side and bottom of a door on the far wall. My eyes make out a shape, Conner, crouching next to me. He raises a hand to the back of his head and moans when noises sound from outside the room—one loud and male, the other, female, rising to challenge it. The voices argue, grumble, and mutter.

"How you feeling, man?" I whisper.

"Okay, I think. I just"—he clears his throat—"came to a couple of minutes ago. I think we're in a back room or something."

"The voices must be coming from where we just were." I turn and notice the dim outline of another door in the near corner, behind us. Probably leads out to the big room, where Abby—

"Abby" I call in a low voice. "You here?"

"Think she's with them."

"Shit."

"Think they dragged us in here." Conner's whisper is harsh, urgent.

I hear him take a deep breath.

"We gotta find her, we gotta—" I try getting to my feet and stumble back on my butt. I can make out the shine of pots and pans now, the darker patches of shelves. We get up slowly, grope toward the door on our side of the room.

Not knowing how long we've been here, where Abby is now, the thoughts swirl in my aching head. Is it too late?

We hear more voices from outside and can't make out what anyone is saying. The voices are too far in the next room and echoing. I move in the direction of the voices, running my hands along the wall. I find the door. And that's when we hear the banging. Someone is kicking and banging, but not against this inner door. The outside door! Before we can say another word, the door is thrown open, letting in a blast of light, and there's Abby in the doorway.

"Move!" In her hands and at her shoulders are our packs, and she's waving her arms at us. "Get off your asses! Move!"

I don't have time to feel relief. Conner charges out the door. I'm right behind him. And we're tearing through an alleyway. Not a soul in sight, just a free, blinding-white world. Nothing but the manic sounds of our feet and the wind in our ears. At any second, I expect people behind us, gunshots and shouting. I expect to be gunned down like wild game. *Blam!* And down I'd go. That's the image playing through my head again and again. Abby leads the way, and I can see the car up ahead—the most welcome sight in my life—parked against a brick wall in the alleyway, on the corner with the street. She drops the packs on the ground before jumping into the driver's seat. Conner and I pick them up, throw them in the backseat along with our bodies, head-first, as the engine fires up and Abby's peeling the corner. At the light, we swerve left, and we're on the 395 again, gunning as fast as possible. We're dazed, my heart's racing, still unable to wrap my head around what just happened: I can see that guy Bunting, his boys, the assault rifles, all too raw, like a nightmare we still haven't woken from. In the street, people are gawking.

"What happened?" I ask. "How'd you get out?"

Abby looks at me through the rearview mirror. "That lady. June. Saved my life. The men were getting ready to drag me to whatever the hell ranch that sheriff guy lives on. I didn't know what to do—" She reaches a hand out for us, and we both take it and the three of us clasp hands. She's choking back tears. "You guys hurt?"

"Just banged up but not bad," Conner says, breathing hard.

"You saved our lives, Abby. You fucking saved us."

"I couldn't have done it without that lady. They were about to take me, and she just grabbed a gun, said she'd shoot up the place if they took one step out of that room with me. Then she told me to grab our keys and get our stuff. I've never moved that fast in my life. I jumped in the car, parked in back where I knew they'd locked you guys up."

"Thank you," Conner says, catching his breath. He shuts his eyes. "Holy shit, thank you."

We stay like that, together, hands clasped as we roar up the street. We're out of "Freetown" or whatever this place is called.

Conner leans back in his seat. "Maybe we're in some weird, separatist area right now. I couldn't be sure if those guys were punking us, but with the way the country's falling apart, none of this separatist shit surprises me anymore. You saw that guy's hat, right?"

"The one on Ben, the guy who jacked us? Yeah, I remember." It was dirty, frayed, with a patch on the front of it of an American flag but the stars arranged in a circle and three marks in the shape of bullets inside the circle. "What about it?"

"That's the Three Percenters. Whack militia."

"That's effed up. Never seen one of those."

"We're not in Oberon Heights anymore, son. Tons of outfits like that out here now."

We drive in silence. The town recedes. Land turns flat all around: featureless country with the spine of two mountain ranges running far to the east and west alongside us. Between us and the mountains are miles of tan- and chalk-colored scrub. The country makes me feel exposed. All I want now is to get as far from Freetown as possible.

A bit later and to the right comes a sign: *Bunting Ranch, next right.* Farther on, we pass a service road with an arched, gated entryway. At the top of the arch is the word "Bunting" in white, bold letters. On either side of the archway are signs on pieces of fabric and planted into the ground.: "Governor's Mansion," "Liberty 4Ever," and "Welcome to Freetown Now Get the Fuck Out."

About a mile to the east is a sprawling complex of many buildings, some half-finished, and what looks like a mansion at one end. Farm vehicles, horse trailers, and pickups are parked along the side of the service road or going off-road, raising dust.

None of us says a word. The sight of the place is too threatening, too disturbing, and I turn away. It's like we're passing through a living nightmare. Abby keeps her gaze straight ahead.

"I read about this shit," Conner mutters, partly to himself. "It's happening here and in every state. Thought it was propaganda to scare people into moving into the zones. But it's not."

"What's with this?" Abby says, staring first at the rearview mirror and then behind her through the back window.

A pickup is rapidly gaining on us. It closes in from a hundred feet behind us to maybe ten or fifteen feet in a matter of seconds. *What a prick* is my first thought, and I'm about to wave for him to go past but the driver's got other ideas: there's a horrible jolt, the kind that jars your insides, as he rams into us with his grill. Abby screams, and I turn to see the nose of a pickup following behind our car, close enough to reach out and touch. Conner and I yell, "Shit!" as Abby veers off to the shoulder. But the truck veers along too and slams into us again.

Abby speeds up and merges back onto the road. Any more hits like that and the car could careen into the scrub, and we're screwed. Abby floors it, but the pickup has no trouble bombing ahead of us—Conner flipping them off as they pass—before it jerks back into our lane. The truck speeds on ahead for a couple of seconds and, just when we're thinking it was all a scare tactic, the truck hits its brakes. We lurch forward, and I nearly tumble headfirst into the driver's seat as Abby slams on the brakes.

I feel the car angle toward the shoulder, coming to a stop inches from the pickup's bumper.

Someone jumps out of the pickup: it's that asshole Ben, with the ratty militia cap, and he's got his rifle pointed at me, stepping toward me from the passenger side of the pickup. Three others are out of the truck too: two of them I recognize as Pool Table Boys—both aiming semiautos—and the third is that boy, Daniel, pointing his Glock at us. "Stay in your seats, and don't move," he orders, his voice cracked and thin. Without the gun, he wouldn't be half as intimidating. I do as he says.

In seconds, Ben's come around to the driver's side door and pulled Abby out of the car by her arm. She screams and fights back, but it's no use. He's got an arm locked around her neck, and his rifle trained on me. I half-rise out of the car and freeze, feeling the same helplessness I felt at the restaurant.

The others are chuckling. Our obvious terror is amusing. As Abby struggles against Ben's grip, one of the Pool Table Boys, thin, scruffy-faced, leaps over the hood of the car. He grabs Abby up by her legs and, with Ben gripping her by the arms, they lift her and carry her over to the pickup. The third man is now in the bed of the pickup holding a cord of some kind: a rope, a cable, I can't tell. "She's a frisky one, bring her over," the man with the cord yells, grinning.

"We got a live one here!" Ben says. "Whoo-hoo, man. Hold her tight, Luke!"

Abby kicks the man—Luke—holding her legs square in the jaw and wriggles out of his grip. While Luke is calmly nursing his jaw—more amused than alarmed—Ben yells for her to settle down.

Luke lifts Abby's legs up again, and he and Ben drop her into the bed of the pickup where the third man begins circling the cord around her.

Conner and I both leap out of the car. I know this could be it—I picture myself dead on the road—but there's no way in hell we're about to let his happen. Then I hear the boy, Daniel, grunting, and I find Conner wrestling the Glock out of his hands. Cowering, Daniel drops to the ground, covers his head with both hands.

Conner points the pistol at the men. "Let her go—right now!"

Ben and Luke, their rifles ready, jump down from the bed of the pickup. "You want to play, boy?" Ben approaches, smiling. Probably just for kicks, he fires a round into the field. And again, chuckling now as he does it, like he's mocking us with the last sound we'll ever hear.

"We don't need to do this," Conner says. "Just let our friend go, and no one has to get hurt." His words are even and steady as he points the pistol.

Meanwhile, Luke has his weapon on me, and by his easy grin, he's having the time of his life.

"He wants his little friend back," Ben says. "You're gonna have to come get her, then."

Conner pulls the trigger on the pistol. Nothing but clicks. Chamber's empty.

Luke starts giggling. The man in the pickup is standing now, his own rifle pointed at us. Abby crouches in the bed of the pickup, her head down so I can't see her face, only her hair and the curve of her back.

"Trespassing, evading arrest, absconding justice," Ben says, counting off felonies on his fingers, "and now, threatening officers of the law." He angles his body toward me. "Now you stay still—"

I see ejecta spray from Ben's eyes as his head snaps to one side, recoils, and his body crumples to the ground, the rifle sliding out of his arms.

For a second, I think one of the other guys fired by accident. But then Luke, leaning down for a closer look at his dead friend, also folds in half and slides to the ground, his face shattered..

Now the third man has it figured out at the same time Conner and I do: someone out in the field, hidden in the scrub or behind one of the oaks, is firing at us.

"Shit!" the man shrieks, taking cover behind the lip of the bed. A metallic bang punches into the truck's chassis, inches from him. Then another. Conner and the boy roll over to my side of the Outback, and we stay down. Another bang goes off against the side of the truck.

"Where is that—?" the man grunts, freaked out, desperate. Tucked inside the bed of the truck, he fires his rifle in the direction the shots came from. "Where are you?"

Peering through the scope, he fires again and again. It's just random now. Two more bursts of noise followed by steady hissing sounds tell us the field shooter's hit the truck's tires. I can hear the man in the truck breathing hard now, frightened, furious. A few seconds later, he's made up his mind: he jumps out of the bed, on the driver side.

Head down, he pulls open the driver side door, throws the rifle in, and climbs into the seat. Two things happen as he turns on the ignition: One, I realize he's about to drive off with Abby bound in the bed of the truck . . . and, two, a *phoop!* noise shatters the passenger window of the truck. The man slumps against his side window, does not move. Even from here, I can see brain matter on the windshield.

In the long seconds that follow, all I hear is the whimpering of the boy behind Conner above the dying hiss of the pickup's tires. I break the silence: "Abby, you there?"

No answer.

"Abby?"

"Here!"

"Don't move!" I slide over to the front of the car and, with painstaking slowness, I rise to my knees to get a look over the hood. There's no sign of anyone, not obvious anyway. Beyond the wide field of scrub, there's a line of oaks and aspens about six hundred feet away. That's a hell of an aim, I'm thinking.

"See anything?" Conner whispers.

"Nothing. There are trees but really far away."

We wait another minute. Everything's gone quiet. The three of us discuss whether we should stand up and step out. Maybe the shooter is gone. Or maybe just waiting.

"Either way," Conner reasons, "we're SOL. If whoever's out there wants to kill us, they could do it right now, or they could do it while we're on the road. So—" He stands up, raises his arms, backs away from the car, and marches out to the open.

"Are you frickin' demented?" I yell. "Get back—"

"I'm cool," Conner says, "no worries, all good." He steps out toward the shoulder. "You're right. Not a soul out here."

I raise myself up, cautiously as hell, back on my feet now.

The boy is on his knees, peering out from the car's bumper. I take my chances, pick up Luke's rifle and move over to the pickup. I see Abby working at the cords around her legs with a box-cutter.

There's an open toolbox next to her, wedged beside a plastic tarp, packing crates, and bungee cords. "Here," I tell her, "let me." I climb in, take the blade from her hands and cut the cords, and she shucks them off. She shudders, hugs her arms to herself. She lies down against the side of the bed.

"Abby?"

She doesn't answer, doesn't look at me. She brings her hands to her face and starts to cry. I place a hand on her shoulder. Her crying grows. I lay down beside her. We stay like that until she inhales, and her hands drop away. She's looking at me now, in a funny way, like she's looking beyond me.

"You're good now. Everything's good." I keep my hand on her shoulder. Her eyes, half-hidden by strands of hair, have this rock-steady, here-but-not-here look about them. She sits up, reaches over to grab the rifle I've set between us, and clambers out of the back of the pickup on the driver side. I follow her, curious, worried for her. "Abby? Careful."

She's pointing the rifle through the open driver-side window. Inside the truck, there are fragments of bone and meat everywhere. The body is slumped against the door and half the face is gone, like a blown-open gourd you'd find in a pumpkin field. What makes me want to puke is how the rest of the face looks: completely normal, untouched, not a mark on it, like nothing happened. The remaining eye is open.

Abby's got her finger closed around the trigger. I know what's going through her mind, the storm inside, and know there's nothing I can do. Gradually, her arms trembling, her body tensed, she loosens her grip on the rifle and lowers it. She doubles over, placing the rifle on the road, and begins sobbing. All I can do is put my arms around her as she cries.

Daniel is gone. As we walk back to the car, we see no sign of him. "Took off that way." Conner points back toward Freetown. "Gonna be a long, hot run for that tubby little terrorist."

First, I check to see if the car runs. To our surprise, the engine turns without a fuss. We debate whether to take the rifles because the road no longer feels safe, especially because—if Bunting is to be believed—this whole country is under the control of some crazy-as-fuck militia. But we don't want weapons in the car, no reminders of the people we crossed paths with.

So we toss the rifles into the pickup, next to the body, after taking the magazines out, removing the bullets and chucking them into the field.

Abby and I talk about how the pickup is this dead asshole's coffin now. We can hear Conner rummaging around the back of the pickup. "Our stay in Freetown wasn't a complete loss," he says and holds up a five-quart jug of motor oil.

As for the two other bodies, we leave them where they fell. We don't even want to touch them.

The highway and all the land around are dead, nothing out here but baking heat, turning the grasses and trees into kindling. Since we passed Bakersfield this morning, the traffic's gotten sparse. Maybe because of wildfires up and down the state—you can smell them when the wind blows up from the south—maybe they're all out on the bigger freeways heading east. Whatever it is, it really makes you feel like you're going to die out here, alone.

I'm sure we'll soon come across Bunting or more of his men . . . or maybe whoever it was fired those shots. I dread all the above.

"Anything?" I ask as we settle into highway speed up the 395. "Any signs?"

From the back seat, Conner keeps his eyes roving. "Nothing," he says, and with a groan, he places a hand across the side of his head. "This is going to hurt for a while."

I touch the sore spot behind my ear. The pain radiates out of it, and I can feel the tough mound—what Mom would call "an induration"—where the blunt object collided with my head. "You feel dizzy at all? Headaches?"

"No."

"Nausea? Any ringing in your ears?"

"No, doc."

"I wonder if I should pull over and check your pupils. I got a flashlight in my pack."

"Naw, I'm good."

I return to thoughts of the road. The Outback took a beating—the front left corner, especially, looks pretty banged up—but we're moving and, with the oil topped off and still a half-tank of gas, the car should make it to the cabin in one piece.

By my count, it'll take another four or five hours to reach the lake. I check my phone: it's past three now, so the hike to the cabin tonight is going to be tricky with only the moon and our flashlights to go by. And when we get there, I have no clue what we'll find. For all I know, the cabin could've been demolished years ago by rains, snow, or fire. Wild animals could be living there now.

Weirdly enough, the cabin feels like a safer place to be than out here in a flat, wide-open valley, the mountains like arms opening in the east and west, leading us into the dark, wild heart of the state.

"Maybe it was the lady?" I say, breaking the quiet. "The one who helped you out."

Abby, her arms folded across her stomach, speaks so low I can barely hear. "I don't know."

"No, man, that was military," insists Conner. "Like elite sniper shit. Did you see how freaking *exact* those shots were . . . from, like, three hundred yards?"

"I know. It was freaky," I say. "They could've killed us too. I don't get it. They're probably watching us right now."

"Whoever it was, they're either our angels, or they're biding their time"—Conner's eyes dart from a side window to the rear window then back around to front—"before they do the same to us."

"I'm going with option number one."

Conner laughs. "That's probably wise. No point obsessing over option two."

"I'll feel better when we get there," Abby says.

I nod. She smiles at me. A smile: that's a good sign, right?

"I'll tell you one thing, today hasn't been boring," Conner says, his eyes on his phone. His finger swipes and taps at the screen.

"Getting a signal? What's the latest?"

He shakes his head. "LA is still quarantined. Schools, businesses, everything's closed. Government orders. More cases of that disease. It's military, man. It's got to be. Lemme see." He scrolls and continues: "New cases in Mexico, Bolivia, Turkey. What else? War, riots . . . and meteors. Yeah . . ." He puts the phone away. "Same ol', same ol'."

In the next town, Big Pine, we take a risk: we pull over for urgent bathroom breaks and top off the fuel tank. We've still got half a tank, but there might not be many more chances up ahead. I just want to fill up and get the hell out, attract no attention.

There are few people about, except for the locals. Campers, pickups, and a couple of semis ply the southward road. And we see militia types patrolling the sidewalks, toting rifles, around a pancake house. Seeing them, my first thought is that they're more of Bunting's men hunting for us. But they're not paying us any attention, and, gradually, my nerves settle.

At the station, we discover a single bathroom—dingy and rank—and we go in one by one. Afterward, I hand over twenty bucks to the clerk behind the tiny window and start filling up at the pump as Conner and Abby climb back in.

A man in shades approaches. He's black and has a close-shaved head, stubble face, and a coffee-spotted T-shirt. "You guys going south, by any chance?" His voice is clear and urgent.

"No."

"Think you could help us out? I'm looking for a ride for me, my wife, and kid."

I look past his shoulder and see a small dark woman, Thai or Philippine, her hair in a frazzled ponytail, standing next to a cinderblock wall at the edge of the gas station. She's holding a baby, rocking it, and looking abashedly in our direction.

"We got our car stolen and got robbed down in Freetown. We hitched a ride up here. We really just wanna get down to Barstow and catch one of those buses going out to the new zones, you know?"

"We had some trouble there ourselves," I tell him. Otherwise, I keep quiet and my eyes on the numbers on the pump. When the handle clicks off, I quickly replace the nozzle, anxious to put some distance between us and this guy and this town and this whole part of the state.

"What do you say, man?" he presses.

"About?"

"That ride, man. To Barstow?"

"We're going north. And the last place we want to go through is Freetown," I tell him. "Sorry."

The man seems peeved and confused now. "But north is a dead end. What're you going north for?"

Conner lowers his window. "Hey, man, we can't help you. We're on a schedule ourselves, you know. Good luck, all right?"

"But what're you going north for?" the man asks.

"Look, we'll be back down this way tomorrow," I say, if only to get him off our backs. "If you guys are still here, we can give you a lift down to the 58 or Bakersfield or whatever."

"There is no Bakersfield, man," he replies in a parched and desperate voice. "There is no LA now. It's all in quarantine. They're saying weeks, but it'll be months or maybe never. They say it's in the air, the dust or some shit." He pauses and seems to be scanning us, one by one, behind those shades. "Hey, how old are you guys? You got parents?"

"Up north," I say.

"Hmmm." The man ponders, suddenly saddened, and shakes his head. "Well, good luck."

I slide into my seat, fumble with my keys.

"Hey, listen, guys. I got a wife and kid. Think you could at least spare some cash? Some locals here are getting out tonight," his voice turns low now, "and they're only taking people who can pay cash. What do you say?"

The three of us pool together forty bucks. "Thanks, guys. This'll help." He's about to walk off, back to the woman, still rocking the baby in her arms. "Hold on," Abby calls out, and the man shuffles back. Abby hands him two more fives.

The man clutches the money, nods. As he pockets the money, something comes over him. He sniffs, wipes at his eyes, and thanks us again as he reaches through the window to shake our hands.

"Good luck," I say to him.

"Be careful up there."

As we leave town, we pass a rally in a parking lot: fifty or sixty noisy men are crowded around a pickup. Confederate flags and a banner with a coiled rattlesnake rise out of the crowd, held up on thin poles, and there's a large, bearded man on the back of the pickup, shouting into a megaphone. A decal on a parked F-150 declares "God, Guns & Glory" on the side of the road. This is very much Tod Bunting country.

"Let's get the hell out of here," says Conner.

"Nice of you to give him more money, Ab," I say, speeding up. "Why'd you do it?"

"The kid," says Abby, taking a swig of water. "It was the little boy."

"They either scammed us, or they were legit," Conner says. "Either way, we made their day."

Abby stares out the window as the scene morphs from town to open country. "They were legit."

Every now and then, we check the rearview for Bunting or his men or anyone else in pursuit. But the road stays clear, and we're making progress again.

From above, the sun's roasting everything for hundreds of miles all around. We see now that Bunting wasn't bullshitting: to the west, in the direction of Yosemite, there's a wide brown smudge beyond the Sierra ridge, trailing to the southwest. To the east, all we see is scrub until the evaporated bowl of Mono Lake where the water line's receded almost halfway to islands that stand in the middle of the lake.

Abby's cracked open the map now, careful not to tear the delicate seams even more. "In another hour, you're gonna turn off this road," she says, peering closely at it, "onto a smaller road that goes into that." She points at the mountains, the smudge. "But we should be north of that mess by then and clear it."

"And then?"

"That's it," she says. "We follow that little road till we get there."

"How long?" Conner asks.

"It'll be dark," Abby answers, keeping her eyes on the map.

My phone starts to vibrate. With all the craziness back in Freetown, I'd almost forgotten about my phone. It's not my mom's number. Caller ID says "Unknown." I answer tentatively. "Um, hello?"

The voice on the other end is familiar. "Dev? It's Michael Greene from the ER at LA Memorial. You got a minute?"

There's a tight, urgent tone in his voice. My heart's starting to thud in my chest. "Yeah, sure, what's going on?"

There's a pause before he goes on. "Dev, I've been trying to reach you today, but calls aren't getting through."

"It's okay," I say. "I've been trying to call too. Connection's been bad. I haven't been able to reach my mom."

Another pause. "Your mom checked into the ER this morning, Dev. Not doing too good. High fever, and she was having some trouble breathing. I found your number listed in her files here." My heart is going to explode out of my chest.

"What're you saying?"

"You probably want to get to the hospital," he says. "We moved her to the ICU a little bit ago, so she *is* stable. Resting."

"Any idea what happened to her?"

"We're running tests. We're keeping an eye on her. But you want to get over here."

I don't know what to say. What *can* I say? I realize I'm wavering off the road, and Abby reaches a hand in to correct my steering.

"Sorry."

"Dev?"

"Um, yeah."

"When can you get here?"

"I'll be there as soon as I can."

And I hang up. The act itself shocks me. I just hung up on news about my mom. My mother is in the ICU. My mother is dying. It's that disease. It has to be. My throat's clamping up, like it's strained from holding my heart from dropping to the floor.

"What's going on?" It's Abby's voice.

I'm zoned out. I feel the steering wheel shudder, and the engine start to complain. "Dev?" The voice sounds far away, from the other side of worlds. "Dev!" Abby, clear as a bell, puts her hand on top of my hand, vibrating with the steering wheel. I check the speedometer: I'm doing 95.

I slow things down, slow things down. *Steady, Dev.* I think about pulling over, but I can't stop, not now. The sooner we get there, the sooner we're back, and I can see her, and things can go back to the way they were. I want to chew up as much road as this banged-up old car will let me.

CHAPTER ELEVEN

Winter 2019

Every time Gavin thought he'd cracked the code, Bizarro pulled a fast one. Three and a half years after that first accelerator experiment—when the energy field revealed itself for a brief instant—he was still searching. The invisible mass particle: still a mystery. The energy field: still a mystery. With every collision, a mysterious subatomic mass was releasing a fury of energy. For a millionth of a millionth of a second, it peeked out at him . . . before zapping out of existence and going into hiding again. Harnessing that millionth of a millionth and expanding it to even a touch more—that would mean everything.

The weeks and months following that first experiment were the headiest and most hopeful. Gavin talked Bollinger into allocating him more money to build out a small team, which now included Megan Chen, and making modifications to the accelerator to make more precise measurements. But scores of experiments, hundreds of meetings, and thousands of hours spent calculating and speculating had gotten them . . . nowhere. Nowhere closer to figuring out why subatomic particles extracted from Bizarro behaved as they did.

Then, one afternoon, the boss pulled the plug.

"Three years, three million dollars, and a net return of zero," Bollinger said, forming an O with his thumb and fingers. (Gavin didn't need the extra show of emphasis.) The two sat in Bollinger's office with the floor-to-ceiling windows overlooking the San Gabriel mountains, and Bollinger summed up Breakthrough's next initiative.

"Triton has been popping a lot of champagne bottles lately, as you know," Bollinger said, referring to Breakthrough's biggest investor, Triton Corp. "They just tested their suborbital flights, New York to Shanghai. One hour. Seen these ships? They're incredible. They want to go big too. Flights to the moon and back. Six months ago, I made a bid to design solar-energy fuel containment for these ships. Triton bit. They want us to work with their aerospace division on a proof of concept."

"That's great," Gavin piped in, "but I don't under—"

"There's a catch. Triton doesn't care for, shall we say, this company's less-than-stellar ROI. That includes all the resources we've put into this"—he waved his hand back and forth in a dismissive gesture—"Bizarro stuff."

Gavin sat up to protest, but Bollinger anticipated him.

"I'm all for cutting-edge discoveries, Gavin, but you have to remember I'm also running a business." Bollinger closed his folder with a flick of his wrist. "So, effective immediately, research on your rock is done. I could show you the numbers—"

"It's all right," Gavin said. "I understand." He kept his eyes on the patterned carpet, processing Bollinger's words. He'd suspected for months that Bollinger was going to do this. He had every right to. But, dammit, they were on a threshold. He could feel it. "There's something here," was all Gavin could muster to say. Bollinger didn't answer. Gavin turned to face him, and their eyes met. "You want to know what I think? I think we're about to redefine physics, our understanding of the fundamentals."

Bollinger hatched his thick fingers together on his desk. "You want to know what *I* think?" His eyes steadily held Gavin's gaze. "I think you've been telling yourself that for three years. And you're welcome to keep telling yourself that as long as you want . . . on your own time, as you tinker away in your garage. But there are bigger wigs than me that pay our bills, and they want to see dollar signs. As for me, I want to do more than keep this shop open."

Bollinger rose from his chair and turned to the windows. His tailored jacket and neatly trimmed silver-dark hair gave him the aura of an investment banker rather than the director of a design and technology lab. "You're a good research man, Gavin, a good physicist. But I didn't bring you on board to waste your talents on dead ends. Starting Monday, we get to work on the POC. We've got meetings with the aerospace people. You'll find a lot of homework in your inbox. We good?"

Gavin nodded, unable to raise his eyes and look at the man across the room.

"Good." Bollinger sat back down. "We're done, then."

Gavin returned to his office, fighting every urge to go back upstairs and tell that guy off, the way he'd done with the chair of his department at UCLA. But that stunt had done nothing but land him in professional purgatory: a classroom of bored high-schoolers who'd rather stare at their phones than pay attention to a single word he said. Gavin also knew he couldn't do as Bollinger had ordered. Put all that research in a box, tape it shut forever? No way.

In his office, he stared at the equations and graphs on the whiteboard. Half-erased, layered one over the other, the palimpsest was unintelligible to all but himself and maybe Megan. He knew he'd have to break the news to her and to the rest of his team, but he couldn't bring himself to do that tonight. He'd tell Megan and the rest tomorrow morning.

Solar fuel cells for Earth-moon ships? The very thought bored him. Maybe if he were an engineer, Bollinger's spiel might've interested him, but for Gavin—who'd witnessed a thousand gamma-ray bursts going off for an instant—anything other than working on Bizarro would feel like a massive and tragic letdown. Clicking off the lights in his office, he knew his days at Breakthrough were numbered.

On his drive home, he got a call from Megan: "Bollinger just gave me my walking papers," she said. "Guess you don't need an astrobiologist when you're designing solar fuel for spaceships."

"I'm sorry," he said. "What're you going to do?"

"He said I can go ahead and publish all my notes on Bizarro."

Gavin felt his insides cave. "That's . . . great," he managed.

So it would soon be public knowledge. With no theory to tie it all together, Gavin imagined all their work on the rock—the microbes, the energy field, everything—thrown into the chaos of conspiracy blogs and half-baked science stories on CNN.

Public knowledge: the most grotesque of fates. Because knowledge could be so easily mishandled, and the public was so goddamn gullible.

"I just want you to know that I'm not going to publish anything," Megan continued. "Not until we come up with something."

"Thanks, Meg, I appreciate that. But you discovered Bizarro. And you've got every right to publish. It'll set you up with a nice career. You deserve it."

They spoke about their uncertain futures for a few more minutes, Megan still unsure about which part of the research she would publish, *if* she would publish any of it. For his part, Gavin couldn't see himself continuing at Breakthrough for much longer. Solar energy collectors? His heart wouldn't be in it. Bollinger would can him inside of three months.

After he hung up, his thoughts whirled. Eventually, someone, somewhere would come up with an explanation for the energy field, a new theory of fundamental forces, maybe even win the Nobel for it. A flush of jealousy and panic surged through him as he slammed the brakes on approaching a traffic jam on the 10.

In the history that would one day be written about Bizarro, his name (and Megan's) would merit only a polite mention. Others would reap the glory. In a year, he could be back to teaching high-school physics. The traffic ground on.

Gavin returned home to find a Pokémon episode playing on TV and Dev limping into the living room. The boy crouched down on the rug, his back against the couch, and drew his right foot up close to his face. Gavin found him inspecting the toe, his eyes inches away from it.

"What's wrong?"

"I banged my toe on the table leg when I was leaving to go to school," he said. "Now it super hurts."

Gavin crouched down next to the boy. The right toe was indeed swollen, reddened. When he pressed against the toe, a yellowish pus oozed from the nail fold.

"Ow!"

"Sorry." Gavin backed away from the foot. "Didn't Mommy wash it or put anything on it? Or Jess?"

The nanny, Jess, appeared in the living room, searching inside her handbag for her car keys. "All right, guys. I'm off."

"Did you know about this, Jess?"

"Hmm?" She looked up, her brows pinched with concern. "Dev? What happened, sweetheart?" She came over and knelt to take a look at the foot.

They agreed that it looked infected. Gavin picked up his phone, called Seema, who said she'd put through a prescription for doxycycline and pick it up on her way home. She asked to speak with Dev, who put on his best hurt-little-boy voice on the phone for his mother. In the meantime, Gavin's thoughts returned to his conversation with Megan, the utter loss about to happen.

After Dev hung up, Gavin washed out the injured toe, applying antibiotic ointment and a Band-Aid on it. "That'll tide you over till Mom comes home with the medicine."

As Dev followed his father into the kitchen, he kept his eyes on the hobbled foot. "How did this happen anyway? My foot was fine this morning."

"Give 'em a chance, little man, and the germs will get in."

"How'd the germs know? How'd they know to get in?"

Gavin laughed. "Germs are everywhere. Just hanging out. Remember what Mom was telling you? Once they get in your body, they go to work, start making copies of themselves. And the body and the germs start fighting. That's why it hurts and looks like that, and you need the medicine."

The explanation seemed enough for Dev, who turned his attention back on the TV screen. With everything on his mind, Gavin wasn't in the mood to put dinner together. He and Dev agreed: pizza was the way to go.

After he called in the order, he went into the kitchen for a beer. And as he stared into the light of the opened fridge, he heard his words play over in his mind: *Once they get into your body, they go to work, start making copies of themselves.*

Gavin could hear Dev in his room, playing with his Star Wars action figures, mimicking explosions, reciting lines. He turned off the TV and sat back with the beer.

For three years, they'd run experiments using grain samples from the rock dubbed Bizarro. And it was isotopes from those globules, those round shapes in the rock, that had caused the lab-shattering result in 2015. Gavin and Megan had thought the shapes to be chondrules, molten bits often found inside asteroids. Though experiments since that first one had come back with mixed results, it was that first experiment that needled at his brain now.

His words came back to him: "When they get into your body, they go to work." Otherwise, germs were dormant. A few cocooned themselves in endospores, safe until they found themselves in an environment where they could thrive and reproduce, at which time they shed their endospores—and . . . went to work.

Those grains weren't chondrules.

The doorbell rang. Gavin got up, reached down for his phone. Again, the doorbell rang. "Be right there," Gavin shouted. He could hear Dev come thumping out of his room. "Pizza!" he cheered, bopping on his hobbled foot for the front door. He opened the door and greeted the delivery boy.

"Just a sec, Dev," Gavin said. He dialed up Megan. When she answered, he dispensed with pleasantries and got right to it. "There's one more experiment I want to try."

Megan peered through the lens, adjusting focus knobs. Perched on a stool, Gavin felt the crimp of the face mask and the latex gloves he wore. Impatient, he tried to turn his attention to his breathing, the soft rasp of the air against his mask. Neither spoke. In the after-hours silence of the UCLA microbiology lab, Gavin could pick up the noises of cooling fans, even the beeps and chirps of temperature-controlled incubator cabinets. On the stage of the microscope was the blood agar plate.

"Well?"

"Never seen anything like it." Megan turned away from the microscope. She backed away so Gavin could lean in and take a look.

As he peered through the eyepiece, his breath caught in his chest. In twelve hours, the microbe—if that's what this was—had not only shed its spore—if that's what *this* was—but also consumed the blood agar, leaving iridescent blotches and trails throughout the plate.

Megan said exactly what he was thinking: "It's alive. I've never seen that color either." She turned the plate over in her hand, inspecting the glowing crisscrossing patterns and patches. "Could be a metallic by-product of reproduction. But I wouldn't know until I analyzed exactly what these little buggers were made of."

"Whatever happened, it was fast, wasn't it?"

"Hungry, maybe." Megan continued inspecting the plate, murmuring to herself about the shedding of nickel or iron. "Running another mass spectrometry might help us."

"Not now," Gavin insisted. "Let's move on with what we planned."

A minute later, Megan came back with two additional sealed agar plates, fetched from the incubator in which control samples of bacteria were stored. She produced a clean new slide from drawers in a tabletop cabinet and drew three dime-size circles on the slide with a grease pencil.

"Heat it up," she told Gavin.

On cue, Gavin inserted a wand with an attached wire loop into a microincinerator, a heating unit that looked somewhat like an electric pencil sharpener perched on a stand. Ten seconds later, Gavin handed the hot, now-sterilized loop across to Megan.

As she waited a few seconds for the loop to cool, she and Gavin took a deep breath together, exchanging nervous looks. She dipped the loop into the agar plate with the track marks in it, taking a millimeter-size dollop and smearing it onto the center circle of the slide.

They let go of long-held breaths.

Megan handed the loop back to Gavin, who sterilized the loop by inserting it back into the incinerator, then back again to Megan. They repeated these steps two more times, once for each of the additional plates, sampling tiny portions of two different bacteria, the two controls: one a spore-producing one, the other not.

The staining came next. Gavin looked on as Megan applied droplets of two different, dark-colored dyes—the stain and the counterstain—rinsing the slides in water between each application of dye. The two waited as the slide was heat-fixed on a wire tray on a ring fixed above a burner.

Gavin paced around the lab, restless, joking that he hadn't felt this nervous since he was in the hospital waiting for his son to be born. Several minutes later, it was time.

With halting steps and a pounding heart, he approached the laminar table where Megan was now scrutinizing the slide under a microscope. He found her adjusting the focus knobs, the coarse first, now the fine. He stood behind her for several seconds in the silence. "Well?" he broke in, irritable now. She still said nothing.

Finally, she straightened up on the stool and turned to him very slowly. "We might've discovered the first live extraterrestrial organism."

Megan's words were all Gavin needed to roll up his sleeve to the elbow. Megan fitted an ampoule into a syringe and filled up two ampoules of Gavin's blood. A minute later, using the loop, she'd dropped another millimeter-size dab of the Bizarro blood-agar sample into one of the ampoules.

"When will we know?" Gavin asked.

"Usually, seventy-two hours. Sometimes longer. But"—Megan scrunched her eyes, sliding her gaze toward the agar plate—"I don't think this is usual."

The next morning, Gavin was at a team meeting at Breakthrough. Bollinger was going over a PowerPoint, prepping them for the upcoming conversation about solar cells with Triton's aerospace honchos, when Gavin's phone buzzed. It was Megan. "Your blood is yellow."

Gavin didn't know whether to cheer or be horrified. For a second, he considered the possibility that they'd screwed up somewhere, somehow. "You think we made a mistake?"

"No."

Minutes later, in his office, Gavin was poring through an email from Megan. She wrote that, on closer study, "it wasn't bacteria at all. Bacteria have no structures inside, no nucleus, just a bundle of DNA. These are more like cyst-producing amoeba, except they're smaller than your typical amoeba. And they have fixed body shapes, unlike amoeba. And they're even more complex. Watch the video."

This has to be good, Gavin thought, and clicked the video attachment. On the viewer, grainy gray-scale footage revealed donut-shaped cells—his red cells—huddled and trembling as they floated in a microscopic pond of plasma. Then, like a monster emerging from horror-movie shadows, a shape much bigger than the cells appeared. It looked like a bizarre version of a centipede or beetle, something out of a primitive eon. Numerous spindly legs jutted from both sides of a transparent tube-like body, wriggling, while its "head," two thin pincer-like attachments, swept side to side, propelling the thing forward. The shape swam jerkily through the medium, and when it nosed up to the cells, it became still. Then it absorbed several cells, devouring them. Gavin peered closely as the cells, visible through the transparent body, dissolved from their centers out, each imploding. More of these things appeared and, within a few seconds, every last cell on the screen was gone. The things nudged and wriggled around each other as the video ended.

In her email, Megan said that these pseudo-amoeba tucked themselves into their cysts once they'd finished their meal. No wider than a human hair, the shells looked like the ammonites he remembered from his college biology textbooks.

He turned off the computer and tried to wrap his head around this. To think that, for all these years—all these decades—E.T. had been on a shelf in a university meteorite collection, dormant and embedded in a piece of interstellar rock . . . ready to be cultured back to life!

And that might be enough, Gavin thought, to change the course of history. But given what he'd observed in that first experiment three and a half years ago, there was one other step he needed to take while this knowledge belonged to only two people in the whole world.

Repeat spectrometry revealed ordinary stuff: another carbon-based organism with helpings of hydrogen, nitrogen, sulfur, phosphorous, iron. Yet test after test revealed there was something unmeasurable, an invisible mass. Gavin and Megan knew this information had to go public, at least made available to the NSA or to state and federal environmental and health agencies. Hell, even to their boss. But Gavin knew enough about the secrecy and deviousness of the NSA, and he didn't trust Bollinger, whose only concern right now was shoring up his business. But confidentiality would soon have to end.

A week later, on her last day at Breakthrough, Megan stopped by Gavin's office, her arms laden with boxes. "I wanted to wish you luck."

He swiveled in his chair, away from the whiteboard, and opened his mouth to say, "Thank you," but instead went over to Megan. "Let me help you with that."

They left the building and didn't say a word till they'd reached Megan's car on the far side of the parking lot. They could hear the freeway behind a high wall of cypresses and concrete. Gavin dumped the boxes into the trunk then, after a quick look around, said, "Thanks, Megan. For everything."

Megan shut the trunk and dusted her hands. "Everything ready?"

"No one's in there tonight. Once ought to do it."

"And the samples?"

"Kept them like you said. In the incubator."

"Sure you don't need an extra hand?" she asked.

"Can't have you risk it, Meg."

"What's to risk? We're already this far along. What's one more test?"

"Not this one, Meg. The risks."

"I'm already let go, how much worse—"

"I don't mean to your career, I mean something way more than that. There's no telling what this sample will do. No." He shook his head.

"Fine," she said tersely, opened her car door and got in. "But tomorrow . . ."

"The world will know." With his hand, he sized up the headlines: "'E.T. found inside rock.'"

"Of unknown origin and age," Megan added, shaking her head to absorb those words. She stared vaguely at her dashboard. "That's *huge*."

Gavin propped an elbow on the car and leaned down to talk. To security cameras, they were just two colleagues having a conversation. "After we run the sample in the ring, we'll know what we're dealing with. And then you can go off and publish everything."

"But you'll have Bollinger to deal with."

"I'll handle him." With his palm, he thumped the roof of the car twice and turned to leave as Megan fired up the engine.

"Whatever happens," she called to him, "I want top billing on the paper we publish."

"This was all you, Megan," he told her. "Let me tie this up tonight."

"You're going to need help, Gavin."

He sent her on, though deep in his heart, Gavin knew she was right. He'd need help, someone to help him track the experiment, monitor the results. He thought of calling Megan, telling her to come back. But she wasn't the best candidate. She knew her way around a microbiology lab, but in the collider's control room, there'd be too much of a learning curve. He needed someone familiar with the system, someone he could trust.

Anton Veronin was a new addition to the Breakthrough team. Hired only two months ago, Anton was a systems engineer with a background in quantum mechanics from someplace in Russia or Eastern Europe, Gavin couldn't remember. Anton had been going over and analyzing three years' worth of their calculations—until Bollinger canned all Bizarro research. True, there was an arrogance about him that irked Gavin—but he was a good analyst and technician. And being the low man on the Breakthrough totem pole, Anton might jump at the opportunity to be part in an out-of-the-box, confidential assignment.

From the parking lot, Gavin walked around the main building of the Breakthrough campus and entered the terraced central courtyard (landscaped courtesy of Triton). He scanned the grounds with its various water features, space travel-inspired art installations and an espresso bar and café. He'd seen Anton out here in the evenings, chatting with the admins or the interns at one of the café tables. Not today, though. Next, he took the wide steps of the courtyard down a few more flights on the far side and into the collider complex.

Gavin roamed the floors of the complex for another half hour. He'd given up any hope of finding Anton when he spotted him in the breakroom, crouched behind a vending machine. The machine was scooched away from the wall, and Anton seemed to be trying to take it apart.

Collecting his breath, Gavin approached. "Breaking into Coke machines, eh?"

A wide-eyed, clean-shaven face—it could've belonged to a teenager—popped out from behind the vending machine. He smiled somewhat embarrassedly. "Oh, hello. I'm sorry. I did not notice you there, Dr. Harrison."

"Call me Gavin." He took another step and, leaning forward, offered his hand.

Anton got to his feet. In his hands, he gripped a screwdriver and the grill backing to the vending machine.

"I see you got your hands full. Never mind." Gavin laughed and waved his hand away.

"Machine was jammed," Anton explained with an awkward, apologetic air. "It has not been dispensing, so I thought I would fix."

"How's your day so far, Anton? Here." He took the grill backing from him and set it down in one corner. "Have a seat. Please." Anton complied, sliding into one of the molded chairs at the round table in the middle of the breakroom. Gavin pondered, trying to find a way to broach the conversation, and the best he came up with was: "So, uh, you got anything big going on? I mean besides fixing broken soda machines?"

Anton scrunched his eyes. "Well . . ." He frowned. "We are trying to finish calculations on solar diffraction ahead of modeling the panel design." He bowed his head, his finger fidgeting with a discarded straw wrapper. "But our results aren't good enough. Boss is anxious now. Says we are already behind—"

"Sounds intense," Gavin replied. "JB is going to make us all sweat a little more from now on." Gavin got up and ran some water into a glass, gulped it down. Refilling the glass, he asked if Anton was available to assist on "what should be a very routine test on the collider this evening."

"I don't remember seeing any test scheduled."

"Last minute, very routine."

"I don't understand. I apologize, Dr. Harrison. If it is routine, why test after the complex is closed? We can schedule it next week. I can check—"

"There is no next week. All Bizarro work shuts down now, today. Boss's orders. I just need one final run. Very routine."

Anton fished a bag of potato chips out of a basket of snacks placed in the middle of the table. "So you have no team?"

"It's last minute. Just me and Megan Chen. We need some data before we close the books officially."

"Does Bollinger know about this?"

"Just follow my instructions, and I'll handle Bollinger."

Anton stood up, contemplating, and moved to the vending machine. He put several coins into the slot. "Let us see if it eats more of my money," he mumbled, punching numbers on the keypad. Nothing happened. "Shit," he muttered, his shoulders slumped.

Gavin moved in and gave the face of the machine a smart *thwack* with the heel of his palm. "Sometimes you gotta—" He *thwack*ed it again and pressed a number combination on the keypad. Anton looked on quizzically.

"Which soda you want?" Gavin asked, taking a step back. Anton stared at Gavin then at the machine then back at Gavin. "Go ahead."

Tentatively, Anton pressed numbers on the keypad and a moment later, he heard a metallic tumbling inside the machine before a can of soda rolled into view. As he reached down to collect the soda, he also heard coins clinking into the coin return slot.

"There," Gavin said, "consider that a recoupment."

Anton shook his head, smiled, and collected the change out of the coin return. He popped open the soda, and they both sat down at the table again.

"Help me out, and I'll show how to hack that soda machine. You'll never pay for a Coke again."

"Bizarro." Anton laughed and took a sip. "I have always liked your name for this."

At 2:05 the following morning, a small temblor rolled across the suburbs of eastern Los Angeles. Megan started awake and felt it thump against the walls, shift the floor of her third-story Altadena apartment. Otherwise, the night was undisturbed: the houselights on the hills twinkled and the whooshing of the freeway below continued. A minute later, she turned on the bedside lamp and reached for her phone. *You feel that?* she texted Gavin.

Feel it? he texted back. *I caused it.*

Her fingers tapped: *WTF?*

Equipment held, systems normal.

And?

Megan waited. One minute, two minutes, three. She picked up her phone again and had begun another text to Gavin when a balloon of words scrolled up on her screen: *I calibrated the test for the iron isotopes.*

She recalled that analyses they ran always narrowed down one particular iron isotope found inside Bizarro. These isotopes were heavier than they ought to have been; there was more to their nuclei than was detectable. They'd found the same isotope when they analyzed the cultured blood sample.

Megan typed a reply: *And?*

Two minutes, five minutes . . . ten.

And?

And I think we got us a wormhole.

Gavin and Anton stared with wide-open eyes at a video feed from ninety feet underground. Normally, the feed would show the detection chamber—a copper-red, SUV-sized barrel layered with trackers and measuring equipment—fitted at either ends to the vacuum piping through which protons were blasted. Right now, the screen was a blur, ablaze with light.

A blue-white orb about three meters in diameter, as bright as the sun, surrounded the walls of the detector. The orb expanded beyond its walls but otherwise seemed not to interact with the chamber—nor any other ordinary matter—in any way. The orb just hovered there, pulsing with high-frequency electromagnetic radiance. Gavin raised his hands to grasp the sides of his head, to keep his disbelief under control. Why hadn't this object exploded? It should've vaporized this complex instantly, created gravitational anomalies. It was large enough. Why hadn't it fizzed out instead?

It was energetic, which also meant it was massive. And till now, it was invisible. Gavin sat back in his chair, exhaling, gratitude and relief filling his whole being. He wanted to throw up, to pass out. His heart was pounding. He was okay, he was okay. *Holy shit!* How close had he come to causing disaster? What had stopped it? Here was the luckiest break he—maybe anyone in history—had ever had: the collider was undamaged, he was *alive*, his family was safe, the Earth, the solar system . . . all well. On top of that, he was witnessing something no one ever had.

It had been two minutes since he'd brought the ions into collision and the orb had appeared. Otherwise, the experiment had gone as smoothly and normally as any experiment using the accelerator. Billions of protons had smashed together, pulverizing into quarks and gluons. Anton had tracked the charges, volt-energies and mass densities of this subatomic scattering. All normal, they both agreed, none of it out of the ordinary.

"Can you get a reading of the surface temperature?" Gavin asked.

Anton swiveled in his chair and leaned toward a screen. He shook his head and chortled in disbelief. "Either the instruments are broken or . . ."

"Yes?"

"Twenty-two degrees," Anton said.

"Incredible," Gavin said, shaking his head. "That's picnic weather." It was a far cry from the temperatures in the vacuum tubes, which were as cold as deep space.

Anton checked the digital clock on the wall. "Fourteen minutes. Fourteen minutes? How can that be?" He continued to scan more readings, his mouth open in wonderment.

Since the collision, the field's mass readings had them boggled too. "The composition could be baryonic mass," Anton muttered, half to himself, then louder, "but this mass number is not only baryonic. There is more here."

Gavin scrambled for explanations. "Maybe the chamber got corrupted with gases we hadn't cleared out. There are always stray atoms from outside."

"Stray amount of mass would not generate this kind of energy."

"It's too much," Gavin had to admit. If their readings were correct, the field was generating enough power to rival the hearts of supermassive black holes or the most spectacular neutron stars. Impossible!

Anton giggled. "Why are we still alive right now?"

Indeed, something within the orb was balancing out its explosive energies and following all the textbook laws of conservation. And something else bizarre: it wasn't nearly as dense as its volume suggested. In fact, the orb was hollow. Where were all the x-rays and gamma rays? The radiation that should've set Southern California aglow?

As he was pondering all this, the orb blinked out of existence—vanished. No, it more like—*folded*. Folded in on itself.

Anton sat bolt upright and muttered something in Russian.

The video feed was back to normal, displaying a scene of the detection chamber, as if nothing had happened. Looking at it, Gavin felt both relieved and devastated. The orb was gone, but at least now any potential dangers had passed. His next thought was whether he'd ever be able to duplicate the experiment. He panicked before remembering that he had the footage, the video feed, he had the measurements, everything recorded and preserved. There was data here to last a lifetime.

Anton was deep in his own murmurings and thoughts, making sure the readings had been logged, how he couldn't believe he'd been here to witness this. He asked if he should put a call through to Bollinger.

"I'll take care of it."

"This is too important," Anton said breathlessly. "We must notify everyone—" He picked up a phone on the console.

"Put the phone down," Gavin said, gesturing with his finger at Anton. "Am I going to regret you being here?"

Anton put on his glasses, his face expressionless. "No."

But Gavin was beginning to feel regret. He was aware of the risk; for all his smarts and dependability, Anton was also young—and young meant stupid. "*You* are not going to say a word about this. Do you understand?"

Anton mumbled a few phrases then shut this mouth and nodded curtly. His eyes were blank, his face wore a sour expression.

"*Child*," Gavin said under his breath. He needed to think, to look at this data, come up with a workable hypothesis, a starting point.

He backtracked: they had awakened dormant spores, cultured the germs, collided atomic nuclei derived from molecules in the petri sample. The result was a self-contained, hollow, cool, yet intensely high-energy sphere.

How to explain this? Strange, he thought. *Strange.* Maybe that's it. Could this be what particle physicists called *strange matter*?

Gavin rose out of his chair as if boosted up by his own thought. His mind roamed the heights of exotic physics now. It was his best guess for what this data told him, for what he'd seen. When the rest of the heavy ions in the sample were smashed and scattered, maybe this is what was left—the heaviest stuff, the so-called strange quarks neutralized by their counterparts, the anti-quarks. Denser than ordinary matter, the "Strange Orb" could easily have annihilated everything around—all of matter, frankly, were it not for the anti-quarks.

He turned a corner in his mind: And where were those anti-quarks coming from? It was all in the data, the data had to be parsed out. The secrets were there.

After the two had made sure the data was secured in Breakthrough's servers, Gavin thanked Anton for his help, told him he could leave.

Gavin could tell from the brusque, silent manner with which Anton went about his business that he was still smarting. "And I'm sorry about laying into you there," Gavin said. "It's important that we not say anything yet. Not till I've come up with a working hypothesis. Once everyone knows, it's over. Do you understand?"

Anton shrugged and nodded.

Gavin watched him take loping strides toward the doors, picking a cigarette out of a pack and putting it in his mouth. Beeps sounded as he jerked open one of the doors and left. Gavin's regrets began to grow. He needed to keep an eye on Anton.

He checked the wall clock: 12:43 a.m. He'd better get home. Seema would be asleep, but he sent a text anyway: *Sorry to be so late. Things went well, better than well.*

The security guard opened the door. Gavin told him he was on his way out and sorry to be so late. Grabbing his jacket and notebooks, he thought about how he was either telling people to keep their mouths shut or apologizing to them for the consequences of his secrecy. He felt like a CIA agent or robber planning a heist. That made him laugh. He locked up the doors to the control room and made his way up and across the terrace, back to his office for his laptop and bag.

The energies were beyond anything he would find in a heavy-ion collision. The Breakthrough collider was a state-of-the-art machine, but it wasn't designed to generate field energies of this order. If the data were to be believed, the orb was generating something like a quadrillion electron volts. The more these thoughts spun around in his head, the faster he walked. It took a few minutes to realize he'd walked right past the main building.

The lights in his office blinked on. The emptiness and quiet of the hallways in this deep-night hour made him feel that much more like a fugitive. He put his notebook and laptop in his bag, but he couldn't bring himself to leave. Just a few minutes more to think this through. He slumped in his chair, aware of how tired he was, but not feeling the least bit sleepy. Seconds later, he was on his feet again, taking up a marker and scribbling mass-energy equations on his whiteboard.

The energy released in that experiment should've destroyed the collider. But something contained it. For that to be the case, whatever that "something" was had to have a source. A source abundant enough to neutralize the outward momentum of the orb, the same way the Sun's gravity checked its expansive fusion energies. So, could this orb too be held back by an unusually strong source of gravity? Or could it be a kind of negative energy—the yin to the yang of the positive energy?

He took a step back from the whiteboard, capped the marker, and looked over equations. He shook his head. There was no doubt they'd tapped into mysterious sources of power, one arising from the germ and the other from . . . where? He erased a portion of the board and drew a graph, but the arc plotted from the numbers made no sense. As he worked away with the marker, he felt something he hadn't felt since he was a student at Cambridge, poring over equations: the sense that he was scratching at the door of the universe, dwarfed by its unimaginable scale.

Knocking at his door woke him. He heard the turning of the doorknob just as his eyes flickered open, and realized he'd dozed off in his chair. "Gavin?" It was Bollinger's voice. *Shit,* Gavin thought as he sat up and swiveled around in his chair to face the door.

"JB," Gavin muttered, rubbing the sleep out of his eyes. "My God, how long have I been out?"

Bollinger didn't answer, only stood there, glaring. Sooner or later, Gavin knew, he'd have to confront his boss over the experiments and all they'd been keeping from him. *Okay, bring it on,* he thought. *What's he going to do? Sue me? Ruin whatever is left of my career?*

"Got a call from technicians telling me about a trove of data uploaded into our servers," Bollinger said. "It doesn't correspond to any scheduled test. Date-stamp is last night. You wouldn't know anything about it, would you?"

Gavin stood, stretched. "I do. I know everything."

"After I told you research on Bizarro was over, and we were moving on." Bollinger's tone grew louder. "What you did was a serious breach. On so many levels."

Gavin held up one hand. "Say no more," he said. "I'll be out of your hair." He picked up his jacket and bag off his desk just as a security guard appeared in the doorway. "Wow. An escort."

At the door, he turned to Bollinger. "But before you clear out this office, JB, don't erase the board till you take a good look at it." He nodded toward the board, crammed now with a series of equations, a graph and a curious diagram of a sphere inside of which sets of numbers emerged like spokes in a wheel.

"What's all this?"

"There's a pattern."

After Gavin left, Bollinger stayed on, staring at the board. He read off the equation on the top line under his breath. He considered the solution circled in blue marker and taken up inside a new equation beneath it. He backed up a step, tracking the integers and symbols of the formulas with his finger as a musician might track the cadence of notes on a piece of sheet music. His arm slowly dropped to his side.

Without taking his eyes off the whiteboard, he picked up the phone at the desk and punched a few keys. "It's Javier. Can I get a couple of guys from the control room up here in Harrison's office? I need fresh eyes on something."

—✶—

Gavin sat in his office at home, resisting the urge to simply close his eyes. Sleep felt as tempting as an immersion in a warm bath. He shook the thought away, sat up in his chair, and pulled up a picture on his phone. It was a picture of the whiteboard, a series of pictures actually, detailing his equations, the graph and the diagram he'd rendered.

He pulled open a drawer, rooted around until he found a black, cardboard-bound sketchbook. He preferred sketchbooks to journals; the blank sketch paper, unfettered by lines, allowed Gavin to puzzle out ideas, theories, concepts freely. He opened the book to its first page, took up a pen and, glancing now and again at the pictures on his phone, began copying down everything he'd written on the board.

Just then a text came through on his phone: *How is this possible?*

I'm working on it.

Get some sleep first, the next text read. *Then get back here.*

—✶—

It took the better part of the following day to bring Bollinger fully up to speed on recent events up to and including the appearance of the Strange Orb (as Gavin had dubbed it). Megan and Anton were present along with a few senior members of Breakthrough's particle research team. Many at the meeting were furious that testing protocol had been breached and the facility—hell, the whole city at the very least—was put at risk. And it took a while just to smooth out hard feelings, but Gavin managed it, urging everyone instead to focus on the extraordinary results. The orb itself was enough to get everyone's attention, and the conversation turned to the road ahead. They agreed that everything—the rock, the amoeba, everything leading up to and beyond the energy field itself—was shrouded in mystery.

"I want both of you on this," Bollinger said, waving a finger at Gavin and Megan. Gavin had to admit the boss seemed intrigued, even humbled. But he also knew there were better than even chances that they'd be kept on as consultants or as bottom-feeders in the new team hierarchies.

Bollinger and Gavin identified areas that needed the greatest focus and resources, delegating a half-dozen teams to zero in on them. Then, to Gavin's amazement, Bollinger appointed Megan as leader of the team assigned to analyzing the rock itself and the organism found inside it. Others would lead up efforts to analyze the isotope and peer inside it as more tests amounting to billions more collisions were plotted. Gavin and Bollinger would focus on analyzing the nature of the orb itself: its composition, what sustained it, and how.

Pizzas, salads, beers arrived, but most of the attendees stayed clustered around their laptops and whiteboards, around projection screens on which collision results were displayed. Eventually, though, people made their way to the food, cracked open the beers, and gave in to a mood of celebration as the full implication of what they'd found and what they'd soon be undertaking started to take hold.

"Any other outstanding issues?" Bollinger asked, standing at the head of the table. A few questions were brought up about the solar-cell project and other parallel developments at Breakthrough, which Bollinger took up one by one.

"Let's listen to it." Gavin realized he'd spoken his thoughts out loud.

As the meeting began winding down, his mind had started drifting back to the diagram he'd made on the whiteboard and copied into his sketchbook. Others in the room stopped and turned to him.

He noticed Bollinger staring at him too, his expression curious, peeved at the interruption. From across the room, Anton gazed at him, puzzled.

"Listen to whom?" It was Megan. She'd come up behind him with pizzas for them. She pulled up a chair next to him, took a swig from a beer.

Gavin stood and crossed to the far end of the room where a projection screen displayed the collision data. "I was just thinking something."

From his jacket pocket, he fished out the sketchbook, opened it to a diagram scrawled in ballpoint pen. To a layperson, it resembled convection patterns flowing out from a central source, traced in dotted lines and marked at intervals by numbers. "When the orb appeared," he said, gazing down at the diagram, "Anton and I, we started measuring for radiation. I was sure we'd find gamma and x-ray, but"—he shook his head—"instead we found these patterns." He held up the book for everyone to see. He began tracing the patterns with his finger. "These are radio waves following what I think are slight, very slight variations in mass inside the orb. The waves reach the surface, permeate it and escape right out."

Anton stood up, his hands grasping both sides of his head. "There is software patch for this. Developed so engineers with little funding could convert and amplify digitized EM waves into sound waves."

"So, what you're saying is . . . we have an app for that."

Chuckles made their way across the room.

"We have," Anton said. "Illegal, yes, but we have it."

The idea percolated in his mind briefly before Gavin posed the last remaining question: "Does anyone have a set of speakers?"

A half-hour later, crowded around Anton's cubicle, just across from the accelerator control room, Gavin, Bollinger and the rest listened intently to a block of converted low-frequency waves from a pair of speakers borrowed from a technician and proceeded to hear . . . nothing. Not *nothing* exactly, rather an unremarkable hissing. They boosted the signal and now, above the hiss, they picked up a faint murmuring, rising and falling, peppered with bits of static. Everyone's ears pricked up. But, after a minute of strained listening, people started to shake their heads. A few around Gavin frowned and explained that the noises were just interference. "The generator," one said. "Or the electromagnets," said another. "Maybe contamination in the vacuum tubing."

Sensing interest around the cubicle waning, Bollinger announced he wanted everyone back in the morning for more meetings. "There's a lot more to get through," he said, "but above all, I want people to keep a tight lid on this. No doubt we'll have to release aspects of our research," and here he nodded to Megan and then at Gavin, "but I trust you all agree that word of something like this can get out of control in the press very easily. Lots of misinformation and, for the sake of security, I want to keep this under wraps until our media team can nail down a press release."

Bollinger's words had a soothing effect on Gavin. Keeping the media at bay for as long as possible was going to be essential as they continued their research. And not just the media, there were many other parties who'd want a piece of this discovery.

Gavin watched as people slowly filed out. In the end, only Gavin and Anton stayed behind; Anton had calculations on another project to double-check.

Gavin listened now with headphones he'd borrowed from Anton, adjusting the output as he did. The static in the front and the hiss in the back were undeniable. But the ebb and flow in the middle. It could be the generator. There were lots of obvious causes. Or was it the sounds of something else? Of some*where* else? Gavin put the headphones away and reflected. What was he hearing if not interference?

He remembered the text he'd sent to Megan while he and Anton were running the experiment two nights ago, once the field had appeared. *I think we got us a wormhole.*

There was nothing about the field to suggest that it was a wormhole, and nothing to suggest that it was not. If it were a wormhole, then the field was a window that the particle experiment had blown open.

The more he listened, the more Gavin became doubtful about any easy explanation for the noise he was hearing. This wasn't electrical interference. It was a discrete rise and fall. And what was that? Swirls laced into the weave, a downward then an upward pitch.

"Let's drop something in next time," he thought aloud.

"Dr. Harrison," Anton said, "you are suggesting that the audio waves from that orb are not, uh, normal interference?" He ended his question with a grin that Gavin couldn't quite place.

Not yet, Gavin thought. "I don't know what I'm suggesting."

I think we've got us a wormhole. It wasn't too far-fetched a notion, was it? Was it any more far-fetched than discovering an asteroid more than twice the age of the solar system? An asteroid that contained dormant amoeba that, once awakened, could ravage one's blood cells? Amoeba whose molecules contained isotopes with subatomic particles that couldn't be detected? Particles that, once collided, produced a stable—*stable!*—energy field never before observed, so energetic that it vied with the frenzied output of neutron stars?

He thanked Anton for the use of the headphones and started for home.

The applications for the real world were obvious: an energy source that could power all of Triton's tech ambitions for centuries. Bollinger would be quick to latch on to them, monetize this discovery, channel it into new technologies that would give him leverage over Triton. It would put Breakthrough on the map.

But for Gavin, it was about much more. Physics had always made him a feel like a safecracker. Each proven equation and theory was a turn of the dial, one in an infinitely complex combination that scientists had been cracking one number at a time for thousands of years. One day, in his lifetime even, someone would open this lock and lift the lid on the universe. They were *almost* there: less than a trillionth of a trillionth of a trillionth of a second away from the instant of origin.

The sounds could've been routine interference, of course. Or they could've been the final clicks of the dial before the lock sprang open.

Dev was sleeping soundly when he got in. He leaned down and kissed his cheek, afraid he might wake him up. The boy mumbled something in his sleep, rubbed his nose, and turned away.

Seeing his son after what had been days had a calming but contradictory effect on Gavin. He felt the pangs of guilt for being absent for so long, but being in his son's presence was nourishing too, like finding a cool spring after a long trudge through a desert. He propped himself up on a pillow and lay next to him for a few minutes, watching him sleep. His eyes scanned the room. In the dim light of the hall, he could see the posters of planets on the walls, the microscope on the bookshelf next to shells found on the beach, the models of dinosaurs and superheroes.

On a far wall was a diagram that Gavin had drawn on a sheet of black construction paper: It was a timeline done with a color pencil. On the far left, marked "13.8 bya," Gavin had drawn a crude starburst and the words "Our Universe Is Born" above it. There were lots of milestones after that: "First Light" came 380,000 years later, then "First Stars," "First Galaxies," then at "4.6 bya," "Our Sun Is Born,"

"Our Solar System Is Born." At "3.8 bya," Gavin had written in "First Bacteria," followed billions of years later by "First Fish" then "Dinosaurs Are Born" then "Meteor Kills Dinosaurs," on to "Ancient Egypt" (because Dev loved mummies), "Dad Is Born," "Mom Is Born," all the way to the far right of the timeline: 2013, "Dev Is Born."

With that timeline, Gavin had wanted to give his son a sense of the grandeur around him and of his place in it. Maybe he'll understand, he thought, when he's a little older. And with everything happening back at work, he also wondered giddily if he weren't on the brink of having to elaborate further on that timeline. When would he be able to tell his son about this? And how would he explain it?

A few minutes later, Gavin joined Seema in a glass of wine. He wanted to tell her everything about what they'd been up to at the lab. But it wouldn't be fair; after all, he'd been more insistent about a code of silence than anyone else. The least he could do was to honor it, now especially.

Seema did press him, though, about what he'd been up to, enough so that Gavin dug around on Google and found an article from the online archives of a rural California newspaper called the *Lone Pine Register.*

"This is the only hint I can give you," Gavin told Seema. "This is as far as it goes." The article was scanned in, dated July 28, 1981, and was only a few small paragraphs long.

It told about a rancher named Hugh Goodman. For several nights, Goodman had been noticing more meteor activity than usual. He witnessed three come blazing out of the nighttime sky and land on his property. The meteorites varied in size from an oyster to a small dinner plate. Beside the article, there was a black-and-white photo of Goodman, a genial-looking soul in a plaid shirt and straw cowboy hat. He held in his hands the very rock that Gavin would later call Bizarro. Seema scanned the article but was not particularly impressed.

"So . . . you're collecting rocks?"

"Not just any rock," he said, smiling slyly. "*The* rock."

"Whatever keeps you nerds out of trouble," she said, kissed his cheek and went back to her own reading.

Gavin was about to close the article when he noticed "Related Links" on the side of the page. One of them was to an article headlined "Local Rancher's Death Baffles Local Health Officials" and dated "August 9, 1981." He clicked and read on:

> LONE PINE, Calif. Local rancher Hugh Goodman passed away at Desert Regional Medical Center today, aged 46, from what medical authorities are calling a rare and severe form of encephalitis.
>
> Goodman was admitted into the medical center on Aug. 2 complaining of headaches, fever and blurred vision. Tests for bacterial and viral infections came back negative. Three days after his admittance, Goodman experienced seizures and lapsed into a coma before succumbing to the illness.
>
> While doctors are unclear as to the exact cause of Goodman's death, their best determination is a brain inflammation caused by an environmental or waterborne pathogen. They blame windborne or waterborne parasites known to be most active in the warmer months.
>
> Goodman's symptoms appeared a day after a windstorm swept through the area, and that may have stirred up fungal or bacterial spores, say county health officials. The well water on the property is another possible culprit. While infection is

> rare, they are urging caution when swimming in warm-water pools or traveling in the desert during or immediately after windy conditions.
>
> Two weeks ago, the Lone Pine Register ran a story on Goodman's discovery of three meteorites on his ranch, which his wife Beverly Goodman has donated to the Mojave Historical Society.

"That's terrible," Gavin said.

"What is it?"

"The guy who discovered our rock died back in 1981. That's a bummer," he said, closing his laptop. How sad, too, to have died the way he did. Gavin had hoped to look Goodman up and tell him how his rock was going to change the world.

CHAPTER TWELVE

Eagle Lake, south of Lake Tahoe

October 26, 2030

The wind is a howling beast. It's been sweeping out of the west ever since we turned off the 395 and began the twisting, turning climb on the 89 then the 50 to Eagle Lake. The winds remind me of what we encountered back on the Grapevine last night as we were leaving LA.

The car's been driving okay since we topped off the gas and oil down in Big Pine. But the shuddering when I speed up, the oil leak from earlier today, are making me unsure. Then I think of Mom in the hospital and buckle down, step harder on the pedal.

Abby straightens in her seat and points. "Right there!"

I swerve in the direction she's pointing, and the headlights find the narrow turnoff, and we take the bend in a split-second operation like we rehearsed it a hundred times. The turnoff takes us from the highway onto smaller roads toward the lake.

If it weren't for our headlights, we'd be SOL—plunged in almost-total darkness out here. All we can see are the black reaches of pine forest against the even blacker heights of the Sierras, and everything against the blue-black sky. The headlights are our angels, I'm thinking, protecting, guiding us out here. The moon is the only other light source, laying down a pale sheen on the higher granite and tops of pines. It feels eerie, lonely, like we're fugitives.

"Keep your eyes out," Conner says, joking, but I can tell he's freaked about the same thing I am: that some humanoid creature is going to charge at us out of the black. We'd be dead, for sure. After what we saw at the gas station, I don't ever want to see one again.

The final stretch of road ends at a small, circular parking lot on the eastern side of the lake. This lot is probably packed during the summer months, but right now, it's desolate. It's like we're trespassers on the whole land.

Along the east and north sides of the lot, there are low buildings. Conner says there could be a market there, but we won't know until morning. Maybe on our way home, we'll pick up food with the last of our cash.

The headlights pick up the docks—not a single boat tied out there—and the water's leaping and smashing against their posts, making me think of wild, frantic cats. The wind's a massive presence too, carrying ghost-clouds across the waxen moon. Scrubbed clean by gusts, it casts a spotlight in the middle of the lake, and in its light, the water's furrowed face churns with whitecaps.

The instant we get out of the car, the wind bullies us. We slip on jackets and, taking up our packs, food, and water bottles, we leave the car and make for the trailhead which I know is on the far side of the lot.

"How far?" Conner shouts over the wind.

"Half-hour. Less, maybe? Looked about that far on the map." From old pics, I know that the cabin is due west, at the foot of Eagle Peak.

The trail is wide and visible only when clouds aren't blocking out the moon, so we keep our flashlights on. Their beams are spears in the black. It's not thickly wooded here, and, in the on-and-off dance of moonlight on the scrub and small trees, it feels like an alien world, a blustering planet where no light and no humans exist, where the trees are conscious, animate . . . and watching us. Except for a few pines along the lake, there's no buffer to our left so we get the winds head-on.

We keep our flashlights roving side to side, bracing for one of those crawlers to jump out from the side of the path.

"See anything?" I say to Abby, who's next to me.

"No. Let's hope it stays that way."

I keep an eye on the lakeside. Now and then, we pass cabins along the shore, all dark, empty; this sense of human abandonment is everywhere. The pines up the slope on our right are swaying in the gusts, screaming like they're all possessed.

"This has to be it," I call out. Off to the left, down a short slope, is a shape that matches what I've seen in photographs: a compact-looking house with a high, peaked roof. We shine our lights at it and make our way down, aware now of the sound of wind chimes. This is it. I recognize the small bay window on the ground floor and the dormers up on the second. The wind surges again, and the chimes go crazy. As I'm trying to locate the chimes, I trip over the ledge of a small, wooden deck. "Whoa!"

Abby and I train our flashlights up at the cabin. The chimes seem to be sounding from a corner of a canopy hanging over the deck. The flashlights show a place in need of a paintjob. The canopy and deck are covered in leaves. And it looks like an upstairs window is broken. And check this out: under the canopy, on a small round table and the floor behind it, I see flowerpots and decorative ceramic shit that I recognize from old photographs. I'm three or four, with my parents and my old black Lab, Rohan, who died when I was eleven.

Conner's attention, meanwhile, is on the back door. "You guys ready to pick this thing?"

I train the flashlight on Abby as she fishes out a pair of bobby pins from her backpack. Conner bends one of them into an L shape, plants his feet and crouches down to get a look at the door handle. A couple of seconds later, though, he straightens up. He tries the door handle. It's wobbly, turns freely. The door opens. We look at each other: Shit. Who's been here and when?

The door opens into the kitchen. Our flashlights pick up cupboards and drawers and the pantry, all lying half-open. A mouse darts out of range of the flashlights. Utensils, canned goods, bottles, cracker boxes and cereal—everything untouched for ten years—are everywhere. The linoleum is like gravel, our feet crunching on saltines and cheerios. Also, it's freezing in here, an ice box.

I reach out an arm and block Conner and Abby from walking any farther. "Hey," I whisper, "whoever did this might still be here. Grab something and be careful."

Abby takes a knife off the counter and Conner finds a screwdriver. I go for the broomstick, detaching the stick from the bristles. Our weapons out, we go from the kitchen into the living room—where we find sofa cushions upturned, the tables pulled away from the walls, everything in shambles—then up the stairs to the bathroom and two bedrooms. It's like a bear came through here, ransacking. Whoever came through, we decide, isn't here anymore. "But who the hell were they?" I ask.

"Maybe the same people we saw following us. But if they knew where this cabin was, why follow us?"

"They didn't come through any time recently," says Conner, stooping down to inspect the dresser drawers.

"How do you know?"

"Check it out." He extends a hand to the drawers on the floor. He pulls at cobwebs in the corners of the drawers. "And I saw ants in the pantry. And I think we all saw the mouse in the kitchen. Whoever came through here left days or weeks ago."

"So they came here first," I find myself saying out loud, "before they came looking for us."

"Maybe."

"This place is creeping me out," Abby says. "I'm going back downstairs."

In the kitchen, there aren't any more signs of mice or—possums or raccoons, either—so I dig out a couple of lanterns and a can of kerosene.

The lanterns don't give off the strongest glow, but the light is warm and comforting. You need light to have any hope. Are hope and light the same thing? Is light the physical manifestation of hope?

There's no power here, no refrigeration, heat, or running water. The snacks and cereal are stale. But there's canned chili, which we pop open and pass around, and we finish up the rest of the fruit and snacks we brought along.

I turn on my phone long enough to check the time. It's past eleven. We decide to get some sleep. We want to be up at first light and see this through, and by the afternoon, I want to see my mom.

We brush our teeth, being spare with the water we've got left, and find sheets and blankets tossed around on the floor of the linen closet and make up beds in the living room. Conner considers taking one of the bedrooms upstairs but decides against it; it just feels safer for us to be together downstairs.

I settle down on the bedding, still dressed in layers against the biting cold of the cabin. "Guys, I couldn't have done this without either of you. I don't know what I was thinking. Thanks for being here with me."

"Well," Abby says, lying under a blanket and propping herself up on both elbows, "you didn't know you'd come face to face with werewolves."

Conner spreads out a comforter in a corner of the room. "Or, you know, get abducted by the sheriff of Crazy Town, USA."

"Speaking of which, how's your skull?" I ask him.

Conner grunts, rolling himself onto his butt on the blankets. He touches behind his head and gasps. "Hurts when I touch it. Tender. Headache's gone, though. What about you?"

"Same," I say. Whenever I move my skull, the pain radiates from the lump above and behind my left ear. It's like I'm touching a fragile egg embedded in my skull. I think of horror movies of alien creatures spawning inside human victims.

"Like I said, I couldn't have done this without you. Sooner we're out of here and you guys are both home, the happier I'll be." I lay back and stare up at the ceiling. The others are silent. "I'm just sorry about your families."

"I know," says Abby.

"It's all good, man," Conner says with a yawn. He's sitting with his back against the wall. "All considered, I'd rather be here than trapped in the quarantine. Who knows what's going down in the city."

"It's horrible," I say, and, for the first time since getting the call from the hospital this afternoon, I feel like the tears are going to break. "Just thinking about my mom, more than anything."

"We're doing the right thing," says Abby. "I know it."

"I feel like we are." I prop myself up on my elbow and face her. "But what makes you so sure?"

Abby glances at me and then at Conner. "I just am."

We turn off the lanterns. I lie awake, listening to the noise of the wind howling and rattling the windows. I hear knocking and scraping from what could be branches against the roof of the cabin, and the crazy chimes whenever the gusts swirl around the back of the house and catch them.

"Dev?" Abby whispers next to me.

"Yeah?"

I hear the rustling as she turns over in her blanket. "It's because I had the dream too. The same dream."

I'm too stunned to respond.

"It's like you said," she whispers. "I saw a man high up on a rock. It was your dad. He reached down under the rock and brought out this box. It said 'Find Bollinger' across the top of it. And it was like you said. Like I was separate from the dream, more like watching it unfold."

"You're messing with me, right?"

"It's what made me think we were on to something. Even after I got the call from my dad. It was just . . . too weird."

Silence between us.

"Look, Ab, you're having the dream because I told you about it. It's stuck in your head, so you dreamt it." Dammit, now I feel like Conner, the devil's advocate.

"Could be." Abby lies back. "But it didn't feel like it."

I jolt awake. My heart's hammering away. I put my hand on my chest and try to calm down. The windows are rattling. I reach over and turn on my phone: 3:30 a.m. I turn it off again.

In the corner, Conner's sleeping as soundly as he was hours ago, when I heard him snoring away. Abby's asleep too, her back to me, bundled into her blanket and the hood of her jacket drawn up over her head. Through the curtains on the lakefront side of the room, moonlight slants in. Her hair, visible around the fringe of her hood, is lit up like silver filaments.

I have to take a leak. The bladder won't be denied.

I sit up, pull on my shoes, pick my way toward the stairs. The railing wobbles under my hand and each stair creaks in an uncertain way. The wind thumps against the side of the cabin.

The bathroom is at the top of the stairs. I pee into the compost toilet, listening to urine hit the plastic valve at the bottom of the bucket. There's a small window above the toilet. Moonlight sieves in, through the scrim of madly blowing pines, to make this kaleidoscope of light and shade. It's some eerie shit. And that's when I see the boat.

I zip up my fly and lean closer to the window. Through the trees, there's something about a third of a mile to the north moving across the chop. For a split second, I humor the possibility that it's a bird or a fish or even the Loch Ness Monster, but this is a motorboat and it's moving rapidly from the far side . . . to this side of the lake. Its wake shimmers. And just as I'm sure about what I'm seeing, it disappears behind trees and a high bank.

Why would anyone be out on the water this time of night, in this weather? I decide against waking Abby and Conner. Let them sleep. I lie back, pull my hood back on, and try to push any thoughts of the boat out of my mind.

Daybreak. And the wind hasn't let up a bit.

We listen to the thump and rattle of the windows as we share the last energy bar from Conner's backpack, drink the last of the water. "Make it last, guys," Conner says. "No food, no water till we get back to civilization."

We pocket our phones and hoist up our packs. With the food in our bellies, the water bottles empty and wearing everything we brought along, the packs are a lot lighter. I take one last look around.

"Guys," I call out. "Slow up," Before we head out, I tell them about what I saw through the bathroom window.

"If you did see something, someone," Abby says, "they'd be here by now, wouldn't they?"

"Maybe, but honestly"—my recollection is foggy, like I dreamt the whole thing—"I don't know what I saw anymore."

"We're gonna find out either way," Conner says, zipping his jacket up all the way. He flips up his collar so it wraps around his neck and thrusts open the door. "Let's go."

It's a gloomy, gusty morning, a lot darker than I expected. The first thing we hear are the chimes hanging off one end of the canopy. The other half of the canopy collapsed during the night. The canvas is flapping like a raggedy sail from the end of two metal struts. The clouds are marching in too, armies of them, over the lake and over the thousand-foot granite slopes above us.

I take the lead as we walk in single file from the porch back up a short slope to the trail. Not far away, the trail cuts off and climbs. We follow it as it switches back and forth, between ledges of grasses and rock. It's impossible to keep up any kind of conversation because the wind blowing through the pines and shrub sounds like tidal waves of static, so we keep quiet.

The path gets stonier, steeper, and pretty soon, our chest and legs are burning with the climb. Sometimes, the path will disappear and reappear a minute later, sometimes it widens out into clearings, hemmed by thickets and the naked trunks of long-dead pines. The higher we go, the less it's a hike and more a climb up walls of granite.

Sometimes, we stop and look around. The lake is a shifting play of slate and gunmetal and gold where sunlight stabs in through openings in the clouds. Beyond the front rank of cloud scraps, there's a charcoal-black mothership of a cloud as wide as the horizon moving our way.

"Look, over there!" Abby shouts. About two hundred feet above us and to the south, we see a fluttering piece of fabric: the flagpole on the peak!

The sight of the peak makes me forget my exhaustion. I scramble to find wedges between boulders, grab hold, and push upward as fast as I can. Abby follows right behind and Conner just behind her. No doubt about it—just like the dream, there's a flagpole planted there. "I know this path," I mumble out loud. "I know this path."

"Easy," Conner shouts as the wind picks up, knocking me off-balance. I panic and regain my footing.

The thumb of granite sticking out, this ledge I'm negotiating, the path flattening and rising as it does, and the way the roots of that fallen aspen splay out over the edge like that, I know every detail. It's freaking me out, yet I feel completely at peace at the same time. I'm both in a trance and completely here.

The ground starts to even out, and a stony trail loops sharply to the left. A couple of minutes later, and I'm on the ridge. My chest aches, my leg muscles are wrecked, so I stop for a second and wait for Conner to catch up. Turning into the winds, I see the sky is black now, the lake pocked with millions of white caps.

We break into a run, anxious to put this past us. The flagpole is up a short rise. It's come down to this. Dreams brought us here, their details blending with reality the way a traced image lines up with its original. I feel a hand, Abby's, as we struggle up the rise, and hold it tightly. We walk the last steps together.

"Unbelievable," Conner says, panting. "This is blowing my mind, D. Is this exactly what you were dreaming?"

"So far."

The Stanford flag, faded, in tatters, snaps atop seven feet of metal pole wedged into a mound of rocks. Abby lets go of my hand. She looks at me then at the mound, nods to me. And the whole world condenses down to this.

I take one step, another, climb the mound. I lower myself to my knees, exactly as I'd seen my dad do over and over. There are small differences: crumbled bits of fallen rock, clumps of overgrowth where there weren't any in the dream. I brush away stones, branches, and see it—a flat rock jutting a bit farther than its neighbors.

It doesn't come away as easily as it seemed to in the dream, but, with some effort, I pry it out. For a second, I'm frozen in place, this rock in my hand. Conner, his eyes wide, is crouched behind me now and peering into the rectangular hole left behind by the rock.

It's not possible. This is not possible. Every event that got me here, every instance of the dream—every thought, denial, and conversation about it—flashes through my mind the way you hear people say their lives flashed before their eyes seconds before they thought they were going to die. How can the real and unreal, the possible and the impossible, exist side by side?

"Dev?" Conner is peering into the niche, his flashlight aimed into it. "There's something in there."

Conner reaches his hand in, yanks it away.

"Shit, what happened?" I ask.

He shakes his head. "Nothing." He's wiping his hands on the front of his pants. "Just freaked out a little."

"Here, you hold the flashlight," I tell him and position myself in front of the opening. In the shine of the flashlight, I can see the corner of an object. I reach my hand in and pull out the rocks and gobs of dirt. Finally, carefully, I pull it out: a gray metal box, flat like an instrument case, covered in dirt.

I brush aside the cool, caked dirt on the surface of the box. Bugs in the dirt scatter. It's like we're treasure hunters who've dug up some artifact out of old legend. That feeling grows as I wipe away more dirt to uncover letters, one at a time, forming the words *Find Bollinger*, scrawled in black marker in Dad's handwriting. I know his hand; I've seen it on lists and notes left around the house, odd and random things that I collected in a box in my room. "It's exactly like what we saw," Abby says, half-laughing, half-crying. "Dev, this is, this is . . ." She covers her mouth with one hand, takes a step back.

There's a hasp and copper-colored padlock closed over a loop, securing the lid. Do I break it open? I'm considering this when Conner says, his voice raised above the wind, "Let's break this thing open!"

"No," I tell him.

"Look, after everything we went through to get up here and find this," he says, looking first at me then at Abby, "I think we earned the right to find out what the hell is inside."

While I mull that over, Conner fetches a fist-sized rock. "Here. I got this."

I shield the box. "No. It wouldn't feel right. The box isn't meant for us, we're only meant to find it and deliver it. The dream trusted me to do that."

"After all this? Come on!"

"The dream got us here."

"It's a message," Abby cuts in.

"Makes no sense." Conner throws his hands, the wind raging at his hair. "This is crazy."

"'Find Bollinger,'" I say. "That's what we, what *I*, have to do."

Conner nods. "Can't be any harder than finding the box."

Abby holds out her hands for the box. I jump off the mound and hand it to her.

The 360 here is insane: we're on a dome-shaped peak on a long ridge of granite, a bare spine topped by a bald crown. There's hardly any cover, and we're getting the full brunt of the wind. The eastern side of the ridge is covered in pines, cypresses all the way down the slope to a patchwork of green and brown carpeting the valley beyond. Lake Tahoe to the north is as dark as a blackboard, its surface chalked by furrows.

The gusts rise, tipping me off balance, and I feel a hand at my shoulder, helping me steady out: Abby. She shoves the box inside my pack, zips it closed. I feel a cold splat of rain on my forehead. Another on my hand. "Come on," Abby says, "we better move."

Conner's already at the ledge. "Back to the trail!"

Within seconds, the drops have turned into a slanting drizzle, pelting us as we pick our way down the stony path and scramble over the first boulders.

"Careful," Conner shouts, "this wind could knock you on your ass and next thing your head's split open and— Hey, Abby, what's that dessert your mom makes at Thanksgiving?"

"Peach cobbler?"

"That's it. One wrong move, and you'll end up looking like peach cobbler down there."

"Ugh," Abby replies. "Don't be gross."

"Seriously, though, that peach cobbler was fly." Conner is on top of a slab of granite, smiling and goofing off, but at his feet, on the other side of the granite, there is something else: a head darting up and down, eyes wide, but it's the bristles of hair that make me stop in my tracks. Its hair blows like a horse's mane in the wind.

"Conner?" I yell. "Conner!"

He's still smiling at Abby, and now Abby sees it and stops.

"Behind you." My words are as sharp and clear as I can make them.

Conner blinks back at me, confused, and slowly turns around. That exact moment, everything goes to shit as the thing—again, the size of a child, like a ten- or twelve-year-old—hoists itself up onto the slab in one go, grabbing Conner's leg. Conner shrieks, wriggling loose from the thing's grasp, and leaps back to the ground. The three of us start running back uphill.

I stop to grab rocks, turn to see the crawler hunkered on the slab, monkey-like, half-naked, just tattered pants and shoes, shags of hair covering the upper body. Its eyes glare, do not blink, and it bares its teeth like I've seen demented animals do. The sight freezes my blood, but then it's off the slab, charging at us on all fours. We take giant strides back up the slope, all I can hear behind me are feet scuffling in the dirt, the thing growling, screaming in a high-pitched rage.

Then comes a crash: Abby's on the ground, and the thing's got its arms wrapped around her legs. Conner and I surround her, trying to pry the thing loose, but it's strong as hell.

Conner's screaming. Abby spins on her back and launches her foot at the thing's face. Once, twice, the third time, the thing loosens its hold, and she wriggles free. We grab each other and even before we're running, it's at our heels again. I spin around, three rocks in my hands, hurl the first: it bounces off its shoulder. The second goes wide. Abby and Conner are up ahead, yelling my name. As the thing, its eyes flaring and furious, teeth bared, jumps at me, I heave the third rock at its face. Direct hit to the mouth! It stops in its tracks, letting out a long whine like a hurt child, covering its face.

I turn and run after Abby and Conner. My legs are burning, adrenaline's going to boil out of my chest, and then we're back on top of the ridge. Naked, exposed to the world. Conner, up ahead, turns to make sure we're behind him.

The three of us are huddling together when the gunshots go off: three of them. We hit the dirt. The air is silent except for the wind, the faint tick of rain on rocks.

Out of the corner of my eye, I see a tall man. He's in front of the mound, wearing a hooded camouflage poncho, a rifle braced at his hip. We get to our feet, staying close to each other. The man keeps his rifle poised for a few more seconds, then blows out a deep breath and, setting the rifle upright at his feet, he takes a seat on the mound. Finally, he looks up at us and pulls back the hood of his poncho: the man is bald and has square metal glasses and a dark, coarse-looking beard.

Abby, Conner, and I turn to each other. *What the hell just happened?* The man looks at us with a faint smile and waves us over as he sits there, his arms lank at his knees, the rifle resting now in the crook of his arm. He stretches his neck from side to side like his muscles are stiff. He pulls on the hood of his poncho, drops his head, and sits there, in no particular hurry.

Haltingly, we approach him, climbing the slope toward the mound. "At least they're easy enough to kill. Two–three bullets usually does it," he says, his voice deep, raspy but nonthreatening. "That's the third of those little devils I killed in the past two days. LA is crawling with them now. But the police and National Guard have things under control."

"Who the hell are you?" Conner's tone is brash, incredulous.

"You've been following us, since LA, haven't you?" Abby says.

The man tilts his head in our direction, squinting through the rain, and smiles in response.

"Thank you," I say, "for killing that thing. What are they, anyway?"

"The CDC has a word for them. Simianoids. Word's caught on now. But I just call them devils. I understand you kids have a lot of questions. Right now, though, we have to move. Or we'll see more of them." He points at the dead shape, matted with shags of hair, dirt, blood. "They'll smell that one for sure. And if they're close, they can smell us too."

"Simianoids," Conner says. "Like half-man, half-ape?"

The man nods, stands. He's towering, six-five at least. His arms and legs are like tree limbs. "Franklin Dix, by the way." He holds out his hand to me. "And that's an affirmative. I've been trying to track you down since LA."

"What're you?" I ask, shaking his massive hand. "FBI?"

"At your service."

"FBI," Conner says skeptically. "Right."

A smile plays over Dix's bearded face. "Proof. Of course." He reaches into a pocket and fishes out a wallet. He flips the wallet open to show an FBI badge and ID, tucked inside a plastic sleeve. Conner takes the wallet, frowns at it and hands it back. The wind and rain lash away.

"You're following us?" I ask as we begin walking down the slope.

"Naturally, Dev. Been on your trail since you left LA. It's a journey you've been thinking about a lot, haven't you? And now you've reached its end." As he lopes along, he produces a handkerchief from a pocket of a black jumpsuit he's wearing beneath the poncho and wipes his glasses with it. "I'll be happy when we're out of the rain." Shouldering his weapon, he leads the way. At first, I think he's hunchbacked, but then realize it's probably a pack he's carrying under his poncho.

"Hang on," I say, following after him. "What for? What're you tracking us for?"

Dix keeps walking, turns slightly toward me. "Dev, you're not the only one who thinks your father's death doesn't add up. Even the Bureau has him listed technically as missing. I wasn't convinced, not since the night of the explosion."

That's it! I recognize this man. "You were there, weren't you?" My mind flashes with the image of the bald, black-suited agent. "In my house. You were one of the agents in my house that night."

"Funny how memories from childhood never fade, isn't it?"

We follow Dix past that dead . . . *creature*. If it weren't for the taut ropes of muscle and the heavy clumps of hair on its body, this could be the body of a dead child. Its face is grimy, smudged with blood, and, even now, minutes since it was shot, the body twitches.

"The pathogen hijacks all the electrical pathways," Dix says without turning around. "Its brain is dead. Believe you me."

"Pathogen?" Conner says. "So, what, like these are infected people?"

"It invades and re-engineers our bodies from the inside out. The lower brain, the amygdala, the adrenal glands all go into hyperdrive. It gives victims increased strength, everything several times normal.

They're fast as hell, if you haven't noticed. But almost all the victims die before the transformation even begins. Overwhelms the body. Ninety-nine percent mortality. And if they don't die early, then it's a lethal injury or bullet that kills them off."

"I've seen them scale walls," I say, almost under my breath, like I'm recalling a nightmare.

Dix stops and turns. I almost bump into him. "Like flies."

I nod, still chilled by the thought. I tell him about the incident at the gas station the other day. He ponders for a few seconds. None of us move.

"It's an adhesive fluid expelled by the sweat glands."

"What's infecting them?" Abby asks. "Have they figured that out?"

"FEMA is betting it's whatever exploded over LA and South America and parts of eastern Europe. News says it's bioweapons. But it's a mystery. We don't know who did it."

Meanwhile, the rain has picked up since we left the peak. It's not as blustery, but it's enough to make me nervous on a hike this steep. The rocks and ledges are getting slippery, and the path's turning to mud. I'm watching both the path and Dix, in case he makes any moves with his rifle—not that he couldn't have picked us all off a dozen times over since we left LA, if that was what he wanted.

Dix is moving quicker than I'm comfortable with in all this rain. It's scary, this guy's agility, the way his arms vault him up and over boulders, and how he leaps from one ledge and down to the next while it takes the rest of us minutes to negotiate that same terrain. Dix is patient, though, and uses the time to scan the surroundings with binoculars. And once, he somehow jumps *back* to us and saves Abby from what could've been a bruising fall. I was right next to her and barely had time to reach for her.

About halfway down, Abby whispers from behind me, "Dev?" I slow down a step. "You think he knows? About the box?"

"No clue," I whisper back, "and I'm not going to say anything."

"Stop," Abby whispers and, letting Conner catch up with us, we stand in a huddle in the middle of the path. "What're we doing?" she goes on. "Why were we letting him lead us?"

"We do need to get out of the rain, don't we?" I answer.

Conner catches his breath. "Okay, as soon as we get to the bottom, we need to think fast."

We stay quiet the rest of the way, and at the bottom of the trail, at the T where a separate path cuts down the slope to the cabin, Dix halts. He pivots to face the cabin, then back at us. "Why don't we rest up, eat something, dry off, and then we can be on our way?"

"How'd you know about the cabin?"

"I'm FBI. We know everything." He smiles in a sly but harmless way. He proceeds down the short slope, and we join him at the back door of the cabin. The half-broken canopy sags crookedly, draining rainwater onto the wooden planks of the patio.

He removes the hood of his poncho and, pushing the door open, he ducks his bald head a good six inches, and steps inside.

The place feels even colder now than it did last night. The walls thump and creak, the windows rattle, and the rain patters noisily on the roof.

We hang up our jackets to dry here and there—lampshades and on the backs of chairs—while Dix goes over to the window, slides the drapes back and inspects the lake, the gusting trees. "Shit," I hear him mutter, "that's some chop. The sheer's going to be ugly."

Conner begins scrubbing his drenched hair with a kitchen towel, flicking the water at Abby. "Stop," she tells him flatly, her eyes focused on her phone.

"What'd I do?" Conner keeps at it.

Abby puts her phone away, grabs the towel, and snaps Conner with it.

"Ow! Not cool."

I tell Dix about how we found the whole cabin in disarray when we got in last night. "That was you guys, then?"

Dix turns from the window. "Possibly," he says, his head coming to within a foot of the ceiling, "but it wasn't me." He takes off his glasses again and wipes them. His eyes are gray-blue, and the skin around them is weathered, lined, like he's been out in the sun too much. There's a piercing, haunted quality about them, but nothing sinister.

He proceeds to sort through his pack, comes up with three bags of trail mix and half-liter bottles of water, and hands them out to us. We're famished and waste no time emptying the bottles, tearing open the bags.

"Tell us how you found us up there," Conner asks before shoving a handful of the mix into his mouth.

"Found your car this morning, by the landing on the east side of the lake. Picked up your trail. By luck, I saw you guys leaving and start your hike up the peak. I simply took the long way around."

"So you know why we were there, what we were looking for."

"I didn't know what you were up there to find. But I had a hunch it was something"—he struggles for the word—"*useful*, based on intercepts I made."

"You mean the bugs," I say, and that gets him arching his eyebrows.

"You found them." Dix smiles, baring gapped teeth.

"You wanted us to lead you here," Abby says. "What's your plan now?"

"Bring you to safety . . . along with the contents of that pack." Dix points to my backpack.

"Where?"

"The authorities. I call in our pickup location, and we get lifted to Sacramento."

"Sorry," I tell him. "We've got families to get back to."

"LA is on lockdown, in case you don't know. As far as your families, we'll get you all back with them as soon as we can. Probably in a day or two."

"What is it they think we have?"

Dix shakes his head, shrugs.

"You've been investigating my father, my whole family, my friends for ten years, and you can't tell me?"

"I don't know myself. But whatever it is, the government considers it important enough that we deliver it over to them asap. My job—and this is all I know—is to bring you in so they can talk to you and analyze the contents of that box."

"It's not for them," I tell Dix firmly. "It's for whoever this Bollinger guy is."

Dix's eyes narrow behind his glasses.

"I think he was one of my dad's friends."

"Bollinger is dead."

My breath catches. I'm jarred. But I don't feel surprised. The instruction in the dream—"Find Bollinger"—was clear enough, but that didn't mean it wasn't ancient and out of date. Maybe the dream was "made" some time in the past when Bollinger was still alive.

"Did you know him? Bollinger?" I ask.

Dix unscrews the top off a canteen and swigs from it. "We investigated him right after your father disappeared. He was the head of the company your father worked for. We questioned him about his company, what they were up to. Got us nowhere. Then a year later, we found his body burned to a crisp in a car wreck on a road north of LA."

Dix stands up, digs into a pocket of his black jumpsuit, produces a cigarette. "You guys don't mind, do you?"

Conner crumples the empty food wrapper in his hand. "We do, actually."

Dix smiles. "Right." He jabs the cigarette in his mouth, pats his hands around the pockets of his jumpsuit and find what he's looking for: his lighter. "I'll smoke this outside. You kids sit tight. Our ride will be here soon." His rifle slung at his shoulder, he goes to the door, then turns to me. "What the Bureau wants is simple. Secure the item you found, and make sure it doesn't fall into the wrong hands. Because, trust me, there are lots of . . . less-than-honorable people who want the contents of that package. All we ask is for a day or two of your time. You'll be doing your country a great service."

He throws opens the door, lights up. "And I can finally stop chasing after you." He inhales and blows a cloud of smoke through the doorway. "You're tiring me out." The door squeaks shut, and he disappears.

We stare at each other in silence, each of us thinking the same thing: What the hell is going on, and what do we do next? Abby moves to the back door, pulls back the drawn blinds, and peers out.

"What's he doing?" I ask.

"Sitting in a chair under that broken-down awning. Smoking his cig. Oh, wait." She watches a few more seconds. "He's on his phone now."

"Probably calling in the cavalry," Conner says worriedly.

"Okay, he's off the phone."

Conner goes to the big window that looks out on the lake. The dribbling on the roof comes and goes in waves, like the storm can't decide whether to stick around or move on.

Abby sits down next to me on the couch. I check my backpack lying at my feet: the box is still inside. I stare at the padlock and the name *Bollinger*. "You guys believe what he said about Bollinger? That he's dead?"

"Nothing about the guy tells me he's bullshitting—*yet*," Conner says in a hushed tone.

"Nothing about him tells me he *isn't* bullshitting," Abby says, keeping her eye on the door.

Conner drops to his haunches at the foot of the sofa. He pushes his fingers through his matted, towel-dried hair and proceeds to boot up his phone. We're all dog-tired, achy, stiff, and can't believe it's not even 9 a.m. yet. The morning's been intense enough, and we just want to curl up in a real bed and pass out for twenty-four hours. Conner makes a clicking noise with his tongue. "Shit, can't call out, no internet. It's like we're in Siberia or something."

"Let's just ditch this guy," Abby says. "I say we grab our stuff, get to the car."

"How do you propose we do that, Action Jackson?" Conner says, leaning back on the sofa cushion. "Dude's got a sniper rifle, and he's a damn good shot from what I saw, and he's FBI, according to his very convincing badge. Top it off, we got those *whatever-the-hell-you-call-em* out there."

"Look, something brought us all up here," Abby says testily. "I can't explain it, you can't. Every detail has been proven true. And now it wants us to find Bollinger."

"But the message is—could be—obsolete," I say, my heart aching at the possibility that Dix is correct. "Bollinger is dead."

"I'm going to go with our original plan, D, over some smelly weirdo who pops up out of nowhere and tells us to fall in behind him because he says so."

"I agree," Conner says, surprising Abby. "He does smell like BO, coffee, and gun powder."

Abby stands up.

"We don't have a choice," I interject. "LA is in quarantine. The only option is to take Dix at his word and go with him. The Feds could probably fly you to Chicago too."

I lay my head back on the sofa, stare at Abby's hair as she undoes the band, lets the hair fall. She sits back down, her palms joined, and her face resting in the crook between her thumbs and fingers, mulling things over. I feel lucky to have her with me. But this isn't a situation she needs to be involved in now.

Conner gets to his feet. "He'll be back in here in a minute." Long seconds of silence pass. Finally, sighing heavily, he adds, "Why don't we offer to give him the box? We give it to him on the condition that he let us go. That's what the government really wants, right? The box?"

This much I know: abandoning the box is not an option. Abandoning the box would be a betrayal of the dream, a betrayal of a message my dad sent directly to me. "I can't do that."

"That dream was intensely and weirdly accurate," Abby says. "Every detail, every rock and tree we saw up there, the box itself, matched it. We didn't come all this way to give up on it."

Conner gives me the side eye, then his gaze slides over to Abby. "You talk like *you* had the dream."

"She did," I tell him.

"When was this?"

"Two nights ago," Abby says. "No clue why. But it was the exact same as Dev's."

"Guys," I cut in, sensing Dix is about to walk back in. "If he planted the bug in our houses . . . then who wrote that note?"

The answer comes from behind us: "I did."

CHAPTER THIRTEEN

She's crouched at the top of the stairs, hidden in the shadows. I make out dark hair, pulled back. Her hands in fingerless gloves rest on her knees, the fingers hatched together. "This man, Dix, is about to take you to a rendezvous point where transport from the federal government will try to collect you."

I feel my grip on my backpack tighten. "Who the hell are you? How did you—? How did you even get in here?"

"I suppose it's too much to ask you, Dev"—her voice is low, under control—"if I can hold on to that package inside your backpack? For now. Safekeeping."

I run my arms through the loops in the backpack. "Not a chance."

"Right," she says in a tone that's a bit sarcastic. She rises, takes two steps down so an angle of light finds her. Not young but not old either. Dark skin, a lean, taut face, pretty. Her hair is tied back over a black scarf wrapped around her neck and tucked into an army jacket. Black eyes like darts nail us in place. A hint of a smile now. "You're on a mission, aren't you?"

"We asked who you are," Conner says before I can answer. "How do you know us?"

She doesn't turn her gaze from me. "I work for Bollinger."

"Bollinger is dead," I tell her.

"Believe nothing Dix tells you. And under no circumstances should you turn over that box to him. Do you understand?"

I mumble a few half-assed words questioning her authority when she interrupts, "Look, I wish we had time for a coffee and a long chat right now. When you get to the rendezvous point, wait for my signal, got it?"

She starts, gets up, and ducking her head, strains for a look out the window. There's a coiled sense about her, like she could either attack or escape with one lightning move. She plants one foot behind her, on the topmost step. "Wait for my signal," she repeats. "Good luck."

From the distance, we hear what seems like artillery or thunder, but, no, it's the guttural chop-chop of a helicopter. It gets louder, turning into a metallic whir, as it rushes over the lake. We see it through the opening in the drapes, like a monster-sized mechanical dragonfly zooming toward the south end of the lake. I turn back to face the woman on the stairs, but she's gone.

The rain's let up a bit, slowing from a downpour to a drizzle. Thin sheets of it peck at our faces and at our backs, depending on the shifting wind.

Abby, Conner and I walk in single file, keeping close to each other, while Dix takes the lead three or four yards ahead. He keeps his rifle out, braced at his side, and scans the surroundings.

There are clusters of pines, aspen, and scrub on both sides, but other than that, we're out in the open. The granite shoulders of the ridge rise to the left and, out beyond the trees and cabins along the shore, the lake ripples and roils.

The layered clouds, the darkest and heaviest skimming so low they touch the far peaks, remind me of these Winslow Homer paintings of storms at sea. I studied a lot of them once for this mixed-media art piece I did for a competition. I won the competition, but, in my mind, I didn't win; I didn't come close to Homer's storm paintings. No one can.

Dix says a few words into a wire attached to an earpiece. He's been getting updates from the helicopter pilot, who's been unable to land in the parking lot because of the winds scooping into the valley. Dix says he tried once and had to abort. "He's making a sweep of the valley and going to try again," Dix adds, standing on the edge of the trail, scanning with his binoculars, a cigarette drooping from his lips. He puffs the last of it and staunches it under his feet. "Don't worry. We'll get you outta here in a jiff."

"Not going anywhere with you," Abby grumbles next to me.

"I think anything we do at this point," Conner murmurs to us, "is less about believing that commando lady over this guy Dix, and more about saving our own skins, know what I'm saying?"

"What was all that about 'wait for my signal'?" I wonder. "What signal?" I look around at the ridge, the lake, the trees. There's no sign of anyone else about.

"She probably knows exactly where we are," Abby whispers, "tracking us right now."

Dix, still several paces ahead, swivels his head around. He cocks his chin at us and smiles. "Doing all right back there?"

I wave at him. "Doing fine."

"I know you guys are tired. We'll have you out of here in a few."

The drizzle is a fine mist screening out the world. The trees sway and bend like tipsy drunks, and the path, snaking toward the trail-head, squelches under our shoes. We can't be far now, only minutes from the trailhead. The greenery is getting thicker as the path cuts through, looping a couple of times and dipping down toward the first dock and the lot beyond. The rooftops of the low buildings we saw last night come into view.

"See that?" Abby says.

I look to the trees on the lakeshore side and see shadows, two at least, darting from one tree to the next.

"That's one big squirrel," I say. Abby laughs abruptly, nervously, then I shout, "Mr. Dix."

"Only a couple of minutes now, guys. Be cool."

Through the mist, in a clearing between treetops, we see the helicopter approach from the north. It makes me think of a splotch of black on a dust-covered gray canvas. The chopping jag of the rotors arrives seconds later, muted at first then louder, a persistent part of the background noise.

As we round the last bend, dropping through pines toward the lot, I grab Abby's hand. She closes her fingers tight around mine. "Want to make a run for the car?" I whisper to her.

Her eyes, unblinking, lock on mine. She half-nods. I turn to Conner. "What do you think?"

"It's dangerous as shit, bro, but . . ." He nods. "Yeah. Think you can fire it up fast enough?"

I mumble, "Yes," as the trail turns to pavement, and the trees clear out to reveal the parking lot. After thirty feet or so of open space, the paved lot splits like a pair of legs extending from a torso. The leg on the right becomes a path running alongside the landing, the left half becomes a row of parking spaces. Between these legs is a clearing of mud and grass, backed by a rising slope of pines and dead aspen trunks.

In the middle of the paved space, we see Dix facing the lake, waving both his arms over his head at the faraway chopper. I glance at the Outback. Slumped on low tires, its body dented and mud-streaked, it's a starved and bruised-looking beast, but what a welcome sight, a reminder of home. I feel kind of guilty, knowing I'll have to spur this sad thing awake and burn some road if we're going to get out of here.

As we walk, I keep an eye out past the landing—a lineup of empty docks and the breakwater farther out—to the helicopter, now making a wide circle from east to west above the spray and frenzy of the chop. It's as good a time as any to make a break for the car, but Dix, right at that second, begins striding toward us and shouting, "I'm going to have him put down right there." He points to the grass clearing between the parking spaces and the landing. He takes big steps toward us, and he's got his eyes on us now.

I glance from the car to my far left to the rifle in the crook of Dix's arm only a few feet away. Gusts pour over the western ridge, plunging and shearing across the lake, as the helicopter makes its way toward us.

The chopper pilot negotiates the pockets of up and down drafts, but, gradually, he draws up over the lot, sending out fresh, cold gusts and peppering rain. The chopper is sleek, black, and has no markings on it.

Dix signals for the pilot to put the thing down in the grass clearing. But the pilot is having trouble steadying out the chopper, and the thing just swirls and bobs there, about ten feet above the ground, sending out concentric ripples of grass beneath it. Dix gestures impatiently for the pilot to touch down, but the chopper, swaying unsteadily, keeps hovering, unable to descend the last few feet.

This is our chance. "Go," I tell Conner and Abby, pointing at the car. "Go now."

The engine fires up on a dime—like the old Outback was ready to spring back to life, like it knew what it needed to do all along. I toss my backpack in the backseat with Abby. The wipers slash away, and I peer through to see the helicopter still hovering there like it's under a spell. But Dix has seen us, and he's shouting something, gesturing. He's striding our way.

I crank the stick into reverse, back away from the curb, throw the gear into first, and we're on our way. But we're plodding, plodding, the engine whining. I kick into second, aware of Abby and Conner, hunched down in their seats, shouting, "Go, go, go, go!" But the car can only go so fast, and, in third gear, we're already about to round the parking lot exit.

The rear window shatters, and it's not even there anymore. The car jolts.

"God*damn*!" Conner shouts. "He's taking shots at us now!"

We plunge out of the lot, taking the first hairpins as the road winds through a pine forest, leading us back down to the local highway.

"I knew he was bullshitting us," Abby says.

We're doing okay for a minute, but then the car starts shaking, and it's harder to keep control of the wheel. Still, I hit the gas harder, knowing full well we'll never give that chopper the slip, not even with the forest cover.

"Guys," Conner shouts at us.

Abby and I look behind us, through the open hole of the rear window. Crawlers! My heart freezes and Abby screams at the sight, three of them, bounding after us on knuckles like chimpanzees. Scrambling out of the forest and onto the road, twenty or thirty feet away. And they're fast! I'm doing fifty, and they're closing in.

We hear the roar of copter blades, whirring over us, past us. There's a thump on the roof, *thump-thump-thump*: one of them jumping up and down above us. Conner's scavenging around the cargo and comes up holding an orange pistol and black nylon bag. "Check this shit out," he yells just as we see a gnarly-looking, upside-down face drop into the frame of the back window. I swerve, skid, and manage to steady out the wheel as the thing, hissing, begins slithering through the open window.

Conner's fiddling crazily with the flare gun. "Kick him," I scream, "push him out!"

"Conner!" Abby's twisted around toward the back seat. "Kill that thing!"

Next I hear a sharp pop like a paper bag exploding next to my ear, but it's from behind me. The crawler's gone, like it was never there, and Conner's whooping. "That's what I'm talking about!" Through the rearview, I watch as he loads another cartridge into the barrel of the flare gun.

"Another one there!" Abby shouts, pointing out the rear left window.

Conner takes another shot—I hear the crack of the gun. "Shit!"

"Try again!"

"There aren't any more," Conner says, shaking the bag in his other hand.

Another upside-down face appears right in front of me through the windshield, its hand clasping the glass. And I can see smears of a clear, sap-like nastiness oozing from its fingertips. There's one thud, then a succession of hard thuds against the windshield: The thing is bashing its head against it like a maniac trying to break through. Where its head impacts, we see a splat of hair and residue, getting wider and wider till the safety glass begins to split.

"Ohh!" Conner screams, gripping the back of the front seat. "Stop!"

I missed a hard curve to the right, so we're about to plunge off-road into gravel and a stretch of brush. The wheel shudders like mad and, in spite of my grip on it, the car veers, I brake, the tires lock. We careen, and now I jerk the wheel away from the stand of pines we're headed for.

The wheels screech, the car slows but still way too fast, and it crumples into tree trunks. For a millisecond, I'm aware of airbags exploding out of the steering wheel and dashboard before I black out for what feels like a few long seconds. It's like I got cold-cocked by a gloved fist.

Shit, I'm thinking, *that's it. We're done.* I have one more coherent thought: *Sorry, Dad. Sorry I totaled the car.*

I hear things: Abby screaming my name as I'm pulled by rough hands from my seat into the rain and the bashing wind. The smell of wires burning, the smell of rubber and gasoline mixed with drenched earth and pine resin as I'm dragged by an arm under my chin and armpits.

Fight it! Crawl away! Get up out of here.

But I'm being pulled in, undertowed, like in that churning lake. Hands press me down onto a seat, restraining me with a strapped buckle. *Crawl out of this!* I hear a metallic door slam shut. Conner's and Abby's voices pierce the fog in my head.

I'm starting now, starting to pull myself out, free of the undertow, gasping for the surface. I want to get back to the car. Totaled. *Conner, Abby—!* Shaking my head brings me back to my senses.

"It's all right, Dev. Breathe. Can you hear me?"

"Dev— Yeah," I mumble, the fog lifting.

"Easy there," a woman's voice says. I feel buckled back in, my backpack at my feet. My head clears, and I sit up to find Abby climb in next to me, slamming shut a car door—but which car? Abby has spatters of blood on the side of her face. Her hands are shaking, both clutching a bloodied jackknife.

"It's okay," the woman says to her, holding out her palm. It's the woman from the stairs. She's in the driver's seat, turned around to face us. "Give it here, Abby," she says in a soothing but direct tone.

Abby doesn't move, she breathes in deeply, her eyes blinking. A hand moves in from my right and gently takes the knife from her. It's Conner, sitting to my right, tucking the blade back inside the handle and passing it to the woman.

"This lady saved your life," the woman says to me.

"What happened?"

"You were blacked out," the woman explains. "One of those creepy-crawly SOBs was about to turn you into its next meal. I passed a weapon over to her and—"

"She sank that knife into its skull," Conner cuts in, a note of admiration in his voice. "Whoever you are"—he's looking at the woman now—"I owe you a thanks, too. These guys saved both our lives, D. She blew the head off the other one."

"Just doing my job." She starts the vehicle—it looks like we're in an SUV—and begins peeling out of this clearing and onto the smooth surface of the road. I scan my surroundings: forest, brush, the last things I remember before getting knocked out by the collision. I turn my head and behind us is the smoking ruin of the Outback, smashed against the pines. I see limbs shaken loose and bent. I see the smashed brush and the scar marks of skidded tires in the gravel. As I'm taking this in, I hear Conner ask, "And what's your job, anyway?"

The woman doesn't turn. "To bring you and the contents of that package to Bollinger." She jerks a thumb toward the backpack at my feet.

"Who are you?" I ask.

"Name's Magnussen." She whips out a few Kleenexes from a tissue box and hands them to Abby. Absently, she takes them and starts wiping the tissues against her hands.

"Here." I take the tissues from her and wipe away the dots of blood from the corner of her face.

"It was . . . it was just a kid." She closes her eyes, trying to banish the thought of what she saw and did.

"Shake it off," Magnussen says steadily from the front seat. "They're not people, not anymore."

"What are they, then?"

"Infected. When you contract the spore, breathe it in, most likely, you got two paths in front of you. You die a horrific death, or you turn into one of them." We drive in silence for a while. "People with healthy immune systems—you and me, say—it kills off within hours or days. People with weak immune systems or the young or the old, it holds on to, and takes up residence in. It bio-morphs them into these . . . these . . ."

"Simianoids?" I offer.

"Yeah. Like ferocious, primitive versions of people. They're agile, fast, superhuman, you could say. But killable. So far. Killable."

"So far?"

"Scientists have found rapid adaptive responses in these things. So that one kill method loses its ability to kill after a short time, like drug resistance in bacteria. One by one, every antibiotic, every pharmacological weapon loses its power. Soon, a knife or bullet won't be enough to kill them."

We drive in silence. The rain has thinned to a sparse drizzle, though the winds are still gusting away. *The copter*, I wonder. Could they fly that in these winds? Maybe it stayed back on the landing. "What happened to Dix?" I venture to ask. "You think he hung back with the helicopter at the landing?"

"I'm sure they're planning their next move," Magnussen says. "We haven't seen the last of them. So keep your heads down and sit tight."

The gusts ripple across the pines, making them dance. They remind me of the fan-blown tube men with the jittering fingers outside the car wash near our house. The thought makes me laugh.

"Speak of the devil," Magnussen says as she brings the SUV to a slow stop.

In the middle of the road, about fifty feet ahead, is a standing figure: tall as a power forward, dark, cloaked in a hooded poncho. We can see he's got his rifle leveled at us.

"Where the hell did he come from?" I blurt out.

"There's a lot you don't know about Dix," Magnussen says.

Like he's out for a Sunday stroll, Dix moseys over to the SUV. As he gets closer, Magnussen lowers her window. "Agent Dix," she calls out with mock cheerfulness. "Fancy seeing you here."

Dix ignores her and instead levels his stare at me. "You should've listened to me when you had the chance," he shouts above the wind. "We only wanted the package and a few minutes of your time."

"Keep the boy out of this," Magnussen tells him.

Dix turns to her calmly, and it's like he's seeing her there for the first time. "Nice to see you again, Agent Magnussen." He approaches till he's only a few feet away from her car door, at which point she trains a pistol at Dix, steady, aiming it at his face. "Back up."

Dix smiles and, to our surprise, backs away from the SUV. "I ask only for a moment of your time."

Magnussen gestures with her pistol. "Keep on going."

When Dix is about twenty feet away, I expect for Magnussen to hit the gas and make our escape. Instead, she looks the three of us over. "If anything happens to me, take the wheel, and go west to Playa del Luz. Find a place, sit tight, wait for instructions." Before any of us can respond, she steps out of the car and shuts the door.

Rain prickles on the windshield and the roof of the car. The truck waits cat-like, its engines running.

Through the windshield, we see Magnussen step up to Dix. She's a foot shorter than him but doesn't seem intimidated in the least. Her arms are at her sides, one hand still gripping the pistol. They're talking now, about two feet from each other.

As the two of them talk, Conner says to me, "Do me a favor. Hand me your pack."

I pass it over. Conner unzips it, makes sure the box is still inside. "Abby, can I see your bag?"

"What're you doing?"

"Just hand it over and trust me."

Conner takes the box out of my backpack and, taking out the clothes from Abby's pack, puts the box in hers. He puts Abby's stuff in my backpack and hands it back to me.

"What was all that for?" I ask him.

"Security."

Then it all happens, too suddenly.

Magnussen turns around and starts toward the SUV. She's only come a few steps when Dix grabs her by the back of her head and plows forward like he's going to slam her head against the hood of the car. But Magnussen pulls some kind of jujitsu move, spinning out of his hold and yanking Dix's arm so that it's twisted behind his back. We see Dix grimace as he swats Magnussen's pistol-wielding hand away before the weapon fires inches from his head.

Dix frees himself of her grip, but she tries to neutralize him with punches lethal enough to break anyone else's face and ribs. It doesn't faze him, and he takes a swing. Anticipating it, Magnussen ducks, rolls beneath Dix's legs, and is on her feet again. Dix spins around, swings again, his fist glancing across Magnussen's face. She recoils like a spring, and now the two are grappling over the rifle. Her hands are closed over it like a vise as Dix tries to twist her hands away once, twice—the third time, he lifts her off the ground and, slinging the rifle hard around, sends Magnussen—I see her airborne—smashing across the windshield. The SUV shudders. Magnussen tumbles off the hood and falls over the far side. We can't see her. Seconds pass. She doesn't get up. No sign of life.

This is my cue: I scramble for the front seat. As I'm turning the ignition is when I feel Dix's fist crack the side of my face like a mallet on cheekbone. Shit gets blurry, and there's a flood of pain. Before I know what's up, I'm being dragged out of the SUV and thrown to the road. I'm pulled onto my feet and pushed onward, my feet stumbling, eyes bleary in the wind, back up the road.

From behind me, I hear Abby's voice cry out, "Conner!"

I spin around and see Conner, his backpack at his shoulder, sprinting from the SUV, across the open ground between the road and the forest and then disappearing into the trees.

Dix mutters something, standing there, squinting. Dix has my backpack in his hand. He drops it, opens it, and snarls, "Little bastard." My pack—the box missing—falls at my feet, snack wrappers, a half-empty water bottle, flashlight, and extra clothes inside all spilled out, and I'm pushed to the ground.

I look up to see him taking aim through the scope of his rifle. Before I can lunge at him, he fires. The shot misses, shredding tree bark. Conner is gone.

Dix glances at me and toward the SUV and, a second later, takes off into the pines with his rifle.

"Abby!" I call out as she jumps out of the car.

"We gotta go after him."

"Wait here."

We hear a groan and the thump of a hand on metal. Magnussen pops into view across the hood of the SUV. It takes a second for her to regain her balance, but she shakes it off. "No," she says, breathing hard, reaching down to pick up her pistol. "You two wait." And like that, she sprints to the trees.

Abby and I look at each other. No way are we leaving Conner out there alone. Together, we take off into the trees, following what we guess is the path that Conner took. We run upward, but the roiling thicket of pines and undergrowth make it hard to see. I slip once on moss matting a trunk; my shin barks, and I spit-curse, "Shit!" Abby grabs my hand, and we're off again. I peer through the rain for signs of Dix's camouflage poncho, listen for the sound of voices, dreading the sound of another rifle blast. For a flash, there she is: Magnussen up ahead, forty feet maybe, before trees hide her again.

The forest is climbing. It's like the climb back at the lake, except no path, no boulders, just dripping pines, drenched earth, fallen trunks; it's a goddamn obstacle course. No sign of Conner or his pursuers. We keep climbing for minutes more, stopping to catch our breath as the ground levels out before climbing again a few more yards.

I slip off the hood of my jacket, scan the slope, panting. "See anything?"

Abby, breathing hard, shakes her head then freezes, points: "There!"

We've kept pace behind Magnussen. "Hey!" I shout. "We're coming!" But she ignores or doesn't hear us and continues pursuit.

We find ourselves jamming up the slope, tripping, cutting ourselves on nettles and thorns. Magnussen is gone from view, but we climb in her direction, hopeful we'll catch up with her any second, when Abby thrusts her arm out, cutting me off: "Wait! Hear that?"

We stop, strain for any noise. And, yeah, there it is: a loud, calling voice. It's Dix. "Nowhere left to go" we hear him shout, and "Give up now!" There are more calls, getting angrier. There's a long silence punctured by a rifle blast then an exchange of gunfire: a battle between the rifle and what I assume is Magnussen's handgun. About eight or nine shots later, a dead quiet falls over the forest save the whistle and roar of the wind.

Tree limbs, tall shrubs, slashes of rain, and the slope itself are keeping us from seeing anything beyond twenty yards. We pump our legs with the last ounce of our strength up a final rise.

As we approach the top, the vegetation thins out to a stretch of mud, scrub, a wall of boulders. One last push, and we'll be up and over. Conner, just need to reach Conner! That instant, I almost fall as the ledge ends steeply, diabolically, behind granite shoulders.

Magnussen's arm lunges out, barring both of us from taking a very unexpected and brutal dive into—I look down to see—a broad, rushing river, swollen from the rains. Water courses around a bend from the north, swirling and foaming around the rocks below, and bends to the east. I look around frantically: there's nothing here but walls of granite and clumps of green, and the purling gush of the river.

Tahoe goes up and down like this now. A few years ago, the water level dipped like there was an opened drain in the middle of every lakebed, back when the names of water channels on the map pointed to dust-and-weed-choked arroyos and the small lakes had turned to basins of clay. Then it all turned: the jet stream shifted again and now flash floods like this get triggered. It'll rage like this for a few months off and on this time of year, flooding an arid waste.

"What happened up here?" Abby asks.

Magnussen points to an outcrop about ten yards away. "I saw Dix there. Your friend was farther out, over there"—she points to a boulder much lower, looming about twelve feet above the water—"trying to climb over that rock. I think his goal was just to lose Dix and he didn't figure on running up against the river."

My heart is starting to clench.

"I saw Dix draw down on him. Your friend said something—"

"Conner," I murmur. "His name's Conner."

"I aimed my pistol at Dix, hoping to knock him off balance, but Dix fired first. I saw your fr—*Conner* go over, into the water. I don't know if he was hit." Abby gasps and brings a hand to her face. "Dix saw me, turned, and we exchanged fire. My last two shots got him. He lost his balance, fell to the lower rocks. I know I injured him, but he waded out in that water. Dove in, next I saw him, he was on the other side, injured for sure, limping, but alive."

"How the hell is he alive?"

"I told you. You don't know this guy."

"Conner," I ask, my breath catching. "No sign of him?"

Magnussen doesn't answer. I feel a cold terror and start climbing down toward the water. Magnussen yells after me, telling me to stop, but I'm hardly aware of it.

The rocks are steeper here than at Eagle Lake. If you jumped out far enough, you could drop to the bottom without hitting a single rock on the way down. Minutes later, I'm at the base of the slope, my eyes scanning the near and far shore. Knobs of rock on the far side make a dark, shining slope—shelves of rocks stacked on top of each other—till it ends in a lip of ferns and bracken bordering the foot of the pine forest. The gusts heave and tear through the forest, whipping through the pines. I can't see anything through them. And this flood river is a beast, churning and scouring away everything in its path. It's not that wide, maybe thirty feet or so, and everywhere in it are blocks of rocks scattered like booby traps.

"Anything?" shouts Abby, climbing down behind me.

I shake my head.

We pick our way east, along the river, up and down granite slabs, helping each other as we go. Magnussen is just above us, about ten feet, negotiating the higher rocks.

"Did you see him swim this way?" I shout to her. She doesn't answer. She leaps off one rock, onto another. I see her freeze. She points, directing our gaze to something in the water. And there it is, wedged in between the rocks there.

I take off my shoes, step into the current. The force of the current is shocking, but I keep upright, navigating the uneven bed across the channel. Squinting at the object, a few yards out now, I see what it is: his jacket, sodden, swaying in the current. I take a huge step forward, the water now up to my chest. It's not much farther.

If it weren't for me bearing my weight down with all I had, I'd have been carried off instantly.

I reach for the jacket and yank it free of the rocks. But the effort knocks me off balance, unmoors my legs, and I feel myself carried, panicking. My legs pump, trying to get upright again, but I tumble, get dragged by the current, and think of when I was a kid at the beach and the wave overtook me, almost drowned me, but I pulled out of it. Now I will my legs to plant themselves on the bed of the channel, find my balance. Holding the jacket up above the water, I wade back to Abby waiting at the shore. The water is *determined*. But I'm more determined.

CHAPTER FOURTEEN

We search the area, Abby and I in a daze, in shock. Farther down the river, the channel narrows enough that the three of us can wade across. We figure maybe we'll see signs of him: footprints in the mud, scraps of clothes, even blood, leading away from the water. But we find nothing.

We climb up the far slope, search the forest, and cross back again. After an hour, maybe two, of searching, we know it's over. And I'm too numb to think or speak. Magnussen says we need to start moving.

I feel rage at this. "We're not going anywhere till we find him, all right?"

She says, "Dev, he's gone." The same words my mother used about my dad. "And if you want to stay alive and have any chance of finishing what you started, we need to move."

I'm aware of nothing after that, not in any detail. Here I am, schlepping through the woods back to the road. I'm climbing into the SUV. I'm holding a water bottle, drinking from it. The less I think, the better chance I have of getting through this. Magnussen grabs the backpack on the floor—Abby's backpack, still here—and unzips it, lets out a sigh of relief; the box is still inside. That goddamn box. I glance at Abby. She hasn't said a word since we found the jacket. I'm drained, drenched, and beyond that, there's this void, like I'm looking into the eye of a black hole: in my arms is the jacket. Except it isn't just a jacket anymore. It's a void. And if I stare at it, my mind will enter it, swallow me up. I grip the jacket but can't look at it.

On the edge of my sight, I can see the woman—blurry in the rained-out windows—darting from place to place around the SUV, doing what, I can't tell. I hear her opening and closing the gas cap, thumping the metal undersides of the wheel wells. Abby buries her face in her hands. Quietly, she whispers, "Oh my God. Oh my God." I know she's crying, and there's nothing I can do. I feel helpless, rotten, as I circle my own depths.

The driver-side door slams shut, the engine revs up, and my backpack falls to my feet, retrieved from the road. Magnussen hits the gas, and we're speeding down the highway, going fast, faster than feels safe through blind curves and corridors cut through pine forest. Honestly, right now, I couldn't care less if we swerved right off the road.

"Better change into those clothes I saw in there." Magnussen is staring at me through the rearview. "I don't want you getting the seats soaked."

I feel cold suddenly. Wet. Miserable. And remember the water. Unzipping my pack, I pull out the jeans, T-shirt, and pullover I'd packed.

"After you're dressed, get some sleep," says Magnussen. The wipers slash angrily. I can only make out blots of forest through the gray rain. "You're in shock, and you're exhausted. Get some sleep."

Are we speeding away from Conner right now? Is he alive, and we're abandoning him? Could he be back there, hurt, hiding somewhere we didn't check? Or is he dead? Did Dix capture him? If he did, maybe there's a chance we can still save him. I think of the river, the nauseating drop. He's dead. I feel it. I can't even wrap my head around the words.

"I can't even think," Abby says.

"Me neither." I slowly change out of my sodden clothes, vaguely aware of the lack of privacy and not caring. It's not that my mind is spinning. Just the opposite. It's frozen. He died. The words are as plain as day. He died. My brain speaks the words to my soul, but my soul is too shocked to answer back. The rain picks up as we drive west, and soon, the sounds of the slashing wipers, the steady whine of tires lull me to sleep.

The last thing I remember is Abby asking Magnussen questions. "What the hell is all this about? Where are you taking us?" And Magnussen keeping her gaze out the windshield. "You'll know in a few hours."

I wake, and the storm is gone. We've stopped moving. There's a dull ache in my left temple, my neck's stiff, my mouth dry. There's no one in the driver's seat.

The horizontal blue-gray of the Pacific, edged with the red and gold of sunset, is directly ahead of us, behind fencing and high grass. Clouds in piles and tatters take up the rest of the sky as the backside of the storm moves eastward.

A knocking on the window startles me up in my seat. It's Magnussen, pointing to what looks like a coffee shop on our side of the street, not too far in the direction of the sea. She opens the driver-side door. "You'll probably want some food. There's a place right here."

"Where are we?"

"End of the road. About ten miles south of San Francisco."

"What're we doing here?"

"We wait. Shouldn't be long." She opens the passenger door and gestures for me to hand her Abby's backpack. The goddamn backpack with the box. I'm only too happy to hand it over. Before she can shut the door, I ask her who or what we're waiting for.

"Clearance," she says, "before we go the rest of the way."

Next to me, Abby is stirring out of her own sleep. I touch her shoulder, and she opens her eyes. It takes her an instant to snap out of the peacefulness of sleep and realize the shit we're in. She gasps when she doesn't find her backpack at her feet.

"It's okay. She's got it." I point at Magnussen, who's standing in the storefront arcade. "How'd you sleep?"

"I forgot for a while," Abby says and stares down at her feet. "There's that."

The pain is so raw. And the worst of it is the helplessness against it. It takes her a minute to get herself together before we both climb out of the SUV.

We're in a cul-de-sac, sloping down to the beach, in what seems to be a small seaside town. On the near side of the street, the storefront arcade is mostly boarded up. On the opposite side is the remnant of a defunct, graffiti-scarred stucco building. Sheets of plywood cover up the doors and windows, and a faded blue-and-white sign, smeared with spray paint, reads "United States Postal Service" and bears the emblem of the eagle. A few trucks and cars rumble past at the top of the street. There's a panhandler or drunk—I can't tell—crouching on the curb about ten or fifteen feet behind the SUV.

Other than that, there's no sign of life here but the water. Water is everywhere, running in channels along the sides of the street, collecting in this roiling lake of floodwater at the bottom of the street. The water churns, spreading up beyond the beach fencing and running in either direction at the T, as more water gurgles up out of backed-up drains.

Abby takes two steps then abruptly spins around, shrieking, "Oh my God—it's them!"

"It's okay," I tell her. "It's just a man. He's not one of them. It's okay."

She lets out a long breath, takes one more look at the man on the curb and nods. I see how drained she looks, her eyes and cheeks hollow.

We breathe in gusts of sea air and slosh our way around the SUV and onto the arcade toward Magnussen, who cocks her head toward the bottom of the street. There's a neon sign there spelling out "Seashell Café" blinking on and off. It's cheerful and gives me the feeling that the world is normal—that it *can* be normal. As we walk, I start at a sound, like a far-off gunshot. But it's only thunder from the scattering clouds.

The Seashell isn't too crowded. There's a line of dejected-looking men and women at the counter, smoking, reading, drinking coffee out of paper cups, whiskey out of bottles. Magnussen points out a small table in the near corner.

Abby and I sit close, next to a row of huge, sea-facing windows. Only two of them are exposed, though; the others are boarded up against the rain. Magnussen takes a seat facing us, keeping her eye on the counter and the door.

Through one of the windows, the clouds over the Pacific are like rows of ragged steps climbing the sky.

Behind the counter, a pear-shaped lady gabs and moves back and forth with a pot of coffee. Around the room, more homeless types, truckers, and a teenage Hispanic couple sit on sagging couches or along the bench on the back wall. It's not the most encouraging sight. They could all be out-of-work locals, they could be exhausted travelers, broke, starving. It's hard to say. If this weren't a place of business, you might think it was some detention facility or the customs room of some fetid airport in the ass-crack of the world.

"What're we doing here?" Abby asks in a low voice.

Magnussen doesn't answer. She's scanning the room, craning to get a look around, a corner of her mouth turning up in a sneer. A man in a tan windbreaker, thick black glasses and beard emerges from the bathroom. He shuffles over to a stool at the counter and goes back to reading a newspaper. The counter lady refills his coffee.

"Let me get you something," Magnussen says, getting to her feet. She goes over to the end of the counter. We see her exchange words with Counter Lady, who shakes her head.

There's an Asian family: two school-age kids, parents, and an old man—the grandfather, maybe—squeezed together at a table next to one of the boarded-up windows. They've got suitcases with them. The parents look tense, worried. The dad keeps pacing between the door and table, where he and the mom snap at each other. The dad shrugs, checks his watch. No one in the shop is paying much attention to them.

Finally, I see a van pull up outside, your typical minivan but this one's seen its share of fender-benders. Its arrival gets the family scrambling to its feet. The mom yells at the kids to put away whatever they're eating and grab their suitcases. The dad helps the old man off the couch. The van honks twice. The family, loaded up with suitcases, are having trouble with the door so I get up and open it for them. The van honks again. They trudge out of the shop, and I watch them from the door.

The dad hurriedly slides open the van door and pulls open the hatch. As the mom, grandpa, and kids get in one by one, I can see the driver, a white-haired Hispanic guy, climb out of the van and speak with the dad behind the van. I wonder if they even understand each other.

The dad hands the driver a wad of cash. There's a quarrel. The driver's just throwing his hands in the air and shaking his head. He pops open the hatch and starts unloading the luggage.

Frazzled, pissed-off, the dad goes over to the mom inside the van. They quarrel as the mom digs more money from her purse and hands it all to the dad. Defeated-looking, the dad returns to the driver and gives over the money. The driver pockets it while the dad, scowling, puts the luggage back into the van.

Everyone inside, the van fires up, makes a U-turn, and starts rumbling away. A dog barks. Water dribbles off the covering of the arcade.

"Hope they get where they're going," Abby says to me after I sit back down.

"Canada," I say. "Maybe Canada?"

"Unless they've closed the border."

The world is a building on fire, and they're locking down the exits.

Magnussen reappears, setting down paper cups at the table. "Coffee. And I bought these off a fellow at the counter." She produces two bottles of water.

Abby and I go for the water, opening the caps, while Magnussen sits down, one arm wrapped around the pack. "They don't have water here?" Abby asks.

"I wouldn't drink it," Magnussen says. "Can't trust the water in the system anymore."

We drink down the bottles. The coffee is like cigarette ash. But at least it's hot. In the silence, Abby and I look at each other. Looking at each other means looking away from the black hole that's opened up in our lives. It's unbearable this void, this missing.

"Look, you have the box," I say to Magnussen. "It's yours. Take it over to Bollinger. Take it wherever the hell you want. Just let us go. It's already cost us enough."

Magnussen looks at me steadily, calmly. "My job is to bring you both in."

"Or what?"

"Or you'll both be hunted down. And by parties who aren't going to be nearly as nice to you as I am." She sips from her coffee.

"Yeah, that was Dix's line too."

She sets down her cup, keeping a grip on it. "Look. I'm sorry your friend got himself killed. That wasn't part of the plan. But what you're involved in now is much bigger than your friend. What's in this"—she nods at the backpack—"is bigger than any of us."

"How long have you known about us?" I ask. "About my dad, his work?"

Magnussen looks at me hard, her mouth clenched. "As long as Dix has."

"You were there," I say suddenly. I don't know how I know this—not for sure—but I have a gut feeling it's true. "The night my dad disappeared. You were at the house. With Dix."

Magnussen nods once. "He and I were assigned to investigate."

"What? You went rogue or something?"

"I left the Bureau. Then Bollinger hired me to watch you and to find this."

Abby laughs darkly. "I swear, this is like out of some cloak-and-dagger show I've seen before."

"Think I've seen that one too," I say.

Magnussen's eyes dart to someone to her left. I follow her gaze and find a man in a raincoat at the counter with a small flip-phone to his ear. The man says a word, pockets the phone, closes a newspaper opened on the counter in front of him and leaves the coffee shop. It's some kind of cue because Magnussen turns to us now, nods once. "Time to go."

At least we're moving. At least we're nearing the end of the road.

We drive away from the beach, keeping fifty feet behind a small Honda hatchback as it putters up the street. We cross over an empty freeway—the asphalt cracked and sprouting weeds—traveling into the quiet streets of the rundown-looking beach town. The yards are overgrown, dogs roam the streets, and the only people we see in these neighborhoods are boys in baggy clothes and knit caps, girls in skinny jeans and hoodies. They stare at us from corners, passing blunts.

"Where is this?" I ask from the back seat.

"Town called Playa del Luz."

"What happened here?"

Magnussen makes a noise like a laugh. "This town was a casualty of the drought, the crash. Jobs moved on. Lot of people left for the new work zones going up," she explains. "This is what's left."

Pines jut up in the hills behind sagging homes, an empty strip mall, an elementary school where kids jump, scramble, and slide on rusting playground equipment. They don't care. They want to be kids. Everything that's happened, will happen, is still lost on them.

We make a few turns, and the narrow road climbs up the hillside, curving into a neighborhood where the pines are taller, the homes sparser. The heavy clouds above the town make it look bleaker than it already is. The hatchback in front of us keeps on climbing till we lose sight of it around a bend. Magnussen slows down the SUV a bit then pulls to the side of the road and waits, drumming her fingers on the steering wheel. A full minute passes during which neither I nor Abby say a word. Clearly, this is some kind of ritual or protocol.

I look over at Abby, and she looks so desolate, I whisper, "I'm going to get us out. Get you to your family."

She wipes at her eye. "They're probably in Chicago."

"That's where we'll go."

Magnussen pulls away suddenly, continuing up the hill. After the bend, she turns into a driveway of a two-story ranch home. It looks like any other home in the neighborhood. The garage door opens as we approach, and she rolls right in beside the Honda hatchback we'd been following all the way up the hill. There's no sign of anyone else in the garage.

Magnussen cuts the engine and grabs Abby's backpack. "Let's go." she says, sliding out of the truck. Next to me are the clothes I'd changed out of, still damp. I shove them into my pack, along with Conner's jacket, before Abby and I climb out and into the harsh glow of floodlights mounted high up on the back wall. The garage door groans on its tracks, closing again.

It's stuffy in here. Smells of earth and motor oil. Shelves of paint cans, power tools, and a bucket of paintbrushes line one wall. There's a rack for push-brooms and rakes, and a ladder lies on its side next to jerry cans and plastic bins. A perfectly ordinary garage.

Magnussen stands in front of the inner door, staring at a camera mounted above it. She waves us over. I stare up at the camera as Magnussen punches a few numbers on a keypad on the wall. The pad beeps, and she quickly opens the door and ushers Abby and me through.

A ceiling light snaps on automatically, and we're in a damp storage room. Boxes and household junk are stacked up in the right half of the room. The floor is made up of large square cement tiles. Magnussen steps to the middle of the room, crouches, and feels along the edging of one of the tiles there. Finding a notch, she lifts open the tile on a set of hinges. It opens onto a vertical tunnel with a ladder fixed to its side. A dim light glows from the bottom of the tunnel.

Magnussen stands. "Down we go."

There's room enough for one person to descend at a time. From the way Magnussen's looking at me, I'm to go first. Abby and I share a blank look, and then—here goes nothin'—I'm descending rung by rung into whatever's below.

I go down about ten feet, dropping myself into a cement corridor—a tube really—between six and seven feet in diameter. I'm at one end of a tunnel that extends a long way to my left. Globes of lights are bolted to the ceiling, running the length of the tunnel and casting a murky, half-hearted yellow light.

I hear Abby following me down the ladder.

Panic rises. What if Magnussen wants to trap us here or lead us into something horrible?

Abby drops lightly to her feet and steps over next to me to wait for whatever Magnussen has in mind.

"You okay?" I ask.

Abby nods. "You?"

"I don't know if I like this woman," I whisper.

"She's all we got," she says.

We turn to peer down the tunnel. It goes on a good fifty feet, going by the weak light that pools every fifteen feet or so, and it slopes upward to the outline of a door at the far end. It'd make a good setting for a horror movie.

From above comes the faint creak of the hatch as Magnussen closes it. Moments later, she's down in the tunnel and leading us to the door at the far end. The slope is angled at what feels like a steady thirty degrees toward higher ground. I want to ask her about this whole setup: the room behind the garage, the hatch, this tunnel. "You think all this is enough to keep Dix out?"

"It has. So far," Magnussen says, "but that's because we haven't been detected or followed or in the least suspected. After what happened in Tahoe, that could change real soon."

As soon as we reach the metal door—and the camera perched above it—there's a buzz as if it's been remotely unlocked. Magnussen pulls on the handle, and we're through.

I expected to see another dark chamber on the other side, so it's surprising to be back out in the open: trees everywhere rustling in the dark wind. We huddle into our jackets. Magnussen leads, shoulders squared, arms swinging, not the least fazed by the chill.

The door behind us clangs shut, and I notice that the door is encased in a cement wall that runs in either direction, curving out of sight. It's dark gray, looks ten feet high. It's the kind of wall you'd see blocking a dead-end street from a freeway. And it goes till it either curves out of sight or gets lost from view by the tree cover. I look back and notice razor wire running along the top of the wall.

We wind around dripping trees and a stretch of muddy, rocky ground for a minute before we reach a paved road, cracked, sprouting weeds. Another minute of hiking up this road brings us to a large green sign:

Property of Department of Defense
Authorized Personnel Only

The edges of the sign are chipped, the lettering faded. Magnussen's pace doesn't flag. I don't bother asking her anything yet. And it sure as hell doesn't look like she's in the mood to do much talking. I realize that since we met this morning, she's hardly told us anything. Only a few details. No conversation.

The growth along the edges of the road has gone unpruned for what seems like years; overgrown brambles and trees stick way out into the road, blocking any view around the bend. Before we even see the facility, we hear it in the form of a bleating alarm: *Whomp! Whomp! Whomp!* We cover our ears and see a low cement structure about the same square area as a modest house but half as high.

Set in the middle is a recess allowing for a few steps that lead down to a door. On either side of the recess, there are narrow screen windows, all encased in metal grillwork. As we approach, the *whomp-whomp* stops, the door opens, and a round, middle-aged, stubble-faced man with swept-back graying hair and black glasses steps out. He spreads out his arms like he's welcoming us to some island paradise. His voice booms, "We meet at last." He's wearing army-green cargo pants, a short-sleeve Hawaiian shirt, and flip-flops. He's older, grayer, fatter than in the photo, but I know it's him: Bollinger.

"Javier Bollinger," he says, holding out his hand. "We've gone through a lot of trouble to find you, and you and your friend have gone through a lot of trouble to get here."

I shake his hand. "Friends," I correct him. "We lost one coming here."

Bollinger's brows bunch together and he frowns. "It pains me to hear that," he says, and pats my shoulder. "I'm glad to see you two are safe." He shakes Abby's hand.

She introduces herself, a faint and tired smile on her face. It's now that I notice that the roof of this structure is flat and covered in greenery spread over a layer of tarp. Magnussen moves to hand the backpack at her shoulder over to Bollinger when something inside me takes over: "I've got it," I say and grab the backpack from her hand. Before anyone has a chance to say anything, I'm down the steps and through the door.

On the other side of the door, more stairs: these lead down a couple of flights to what looks like a common room with whitewashed cement walls. The ceiling feels lower than it is because of ventilation tubing and electrical wires running through it, wall to wall. The whoosh of an air-cooling unit and, underneath that, the buzzing of a generator merge to make the background noise here.

Half the room has tatty couches and a TV on a stand running news images on mute. A doorway at that end leads into a darkened hallway. The room's other half is a kitchenette with a counter, cabinets, and all the basics like a hotplate, coffeemaker, microwave and a low, boxy fridge on the floor. A long black table, chipped and scratched, with chairs stands off the kitchenette. The place has all the charm of a budget motel room.

Two black-and-white surveillance monitors, one mounted above the counter, the other in the corner of the ceiling next to the far doorway, show pictures of the complex: six panels looking out on the road, the wall, various rooms, the tunnel we just emerged from.

I go to the table, feeling waves of anxiety and exhaustion wash over me, and open the backpack. I take out the box. *Find Bollinger.* Seeing those words, the words my dad wrote with his own hand and thinking of Conner's jacket fills me with anger. *I did what you told me to,* I want to lash out. *It killed my friend if you even care.* I drop the box onto the table. I feel the others behind me now: Bollinger and Magnussen and Abby. I hear the shuffle of feet and a hand pressed to my shoulder.

"Take it," I say, keeping my eyes lowered. I don't want to look at any of them.

I find myself alone in a corner of this weird underground room that smells vaguely of disinfectant. I expected to feel some enormous peace once I delivered this box, a weight lift from my soul. Instead, I feel wrecked and used. Like I've been run through a machine and spat out the other side.

I turn to find two more people in the room. A dark-haired Asian woman in nerdy black glasses and a thin man with a wispy, reddish beard. Both are wearing white coveralls with their hoods pulled back—the kind you see biohazard workers or rocket scientists wearing in cleanrooms. They and Bollinger stare at me then at the box on the table then back to the me again. "He wants you to have it," I tell them.

Bollinger hesitates for another second before rushing to the table and snatching up the box. He turns it over in his hands while the two others huddle around him, eyes wide, like it's goddamn Christmas morning. Bollinger looks at the man. "Get something to open this with."

The man looks left and right, then snaps his fingers. "There is one hammer. One minute, I will just go and get. Here somewhere." He has a Russian accent.

"Go, go," Bollinger urges.

Seconds later, the man is back with a small hammer. He tries hammering the lock open, but that does nothing except fill the room up with an obnoxious clanging. When the noise is too much, Magnussen swipes the hammer out of his hand.

She grabs hold of the padlock with one hand and starts tapping it rapidly, twenty or thirty times. She hands the hammer back to the man, slides the padlock off the hasp. Grasping the box in both hands, she goes to hand it over to Bollinger. Before she does, there's this moment where even she's overwhelmed, the breath catching in her throat. She exhales and passes the box over. Bollinger looks back at me. "Thank you," he says in a cracked voice. But all I can think of is Conner.

Bollinger opens the box. He looks inside, turns to glance at the man and woman once, then reaches in and pulls from the box—a book. It looks like a cardboard-bound journal. Bollinger gives the box to the man, undoes the rubber band around the book, and thumbs through it. His eyes scan the pages, roving, as he mutters something inaudible.

"What is it?" the Russian-sounding man asks.

"Harrison's notes. All here. He transcribed everything, all the formulas, all the findings." Bollinger turns the pages, his eyes dancing back and forth on the pages, till he reaches the end. He shuts the book, and after a pause, looks first at the man, then at the woman. "We're close," he says.

CHAPTER FIFTEEN

"You must be hungry, thirsty. Please sit down. Anton, some snacks." Bollinger waves us over to the table as the bearded, Russian-accented man goes to the counter where there's a fridge, a microwave, and cabinets. The man opens the fridge and takes out several water bottles.

"Where are we?" Abby asks. "What is this place?"

The sight of her face grounds me. I sit next to her, open a water bottle and gulp half of it down right away.

With everyone's eyes on us, I'm beginning to feel very self-conscious. Abby and I glance at each other; I think she's feeling the same.

"Hope you'll settle for some snacks for now," Bollinger says. "After you've rested, I can put together a meal."

The man—Anton—brings us fruit, a bowl of pretzels, a tin of peanuts.

"As to where you are." Bollinger extends his arms again. "You're inside what used to be a Defense Department lab from back in the sixties. It got shuttered, and the land got turned over to the state. My bank account isn't what it used to be, but I bought this plot of land eight years back through some Sacramento contacts and, well, you could say I've been squatting here ever since. I talked these two into squatting here with me. Welcome to Breakthrough Concepts 2.0." He laughs to himself. "Meet Anton Veronin and Megan Chen."

The two extend their hands, so we shake them.

"You guys hide out here?" Abby asks. "Like fugitives?"

Bollinger shakes his head. "*Technically*, we were persons of interest." He fixes his eyes on me. "After the incident with your father, Triton turned us over to the FBI. They spent a year questioning us, our research. But they didn't get a thing out of us."

"Do you know what happened to my dad?" I cut in. "Did he die that night?" I realize the sudden finality of what I've just asked. I brace myself.

Bollinger stands there with the other two, trading unsure glances, before he pulls out a chair across from me and sits, placing the book in front of him and interlacing his fingers on the table. "We don't know. That's the best answer, for now. Maybe he's dead, but if that's the case, no one's found his remains. Maybe he's in hiding." He leans and looks to his cohorts standing behind him. "But we have another theory, which in due time—"

"Your father was desperately trying to save our work from being stolen," the woman, Megan, speaks up, "and he was willing to do everything to protect it."

"He succeeded," Bollinger says. "But he also disappeared with all our data. Gone. And without it, without Gavin, we had to retrace our steps. Imagine a writer losing the one and only copy of his masterpiece, all thousand pages of it—overnight, *poof*—gone, like that, and then having to sit down and rewrite it all from memory. That's what we've been doing here."

"Javier," Anton says tentatively, gesturing toward the book on the table. "May we?" Bollinger nods, hands it over. Anton blinks and takes a deep breath before he begins thumbing delicately through the pages. Megan looks over his shoulder, intent and curious.

"So, this is, like, your bunker," Abby notes, glancing around the room. "And who owns that house we came in from?"

"I own that too," Bollinger says. "As a front, it's worked amazingly well."

"And that's some James Bond entrance you got too," I add.

Bollinger booms out a laugh and says, "Took a year for a team to dig that out and put in some basic security. Now tell me"—he swivels his belly toward Magnussen—"how was *your* journey? Anyone follow you?"

Magnussen strides around the table to stand behind Abby and me. "As Dev told you, we lost one member of the party—their friend, Conner—during an engagement with Dix. I intercepted him as he tried to extract these assets and managed to escape with them, but he caught up with us. There was a confrontation between Dix and me, then Conner instigated a chase . . . that ended in his disappearance. We think he may have died in floodwaters not far from the lake."

Bollinger rubs his grizzled cheek with the flat of his palm. "I see. And Dix? You lost him?"

"No trace of him after we lost Conner. He disappeared too."

"Drowned, you think?"

Magnussen gives a short, cynical laugh. "Dix doesn't drown."

"He's a tough customer," Bollinger says then turns to me and Abby. "I'm sorry again about your friend. Glad you're both safe."

"Unbelievable," Anton mutters, his eyes on the pages in his hand.

"What do you think, Anton?"

He glances up. "I'll need to analyze the last of Harrison's equations, but we could have our answer very soon." He breaks out in a smile showing straight but cigarette-stained teeth.

Bollinger slams his palms together. "Yes! I like you, Anton. I knew I always liked you. Now—" He opens his palms to Anton like he's pleading to hold an infant. Anton hands back the book.

Bollinger flips through its pages, smiles, and clasps it with both hands like it's a sacred object. Closing his eyes, he bows his head against the cover. "Tell me," he says, his face obscured behind the book, "how did you know? How did you know where the book was? And why did you set out looking for it when you did?"

I don't say a word, either because I don't trust anyone here, or I'm afraid no one will believe me if I tell them.

"Dreams," Abby says. "Dev had dreams where his dad told him where to find that box and to find you."

Bollinger's eyes become beads behind his glasses. "Dreams brought you here?"

"That's right," she says, plainly, almost defiantly.

Bollinger tries to blink away his disbelief. "Um, how long did you have these dreams?"

"Three months," I say, "off and on."

No one seems to be smirking or staring at me like I'm crazy, though eyes are shifting nervously from one to the other.

Bollinger clears his throat. "And this." He turns his attention to the box on the table, picks it up, and holding it at arm's length so his eyes can focus on the words through his glasses, says, "'Find Bollinger.' I'll be damned."

"We followed the dream. To the exact spot where that box was hidden. And that's when that guy, Dix, showed up," Abby continues. "He told us he was a friend and needed to get us to safety and that the FBI wanted to talk to us."

"I told them not to trust a word out of Dix," Magnussen chimes in.

Bollinger turns his head toward Magnussen, nodding once.

"What's his deal?" Abby asks. "Who's he with?"

"He's FBI as far as we know," Bollinger answers. "Real question is who is the FBI with?"

I let that one go as Abby asks, "So this guy, Dix. He some kind of super soldier or what?"

There's a quick snort of a laugh from Anton, but Bollinger's quiet, his expression dead serious. "He's human. Fundamentally," Bollinger says. "But we think he's been enhanced somehow, a product of government experiments, editing out human genes and replacing them with simianoid genes from infected human hosts. We don't have confirmation of that, but you saw with your own eyes that Dix is not . . . *normal*?"

I look over at Magnussen, whose face is still bruised, and the cuts near her eye and lip are vivid. "Yeah, we got a demonstration," I say. "Magnussen will tell you. I'm sure she's not feeling too hot about it."

"I'm fine," she says. *Fine?* I saw her get thrown against the SUV and take a beating that would've cracked ribs, broken bones. But, aside from a limp when she walks, she looks like she's got a lot of fight left in her.

"But you shouldn't be," I tell her. "You should be dead. Are you enhanced too, like Dix?"

"No," she says, shaking her head. "Just lucky."

Bollinger rubs at his gray stubble, opens his mouth to speak when Abby cuts in. "I had it too. The dream."

Silence all around the room. Megan and Anton glance at each other, nodding.

"Same dream?" Megan asks.

"Exactly like Dev's dream. I only had it once, though. Two nights ago."

"Wherever my dad happens to be," I say, "he's been beaming these instructions into my head for months. Over and over. Who can explain that to me?"

"Beaming them from wherever he is," Anton says carefully, under his breath.

"Where your father is," Bollinger says, pointing at me with every word. "That's the question we've been trying to solve. And mark my word, Dev, we won't rest till we do."

It all sounds like a bogus pipe dream right now because, while they tinker around with formulas, Conner is still gone, and Abby is cut off from her family. In Abby's eyes, I can see she's in the same place I'm in—with this box, the journey to getting here, all of it. Exhausted.

"Good luck with that," I tell them. "But you got your box." I turn to Magnussen. "We need to get to San Jose. Abby needs to get to Chicago. I need to get back to LA." Magnussen darts a glance at Abby then over at Bollinger, who sits there staring at his hands like a guilty kid in the school office.

"Flights out of San Jose, San Francisco, are delayed many days," Anton says softly, like he's apologizing. "Los Angeles is"—he makes this sweeping movement of his palms, fanning them out—"cut off. No communication."

"They're right," Magnussen chimes in, rubbing at a scar near her mouth. "I wouldn't recommend it."

"The city was already a powder keg," Bollinger adds. "Like the rest of this country. Rest of the world, really. The rich in their luxury yachts and island getaways while the rest scratch out a living doing whatever comes to hand. Only a fool thinks we have a functioning government. It's just a bought-off PR firm for super-rich sons of bitches to fool the people. When I heard LA went up in flames, I wasn't surprised. Whole city was ready to blow. Just needed the spark." Bollinger pushes back his chair and stands. "And what a spark it was."

"My mother is sick," I blurt out, the words almost catching in my throat. "I need to get back."

"I'm sorry, Dev. The infection is out of control there."

"Yeah, this infection," Abby says. "What the hell is up with that, these . . . these creatures? We saw them, bunch of them. Almost killed us."

"Simianoids," Megan says over my words. "A parasite."

"Yeah, that's the word. You say it's from a parasite?"

Shuffling to the kitchenette counter behind the table, Bollinger says, "That parasite is really where it all starts." He picks up a tablet off the counter, taps his finger on the screen as he takes a seat at the end of the table. Instantly, a 3D projection from a hockey puck–size disc in the ceiling appears in the middle of the room.

Megan, Anton, and Magnussen gather near us, everyone's attention on the projection, which I realize is of the solar system. The inner planets rotate slowly around a tennis ball–size sun, tracing slow, elliptical paths.

A cluster of red, pebble-size shards enter from the top-left of the projection, moving in a long line from the outer solar system toward a familiar blue-green, marble-size orb labeled Earth. The little shards stream toward the marble, reaching it before the whole projection starts again in a loop.

Bollinger must've noticed Abby and me looking wide-eyed at it, and there's a hint of pride in his smile. "Like the tech? I had AR prototypes made up at Breakthrough. Never went to market. But I kept a few around for myself." He points to the swath of red shards. "Those tiny dots, hundreds of thousands of them, are rocks. We all thought they were some rogue group that broke away from an existing stream."

"They are from no known stream," Anton chimes in.

Bollinger takes a deep breath. "The rocks range in size from, say, ten feet across to maybe two hundred feet. All those air bursts we've been seeing lately"—he turns to us now—"that's them. We've observed signs of them out to trans-Neptunian regions, but we still have no idea how far it goes."

"Where are all those rocks from?" I ask.

"We don't know. As you can see, they are well above the ecliptic."

"Javier," Megan says, "these aren't astrophysics majors you're talking to."

Bollinger clears his throat. "*Er*, sorry." He points to the stream of rocks. "See how the rocks don't line up with orbital planes of any of the planets. They're coming in at an angle."

"It's fine," I cut in. "Abby got an A in astronomy, and I spent enough time with my dad's books and watching YouTube science vids to know the jargon okay."

Bollinger laughs. "You remind me of Gavin." He rubs his hands. "So, we think these asteroids got dislodged from the outer edge of the solar system a few billion years ago, or . . . they're from *outside* this solar system."

"You're saying these rocks from outer space are bringing in, like, these *zombie* parasites?" My mind is boggled, racing. "Is this real or . . . science fiction?"

"It's real, and we're running a tad low on time. That's why it's maybe the greatest blessing you showed up when you did—with this." He pats the book reverently, like it's a holy book or something.

"What's this book going to do?" I wave at the red shards. "Did my dad know all this?"

"Megan?" Bollinger takes off his glasses, wipes the lenses with his shirt.

"Your father and I discovered that organism fifteen years ago, embedded in what we thought was an ordinary meteorite. The more tests we ran, the more we realized that the organism was . . . very special."

"Special is a kind way of putting it," Abby says with a smirk.

"We ran experiments on the parasite," Bollinger says. "We have . . . we *had* a cutting-edge accelerator on-site." He sighs nostalgically and goes on: "We isolated ions from the sample, collided them, and let's just say we weren't prepared for the results."

"What happened?"

Bollinger's eyebrows twitch. He grunts out a syllable or two, interrupted with mumblings from Anton and Megan:

"We're not su—"

"We think it's—"

"Hard to say—"

Bollinger gestures with both palms up. "Stop!" When the room is quiet, he says, "Wormhole. We think there is a hidden mass inside the atomic structure of the parasite that . . . opens a wormhole."

I can tell he feels as ridiculous saying those words as I do when telling people about my dreams. "That's unreal," I hear myself mumble.

Wormholes aren't possible. Einstein said they could only exist on paper, but that nature would or could never allow them because they broke all kinds of laws about matter and conservation or whatever. Still, some trippy shit—

A wormhole?!

"Unreal is what I thought, too," Bollinger says. "As far as we can tell, colliding the parasite's atoms unleashes an energy field that matches the output of"—he shakes his head, calculating—"*billions* of suns. The microgravity of the field's core collapses, leaving us with tiny tears in the fabric of space-time. These tears open out to become . . ."

"Wormholes," I finish where he's going. "Where do they go?"

"We don't know. Yet."

"Your father was on to something," Megan says. "His calculations were ahead of the curve, and after a couple of years of research, we knew we had something. Something that put us light years ahead of every other cutting-edge solution to energy. Fusion, ion, plasma—"

"Earth to Proxima Centauri in weeks with that kind of energy, can you imagine what we could do?" Bollinger interrupts, giddy in his own thoughts.

"We were instantly centuries ahead," Megan goes on. "It could turn things for the better, but if it got in the wrong hands—a shady government or corporation—they could weaponize it. and we'd all be screwed."

"All it would take," Anton says in his Russian accent, "is sample of the parasite. All it would take. It would then be only matter of time before they learn how to stabilize the field, harness it."

"That's what made us go dark," Megan adds.

"So the very thing that's going to revolutionize, like, the universe," Abby says with an up-from-under look, "is the very thing wreaking havoc across the world right now?"

Bollinger nods. "Nature always did have a sense of irony."

"How old was the meteorite that you guys pulled that sample from?" I ask.

"It was found by a rancher in the early eighties," Megan tells me. "But the meteor itself"—she exhales, contemplating—"could be as much as ten billion years old."

My mind is putting the puzzle together now: my father's meteorite specimen, the parasite inside it, the meteors over Earth now— "You're saying that the meteors that hit Earth a couple of days ago . . . are the same kind you found that landed in the eighties?"

"Yes," Bollinger cuts in. "We know it is. The organism is the same. Have a look." He taps and swipes his fingers on the tablet. The image of the solar system disappears and now a black-and-white picture of what looks like a parasite takes its place. It's gnarly looking, curved like an S, with pincers at one end. "That's the critter found on our meteorite." More finger taps follow, and a picture slides to the right of the first one. "Beautiful." Bollinger's face flushes with wonder and pride.

This second picture is a 3D image of what looks like a colony of nasty mites, but on closer look, these aren't mites but more of the same parasites. "And there's a CDC image of the parasite found in a victim's blood sample three days ago. Truth be told, the government's known about these rocks, the parasites, and what they do to humans for decades. They've just kept it under wraps. But as deadly as they are, they also open up a gateway—literally."

"And after you guys broke physics and your parasites spawned wormholes, that's when Triton came snooping?" I ask.

"And other people," Magnussen says, her hands behind her back, her foot sweeping away something on the floor.

"We knew our days of working without interference, in secrecy, were over," Bollinger says.

I wait for him to go on. I'm intrigued now. But Bollinger takes a breath and goes quiet, tucking his tablet into the crook of his palm. "But more on that later. I want to make sure you two get some rest—"

"Look, you've got the book," I interrupt. "Is the idea just to keep it away from Triton? The bad guys? If that's all, can we go?"

"A bit more than that." Bollinger smiles and steals quick glances at Anton and Megan. "You asked about your father's whereabouts." His eyes narrow like he's mulling something over. He rubs at his stubble cheek. "Why don't you come with me? Won't take long."

We're led down a white-painted passageway and down some stairs. Halfway down the next hall, Megan and Anton shake our hands again, tell us thanks, that they need to get back to work. Bollinger hands them the book, tells them he'll join them shortly.

As they're about to disappear into a meeting room, Megan stops and turns to me. "Thank you, Dev." She touches my shoulder, and her eyes have a soft, sorrowful look to them. "I'm sorry about your friend. What you guys did . . . you turned the tide."

"Our work lives to see another day," Anton says, smiling, standing behind her.

Megan gives me and Abby hugs, and I feel myself warming to these people a tad. They all knew my dad, after all. They were his crew for years and years and knew him as well—if not even better—than my mom and I did. That right there was the best argument for giving them the benefit of the doubt.

Bollinger leads us down a hallway and around a corner, lit spottily by ceiling tubes of white light. We can still hear the whoosh of air purifiers and generators from the common room.

The air smells vaguely of antiseptic and fresh paint. Most of the doors we pass are shut, and there are piles of crap everywhere: cabinets, binders, boxes, and *Property of US Government* stamped on everything. Ancient-looking equipment that Bollinger tells us were encoding machines, early primitive computers, lie in dark rooms, entombed in plastic tarp.

At the end of one hallway, we get to a wide elevator, like a service elevator you'd see in older hospitals, with a collapsible gate. Bollinger presses his thumb on a thick round button, which triggers a clang and hum and, through the crosshatch of the gate, I see the dim light of the car rise into view.

It's a slow, wheezing descent, and I start to notice that it's getting colder. Not freezing exactly, but enough that I'm bracing myself.

That's when I notice the green parkas hanging on hooks in the car. Bollinger hands one to each of us, puts one on himself. "We keep it colder down here, where we run experiments, do the trials."

The elevator shudders to a stop and, as Bollinger swings open the gate, we see another hallway leading to a heavy-duty steel door at the far end. There's a row of several doors along both sides of the hallway, all closed, all gray. Fluorescent tubes light up the place with a queasy paleness as we make for the end of the hallway.

"Meat locker down here," I whisper to Abby. She's got her arms wrapped around herself, but her eyes are on Bollinger, like she's scrutinizing him with more than a little suspicion. I can tell she's afraid. And that gets me worrying again: till a half-hour ago, we'd never seen him before, and Magnussen, she led us here. What do we even know about her? If this goes south, if Abby gets hurt, it's on me. I take a deep breath, try to push those thoughts away.

Above the steel door, set inside a grill, is a red lightbulb—off right now. As we reach the end of the hallway, Bollinger fishes out a set of keys. Instead of opening the steel door, he goes for a side door and ushers us into what looks like a control room. There's a long glass window along one whole side and, beneath it, a long console where laptops and monitors are set up. Equations, parabolas, charts are scribbled on notepads, post-its, and a whiteboard standing in a far corner. The room reminds me of the announcer's booth the night of the airburst, and how wrecked that whole place looked. Bollinger hits a switch next to the window and a room beyond the window lights up: it's no bigger than a garage, empty except for one object.

"*That* is what all the fuss is about."

Abby and I lean over the console, peer through the glass. It's perfectly spherical, a silver-metallic orb the size of a smart car, elevated on this metal scaffolding. On its bottom is a hatch-like square with rounded edges. Running along its circumference are double rings mounted on thick steel brackets.

"Some kind of drone?" I ask.

Bollinger explains that what we're seeing is a portable collider, made right here from parts he smuggled out from Breakthrough's contractor in Japan. "See that?" He points to our side of the orb, at a shoebox-sized compartment. "That's the insertion chamber. We ionize our subatomic particles from the parasite inside magnetic bottles, insert the bottle into that chamber. The particles then accelerate around the two rings you see around the orb. The entire process is controlled from inside the cockpit of the orb."

"Does it work?"

"Technically, yes," Bollinger says, "but so far not in the way we want. Take a good look. Nothing like this exists anywhere in the world. Only been one other like it. And your father vanished in it." He laughs hoarsely. "He put together the first prototype. Neither he nor that prototype's been seen since that night."

I stare out at the orb, stunned. "Wait. Are you saying my dad took a machine like that on the night he disappeared, and that's the reason he's gone?" It's starting to come together like a bizarre dream I've been trying to remember for the longest time.

"That's the theory, anyway."

"People don't just vanish into thin air," Abby says. "Where did he go?"

Bollinger laughs this amused, throaty laugh. "That's why we built the second one. To find out. We really have no idea."

"The wormhole?"

Bollinger nods, rubbing his stubbled chin. "Mm-hmm."

"So . . . what? He's some time traveler, and he's been sending me messages back in time?"

"Your guess is as good as mine, Dev. All I can say is that we know this technology has the ability to work. Your father might've proved it the night he vanished. But"—he slumps down into a chair, suddenly looking deflated—"he also took the secret with him."

I step away from the console, my hands clasping my head.

"This is . . . this is . . ." I can't finish the thought—don't even know how.

"Exactly."

Abby turns away from the glass. "Except now you got the book, right?"

"Except now we've got the book." Turning back to the orb, he makes a circling motion with his index finger. "Once the protons inside the rings achieve near-light speed, the—well, *pilot*—presses the command, and they smash together there at that vacuum chamber—" He points to the orb's far side where a pipe connects the inner ring to the outer ring, and the outer ring attaches to what looks like another shoebox-size block.

"And then what happens?" I ask.

"The collision generates an energy field. Usually, it's only for a split second before it fizzles. The only exceptions to that were lucky accidents and that final run that Harri—your father—made ten years ago. We haven't seen that kind of stability since."

"Why haven't you?"

"That's the trillion-dollar question," Bollinger says with a shrug. "Maybe the book will tell us." I look more closely at the orb: cables run from the insertion chamber down along the floor, through the wall and into this room through plates in the floor. The cables, some as thick as garden hoses, others resembling DSL cables, are patched into a heavy-duty server, the size of a wardrobe closet, sitting in back of the booth.

"The invisible mass creates extraordinary energies, even in low-velocity collisions. The trick is to create a stable enough wormhole—*er, energy field*—and find out if it leads anywhere."

"My dad knows."

He leans his hands against the edge of the console, nods as he turns to me. "The last energy wave, into which your father vanished, lasted for almost a minute. We've tried to reproduce that experiment. Over and over. Hundreds of times. Came close. No cigar."

"Why couldn't you?" Abby asks.

Bollinger's lost in a fog of his own thoughts before he answers, "We don't know." It's like a fuse suddenly trips in his head, and he pounds both fists on the console. "We. Don't. Know." He straightens, blinking like he's just woken up from a bad dream.

"Maybe we will," I tell him. "Now." And it's like my father is here, somewhere in the room, as I say those words.

In a calmer voice, Bollinger tells us they have rooms made up for us so we can get some rest. He tells us sorry again for the loss of our friend, and the mention of it is like the bottom caved out of my heart again. He switches off the lights, leads us out of the booth.

They've set aside a couple of offices for us, across from each other and near the common room. Both rooms have couches with piles of pillows and blankets on them and small, high windows letting in a gauzy evening light. From above comes the faint boom of thunder and now the prickling of rain against the window. Two small office lamps offer weak pools of light.

Abby is staring at her phone, frowning. "Nothing."

We sit together for a quiet minute in my room, trying to wrap our heads around everything that's happened in the last twelve hours. I check my own phone on the off-chance there's a signal or a message from the hospital. Nothing.

The light outside is failing. All we can see are the dark, shivering shapes of trees. For a second, I panic and can't shake the feeling that I'm trapped. *You're just tired, Dev. You're just tired.* I look away from the window.

"Hey, Ab?" I call as she's heading out of the room. She turns. "Nothing . . . um, good night."

I have no idea where the others are. Suddenly, both lamps go out; the generator goes quiet. I can make out where the couch is, enough to feel my way over and sit down. I bury my face in my hands, try to imagine LA—the roads shut, tear gas, rioters, half the city running on generators, and hundreds dying. What about the rest of the state? The rest of America?

Someone shouts in Spanish out in the hallway, shards of flashlight pass by under the door—reminding me of the FBI agents who'd come to loot my dad's office that night—and, seconds later, the generator powers back up and the lamps blink back on.

Nothing is the same anymore, I think. Normal is an act.

No dreams. That's my first thought as I wake to pale light in the window. From the common room comes the steady, cold churn of the generator. I turn on my phone. Seven a.m. I've slept twelve hours. Thoughts of yesterday: the cabin, Dix, the chase, Conner, arriving here, everything comes flooding back to me. Abby. I move to get up and notice the strands of spider webs dancing from corners of the ventilation panel on the opposite wall, and it's a relief to know we've got air circulating. There's a knock at the door. I yank my pants up as Abby opens the door and pokes her head in. "Hey," she whispers.

"When'd you get up?"

"Little bit ago. Coffee's not bad."

Minutes later in the common room, after I've poured myself a glass of water and a coffee, grabbed two donuts from a pastry box on the counter, I take a seat on the couch next to her.

The security monitors in the corner and above the kitchenette shuffle black-and-white images of the front entrance, the grounds, the tunnel connecting the compound and the house. Nothing but empty spaces.

We hear a door open, and two guys in coveralls emerge from the generator cage near the foot of the entrance stairs. They look Hispanic and mutter words to each other in Spanish. One of them smiles at us as they cross to the hallway. Whether he's shy or nervous, I can't tell. Either way, I get the sense neither of them speaks English.

After they're gone, Abby half-whispers, "Hey, besides those guys just now, have you seen anyone else here besides Bollinger and those other two?"

"Not yet."

She takes a sip from her coffee. "This place is starting to give me the creeps."

We lean back on the couch, sipping slowly. She asks if I've had any more of the dreams. I shake my head. "No. What about you?"

She shakes her head. "No, but I've had other ones though. Bad, like nightmares."

"What about?"

"I'm on this plane, and I'm on my way to see my parents and Danny. And I'm feeling really anxious. I'm looking through the cockpit and everywhere I look are overpasses and freeways, like ribbons in the sky, then the plane rolls down this steep downhill ramp, gaining speed, and it swoops straight up off the end of the ramp and climbs and climbs and barely clears a skyscraper, missing it by that much. After that, I'm flying over mountains and oceans, so close I can touch them, thinking any minute we're going to die. That I would never see them again. It was messed up." She lets out a breath. "Yeah, so not a great night's sleep."

"I can understand you having that dream, though. You're trying to get home, and things everywhere being a mess. I get it."

Abby leans her head on my shoulder, resting it there. "If Conner were here, he'd say things were unfolding exactly as our owners wanted them to," she says.

"Owners," I say, smiling. "He'd use that word. 'Owners.'"

"You think he's alive, Dev?"

"I don't know." I picture the fall, the gun shots, the current. I picture the jacket. But he couldn't have died, couldn't *possibly* have. He was too cunning, too clever, always working a crisis to his advantage.

If he were captured, he'd figure a way to escape. "He's alive. If I know Conner."

Abby wipes a tear from her face. I hug her very close, both of us needing shelter from the same sadness. We stay like that for a minute.

Abby straightens and, setting down her cup, goes to the window. It's high and narrow, showing the last shreds of cloud against the cold blue. "What do you say we get out of here?"

"Let's go."

We grab our jackets and, seconds later, we're climbing the stairs. I fully expect to hear sirens and alarms the instant we open the main door. And we do. It's the harsh *whomp-whomp* from before, but it only sounds for a couple of seconds before it's cut off. The alarm also triggered the red light in the grill above the main door, but that blinks off too. All's quiet. We shrug—happy to catch a break.

Once we're out, we try the door handle and realize we've locked ourselves out. Fine with us. We'd rather be locked out of that dismal hole in the ground anyway.

We follow the slope of the road past the battered sign until we see the facility's entrance down at the bottom of the hill: a high rusted gate with DO NOT ENTER and AUTHORIZED PERSONNEL ONLY signs attached to it, lopsided, rust-eaten. We head into a clearing in the brush, and I realize we're walking back toward the wall with the secret door. The sunlight flickers in through pines, and there's even a faint warmth in it that feels good on our faces. It's hard to believe that two days ago, only a hundred miles away, we were baking in desert heat.

Abby fishes out her phone, powers it up. "Check it out. I'm actually getting a signal."

She's scrolling her social media and news feed.

"We must be near a working cell tower," I say. "Have you posted anything?"

"Nothing. The kinda shit we've seen, it'd freak everyone out."

I power up my own phone. No messages or VMs. I call the hospital, then Michael. Both go to recorded messages. I try my mom's office: voicemail. Home: voicemail. I leave messages at both.

We check the headlines. Riots in LA, water shortages, police crackdowns. The talks to reach a settlement over the Indian Ocean crisis have fallen apart, and now there are reports of people in Gaza checking into Israeli hospitals with symptoms that, to me, seem like a repeat of LA.

"Nothing about what happened at the gas station. Nothing here at all about that asteroid virus at all."

"Parasite."

Abby gives me the side eye.

I laugh. "Sorry. Yeah, it's odd. And that story about people falling sick in Gaza, that's trouble."

"How would you tell the difference between an exploding meteor and a missile?"

I think about that for a bit. I think about Conner and his reasoning about the world: how one side could claim one explanation, the other side claim another, and how we'd never really know the truth for sure. Just believed whatever you wanted to. "Maybe that's the whole point," I answer.

Hands in pockets, we pick our way around the trees, taking our time. I have to admit—compared to what we've just been through, this place is an oasis. No crawlers, no Dix, it's quiet here.

"Something about getting the book here," I say, "seeing people my dad used to know and people who knew my dad, made me feel like . . ."

"Like it's the end? I mean, now that you've done what the dream wanted you to?"

I stop, wondering about her question.

Is this the end? I wish I could ask Dad that now. *Is this all you'll need from me?* I realize I'm starting to choke up but don't care. With the hood of my jacket, I wipe at the wetness on my face. "Whatever it is, it just feels right."

Abby grabs my hand. "If there's any more to this, if your dad's still alive, or if he isn't and there's more to his story, we'll know, right? We'll know when we're meant to know." We keep walking and get to a couple of yards from the wall. Abby scans the top of it. "Think we could jump that?"

"Not without some Franklin Dix skills," I say. "I'd rather have you back with your family in one piece."

"Maybe Bollinger's got a private jet or something lying around we can use. You know he has to, right?"

"LA's on lockdown. It's like that wall in front of us. And my mom is behind it."

After a moment of quiet, Abby says, "You'll see your mom again—"

"Right now, I'd settle for her being alive."

I feel Abby stroke the side of my arm, then her fingers clasp more firmly. "Funny," I hear her say and see her eyes are following something back and forth in the air. She points subtly to what looks like a sparrow or a hummingbird about ten feet away and less than twenty off the ground. It hovers, dips a few feet, making a motorized whirring as it flutters its wings. The bird rises and settles on a branch across from us. Apart from a jerk of its head, it's totally still.

"A hummingbird?"

"I noticed it before on our walk," Abby says in a low voice. "It's been following us."

"Don't even," I tell her.

"Let's get inside, just in case."

Having locked ourselves out of the bunker, I expect to be banging down the front door. Instead, we see Megan waiting for us, the door open and a polite smile on her face. "Javier would like to see you, Dev. Just a few questions."

She shuts and locks the door behind us, and as we're making our way down the steps, she adds, "You're lucky it was me who let you guys back in. I shut down the alarm you set off, told the others it was nothing. Here's the thing, though: you set it off again, I can't guarantee you won't get shot at. That's how some of the personnel here roll. Ex-security from China and Mexico, and they'd have no problem following protocol regardless of who it is. Even you."

Bollinger's down in the bowels of the bunker, so I take that clanging beast of an elevator. It's a long, dark ride to the catacombs, and the hallway at the bottom isn't much more cheerful. It's absurd how the place looks and feels right out of a horror movie—a scene in a morgue or something. It's cold as death down here.

He's in the control room, slumped in an office chair, wearing a parka. He's got my dad's book in one hand, and he's staring at the equations on the whiteboard.

"Ah, Dev, come in." He waves me toward a chair across from him. "Thank you for meeting me."

The monitors on the console are alive with data and graphs and streams of code. Behind me, panels on the server blink red and green, and through the control room window, the lab is lit up, showing the metallic orb perched up on its scaffold. It seems to be "on," if it can be turned on; a soft blue light, visible in the portholes, emanates from inside the orb.

"We've gone over the book," he says. "Up all night, going over your dad's notes. We tweaked our calculations based on some of his notes and ran another test. Sorry about the power loss, by the way. We had a surge, and it killed the lights upstairs."

"So . . . we're good?"

Bollinger takes a deep breath. "Not really. We can't reproduce your father's results." He turns his gaze to the whiteboard, rubbing his stubbly chin. The board is a maze of equations I can't begin to decipher. I see the words "quantum gravity" and "brane worlds" underlined above drawings of what look like sheets of paper. Under that is a mountain of formulas scribbled above words like "distance between branes," "isotropic" and "singularity or bounce still unknown."

He approaches the board, rubs away a number, then writes the same number again, grumbling "Shit."

"You mean the book didn't tell you everything?"

"A lot of what we already knew. We'll keep digging." Bollinger sits back down, leaning forward, his elbows resting on his knees. "Dev, you mentioned the dreams that brought you to this book and then to me. Did your father say anything to you in these dreams?"

I run the whole thing by him again. He listens intently, his eyes glazing over behind his glasses. After I finish, he's silent, and I wonder if he's had a stroke, the way his mouth hangs open, crooked, and his eyes aren't blinking.

Finally, he blinks, his face goes back to normal, and he sits up. "You ever had any other kind of dream? Maybe a dream where you saw that object?" He points out at the orb.

I shake my head. "Never."

"Do you ever talk to him in the dream? Are there symbols or numbers in your dream?"

"No."

He takes up the book again and starts flipping through it. "Was there a note in here that you misplaced? Something with a mathematical formula?"

Again, "No."

Bollinger leans forward. "Now think carefully. Has anyone else touched or meddled with this book in any way since you took possession of it?"

"No," I say. "It was locked the whole time in that box."

"And that's the same lock on the box as when you found it?"

I nod. And I'm starting feel angry and disappointed—that after all we went through to get here, it's come to this. I shake my head. "My only . . . *mission* was to figure out if there was anything to the dreams I was having. And to get the box to you."

Bollinger stands and, after stretching out his arms and shoulders, shuffles to the far end of the console. He manages a smile. "Then we'll keep trying. You're probably freezing down here. Thank you, Dev. I'll let you get back upstairs."

"Could it be . . ." I say, standing at the doorway, "that it's something in the equipment?"

"No, but thank you, Dev. We've got it from here." He gives me a cold, distracted smile as he stands there, slightly stooped.

Shit. The book's come to nothing.

Without another word, I go back to the elevator. I'm seething as the elevator climbs, thinking over my conversation, barely aware of the creaking and the cold. I don't know who to be angry at, I just know I'm angry.

Up on ground level, Abby's waiting for me in her room. Other than the furniture, the room is exactly like mine. I close the door and tell her about the convo with Bollinger, how the book's probably a dead end. Abby's just as puzzled about it as I am. After the dreams and everything we went through for that book and getting it here . . . how can it be?

"There's got to be more to it," she says. "I'm sure they haven't tried everything. They just got their hands on the book."

As we're contemplating our next move, we hear a tap at the door. It's Magnussen, the side of her face bandaged up. She's sipping from a cup of coffee, and it's like she's deciding whether to step into the room or not. She does and shuts the door behind her. "I've been thinking about what you said the other day about wanting to get to San Jose."

"You said it was a bad idea," I tell her.

"I stand by that. Airports are slammed. But I'm also thinking about lockdowns. LA is locked, and a lot of other cities are talking about it too." She paces to the far wall and turns, her cup poised like she's about to take a sip. In a low, steady voice, she goes on, "So I'm going to go scope things out. See what other options we have. How to get you out of here. Give me a couple of days."

"Seriously? I mean, what, are we safe here?"

"For now." She squares her stance. "But Dix might be closing in. And if he knows where you are, others might too. Also . . . not everyone has your best interest at heart. Now that he's got the book, your worth has become negotiable."

"About that. The book is useless. Bollinger told me."

"I always find that things are worth whatever price a person is willing to pay."

I ponder that one. "Tell us if we're, like, in danger here, okay?"

"You're good, like I said. Give me a couple of days. I'll see about getting you out asap."

"You're a godsend," Abby tells her. "Thank you."

"What about—?" I begin. "Can you find out about my mom?"

Magnussen's eyes soften a touch. "I'll try." She touches the door handle but before opening the door, she gives us both a hard stare. "And, uh, let's just keep this between the three of us. I don't want others here getting curious. Cool?"

"Fine, cool," we tell her.

"And you never saw me."

We nod "Of course," and before we can say any more, she is gone.

CHAPTER SIXTEEN

July 17, 2019 – December 11, 2020

The energy field popped into being.

Gavin pressed a button, dropping a tennis ball from the top of the detection chamber and into the field. The ball entered the field and, together, both ball and field vanished, like a flame snuffed out.

Gavin and the team stared at the monitors for long seconds.

"Maybe it rolled out of camera range," Anton suggested weakly.

"Maybe it got fried," Bollinger said. "Likely what happened."

Gavin and his team combed through the calorimeter readings and could find no evidence that the tennis ball got fried. The temperatures inside the energy sphere weren't hot enough to burn one's skin let alone cook food, and the last eV reading didn't register any kind of spike. In every way, the experiment went unremarkably . . . except for the vanished tennis ball.

"It couldn't have just vanished," Bollinger said, throwing up both hands.

A puzzled, expectant silence fell over the control room. Everyone's eyes were on one of various monitors, mounted along the wall or along a set of tables. Bollinger was right: it couldn't have just vanished. That would've violated matter conservation laws—and you don't do that. A few technicians bustled around, checking on systems inside the collider. Everything had worked normally.

After years of experimentation, the team had gotten better at powering up the ions to specific charges and velocities and conjuring the field. But the fields snuffed out quickly. Gavin compared their attempts to trying to keep a kite high up and steady during a strong gale.

This time was different, though: the field vanished—*and it had taken an object with it.* The tennis ball hadn't vaporized. It was gone. Anton grumbled and cursed over their total inability to solve what should've been a simple problem. How hard could it be? The tube was in near-total vacuum, rivaling the vacuum of deep space. There were virtually no foreign particles in the accelerator. Just metal, machinery, heavy ions, and the tennis ball—

"And three point seven grams of . . . atmospheric gas," Megan interrupted. Everyone turned their heads in surprise. "I'm seeing readings of oxygen, nitrogen, and some trace levels of methane and carbon."

"Damn thing's leaking," Bollinger said with a scowl. "Get the QC team in there." One of the technicians hurried out of the control room. "Going to fire all of them."

Gavin wasn't paying attention; he was riding the wave of a new idea. "Megan, what was the weight of that tennis ball?"

Everyone checked their notes at once. "Three point seven," she said, smiling.

"I don't get it," Bollinger said. "The exact amount of gas equal to the ball leaked into the tubing? That's one hell of a breach."

Anton waved at the screens. "There is no sign of a breach. All systems are normal. Perfectly normal experiment."

"So where did the ball go?" Gavin asked, as if posing a question to students in some philosophy seminar. "Where did the tennis ball go?"

The answer came to Gavin while he and the family were spending a long weekend at the cabin on Eagle Lake. It had been a pleasantly warm morning. Dev and Seema were excited and happy to be out of the city. They'd cooked a hearty breakfast, hiked up Eagle Peak, then swam in the clear waters with a few friends from a neighboring cabin. But Gavin's mind was circling around the Mystery of the Vanishing Tennis Ball. Then, as Seema floated in the canoe, reading her book, lost beneath her sun hat, Gavin and Dev hung out along the shore and skipped rocks into the water.

"I can't get the skips," Dev said.

"Like this," his father instructed. "Take a flat rock like this"—he showed his son just such a rock—"and hold it like this"—he showed him how to how grip the rock—"then you throw it so it skims the surface, like this." And the rock skimmed the lake, bouncing over the water once, twice, three, four times before it sank. Dev tried to imitate his father's technique, but his arm could only manage a six-year-old's slightly clumsy forward swing, sending the rock in a twirling parabola, plopping into the lake. Gavin was about to say something about momentum and gravity when a thought hit him. His breath caught in his chest. "Dev, do that again." Again, his son picked up a smooth, flat rock and sent it arcing into the water.

"See? I can't make the rock skim like you can. I'm terrible at this!"

"Wait a second." Gavin stood up, gazing dumbly out at the spot where the rock had entered the water.

"Gav, can you make sure he's got sunscreen on?"

Gavin was aware of his wife's voice calling to him from a distance. He was thinking about the splash. "Uh, yeah," he muttered. "Yeah. Sure. Sweet . . ."

The volume of water displaced is equal to the volume of the mass displacing it. It was physics 101.

The gas had been the exact same volume as the tennis ball. There had been no malfunction. Things had gone exactly as they were supposed to. It was like this water breaking the surface. The field was the surface, the ball had dropped into it, the gas had "splashed" up from the other side. As he walked back to the cabin to get the sunscreen, his son tagging behind him, Gavin was already anxious to listen to the splash-through for hidden clues of the "other side."

That's not static.

Those three words repeated themselves in Gavin's mind as he listened to the audio wave conversion of the EM field. There were two sounds beneath the rough blanket of hiss that sounded . . . sounded almost natural. Like a bird? It was ridiculous. Gavin took off the headphones, shaking his head. Natural and artificial distortions happened all the time in astrophysics research—a weather system or a passing satellite could screw up your readings. But this was a particle collision. Dust was a factor. But this wasn't the sound of contamination. Gavin dropped himself into a chair. What if he built something and included a transmitter inside it—beeping a continuous, unmistakable signal—and sent it through the field as he'd sent the tennis ball?

It wouldn't need to be anything fancy. All their measurements told them that the field contained normal atmospheric pressure and, weather-wise, it was downright balmy inside; they wouldn't need to source nuclear reactor-grade materials to build it.

Days later, courtesy of Breakthrough's on-site designers and technicians, they had a basketball-sized orb sporting silver polymer cladding over a simple PVC shell. It was makeshift but sturdy enough to deflect radiation and any incidental nicks and dings. Inside, Gavin placed two crude bits of technology: a mini mp3 player set to play a Rolling Stones song on repeat, glued to the interior of the shell, and a smartphone-grade camera. The camera was trickier to install because the lens had to be exposed to the "elements," whatever those might be. The engineers carved out a millimeter-wide hole in the shell, attached the lens to it and sealed it with an epoxy glue. Gavin placed the orb in the center of the detection chamber.

Again, the team ran the experiment. Again, the field coalesced into a meter-wide sphere of radiant, spinning plasma. When the orb was pulled into it, it produced a microsecond-long plume of matter that vanished like embers as soon as the field faded. Again, the team converted the EM output to sound waves and, into the night and all the next day, Gavin, Anton, Megan, and any personnel that could be pulled from their labs and cubicles at Breakthrough listened to the hills and valleys of noise. Even to Gavin's ears, there was nothing above or below the static, not even tantalizing hints of anomalies. The signal from the camera was just as unrevealing: the monitor showed gray static. The experiment seemed like a bust.

That is, until he'd gone to sleep that night and begun dreaming.

He saw his wife, his son, his mother, his colleagues as he passed into and out of rooms, plane cabins, and countries that felt familiar, knowing only that he needed to journey alone to wherever it was—either home or a distant place, he couldn't be sure. As he dreamt, the tune came to him, blending into the background: the saxophone warble, organ sprinkled with maracas, the bounce of the conga, and the howl of guitar played on and on till it faded away . . . only to start again some seconds later. And he saw, as if he were watching a screen, a pixelated mosaic, the lightest gray along the top met by jagged borders of deepest black under it and lighter grays under that. What it was, he couldn't be sure.

You've got that song on the brain, he thought. *And you've been staring at the monitor all day. That's all it is.* But he heard and saw it again the following night in a dreamless sleep. This time, though, he saw something in the lower left of the image swaying left to right, right to left.

It was Megan who knocked at his office door and, walking into his office, asked, "Are you hearing it?"

Her question caught Gavin off-guard. He was mustering a reply when she started singing the opening lines to "Can't You Hear Me Knocking."

"You've got that on the brain too, huh? It's natural. You knew I included it."

"But is that how it goes? Is that how the song goes? Because I'd never heard it before. Not before I started dreaming it."

"Come on," Gavin said with a brush of his hand, "you had to have. It's the Stones." He went on, imitating the voice of an old man, "Maybe a bit before your time, kid," and cackled.

Megan stared back at him, eyes wide, and shook her head.

There was a thoughtful pause between them before he asked, tentatively, "Are you seeing it?"

"Yes," she answered. "But just the image from the monitor."

"There's more to it," Gavin said as soon as the thought occurred to him. "It changes. Do you notice?"

He had her attention now. "Interference in the signal?"

"Not like this. It's the difference between natural erosion, say, along a canyon versus a canyon blasted by dynamite. This movement is natural." He wasn't sure what he meant. Gavin simply *felt* this observation to be true.

They searched the campus for Anton. A half-hour later, they found him in the break room, inspecting selections at the vending machine. He looked tired, unshaven as he peered through half-closed eyes at lighted soda options.

"I need caffeine," he confessed. "Been difficult to sleep last two nights. Damn song playing again and again in my head."

Gavin took out his phone, tapped the YouTube app and pulled up the Stones tune. "Is this the one?"

Anton's face scrunched, and he looked like he wanted to throw up. "God," he muttered, then, after a pause, he added, "How did you guess that?"

Gavin turned off the song. "That's the song I placed inside the probe," he said. "Neither you nor Megan knew that tune before, right? But now you're dreaming it." They all nodded. "So am I."

"Are we to be cursed with this song for the rest of our lives?" Anton said, panic in his voice.

"You don't like the Stones?"

"It's not that. But I would like to sleep one day."

"Once the battery on the player runs out, we won't hear it again."

The three sat at a table in the break room, trying to sort out how a song and an image were getting beamed into their sleeping brains from a source (as far as they could tell) beyond the known universe. They were equally baffled by the extraordinary probability that the ball they'd sent through the energy sphere was still intact . . . wherever it happened to be.

"The brain is an electrical system," Gavin ventured. "It's a sender and receiver. Maybe it's receiving low frequency waves. Delta or even Infra. Maybe the way we send things back and forth through that field is by homing in on its exact wavelength."

But several tries later, they were still unable to bring back their basketball-sized "field jumper," as they called it. And the song-signals were long over, fading out a day after their meeting in the break room, just as Gavin had predicted. But it got him wondering how the song-signal crossed over from "the other side" and into their sleeping brains? And how to hold the field steady enough and retrieve the "field jumper."

Like the glint of gold in a pan of silt, the answer to the question winked back at him when he discovered that the waves synced up perfectly with Delta and Infra-Low brainwaves. The second mystery began to shed its cloak when they found that each collision resulted in waves with distinct signatures. Some waves broke down instantly and the field collapsed. But other times, the field held steady, the waves flowing in perfect harmony inside it like the warm and shallow waters of the Caribbean; the team called it the Paradise Anomaly. The "field jumper" had disappeared into just such an anomaly.

Six weeks later, Gavin thought he had the wave characteristics he'd need—down to the last electron-volt—to retrieve the "field jumper." It would have to be a perfect duplicate of the experiment in which the "field jumper" had vanished. They gave it a shot. On the monitor, the team saw the Paradise Anomaly flash on in the detection chamber, hold for almost a second before it blinked off.

The "field-jumper" had re-appeared.

"It's like a goddamn magic trick," Gavin shouted gleefully.

They suited up and descended the ninety feet to the accelerator complex. With the aid of a technician, they opened a hatch in the detection chamber assembly. The "field jumper" looked as normal as could be. They passed the ball around, pressing it, turning it over in their gloved hands, sniffing it, and agreeing that there was nothing remarkable about it, other than the fact that it had appeared and re-appeared through a mysterious energy field generated by colliding mysterious particles of matter. What that implied, the whole physics-bending momentousness of it whirled about in their minds, and the three couldn't help but collapse into giddy laughter and howls of joy.

Fifteen minutes later, the three were huddled around a conference table in the control room, tablets in hand. Gavin moved a stylus around his screen. He drew what looked like an hourglass on its side. In the neck of this hourglass, he drew an arrow leading both ways. In the left half of the hourglass, he wrote BRANE A, and in the right, he wrote BRANE B.

"Somehow," he said, making a circle over the two-way arrow to indicate the energy field, "modulating the collision to create waves with just the right characteristics gives us access to two . . . worlds." He placed the stylus back on the table.

"So long as we can modulate the collision," Anton said. "Not so easy when you are dealing with quantum fluctuation."

"Like riding a goddamn wild horse, I know," Gavin concurred.

No one spoke.

"We are either the luckiest scientists to have ever lived or . . ." Anton began, shaking his head.

"We *are* the three luckiest scientists, Anton—*ever*," Gavin said.

"Yet we know practically nothing, Gavin," Megan said, her gaze distant. She put away the tablet and sat back in her chair, folding her arms. "What is it that's creating these fields? We're no closer to really answering that."

"It is like Newton figuring out calculations for gravity, is it not?" Anton mused. "His laws, they work beautifully, the calculations are perfect. But he still had no idea what gravity was, where it came from."

"What do you think it is, Megan?" Gavin asked. "Any hunch?"

Megan sighed, jogging her thoughts. "Let's take it back to when we isolated the atoms out of the parasites."

"Right," Gavin said, snapping his fingers. "Those guys."

Megan nodded. "The invisible mass was only seen in the DNA of those microbes."

"Only a small fraction of the DNA—" Anton chimed in.

"But even that small percentage was enough to produce an energy field in our experiments. It's rare but . . ."

"It packs a punch." Anton stood and stretched. He cracked open a can of Coke, gulped half of it, burped, smiled at Megan.

"Ugh. Okay, what can we conclude so far?" She got up to pour herself an espresso from the machine on a nearby counter. Gavin and Anton stayed silent. Megan turned from the machine, took a sip from her cup and grimaced. "Exotic particles in the early universe survived eons of fine-tuning and got bound up in the DNA of these parasites on some world that's long gone. It's ancient, that's for sure." She stirred in some milk from the fridge underneath the machine. "Look, Gavin, I know it's a stretch, but . . . dark matter?"

"If it isn't a dark matter candidate, I don't know what is."

"Something in the Higgs field?" Anton muttered. "Something outside the visible spectrum."

Gavin leaned back in his chair and pondered. Bound up within these alien ions, hidden from sight (at least in this, our three-dimensional universe), was the mother of all discoveries.

"So, Dr. Harrison." It was Anton. "What do you think? What's next?"

Gavin got up and began to pace slowly. "The only way to know more about this thing, to know what it is, where it goes . . ." He turned to face his partners. "Let's build one big enough for a human."

Both Megan and Anton looked at him like they'd missed what he said.

"The answers aren't coming to us. We need to go to them."

Gavin got expected resistance to the idea from Bollinger, but his boss signed off eventually, provided that Gavin kept costs to a minimum. It took more than a year to build. At four meters in circumference, the spherical pod itself was just a scaled-up version of the "field jumper," big enough to accommodate an average human and with a chair bolted inside. Besides a five-point harness and the shielding of the

PVC shell and polymer cladding, there were no other protective measures. The passenger would wear a radiation coverall and have their own oxygen supply, but that was it.

What took most of that year and change was engineering the pod's built-in mini-collider. Two vacuum tubes, running the circumference of the sphere, would collide ionized protons collected from the microbial dark-matter DNA. The human navigator would inject the ions into the collection chamber from inside the pod.

The ions would circle the pod a few billion times at near luminal speeds before, on command, they would slam together at a point directly in front of the pod, producing (fingers crossed!) the ultra-high-energy field. The pod would then get sucked instantaneously into the field, like an object inside the event horizon of a black hole—theoretically. Immersed in this low-frequency electromagnetic ocean, the pod would journey to wherever its tidal forces led. If it was a success, it would rank up there with the adventures of Magellan, the Apollo astronauts and the eccentric submariner in his favorite childhood novel. Gavin called their pod Nemo One.

As important as figuring out how to send the pod into the field was figuring out how to bring the pod back. The team's solution, another shot in the dark, was to carry enough fuel—a second ion cylinder —to generate a second particle collision of equal intensity once the pod was on "the other side." If all went as they were gambling, the pod would pop back to "this side" just as the field jumper had.

The difference between this and their prior experiments was it would all be controlled from inside the pod: the ion injection, the calibration of electromagnets and electric charges . . . all the way to pulling the collision trigger. The biggest gamble was that they couldn't test any of this, not without risking the life of the human inside. So, a run-through would also have to be the real deal. If it was any consolation, ramp-ups of the accelerator went smoothly.

Bollinger knew that the secrecy in which he wanted to operate was in breach of his contract with Triton—his investors were legally entitled to be briefed on every ongoing project at Breakthrough at every stage. But for the past two years, Bollinger and his company had succeeded in keeping their discoveries under wraps. Then, in 2019, the less mainstream science and tech blogs began publishing claims of a skunkworks at Triton that had made some "mind-blowing advancements" in futuristic energy systems. The blogs speculated everything from fusion tech to warp drives, and, for a while, these mentions were brushed off as rumor and conspiracies. But then they went viral, and the tweets and videos and blogs wouldn't quit. Bollinger suspected that Breakthrough's file server had been hacked and suspected a mole, one of the technicians or interns. Whatever or whoever it was, it was enough to prompt calls from Triton execs. Bollinger denied everything, said it was all a matter of a journalist misreporting their solar-sail research. "Probably just some yahoo desperate for more clicks," he wrote in his email back to them.

But later, another leak sprang and more speculation bubbled up in the blogosphere, this time about a Breakthrough craft that could "break the space-time barrier." The buzzing in tech and physics forums around the internet was so loud that it reached the ears of Triton Corporation CEO Amanda Agostino, ensconced in her giant campus above Seattle.

Seated at the glossed mahogany desk in her spacious office, lit only by the range of gray clouds beyond the steel-framed windows, and where the blonde of her hair offered the only splash of color, she scrolled through tweets, posts, and videos as every science and tech geek with an internet connection giddily speculated about whether it was a black-hole engine or a time machine that Breakthrough had invented. A moment's thought later, her mind made up, she sprang from her desk, and the following day, she and a top-level team took a private jet to Los Angeles to pay Bollinger a surprise visit.

Bollinger expected just such an ambush. He was ready to greet the Triton team when he got the call that they were at the security gate. He alerted Gavin, Megan, and Anton, who closed down the collider's control room and removed all evidence of their research from their computers. Gavin also shut down access to Nemo One's clean room. If asked, he'd cite de-contamination protocol.

With a warm, bright smile, Bollinger greeted Agostino and her team.

"Marvelous to see you too, Javier," she returned his smile with her own calculated one. "We were down here for a few boring meetings with industry partners and thought we would drop by. Hope it's all right." She showed her straight white teeth, as immaculate as her black tailored jacket, pearl earrings and matching necklace.

"It's my pleasure," Bollinger said as good-naturedly as he could.

He and a Breakthrough representative gave the team a presentation and tour of the facility: the offices, labs, workshops, meeting rooms, the spacious landscaped courtyard, etc. Everything but the clean room. No one, to his relief, asked about it.

Later, as everyone convened around the conference table next to Bollinger's office, Agostino finally broached the subject of the rumors. She brought her coffee halfway to her lips and asked, "You wouldn't be keeping something from me, would you?" before she took a sip.

Bollinger made a noise like a chuckle as he bit into a Danish. "Yes, I heard about those rumors too." And he repeated his guess that a reporter had gotten overly excited over some misinformation, maybe gotten his physics mixed up. They chatted cordially about delivery times for their solar sail project and how excited everyone was about Triton's plans for an interplanetary launch vehicle and translunar space station. The solar-sail team leader gave a presentation and used a scale model of the sails on one of the proposed orbiters to demonstrate how it would work. While Agostino looked engrossed, eager for details, Bollinger was feeling more and more like the proverbial frog in the pot of water. He did his best to not show it.

Bollinger breathed more easily after the presentation when Agostino checked her watch, told him thanks for the visit, and they had to rush back to Seattle that evening. "Don't worry about any more rumors," he reassured Agostino as they made for the door.

Agostino's dark-red lips turned up in a cool smile. "Rumors can be stubborn and ruin everything they touch. Like a stain on a perfectly nice jacket."

"Hmm?" Bollinger noticed the smudge of icing on his lapel. "Oh."

"A pleasure, Javier." She locked eyes with him in a gaze at once cordial and withering.

Feeling slightly embarrassed, he shook the CEO's hand.

In the doorway, she paused. "It's too bad, though. I was *this* sure you guys had invented a light-speed rocket ship." Everyone chuckled lightly. "You'd be gone. But we'd keep the rocket ship." Louder chuckles followed, and the group filed out, their murmurs punctuated by the rap of Agostino's heels in the hallway.

For the next three months, the team took Nemo One through a battery of systems tests. Sitting inside the pod, Gavin ran the collider through its paces. The way the pod was designed, the pilot could do everything from inside it, from prepping the ionization of hydrogen to the injection of protons into the rings on through the ramping up of electric charges, the process that would bring the ions to terminal velocity. Just short of colliding the ions, Gavin—communicating with the team via a simple headset—could conduct the entire operation from his chair, tapping buttons on a console on a swivel arm. It was the DIY, made-in-my-garage version of a futuristic machine.

"And it's damn impressive," Gavin boasted, one December afternoon after they'd finished another run-through, "if I do say so myself." He, Anton, and Megan gave each other hugs and high fives. In a few weeks, after they'd finished a few systems tweaks, Nemo One would take its first plunge into the Paradise Anomaly, a human on board. Who that human would be, they hadn't decided. Anton suggested a fugitive, a hard-up drug addict, or an anarchist/hacker, who'd be just crazy enough to take the job for the money or the thrill. Nemo One was simple enough to operate once its systems were up and running. After that, it was just a matter of following the onboard computer instructions and tapping numbers on a keyboard. They were coming around to the subject of possible candidates when Bollinger called from his office. "Meet me downstairs. All three of you. Now."

He emerged through the elevator doors, zipping up his jacket, and beckoned them with a quick "follow me" gesture as they waited near the security desk. Gavin noticed he had a tablet tucked in the crook of one hand. They followed him across the lobby to the bank of parking garage elevators where he stayed silent as the doors opened, they filed in, and rode all the way down to the garage. They asked where he was going, if he'd slow down and say something, but all he said when he got to his Range Rover was, "Let's go for a ride."

Whenever any of them tried to speak, Bollinger would raise a finger to keep them quiet. They gave up, and let him drive, first across north Pasadena, turning from commercial thoroughfares into residential streets. Thick December clouds had rolled through LA that morning on a brisk wind that promised rain to a city starved for it. They wound their way through neighborhoods bordering on the Angeles National Forest. The change to the land was stark; a minute ago, it was gas stations and strip malls, but here eucalyptus and pines towered above homes and groves of willow and ash. Gravel roads twisted up the foothills into the forest. They came to a stop at the edge of a cul-de-sac, got out, and, in silence, walked past a lowered metal gate and onto a service road that ran along a forest ridge. It was cold.

"Didn't realize this would be a field trip," Gavin said over his shoulder to Megan, pulling up the collar of his suit coat.

"I could use the hike," she said, smiling back.

"I could use a jacket," Anton said, bracing himself against the chill.

"Javier," Anton called, "could you tell us now, please, whatever it is. We really must get back—"

Bollinger swung out his arm in a gesture for silence. The others looked on, confused, as he scanned the skies and handed Gavin his tablet. The screen blinked on and showed a PDF cache of emails.

The emails flowed between CEO Agostino, her advisory board, and a firm called Clean Slate. An email from Clean Slate read that the sender (presumably some data miner) was "attaching files collected from the surveillance and intercepts of communications between members of the targeted party."

The "files" consisted of email exchanges between Bollinger, Gavin, Megan, Anton and the few technicians involved in the experiments. On Bollinger's orders, they'd all kept their email communications vague, nonspecific, and while that gave them all plausible deniability in the event their cover was blown (as it now was), the obliqueness of the emails also gave them a conspiratorial quality. After he'd skimmed the hacked emails, the rest of the PDF was a flurry of questions and directives between Agostino and her team of advisors: "OK, I guess that answers that," she wrote in one. "The data dump shows they're hiding something, and it's big, and they've been working on this for years." Another member of the board confirmed that Bollinger had "clearly violated the terms of their agreement with us." A third wondered what "a swift and suitable course of action is."

Agostino answered that in the next email: "I'm on it. Short answer, we take everything. Their server, the tech, all files. And whatever this Nemo One is. Take it all. And we move fast."

"And Bollinger?" read the next email.

"Leave him with the Feds," Agostino fired back. "Bury him."

Anton closed the screen of the laptop.

"How'd you get a hold of all this?" Megan asked, her face pale and stricken.

Bollinger shrugged. "I hacked them right back."

"But we've got to do something," Anton stammered, somewhat panicked. "I say we turn it all over if we want to keep working on this."

"Agostino isn't going to let us 'keep working on this,' Anton," Bollinger said, an edge of pity and contempt in his voice. "We'll be *persona non grata* if she has any say about it. That's why I don't want any of you near Breakthrough. If we want to protect our work, we suspend research as of now."

Anton covered his face in his hands, cursing in Russian under his breath.

"What does this mean for Breakthrough?" Megan said.

"Breakthrough belongs to Triton." There was a regretful quality in his voice. He was right; Triton was as a majority stakeholder in Breakthrough, had been ever since Triton had bailed Bollinger out of debts and bought out the company. "It's whatever they want to do with it."

There was silence that held as each of them pondered their futures. "Maybe I can find something in Russia or Europe," Anton muttered.

"Why not give Triton what they want?" Megan asked. "You knew they'd find out one day. Hand them our research. No one can duplicate our findings. They need us on board."

"They need the data, Megan," Bollinger told her. "They don't need us."

"Shit," Megan fumed. She raked her hair, grasped at it as she stared out at the overcast city. She was breathing hard now, pacing the dirt, shaking her head. "It's my finding. It's my finding, Gavin." She looked at him pleadingly. Gavin said nothing.

"If we want to keep it ours," Bollinger said, "do as I say and stay away. They'll swoop in in a matter of days. The less you know, the better."

Gavin took a few steps toward Bollinger. "You're going to wipe the servers, aren't you?"

Bollinger dug into the pockets of his jacket for a packet of cigarettes.

"Javier, may I?" Anton held up two fingers to his mouth. Bollinger held out the packet for him, and Anton plucked one out for himself. As Bollinger lit up their cigarettes, Gavin figured out what he would have to do.

"You'll never be able to back up that data, Javier," Anton pressed after blowing out a plume of smoke. "There is too much of it. The research is intricate, and there is still too much we don't know."

"I'm aware," Bollinger said, drawing from his cigarette. "I said stay away and let me handle this. The less you know . . ." A thin, bluish cloud curled in front of him.

"And the authorities?" Anton asked. "They will want to question us."

"And you knew nothing about anything. It was all under my orders. What they know is what we tell them."

Sounding slightly upbeat, Megan offered, "We just tell them we found an anomaly in our experiments that we tried to repeat, but it was a fluke. You know, like a white hole or something."

Anton nodded his head, chuckled.

"Sure, make up something fun," Bollinger said. "Again, there'll be nothing you can show. Tell them everything was my idea, including wiping the servers."

Megan wiped hair out of her eyes. "They probably have the data anyway. If they hacked us, they have everything."

"No evidence they do," Bollinger said. "I checked with IT. Our encryption's solid. There's no breach."

"You'll lose Breakthrough, you know," Gavin spoke up.

"They can have it," Bollinger answered and began moving back down the trail. "We've got something better." The others followed a few steps behind.

"Still," Anton said, tapping ash from his cigarette. "I don't see how we can resume work without our data."

"I can't say when we'll regroup or how or where." Bollinger stopped in his tracks and turned to face us. "But we *will*. Trust me on this."

"So you want us to . . . pack up and leave?" Gavin said. "And then what, we wait for a Bat Signal from you?"

"This is ridiculous," Megan said. "We've gotten so far, Javier. Triton has money, they have clout. They could put some real money behind this, and if we play ball, we could keep spearheading this whole thing."

"No!" Bollinger snarled, and it was like a boulder had dropped in our midst. "They got my company, but they're not getting this." He puffed on his cigarette, started down the trail again then halted. "You know what happens when corporations like Triton take over things like this. Maybe you don't, Megan. You're still young. I'll tell you. You'll be out on your ass, and it'll be over." He stabbed his cigarette at the three of us. "You know as well as I do we'll be kicked to the curb, and this amazing thing we've discovered, it'll be nothing but a part of Triton's defense tech in five years. It'll be a goddamn weapon. And you know as well as I do that a teaspoon of this shit packs a bigger punch than all the nuclear bombs on Earth combined. Is that where you want to take this?" He dropped his cigarette and stamped it out with his foot. "Those guys at Los Alamos couldn't put the genie back in the bottle. I'm not making that mistake." He turned his back and kept on walking.

"Is this really about big bad Triton," Megan said delicately, "or is this about you sticking it to them?" Bollinger didn't answer. They walked on behind him till they reached the car parked in the cul-de-sac. Megan glanced at Anton. Both had worried looks on their faces.

"When we get back," Bollinger said in a low voice. "I want you all to pack up and go home. Triton's lawyers and maybe the Feds will contact you. Tell them what you know, which is nothing. Then get as far away as you can. Wait to hear from me. I've got this under control."

When they got back to the Breakthrough campus, Anton and Megan went off toward their wing, murmuring to each other. Gavin felt sorry for them. Everything they'd worked toward for years had come to a crashing halt, effectively redacted from their CVs, and now they had to scramble—scramble for other jobs (wherever they might find them) and scramble for ways to dodge questions surely coming from authorities. He didn't say another word to his boss, who stalked back to the elevators.

As he opened the door to his office, he remembered his panic years earlier, when Bollinger had found out about their secret early experiments on Bizarro, how Gavin feared it would spell the end of his career. But instead, a golden age of research followed as did the flourishing of an unspoken underground pact to do right by their discovery. That gratefulness mingled with his deepening feelings of loss and sadness now.

Gavin dropped himself into his chair and stared at his monitor. His computer would soon be a husk, emptied of relevant data. He placed photographs of Dev and Seema, random desktop mementos, and his laptop into a shoulder bag. He wiped clean the whiteboard. He placed books, sheaves of notes full of energy-field and Planck-space equations from desk drawers and shelves into a storage box. Things he'd haul upstairs to be destroyed.

When he'd finished, he fished out a small key and opened the lowermost drawer of his desk. There, he found the journal. Gavin wrapped his hand around it now; the solidity of it was reassuring. Between the cardboard covers were 200 pages of notations and equations starting with details on the earliest tests on Bizarro to every single experiment in the collider from the first energy anomaly. The pages also contained branches of thought that Gavin hadn't yet shared with the others, involving the harmonics between the waves generated by the collision and the waves emanating from "beyond" the anomaly. There were times when these two sets of waves—the outbound and the inbound—were brought in sync and magic happened. Why not at other times? What was missing? He had thoughts on that too. The journal was everything now.

He pocketed the book, picked up his things, and, after one more look around, closed his office door for the last time.

Gavin had exited the 10 freeway into Oberon Heights in west Los Angeles when the bad feeling came over him. It was like another presence, a phantom extension of his own mind, telling him not to go near his neighborhood.

He parked a couple of blocks away from his street and walked south down a parallel block so he could approach his home from the opposite side.

He was glad he did.

Parked across from his home were two large black SUVs. Seema was still at work. Dev was in school; the sitter wouldn't pick him up for another hour. He backed away, around the corner, and peered back toward his home. The gate opened, and two figures, a man and woman in black suits, shut the gate behind them and stood conferring with each other. The man spoke into a cellphone, the woman turned her head toward Gavin. He darted back and, seconds later, was hurrying back to his car.

"You're paranoid," he told himself. "That's all this is." But his gut told him to keep away, that Triton was already on to them.

"Seema? It's me," he said into his phone, slamming shut the door of his car.

"Nice to hear your voice, stranger."

"I'm glad I caught you, listen—"

Just then, a black SUV rounded the corner ahead. Gavin crouched lower in the driver's seat. He could hear Seema's voice on the phone. After the SUV had rolled past, he put the phone back to his ear.

"Are you all right? What's going on?"

"Let's say shit went down at work. We got hacked. Javier gave us the scoop. We're shutting things down. But I think we're being watched. Seema, I think—" He craned to look up and down the street. The SUV was gone.

"Gav? Whatever's happened, it's got you all worked up. Are you at the office?"

"I'm home. Near home. I saw two suspicious types in front of our house. There were in black suits—"

"Well, we get those Jehovah's Witnesses at our door from time to time."

A thought alarmed him: What if they had bugged his calls? What if they were listening right now?

"Listen, See. Let's talk later. Maybe you're right. I'm all worked up over nothing."

There was a pause. Then Seema said, "You want to stop by here?" Her voice sounded sympathetic, tired, and he felt sorry for bringing her into this. "I should be finished up—"

"No," Gavin interrupted, "I'm fine. I'll, uh . . ." What to say that wouldn't prompt his wife to call the police? "I'll be in touch. I promise."

Seema said his name, fumbled for words. And against every impulse to hear his wife's voice, he tapped "End Call." Without dwelling on it, he started up the car and drove to his home. The street was quiet. On the front porch, there was no sign that anyone had just been here. The door looked untampered-with. He entered. All looked intact. Now he worked quickly. He found a safety pin, pried out the SIM card inside the phone. Next, he found a pair of pliers and destroyed the SIM card, then, with a hammer, smashed the phone. He put the tools away and threw away the broken fragments. He tried to ignore the panic and ache in his heart, how he'd just severed his line of communication with everyone he loved. But he told himself not to think about it. He didn't have time. He'd need a camera. And then he thought about his son's mini-camera, a knockoff Go-Pro that he'd bought so his son could take videos of himself skateboarding. It was on the windowsill of Dev's room. Rummaging through a drawer in his room, he found the camera's USB charging cord.

Water, he thought. He put several bottles into a canvas supermarket bag along with whatever else he could think of that might sustain him over the next several hours: bags of snacks, fruit, bread and peanut butter.

A box, he thought next. That wasn't too hard. In the garage, on a counter strewn with tools, he found a wooden box full of odds and ends: screws, matchbooks, scraps of notes. He dumped these out. On a shelf, he found a jerrycan of gasoline, which he stowed in the Outback's cargo, and an old Master padlock with a key already fitted inside. He pocketed the lock and key and, box in hand, went back into the kitchen for the rest of his things. He did not leave a note.

Eagle Lake in the middle of December, under cover of darkness, made for a choppy, nerve-wracking boat ride from the south shore landing. He'd parked the Subaru in the lot on the south shore, gathered up his things, and unfastened the covers of the motorboat tied up on the landing and gassed it up. In minutes, he was well out on the lake, making his way toward the boathouse that stood next to the cabin.

With a single searchlight, Gavin combed the far shore for signs of it. A few times, he thought the frigid wind and the waves might send him over. Minutes later, he saw the pair of pines that were familiar landmarks to him; the cabin and boathouse were right in between them.

At first light, Gavin took up his backpack and made his way up to the peak. Flurries started to swirl and whip as he climbed. He knew his wife, his colleagues were probably trying to reach him. Maybe Seema had found the fragments of cellphone in the trash can. He knew she'd be upset, worried. He thought about his son and could hear him in his mind: "Where is he?" "When is he coming back?" With every step, he tried to push the thoughts away as soon as they arrived.

At the top of the climb, he kept his head down against the snow, the gusts, and made his way to the mound of rocks in which the flagpole was wedged. The sun threw spokes of soft gold light between cirrus and a high purple sky. Gavin removed a section of rocks at the base of the mound, cleared out a deep niche. Gently, from his backpack, he produced the box with his journal inside. He slipped the lock into the hasp and pushed the box to the far back of the opening and replaced the rocks, one by one. He looked around: no sign of anyone for miles, and the only noise was the flag fluttering in the gusts. The sparse vegetation shook, trembled.

Standing atop the crown of the peak, he pulled out the video camera, smaller than his palm. After walking down to its base, toward the trail he'd followed to get here, he began recording: First, shots of the lake, the rugged slope below, then, panning across, he caught himself in close-up as he began walking back up the crown. Keeping himself in the frame, fingers grasping the corners of the camera, he walked back up the crown, back to the flagpole. He disassembled the rocks again, revealing the niche. Reaching inside, he pulled out the box and displayed it clearly for the camera. He pointed the camera at two words he'd written across the top of the box—"Find Bollinger"—then slid the box back into the hole. The odds of his recording one day reaching its target were so far-flung, he didn't bother entertaining it. He checked the time and hurried back down the path.

At a rest stop on the 5, Gavin stood face to face with an object as exotic as Nemo One in its own way: a payphone. He dropped fifty cents into the slot and called Seema on her office line. "Gav? Oh my God, what happened? Dev found bits of your phone in the trash can. What's going on?"

"Seema. Glad you picked up," Gavin said, taking a breath, happy to hear her voice. "I'll explain everything—eventually. Just know I'm safe. Have you had any visitors at work or at the house? Any weird calls?"

"No," she said after a pause.

"Good. How're you both doing?"

"I'm holding up. He's been asking about you, worried. You not being home last night and this morning, we're scared. Where are you?"

"About a hundred miles out of LA. Coming back on the 5."

"On a road trip all of a sudden?"

Gavin considered telling her everything, then remembered Bollinger's own admonition that the more others knew, the more they were compromised.

"I'll tell you when I see you," he said. "I'm glad you're both okay." He hung up. Again, he was struck by the thought that they were listening. He got back into his car. *I love you,* he thought to himself. He hadn't told her he loved her, that he loved their son. He hoped he would yet have the chance.

He knew that Megan, Bollinger, and Anton had all likely tried reaching him, maybe asking where he was, warning him that either the Feds had already shown up at Breakthrough or, worse, that Agostino had. When doubts crept into his mind, he thought about Triton confiscating Nemo One and all their work. And a flush of anger would overpower all fear and doubt about what he knew he had to do.

Before Bollinger summoned them with news of the hack, Gavin, Megan, and Anton had been discussing who the first human "guinea pig" would be to traverse the field inside Nemo One. Gavin had a hunch what the answer was then. He was sure of it now.

The rain picked up as Gavin neared the city and pressed east toward Pasadena. The wipers slashed at the rain to the beat of his own panicked thoughts. By the middle of the afternoon, he was driving along the perimeter hedge on the west side of Breakthrough. He swiped his card key at the gate and rolled on through. He dipped into the parking garage. There weren't too many cars here this afternoon, and he wondered if Bollinger had closed the facility, told everyone to go away on indefinite leave. He parked and, as he waited for the elevator, noticed that Anton's, Megan's, and Bollinger's cars weren't in their spaces. The whole place had a mausoleum feel about it that made him more on-edge. Nerves frayed, his brain fogged from too little sleep, he took a deep breath, collected his wits while he waited for the elevator doors to open.

Nemo One was still where they had left it twenty-four hours ago: In its donut-shaped pad in the clean room. There would be no need to foist his way into the accelerator annex; here was a vessel, control room, and collider all in one.

Gavin checked the clock on the corridor wall: 3:55 p.m. He would need five hours—no, six, he thought—to do a full-systems check on Nemo One before its first (and probably only) manned run. Would that be enough time before anyone caught on? He had seen no sign of black SUVs or strangers in black suits since yesterday. He remembered Bollinger saying they still had a few days to cover their tracks. He prayed now—his first prayer since he'd left his parents' home—that Bollinger was right.

CHAPTER SEVENTEEN

I'm on the slope again, picking my way over stones and brush, barely able to see through the mist. Overhead, the charcoal gray clouds seem close enough to touch. Pines along the far side of the ridge are lined up like the cloaked and hooded elders in a temple awaiting the sacrifice. I keep walking, peer through the mist toward the peak and there see the shadow figure, its back to me. I call out, "Dad!" No answer. I climb. The mist, the cold: my bones ache. I climb. For some reason, I hear the surging of the sea, but to the west, see only the descending slope with its boulders and scattered brush. "Dad!" The figure stands motionless, its back to me in the mist. Now, closer up, I see that it's wearing familiar clothes—the hood of the jacket closed over the head—and the frayed jeans. I touch its shoulder. The figure turns. "I'm sorry, Conner," I say, feeling my chest tighten, my face crumple in tears. "I'm sorry about what happened. We left you. We left you." Conner says nothing, his face a blank before a thin smile appears. He opens his mouth, but my mother's voice comes out: "I'm so sorry, son. I wish you'd never left."

I'm in a hallway now: the antiseptic-smelling hallway of a rundown hospital where light panels on the ceiling blinker on and off, where broken EKG equipment, oxygen tanks line the walls. "I love you, Dev. Was it all worth it?" I hear her voice. "No," I mumble in the semidarkness, "I guess not. You were right." I enter her room. She's unconscious in her bed, spaghetti-like tubes running from IV stands and monitors to her arms, her temples, her chest. I go to her side, hearing only the faint beeps of the heart and brain monitors next to the bed. Seeing her, I cry immediately, heaving grief up out of my chest. She opens her eyes to me, and her kind eyes and smile make me feel safe, and right now I can't tell if this kindness is a wish or a memory. It makes me take her hand in mine, sit at the edge of the bed. Her eyes are closed. And the steady alert of the monitor rises in my ears. Voices in alarm crowd behind me: Michael shouting instructions. Now the moment sinks like a weight on my chest, trapping me here when arms lunge. Hands grasp my throat. My mother screams, "Die!"—

"Dev!" I feel hands shaking me awake—"Dev"—and it's like I'm gasping myself out from underground. I'm breathing hard as I look up to see Abby.

"My God," she says, touching my face, "you're sweating."

I wipe at my forehead and chest. I roll off the couch, dazed, shocked by my dream. "God," I groan, turning to Abby. She puts both her hands on my shoulders. "I saw Conner. I saw my mom. Shit."

It's been two days since Magnussen left and no word or sign of her. "I told him I was sorry." Now I can feel tears welling up, my throat choking up. "And my mom, she was in this—" Remembering the dream, I close my hands around my throat. "She was—"

"It was only a dream," Abby says in a low, calm voice. "You and I are both feeling it. I've had dreams too." Looking out the high window, I can tell it's early. The light is pale, the sun barely up. It feels like a prison here. We both feel it. We move for the door at the same time.

The hallway is empty, filled with the noise of the generator and air purifiers. The monitors in the common area flip through images of the facility, soundless and uneventful. CNN plays on the television. The images are hypnotic: guerilla fighters in crumbled towns being shelled by oil-company security forces; a Chinese naval ship, crippled, smoking, torpedoed by an American sub as helicopters airlift sailors and now the scroll along the bottom reads, "Russian ambassador warns US of retaliatory strike in Gulf." The news cuts back to the studio anchor who moves his lips for a few seconds before footage comes on of farmers in the Midwest in a pitched battle with police at the site where one of the Triton zones is being built.

"It's all going to shit," I say under my breath. As I fetch Abby and myself some food and water, I find myself seeking comfort from Conner. He would always make the point that, no matter how shitty the world seemed, it would never get unbearable. If it did, the masses would revolt and our owners and managers would do everything to prevent that, since they needed us around for fodder while they lived on piles of cash and sick yachts. It was his perverse way of looking at the bright side. Right now, it helps stave off any terror the TV wanted me to feel.

We roam the facility, if only to give our legs something to do. Even with all the madness in the news, I tell Abby, all I can think of is the dream, seeing Conner like that, up on the peak, and then my mom. My heart is kind of breaking for her as I saw her in the dream. I want to see her so bad, I tell her. Tell her I'm sorry I left.

We know this place well now, every turn, every sign, every feature. It's pretty much a maze of cement corridors interrupted, at one point, by a bullpen built into a pit and stocked with outdated military-looking hardware. Like the rest of this facility, the bullpen looks lifted out of some old documentary about spies or the space race. The equipment, the filing cabinets and military-gray consoles with their dials, switches, knobs and buttons are all draped in plastic tarp.

We see no sign of Megan, Anton, or Bollinger, but a couple of times, we pass workers dressed in hooded coveralls, wearing protective goggles. I'm about to make a joke about how we're probably getting fried with radiation when I see numbers. They float by in my vision.

I blink, and the numbers are gone. I rub my eyes. "That was weird."

Abby stops a few steps ahead and asks if I'm all right.

I'm telling her about the numbers, what *looked* like numbers.

"Probably just floaters," she says. "You didn't sleep well, and your eyes are strained."

She's got a point. In the last week or so, we've eaten and slept like crap.

That's when we pass the freight elevator, the one that leads down to the lab. Two coverall-wearing guys exit the elevator, walk past us and pay us no attention.

"What do you think?" I whisper to Abby.

"Let's go."

We're on the same page: we've been here for four days, no end in sight and no info. About time we snuck down there and gathered our own intel.

But as we pull open the elevator door, one of the coverall dudes notices and, peeling off the hood of his coverall, shuffles in our direction. He looks Asian and has sparse facial hair. "Elevator, staff only. Please." He gestures us to step away from the elevator. The guy looks no older than either of us. He stands there in his booties, making sure we do as he says.

We pace back and forth in the hallway like we're a couple of caged animals. Abby's keeping her cool, though. Arms folded. She's wearing my button-down shirt, the sleeves too long on her. "You really want to check out what's down there?" she asks.

"I think it's wrong that it's four days since we got here, and we're no closer to any answers or getting out."

"Okay," she says, turning to face me, "go into your room, and wait for the signal." She goes from the hallway, into the breakroom and walks up the stairs to the main door. From the foot of the stairs, she looks back at me, mouths the word, "Go," and waves her fingers like I should slide back into my room. I do, right after I see what she's up to: she opens the door, triggering the red light over the door—and the alarm. A *whomp-whomp* goes off from multiple points throughout the complex. I slip back into the room and keep watch through the crack in the door. I hear shouts and see a blur of coveralls race past. They go up the stairway and out the door. The red light's still on, and the alarm's bleating away.

Before they catch up with Abby, I'm already back to the elevator, pressing the button. The cables clang and whisper, and as it's approaching, the alarm shuts off.

The elevator shudders to a stop. I slide the gate back, get in, and, a second later, I'm in the flickering dark of the well, descending.

It's excruciating because the elevator's going at a snail's pace, but I make it. After sliding back the gate, I step into the corridor lit by cone-shaded yellow bulbs from the ceiling. There isn't a soul around. It's refrigerator-cold down here.

As I make my way toward the end of the hallway, toward the lab and control room that Bollinger showed us days ago, I notice another hallway jutting off to the right. I also pass locked metal military-green doors to the left. There's not a goddamn sound except—wait a second—there are murmurs from the end of the right-side hallway, but it's too dark to tell where they're coming from.

I stop now because the floaters in my eyes are back. I can't blink them away so I turn, backtrack and duck into that side hallway. I crouch down and wait for the shapes to float out of sight. As I wait, I really study the shapes and notice they're not just squiggles, they're not random floaters. I close my eyes, and now there's no doubt: the shapes glow like they're branded behind my eyelids: "*E=1.2407e-31*"

I stare at them, making sure I'm actually seeing this, when a door at the end of this hallway opens. Backlit in a block of light, a figure steps into the hall. He's dressed in a hazmat suit and what looks like a gas mask.

I duck around the corner of the main hallway, crane for a look back and see Hazmat open a second door with a jangle of keys and step through. A few seconds later, Hazmat reappears, now with a syringe and bottles in his hands, shuts the door, locks it, then steps back in through the first door. All's quiet again.

I stand up and turn my attention to the lab at the end of this hall and the adjacent control room. With quick steps now, I make my way, not caring anymore if I'm found. They should know. Maybe it'll help. If I could write down the numbers, they might know what to do with them. It's the last piece, I'm thinking, the last piece Dad wanted me to communicate, and that's when I hear the crash from behind the door of the control room.

The door is ajar. Pressing myself against the wall next to it, I can hear voices. "I think there's something he's not telling us." That was Bollinger.

"What would he know that is not in the book?" That sounds like the Russian guy, Anton. "There is nothing, mathematically at least."

Bollinger again: "What part of any of this has conformed to the principles and laws of physics, Anton? What part of any of this has followed along the lines of everything we ever knew?"

"All of it, in my opinion," Anton answers.

"All of it," Bollinger answers, laughing. "Really?"

There is a pause now, and I hear steps crossing the room. Anton's voice, dry and flat, goes on. "Harrison maintained that no part of the anomaly, none of it broke physical laws. Since we cannot see the full picture—the interaction with the anti-protons contains dark matter, after all—we must guess. But Harrison proved that, with the right calculations, we can guess correctly."

"No gold stars for guessing," Bollinger cuts in.

"Have you asked Dev about this?" Now it's Megan speaking.

"I did. He knows nothing. Or least he's not telling us."

"We keep trying," Anton says.

"At what cost? We've run the experiment twice, and it's a dud."

Megan gives a quick laugh. "You didn't die, at least."

"Not consolation enough," Bollinger says as I hear the spring of the chair, the shuffle of feet, and I'm almost sure I'm about to be discovered. Instead, I hear a groan. "I don't think Harrison disappeared with Nemo One at all. Not in the magical way we like to think. No. I think he knew then what we know now. That it's a dead end. I think Harrison stole Nemo One, and he's been living incognito ever since."

"So, he just lifted the entire vehicle out of the clean room," Anton replies, his Russian accent making him sound even more sarcastic, "got through every security protocol—"

"And set off an explosive device as he was leaving, destroying the lab?" Megan adds.

"And left no trace of him even being there," Anton says. "It takes a master thief to accomplish that."

I'm about to knock on the door and tell them about the numbers I saw, that I'll write them down and report back the instant I see them again. Then Bollinger speaks. "Nevertheless, I think it's the only good explanation. He went rogue."

"That's your official stance?" Megan asks.

"We're turning it all over to them. Effective immediately. That's my stance."

Silence follows, then Bollinger again: "We'll still be involved. They assured us we'd get top clearance, all of us. They need us, don't they?"

"And how much did your 'official stance' cost them?" Megan asks sharply.

"Unless you've got a couple of million lying around, I don't see another choice. Now I thought the book was the answer, but it isn't."

"You," Anton says, "you were so adamant, Javier. This would be our discovery, our research."

"Triton only asks that we share all data, and they agree to fund us indefinitely. Agostino has promised no interference." I hear the others grumble words in protest, then Bollinger adds, "And they want the boy and the girl."

"Sorry, what is that?" Anton asks. "Why?"

I can feel the adrenaline surging in my chest.

"They think they know something, more than they're telling us. Frankly, so do I."

"You think they are lying?"

"Come on, you two. You really believe that nonsense about dreams and those silly messages?"

"It wasn't nonsense," Megan counters. "We had them too. After the field jumper experiment, we had similar dreams."

"Really?" Bollinger shoots back. "Because from my memory, you didn't dream anything, but thought you heard, what, a song?"

"We all three heard it," Anton adds. "I still cannot get that damn song out of my head."

"I think you heard what you wanted to hear. What did you *see*? If I'm not mistaken, you saw only static. Just swirls and fuzz that Harrison convinced you meant something."

"I believe him," Anton says.

"Me too."

Bollinger grunts, and I hear the thump and squeak of a chair. "Wake up, both of you. That boy always knew the location of the book. Or if he didn't, he was told the location, the end-result being for *our* agent to lead him here."

"Told by whom? Triton?"

"The Chinese, the Russians, the deep state. Hell if I know. But I'll tell you the only person who knew for sure the location of that book. And that's Dr. Harrison. He and whoever he's working for. Come on, Megan. You know I'm right."

"Harrison . . . is alive, you're saying?"

Silence. Bollinger goes on: "More parties than Triton are in on this, I suspect. And Harrison and his son were recruited by one of them, as agents."

"Why would Harrison bother with us then, Javier?" Megan asks. "He knows as much as we do. He could just share his knowledge with whoever he's working for. Why come after us?"

"Competition. Locate and destroy the only competition on Earth they have—us three, right here in this room."

"Quite a theory, Javier," Anton says, laughing lightly.

"What's more plausible? My theory or the story that boy is telling us? In any case"—I hear a chair being rolled till it smacks against a table—"the devil you know is better than the devil you don't, don't you agree?" More silence follows. "Oh, don't give me those looks, either of you—" Four or five buzzes go off in the room. A handset is picked up.

"*Yeeeaas,*" Bollinger says like an annoyed parent, then, "Be right up." The handset slams back in its cradle. "That goddamn kid got out, the girl. Kids are like cats." I hear the shuffling of feet and back away from the door, ready to bolt, but Bollinger goes on, "Look, this thing is going to be settled very quickly. Just think, we won't have to live in the shadows anymore."

There's a long silence before Megan asks, "What do you want us to do? We're prepping another run. Pod should be good to go in a few hours."

"Keep prepping. We'll rev it up for a final spin. Agostino will want a demo when she arrives." The door jerks open a slight bit. Words are mumbled in the room, but I don't have time now. I can't make it back to the elevator; it's too far. I take a chance on a door handle to my right. It turns!

I slide in and shut the door to what looks like a musty, lightless storeroom. My heart's pounding. Seconds pass. Footsteps approach, and, through a crack in the door, I see Bollinger move toward the elevator. I listen for the slam of the elevator gate, the clang of the cables, and for silence to return before I dare to turn the handle again.

By luck, good fortune, or—and I can't ignore this—because they *let* me go, I manage to get back to the elevator and back up to the main floor without being seen. In the elevator is when the anxiety is the worst: you're in darkness, hearing only the generators and the ancient cables. Once I'm up, I hurry back to our rooms and find that Abby's door is locked. Weird.

"Abby?" I yell through the door. No reply. I bang on the door with the flat of my hand and yell for her again. I check my room and the common room: both empty.

"You in there?" I try the handle again.

Above the generator noise, I hear, "Sorry, Dev." I turn and find Bollinger standing in the doorway between me and the common area. His thick black glasses behind his pig eyes, the bristly stubble, the baggy clothes over the barrel body all give him the look of a small-time collector who'd shank you over a few shitty bucks. "You knew the rules. No leaving." There are two other guys behind him, and they start moving toward me. I haven't taken even two steps back when I feel someone grab my arms from behind and find myself shoved into my room.

I can tell right away the place has been ransacked, my backpack's been gone through, and the couch cushions are tossed around. Before I get my bearings, one of the men comes forward and lands a punch in my midsection. Nauseating pain. Air gets pushed out of me like when then windows of a plane are blown out, and I'm on my ass on one of the cushions on the floor.

Three men in coveralls loom above me as Bollinger shuts the door and sits down on the edge of the couch, his blunt body towering. "It's an easy question. Who sent you?"

I say nothing. I'm still coughing, doubled over on the cushion.

"Give me a truthful answer," Bollinger says, "and I have the power to change *everything* that will happen to you and your friend in a few hours." He sweeps one arm as if he's erasing an invisible chalkboard.

"Abby," I sputter out, feeling pathetic, as unable to help her as I was Conner.

"You'll see her in due time." He bends toward me, his elbows resting on his knees. "The where and the how depend on what you can tell me now." The smells of sweat and alcohol come off him. "Who sent you?" Bollinger repeats, his voice low, gravelly, tired.

"What's wrong with you?" I try my best sneer. "I told you."

"No." His tone is calm, condemning, like a high-school principal who caught you blazing up in the stairwell. "No, you didn't." I want to flip him off. Why bother trying to convince this prick who's sold us out already? Bollinger leans closer. "Well?"

"My dad sent me."

There's silence for a few seconds before Bollinger lets out a deep sigh. "Okay, then. Have it your way." He turns to the men, nods, mutters something to them. One of them comes at me, pulls me up to my feet. "Phone," he says gruffly. I give it to him, and they all march out of the room. The last one out shuts the door. I hear a lock click and get the feeling I'll be stuck in here for a while.

I miss my phone, worry about possible messages from my mom or a text from Abby. But there's no service around here, anyway. I pace the room for a minute, bang on the door. "Hey, let me talk to Bollinger!"

I shout. No one answers. Once, I shout that I need to use the bathroom, and that they do respond to.

When I'm in the bathroom, which is right next to Abby's room, I run the tap, climb the sink, and call out to Abby through the ventilation duct. I count it as a minor victory when I hear her answer. I go back to my room, satisfied that at least now we've confirmed to each other that we're both alive.

The door locks behind me. I turn to the window high on the opposite wall, but all I can see there is the blank slate of gray sky. I pound on the door some more. No answer.

I take a long look at the ventilation duct. It's on the opposite wall, right above a pair of filing cabinets. Edged with rust, the cabinets are locked and the labels in their frames are yellow, blotted with stains. The labels have undecipherable headings in pencil: *Orion Bio EXP 3.62-11.62* and *Orion Lab SPECIMEN 1.61-5.64*, stuff like that. Both cabinets' drawers are locked, and both loaded with junk, making them heavy and stable enough.

I pull on my backpack and climb up on the cabinets. There are screws securing the cover over the duct, one at each corner. I should be able to use something—a coin or key, maybe—to turn them loose. Then I could push my way through the duct to Abby's room, and the two of us could find a way to escape.

My thoughts get only that far before I realize how stupid that plan is. Escape? How? Where? I wouldn't even fit through the opening.

I drop back on the couch and listen. It's damn quiet out there. I wonder how Abby's doing. I wonder if she's having better luck coming up with a plan to get us out. The generators are an almost-soothing white noise. Slowly, in the quiet, my exhaustion creeps over me.

Noises from the hallway shake me awake. The light in the room hasn't changed much, so I don't think I was out more than an hour. Above the sound of the generator, strange and muffled voices shout back and forth. Metal parts clank, wheels shudder and roll along the hallway like heavy equipment is being moved around. I press my ear to the door and pick up the thump of dollies being dragged up the metal stairs in the common room.

The numbers flash again. I see their outline against the wall of my closed eyelids. I close my eyes again. And they're there, clear as day! I rummage through my backpack and tear out a sheet of paper from a notebook, grab a pen.

It's an equation, drifting by, cloud-like, exactly the way you'd see a floater drift along and reset with every shift of your iris. It takes a minute, but I manage to write it all down: *E=1.2407e-31.* I blink again, and now it's gone. I pocket the piece of paper.

A key turns in the door, someone enters: Megan. I'm about to go off on her, but she gestures for me to keep quiet. She hands me a small notepad with words written on it. They read, "Triton is here. They're taking everything, our research, all equip + Nemo Two. They want u & Abby too."

She takes back the pad, scribbles more words, and shows me: "But be ready—M is coming. Be ready for a signal from me when she arrives."

Finally! News from Magnussen! I start to whisper back a reply when she hands me a pen.

"What about your big boss?" I write. "Does he know?"

"The big boss is nobody's friend but his own," she writes in response. "He doesn't know about M. But I informed her Triton is here. She will contact me when she's near & give me the rendezvous." She hands me back the pad, and I notice her listening at the door, fearful, nervous. Her behavior is starting to put me on edge.

"How's Abby?" I scribble. "Where is she?"

"Fine," Megan writes. "I was with her and gave her the news too." She flips a page on the pad and keeps scribbling a bit more, hands the pad back to me.

"M thought it best not to contact you," the page reads. "Too risky in case your phones fall into wrong hands." She takes the notepad from my hands, scribbles some more and holds it up for me. "I was never here," it reads.

She stops halfway to the door, turns, and hands me back my phone. "Keep it hidden," she whispers. From far down the hallway comes a booming noise—wheels rolling out of the elevator. Megan takes that as her cue and, without a sound, glides back out.

They want u & Abby. The words knock around in my head, and I find myself veering between fear over what it is Triton wants and a slow-boil anger that the bastards of the world—Bollinger, Dix, Triton—aren't going to leave us alone.

As my thoughts are pinging, the door opens again. Two young Asian men wave for me to get my pack and step out of the room. I do so, glad as hell to be out of this prison cell, and feel my fears subside a little when I see Abby in the hallway, her pack at her shoulder. Her eyes are alert, her face drawn, and she's tucking a piece of hair behind her ear. I take her hand. The men bark orders, waving for us to step out into the common room. And that's where we find our welcoming committee.

A blonde-haired woman with high cheekbones and daggers for eyes stands in a black trench coat, arms folded. There's something familiar about her, like I've seen her on the news or videos or something. As soon as she sees us, she extends her arms and her face breaks into a smile that reminds me of cracked ice. "Ah, our guests of honor," she says with affected grandness.

Megan, Anton, and Bollinger, in that order, stand with bags and briefcases nearby. Like a colony of busy ants, security personnel in Triton jumpsuits and black caps together with a few of Bollinger's assistants in coveralls carry boxes piled on dollies from the hallway, up and down the stairs, and in and out of the door at the top.

"I'll be your host on this last leg of your journey," says the woman. The face, the voice, they're familiar: Conner's shown me videos of this woman before, doing TED Talks and lectures for security think tanks and Wall Street fatheads. "Agostino," I say. "You're that woman, the CEO of Triton."

There's that smile again, and the calm, centered voice: "Call me Amanda."

"I already told him everything." I nod toward Bollinger.

"Nah," Bollinger says, shaking his head. "You told me whatever story your handlers wanted you to tell me."

"If you're so goddamn sure," I tell him, "why don't you just tell her who we're working for? Please. Tell her."

"All will become clear," he says smugly. "Am I right, Amanda?"

"*Mmm.*" Agostino nods with pleasure. "And thank you for your demonstration, Javier, you and your team. Sensational work. I wouldn't have believed it if I hadn't seen it for myself."

"I appreciate that, Amanda."

"Don't go keeping things from me again."

"Of course, of course. We're on the same page now."

"Still, considering you were working on a shoestring, you should be congratulated. And this place, this government bunker, secreting it all here, that's enough to get every billionaire and security agency on your ass. You ought to be in prison for holding out on us."

Awkward laughter trickles through the group. Abby and I just stand and stare at them like we're watching parents pretend not to be fighting.

Agostino keeps going: "I always knew you had a maverick streak about you. But you outdid yourself. Can you imagine?" On slender legs, in heels, she walks toward us. "An interstellar something-or-other piggybacks to Earth on an asteroid, we put its protons in an accelerator, and it releases energies that put fusion to shame. Is that about right, Ms. Chen?"

"Yes," Megan half-whispers, uncomfortably.

"We're on the cusp of the next giant leap, maybe the *ultimate* leap, in tech innovation." She lets out a satisfied sigh. "And Triton right in front where I like it. And here's the son of the very man who discovered it. I need to thank you, Dev. But maybe I should be thanking, what, your visions, your dreams, your *whatever* that brought you here with your father's secrets, hmm?" From the front pocket of her coat, she takes out the book. "I don't know what's true and what's not anymore, and I don't really care. As long as we clear out meddlers, competitors, interlopers, I'm good. That's why I came here personally. To make sure the rumors were true. And get a look at you two." She levels a hard stare, first at me, then Abby, back to me. "You cooperate with Triton, tell us your place in all this, the better your odds of seeing your families again."

Agostino shoves the book against my chest and lets it fall. I fumble for it as it drops, secure it in my hands. "Keep it. Useless trinket." She walks back to Bollinger and the others and, turning back to face us, rubs the chill of the room from her hands. "Well, that said, I hope you're all ready for an adventure."

From the corner of my eye, I see shapes moving on the monitors above the counter. I search the screens but see only technicians and security personnel darting across the monitors. I wonder if it's another trick of the brain—or a message.

"Javier?" she says.

Bollinger nods his head once and shoulders his bag. "I'm ready."

And, twice, Agostino shoots him. The blasts are loud. Megan screams. It's only after Bollinger has dropped to the floor like a bundle of laundry that I realize what I've just seen with my eyes: the CEO pulled out a short pistol from her coat and pulled the trigger—twice. Bollinger is now an inert pile between Megan and Anton. She fires at his body twice more.

Agostino hands the pistol to a member of her security detail. The shooting runs through me like an electric charge: I back up next to Abby, my breath caught in my throat. Megan looks horrified, her hand covering her mouth, and Anton's crouched down, calling, "Javier?" and when his boss doesn't move, he starts screaming at the CEO, "Why? We gave you what you wanted!"

Agostino doesn't even look at him. A security member steps through the door at the top of the stairs. "Ms. Agostino, all eyes reporting we're good to go."

"Good. Let's pack up. And pack these people up too. Ms. Chen, Mr. Veronin, boys and girls, you'll find that the more you cooperate, the better Triton will treat you. Who knows? You might even end up working for me."

Megan is consoling Anton, whispering to him, still bent over Bollinger's body.

"Ms. Agostino," calls the man at the top of the stairs. "I'm getting reports of a breach." Pressing his hand to his earpiece as if he's straining to hear, the man points off somewhere to my right and behind me, the southwest side of the compound. "A breach of the perimeter. They're telling me a blast door was breeched."

Before Agostino can reply, we hear gunfire from far down the hallway: echoing *rat-tat-tat* bursts that last about ten seconds, then silence.

"Red team, fall in," the guard orders. "Rest of you, evacuate all assets." He and three others, rifles trained, move past me and into the hallway. We watch them take the corner at the far end, turning left. In panic and confusion, we retreat from the doorway and crouch down next to Megan and Anton.

Agostino, hands at her hips, ignoring us, peers into the hallway, curious. Security personnel are evacuating technicians with their boxes and *thunk-thunking* dollies up the stairs and out of the bunker when more gunfire opens up in a far corner of the bunker. Abby and I cower down, reaching to protect each other.

"Abby"—I turn and look straight at her—"we've got to get out of here."

Metal clangs to the floor. It's a cover to one of the air ducts, and where it was there's now a square hole in the ventilation duct high on the wall. A shadow inside moves, and arms sprout out of the hole. We see it emerging, a crawler, its clothes just rags. Before anyone can react, it drops itself down on the guard below. His weapon falls from his arms as he spins and flails, screaming, but the crawler's holding tight, clawing and gnawing at his face, and it's like the two are locked in a sick dance.

The other guards back away. One of them fires into the wall, peppering it with holes, till another stops him. The blasts are ear-splitting. Two technicians rush in to pull the thing off the man's head, but the crawler's quick and slippery, and it leaps back onto the wall and slithers up and through the opening. His victim staggers, swinging blindly, and collapses and the others keep firing at the duct, at the wall. Where his face was there's something else, flapping, shredded, bloodied. All-out pandemonium fills the room as guards, technicians—both Triton's and Bollinger's—start to scramble and flee up the stairs, falling over each other. Security yells for order—*as if!*—and surround Agostino. Together, they push through the stampede up the stairs and clear the hell out of here. Gunsmoke fills my nostrils.

"Let's go," Abby says to me.

"There's a hatch." It's Megan, grasping my arm. "On the other side of the compound."

"The bullpen?" Abby says.

"Do you know it?"

"I think so," Abby answers. Over the past few days, she and I have walked the corridors of this bunker enough to know every turn, room, and corner.

"Through the hatch, you'll be on the west side of the compound. Go! Wait there for Magnussen!"

Security guards grab at us, but Abby and I grab our packs and sprint headlong into the hallway and, as we do, a crawler's head, eyes bulging, is grimacing from the duct opening. The room is a nightmare of shouts, slamming, fleeing bodies, and gunfire. As we run, I shove my dad's journal into my pack, think of Megan and Anton as we near the end of the hallway. "I hope to God they'll be okay," I say, looking back one last time.

We make our first turn in this fluorescent, cluttered maze. After a right turn, then a left, we're facing the freight elevator—just a wooden gate closed over a black mouth. After a second to catch our breaths, we're going to full steam around more turns, down two flights of stairs, and through hallways. In all the madness, I suddenly lose my sense of direction, but Abby says we're almost there. She points to green metal door with a biohazard sign.

"I remember that door. It's just past—here!"

Once we're in the bullpen, we position ourselves beneath the hatch—a steel bulbous circle in the ceiling about seven feet up with a small wheel on its front. We push one of the desks under the hatch, climb up, and I give the wheel a hard counter-clockwise turn. There's a clang and as I pull on the hatch, it swings downward to reveal rungs that run up about ten feet. We climb them to a second hatch. This one's got sliding bolts, which I pull aside, and a handle, which I give a quarter-turn. The hatch pops open on hinges, and we're looking up at the boundless night sky.

There's this weird sensation that we're breaking out of prison, and we should be celebrating the brisk air and the liberating stars. But the freedom lasts only for a second or two. None of this amounts to anything if we don't find Magnussen. Or she doesn't find us.

About twenty feet away, marking the compound's west boundary, there's the shape of the fence, topped with razor wire. Past the fence, the ground falls off in a slope into blackness. Everything is blotched out by the night. After the madness inside the bunker, the silence is surreal; we can even hear the crickets. We huddle into our jackets, staying close, and walk to the left along the fence, but two minutes later, the way ends in a cement wall. We decide against going the opposite direction; it would take us back to the compound's main entrance, the lion's den. We look through the chain-link for any signs of Magnussen or her truck. There's nothing out there but shades upon shades of black. We can't see a thing.

And that's when the world lights up.

Above and to the north, a meteor tears across the western sky. It's not as bright as the one that exploded over LA that night, but it's enough to light up the pine country for miles around, creating this netherworld of shadow-play. For a few seconds, it's like there's a gigantic klieg lamp overhead. Seconds later, there's the airburst, loud as artillery as it explodes far to the west, miles away, that gets us covering our ears.

"Check that out," Abby says, mesmerized. Smaller meteors are scratching out trails high above in silent pulses. They enter the atmosphere in ones and twos, north to south, east to west. Some track for miles and miles across the night, others appear only for a flash before they wink out of existence, like players crossing on and off a stage, too shy to be seen for more than a second.

I don't know how long we've been staring at them when Abby whispers, "Hey, who is that?" Then sharply, "There!" She points into the darkness at a shape about thirty feet away on our side of the compound. I fumble for the phone in my backpack hoping to aim a flashlight on it when the shape—tall, human, moving in quick strides—comes near.

"Shit. They found us. Let's go for the wall."

But we've gone a few steps when a voice stops us in our tracks: "You won't get far. I wouldn't try it."

The shape is only ten or so feet away, still cloaked in darkness . . . until the sky glows in the satanic illumination of another house-size rock blazing up the atmosphere. It's Dix.

"Run!" Abby yells, and I feel my insides jump as I take big, bounding steps. Maybe, maybe we can make the wall, maybe we can scale it—it was only seven feet or so. To my shock and surprise, we make the wall, take a running leap at it, and our fingers clamp on to the top edge. I scramble like hell to the top of the wall, hoist my body up, even get one leg over when I'm aware that Abby isn't with me anymore. That instant, I hear her muffled shriek.

"Cool your heels, kid, or I'll snap your friend's neck right now."

He's got a flashlight beam aimed at my face, blinding me for a second. "Get your ass down . . . unless you *want* to keep running, in which case you'll be doing it alone."

I climb back down and see that Dix has Abby by one arm. "You got me," I tell him. "Let her go." The thought of him even mentioning Conner and then threatening Abby makes me want to kill him so bad right now.

"Walk next to me," he orders. His voice is hoarse and low like he's getting off on all this. "Try anything, and I will not hesitate to deliver pain on your friend."

I do as he says, keeping to his left as he walks along with Abby on his right, gripped by her upper arm. Dix's flashlight leads the way up the bumpy, grassy path, and this close, I can smell the body odor and cigarettes hovering on him like a disease. Even the slightest thought of grabbing Abby and breaking into a run leaves me when I see the weapon holstered on the strap high on his back.

"You've been slippery ever since Tahoe. And that tea party in there with Triton complicated things. But my hounds gave them a good fright, and I got you now."

His flashlight happens on a pair of feet then takes in a body lying on its back. Like a morbid find in a nighttime scavenger hunt. I wince and can hear Abby's gasp. It's one of Bollinger's guards. A bullet wound flowers on one side of his belly. "Just the man I was looking for," Dix mutters, veering left toward the fence.

The beam of his flashlight leads us to a crudely squared hole cut into the fence. Dix reaches behind him and pulls the weapon—a short-barreled rifle—from its strap. Gesturing with the flashlight in his other hand, he directs us to the hole. "This is where we exit. Go."

I crouch and slide through the opening. The range of the flashlight gives up nothing more than a slope of dirt and scrub. I scramble to one side on my haunches so Abby can crawl through.

"Now you," Dix commands.

The world glows again, another large meteor flashes across the northern sky, lighting up a landscape of pines and cypresses. Shadows shift, my heart pounds, and I cover my head. Through fingers, I glimpse a lone service road, a curve of it at the foot of the slope, and before the blazing head of the meteor booms over the horizon, there's a vehicle. The boom produces smaller booms like a staccato of cannon fire.

"Beautiful," Dix says. "So many visitors tonight."

I hear its hiss before I see its eyes, red glinting points in the blackness six feet from me. I know that's not a raccoon or a mountain lion.

"Dix," I mumble.

He makes a sick, cooing noise from deep in his throat. "That's a nice boy," Dix whispers and makes kissing, clucking sounds. The thing sniffs, responds with spastic noises, a gurgling mix of growls and the moaning you'd hear from a kid with a stomachache. Grass rustles. It scrapes forward from the dark and into the beam from Dix's flashlight, and now I can see it, on all fours, humped like a hyena, with a Mohawk-like ridge of rough hair down its head and back. Dix reaches an arm through the opening, lets the crawler sniff his hands, then he strokes the crawler's head and back. "That's a good boy. These guys did a number on those poor bastards in there. Handling them is a bit tricky, isn't it? Yes, it is. Yes, it is. They're temperamental." Dix slowly pulls back his arm. "One false move, and you're—" He snaps his fingers, and it's like a spell's been broken. The thing leans toward me, inches away, snarling and hissing, his eyes wide and carnivorous. I'm rooted in place; if I run, it's dead certain I'll be shredded in seconds.

"Dev." It's Abby, imploring, anxious. "Do something," she screams at Dix. "Kill it!"

Dix only cackles, his bearded, broken-toothed face visible in the reflected light. "Let him play a bit."

"Dix, we're already cooperating," she pleads. "Call him off."

The thing's face is gnarly, like a nine-year-old's face but with a monkey snout. It screeches at me—its breath is death—and it starts maneuvering around me, lunging once in a while. I stay with it. If I turn my back, I suspect, the thing will jump. "Call it off," I tell Dix.

He chuckles under his breath. "Just having some fun now."

I'm not aware of it until it punctures the cloud of adrenaline in my head, but there's an engine, the sound of an engine. And the grating of tires on gravel. And from my side, there's a burst of light. Another meteor? No! It's headlights!

A horn severs the air as the SUV closes in across the field, tires sawing up the slope. Dix begins firing rounds at it, his laughter rising above the roar of the engine. The crawler grimaces at the oncoming vehicle, twenty feet away now and closing, as I do a rolling leap backward out of the way, hearing the crawler screech. I glimpse back to see it leap headfirst into the vehicle's grill—it's swallowed up instantly—before the SUV plows into the fence. Dix gets off one more shot, the barrel lighting up his grin in flash-frame before he's mowed down under fence and wire, and the whole thing's dragged twenty feet before the SUV skid-stops in a glowing cloud of dust. I get to my feet and rush over to make sure Abby's okay: she is. And seeing her is a feeling like there's still hope in the world. We give each other a moment, pressing each other close, make sure the other's still alive and not a dream.

"No time for that," a voice shouts from the truck.

"Oh my God!" Abby cries. "It's you!"

"Get in."

Abby jumps into the front and gives Magnussen a hug as I slide into the back. I lean forward so I can touch Magnussen's shoulder, making sure she's real too. "You nailed that timing." The thought of Dix and the crawler both pulverized beneath this truck makes me want to puke.

"I did, didn't I?" Magnussen says. "Let's move before Dix wakes up."

I remember Bollinger's words to me now, that first day we met, how Dix was both human—and not.

"Megan and Anton," Abby says, still catching her breath. "We left them inside. Triton was packing the place up when those crawlers attacked."

"They killed Bollinger," I add. "That woman, the CEO, shot him."

Magnussen shifts the SUV into reverse then pauses. "Can't say he didn't have it coming."

"He was selling us out to Triton," says Abby.

"Said we were working for enemy agents," I say. "And we lured you into bringing us here."

Magnussen pauses and looks back at me, slowly. "Are you?"

"What? No!"

"Relax, I'm kidding." She backs up the SUV, away from the tangled mesh of fence, wire, and corpses. I don't even look; a part of me is paranoid that Dix is going to stand right back up, unharmed. Magnussen cuts the headlights and, very slowly, we drive back to the hatch that Abby and I had used to get out of the complex. If Megan and Anton are still alive, we want to "retrieve them," as Magnussen puts it.

"Magnussen, did you find out anything?" Abby asks. "Anything while you were away?"

"Well, you'll want to know your family is alive," reports Magnussen. Abby inhales sharply, brings a hand to her chest. She begins to cry quietly. I reach over the seat and touch her back as she wipes at her face. "I cross-checked their names with the manifests of flights going from LA to Chicago over the past ten days, found their names. I also ran a check on Chicago hospitals, and your brother's name came up. No other news except that's he was admitted."

Abby clears her throat, straightens in her seat, and nods.

"Getting there will be a bit tricky."

"What about Sacramento?" Abby asks. "Can't we fly out?"

"That way is blocked. Whole state's a cluster because of the fires, disease quarantine, and protests. Best thing is to get out of the state. Canada's our best bet. Might be easier to get back to your family if we went that way. We could arrange for air transport from there."

"Did you find out anything . . . about my mom?" The words come out before I'm ready to say them.

Magnussen doesn't answer for a while, then: "News out of LA isn't as cheerful."

My breath catches in my chest, my gut feels in a knot. We're almost at the hatch now. Magnussen slows and stops the truck. After a deep breath, she continues, "It does appear that your mom . . . passed away four days ago. At LA Memorial."

A bomb explodes in my chest.

"How do you know this?" My brain is numb, my words are numb.

"The same hacker I used to get info about Abby's family. He hacked into LA Memorial's hospital records. Shows she died of encephalitis and respiratory complications." She cuts the engine. "I'm very sorry, Dev."

My mind's refusing to process this. I'd dreaded it for days. I'd guessed it too. And, as the days passed, I'd gotten more and more convinced it was true. The dream was a prophecy. I reach for the door handle, and now a thought forms full-grown: I will never see my mother again.

It's a very simple fact, but admitting it to myself now, wrapping my heart around it, is way beyond my comprehension. It's like being dropped into an unfathomable depth and finding your way around with a single, feeble searchlight. I don't even realize I'm crying, don't realize Abby is sitting next to me until I feel her hand on my shoulder, the feel of her forehead against mine. We both cry for a while before Magnussen tells us we need to move if we want to make it out of this place alive and uncaptured.

Abby and I get it together enough to climb out and join Magnussen at the hatch.

"Stay close, just follow me." After checking her pistol, she carefully turns the handle on the hatch and opens it. She gestures for us to keep quiet then lowers herself on the rungs of the chute. One thought penetrates the numbness that's settled in my mind after hearing about my mom: the thought that we have to enter this horrible place again. But it's either this, or we stay out here and chance Dix finding us.

From below, Magnussen gives us the all-clear. We follow. First Abby, then me.

CHAPTER EIGHTEEN

The scene we descend into is creepier than before. It's the same bullpen cluttered with dust-covered office furniture and defunct communications equipment. What we drop into is more a feeling: a creeping dread. The feeling where you know something evil has happened, and you're somewhere you shouldn't be. Like my nightmare of wandering the hospital and finding my mom— Can't think about that now.

A breaker must've tripped, or the lights got blown out by gunfire. Jags of fluorescent light interrupt swaths of darkness along stretches and turns in the corridors. We can smell the gunfire, pungent and smoky, as we go deeper, and Abby and I pull our jackets up over our noses. We retrace our steps, past the elevator, till we get to the hallway before the final corner, and here's where we see signs of the massacre: I don't know if it's the bodies or the blood I notice first, the details are tangled. They're at the far end, human-shaped bundles on the floor, surrounded by smears and blooms of blood, as if there was a deadly fight over a gallon of red paint.

"What in hell happened here?" Magnussen says, slowly and low, the shock on her face obvious.

We tell her about the crawler attacks, the situation in the common room just as we escaped.

Magnussen nods. "Whenever I run into Franklin Dix, those crawlers aren't far behind."

"He commands them," I whisper. "I saw him control that one who almost got me."

"He can. He can communicate with them in crude, simple ways."

Abby and I steal glances at each other. "So, he's like a, what—simianoid whisperer or something?" she asks.

Magnussen shrugs and nods. "If you were a geneticist, you'd consider Dix the greatest achievement in the history of the field."

I store those words away in my mind as the sound of the generator grows louder. In the common room, there are signs of slaughter and evacuation. Bits of food, furniture, and tools like hammers and screwdrivers, packing tape and wrenches are scattered everywhere. The guard with the chewed-off face lies on the floor, slumped against the cushions of the couch like a drunk. The wall above the couch, all the way up to the open ventilation duct, is peppered with bullet holes, stained with blood, with child-size hand- and footprints that lead in and out of the hole.

"Good God," Magnussen says.

Triton didn't take everything; there are still cabinets and files sitting on dollies here. Wooden planks laid down on the stairway create a ramp up to the front door, now closed. They also left Bollinger's body slumped on the floor, near the foot of the stairs.

Abby points to the surveillance monitor above the counter. The six views on the monitor show lit-up areas of the compound and the lab below. The lab cam on the lower right shows the control wall and the pod beyond the glass, its ports glowing blue. Computer monitors on the table are scrolling data of all kinds and blinking messages like "System Operations" and "Nemo2 Online" on and off in the corners of screens.

The upper left panel shows the door in the outer wall—that secret door that Magnussen used to get us all into the facility a week ago. Triton guards, their rifles pointed at Bollinger's workers, shout orders at them, motioning with their rifles for them to step it up as they haul equipment and cabinets on dollies. One by one, the workers disappear through the door followed by the guards.

The panel below it shows the interior of the garage, the one we pulled into when we first entered the compound, the one attached to the house fronting the street. The garage bulb spills light out into the driveway where workers are bustling, stacking equipment, cabinets, boxes into the back of a moving truck.

Then we see a flicker of movement in the panel above it: the one on the open door in the outer wall. Shapes dart from off-screen and charge through the door. They're crawlers, three of them, bounding through on knuckles. The panel to the right of that is a view of the tunnel: nothing at first, just a dim-lit cement corridor that looks like a phantom crypt. First comes the wave of fleeing humans on the screen. Seconds later, we see the crawlers overwhelm them, tackling and gnashing. It's like watching a scene out of the savannah. Abby gasps.

I turn to the view of the garage. Now it's like watching the blissfully ignorant victims of a disaster in the seconds before the disaster hits. As we watch, I see a figure running from the side of the driveway, around the moving truck—Megan! She has something in her hand—the notepad. She steps up to the camera, glances around to make sure no one's watching, and holds the notepad up to the camera. It reads: "They're destroying the lab to wipe leftover evidence. Ten mins? Evacuate now if you see this."

Megan pockets the notepad and hurries back down the driveway when the tsunami of terror hits. Crawlers invade the garage. Guards with rifles start firing, others flee. Three guards are quickly overpowered, they stagger and topple onto the driveway, crawlers gnawing on their heads. The truck, its cargo door wide open, loading ramp dragging, lurches down the driveway, people hanging on for dear life in the cargo. One of them topples into the drive, gets to his feet, and runs like hell as the truck smashes into parked vehicles. The truck rolls out of view followed by two fleeing SUVs. The rout leaves three dead bodies in the driveway, and crawlers tearing at their flesh on camera.

From behind us, we hear a cough and turn to find Bollinger crumpled on the floor, holding out one shaky arm like he's beckoning us. He coughs again, wheezes. Magnussen sits on the bottommost step and helps him get propped against her leg so he can talk and breathe. The effort sets off a coughing fit, but Bollinger manages to splutter out a few words. "Don't let them destroy it." He strains, breathes.

"What's it to you?" I tell him. "You'll be dead anyway."

Now a faint smile appears on his grizzled face, his eyes are lost behind his smudged glasses. He spurts out a cackle. "Serves . . . serves me right. Where—? Megan, Anton . . .?"

"Gone," Magnussen says. "They took them."

The news registers like heartbreak on Bollinger's face. "Then it's over." No one speaks. He's right. It *is* over. "Listen," he splutters. "If you care about"—he coughs—"your father's work . . . save the sphere. If destroyed, all is lost. Because they don't care about the discovery—" He stops to catch his breath. "They don't care to further what we found. They have their own plans. Took a bullet to see it." He emits a short, guttural laugh that turns into a racking cough.

"Easy, easy," Magnussen says.

"How do we save it?" I ask him. "Megan said the lab is rigged to go in ten minutes."

Bollinger listens, thinks, then shuts his eyes, shakes his head. It's a futile gesture of defeat. "Then the future—" he spurts out, "is dark." His chest collapses in a final breath.

Magnussen takes off his glasses and closes the lids of his eyes. She sets him down.

"Destroy years of work," Magnussen says reflectively. "Why would Triton do that?"

"Simple," I tell her, just as it becomes clear to me. "It was never meant to leave here. He said himself they have different plans."

"So . . . blow it up, destroy all evidence?" Magnussen says, puzzled.

"No trace of Bollinger's work was ever going to leave here," I reply. "Easier to let the whole lab go. Have Triton take over and take complete credit."

"'They have their own plans,'" Abby says, contemplatively. "Wonder what that's about."

"They know that Bollinger's experiments all failed here, he's a whack job as far as they're concerned. But they got what they wanted: the drives, the data—"

"Look, we can't worry about that now," Magnussen says. "We've got to get out of here. Best bet is back out through the hatch and hope to hell we don't see Dix again."

Like that, we're on our feet again, hitching up our packs. "Speaking of," Abby says in a singsong, pointing at the monitor. On the garage cam, we see him.

He's inspecting the slaughter and the driveway after the panicked retreat of the Triton team. He lets the three crawlers feed a little longer, patting their shoulders. Then he strides off-camera, just under the cam, in the direction of the trapdoor off the garage. Moments later, the crawlers leap off in his direction. We're mesmerized, rooted to the floor, knowing what's to come. Now the cam in the tunnel shows Dix heading toward the compound. In our direction.

"Dev!" Magnussen's voice shocks me back to life. She's waiting on me and Abby, halfway out of the room. "Now! Hatch!"

We speed out of that room, into the hallway, which feels even narrower now, through dark and lit passages. Down a stairway, around corners, and we're passing the elevator. It's a lightless stretch. We charge on, single file, when I blink. And I see the equation. I slow down, scrutinizing the numbers in the back of my eyelids. *E=1.2407e-31.*

"Dev!" Abby reaches for my hand, I take it. "Come on!"

I dig into my pants pocket and feel for the corner of folded paper. Still there. There's a tube light in the bullpen giving off a weak, white gleam that shows us the way to the hatch.

Abby goes up first. Magnussen pushes me forward under the hatch, her eyes on the hallway. "Go on, Dev." I climb up, make it to the opened lid, where Abby's hand awaits.

And that's when I feel this sudden opposing pull. Like something snagging at my heart, like there is another path.

Magnussen climbs out of the hatch. She and Abby are pulling open the doors of the SUV when I speak up: "I can't do this."

And it's like the world's stopped spinning. Their eyes lock on me.

"Get in, D," Abby says. "We don't have time."

"Why am I here?" I mumble. The news about my mom flickers through my brain. She didn't get to see me before she died. Over and over the past few days, I tried to put myself in her head, worrying about me and admitting herself into the hospital, unsure if I was all right or if she'd survive.

I've wondered, at what point did she realize she would never see me again? Maybe it was exactly when I was dreaming about her. Did she feel as alone as I did when I found out she was gone?

I wish I could've told Conner that he was my best friend. I wish I could've thanked him for saving my life, so I could be here, in this position of choosing my path. I won't have his death be in vain. I can't.

Someone, some*thing* sent me those messages, has been sending them. If it's not my father, it's his spirit then, or a source I can't even imagine, whatever its motives.

The last memory of my father is one he isn't even in: the snap of the hallway light against the outline of my bedroom door, the voices of intruders, the sound of his things being gutted from our home.

I've been walking along the edge of a crater left behind ever since, and what I do now will either save me or condemn me. All this and more is pulling me from getting into the SUV.

"I can't."

"Dev?" Abby looks really scared now, and it hurts to see her pain. She gets out of the truck. "What're you doing?"

I look at Magnussen. "Please take care of her, and please get her to her family."

"So you're just going to ditch me, is that it?" Abby says.

Her anger, confusion, the tears filling her eyes break my heart. "Abby, the pod, it's down there. They were prepping another run before Triton showed. The pod's active, you saw it on the panel. Operational. And in a few minutes, it'll be gone. They'll destroy it."

"Are you serious?"

"If I don't do this, everything will be for nothing. Everything you and Conner went through to bring me here."

She swallows, nods sharply.

"My road ends here." I lock eyes on Abby. "You need to go with her. Your family needs you." Shit. Now *I* want to cry.

We pull into each other. Hold on for what I wish were forever. It's clear to me now, this moment.

My dad studied the origins of the cosmos, and this moment feels to me like what he'd call an event horizon. I'd been drawing toward it from the moment I first had the dreams, the moment we first got on the road . . . maybe even as far back as the moment I first felt my father's loss.

I'm aware of Abby's lips on mine. "I love you," I whisper. Because it's the only and last honest thing I know. She whispers back the same words, and they're enough for me to do what I need to do.

It's pitch black. I use the flashlight on my phone to guide me from the bullpen and into the hallway. Within minutes, the air's stale and close. The generator was either turned off or it shut down; I hated its constant racket before, but now I miss it.

More than once, I get the overpowering urge to turn back, climb the hell out of here. The thought of Abby and Magnussen gone and being alone here triggers instant panic, terror. I shake the thoughts away, keep my eyes on the halo of light from the phone.

My heart's hammering now as I venture deeper into the hallways, recognizing the landmarks of random furniture, files, and, once, the stacked oxygen cylinders along the side of the hallway. I look back—nothing but blackness. Panic rises. I breathe it out. *Don't ever look back again.* To the side, on top of a cabinet, I notice a utility knife. I grab it on impulse.

There it is: the elevator. And my heart sinks. Without the power, how am I going to get down? *Quiet, Dev. One step at a time.*

I swing the outer gate open, and my phone light reveals the shaft. It recedes toward the faint square roof of the elevator, maybe thirty feet down. I reach out and grab hold of one of the cables. It's sturdy, taut, but slippery, so I hold on tight. Like that, I tuck my phone in my pocket, and start clambering down into what feels like the throat of some sleeping beast.

I feel nothing, just numbness now, powered by a weird internal battery in my brain or my heart that keeps me going. *One step at a time.*

As soon as my feet land on the steel roof of the elevator, I pull out my phone and locate the ceiling hatch. There's a rusted brown handle along one side of it. I get a good grip of it and pull. The hatch opens on a hinge and emits the loudest, nastiest creaking noise you want to hear right now. I drop down into the elevator, and it's absolute black down here.

I feel like an undersea diver in the depths with my light. The darkness has a solidity to it, it's a living thing. I shine my light through the elevator's gate and into the hallway. Nothingness.

I roll open both sets of gates, step on through. It's a straight shot now to the control room at the very end. The air is warm, hard to breathe, now that the climate control is out, and the hallway feels even longer in the dark. A metallic clang sounds from the ducts, somewhere distant. I freeze, strain to hear more, my heart beating. Seconds pass. Silence again.

I continue, one step and then another. My phone light is an angel in the darkness. *Photons are brave.* A hallway juts off to the right, the light revealing a dingy gray corridor. Every door along it is bolted shut. I keep walking, my breath quickening. At the end of the hallway, I try the door to the lab. Locked. I try the control room door. It turns open. Like it was waiting all along.

The phone light finds the room ransacked: in the rushed evacuation, a couple of monitors lie abandoned on the console, one face down, the other with its screen shattered. But the cables, files, the cabinet-size server, all that's gone, hauled away. The board in the corner's been wiped bare, the table, chairs, cabinets, everything's in shambles.

On the other side of the window, in the center of the lab, is what I saw on the panel on the monitor up in the common room: the pod with its interior glowing an electric blue, propped up on a scaffold. It's like a spaceship that's landed in these ruins.

I peer into the hallway. The phone light barely reaches the elevator gate. I can't see anyone or anything beyond it.

Go, Dev. Go. What're you standing around for?

I go.

Back in the control room, I pocket my phone, haul the console out of the way, and grab a chair off the floor. I swing it against the window once, twice, three times before the panel begins to crack. I set the chair down to catch my breath. A piece of metal clatters on the floor along the back wall, and I jump back. My hands fidget around in my pocket for my phone. I shine its light toward the noise, suspecting the source before I see the repulsive face, the bristling mane. The crawler hisses at the light and springs back to pounce.

Adrenaline runs like battery acid through my arms and chest as I give the chair one more swing, everything I got, and the window blasts open. The hole's big enough. I jump into the lab and hear the snarl close at my heels.

As I race toward the pod, I can see that it's up on girders about five feet off the ground. Its blue light spills out of a port that—shockingly—lies open on the pod's underside. I pocket my phone, guided now by the blue light of the pod's interior.

I slide through the scaffolding and, jumping, grab hold of the rim of the opened port. I pull myself up, propping my elbows on the rim. I try to hoist myself through the port when I'm pulled down by a massive force. I'm yanked through the port and land on the floor so violently that my breath gets knocked out of me. The crawler's got me by the legs. I flail and kick as hard as I can and get the crawler off me for a second. It hisses and blinks its coal-red eyes, as I scramble, crab-like, on my butt and feel a hard object in my back pocket: The utility knife.

The crawler writhes and rolls onto its hands and knees, leaps at me, but not before I've managed to slide out the blade. In a blinding rush, I slash and make contact with gristle. I slash again and stab. The knife plunges into the thing's throat.

I can smell its mouth: a smell like rotting death.

I hear myself grunting with anger, with terror, with every ounce of energy I have as I slash and drive the blade into the thing's mouth, face, its throat. It gurgles and goes slack. And with one last gurgling gasp, I swear I hear it speak-hiss a human voice behind the burr of in-human noises. Close to my ear, it sinks, stinking like decay, dropping to the cement, and the words "thank you" rasp out of its throat. Then more clearly, so there's no doubt, with its last breath: "Thank you." And it turns its head away and goes limp, eyes open.

Hitching up my pack, I jump through the port.

CHAPTER NINETEEN

There's a T-bar on the hatch door that I turn clockwise, sealing the pod shut. The pod itself is a perfect sphere, and the blue glow I'd seen comes from a pair of computer monitors mounted before a seat bolted to the floor. There's a platform for a keyboard and, behind the seat, what looks like a stainless-steel cylinder inserted into a piping system that leads out, I'm guessing, to the collider apparatus. The cylinder must be the ion bottle used in the proton collisions.

I set my pack at my feet and place myself in the seat. There's a blizzard of readouts on both monitors in discrete panels: life support, pod-pressurization readings on the left monitor; collider stats on the right. At the bottom of the right-side screen, a message reads: "Click START to initialize collider sequence." Using the trackpad on the keyboard, I point the arrow on the screen on START and click. Nothing happens. I click again. Nothing.

Then I realize there's a red error message next to a blank field on the screen: No Value Entered. I click on the field, my mind scrambling. It's a set of fields under the heading Wave Energy Dynamics. There are three fields, one with u, one with l, one with E next to their fields. Frequency. Wavelength. Energy.

Energy! I pull out the paper from my front pocket. Unfold it. *E=1.2407e-31.*

My hands shaking, I tap the keys, entering the number into the E field, one by excruciating one. I hit Enter. The other two fields auto-fill with values for Frequency and Wavelength. Now there's a progress window as a red line starts filling a gauge from left to right. Under the gauge, a message reads: Configuring Collision Dynamics. Holy shit! This thing works!

I fumble with the belt system and figure out how to fasten the shoulder and crotch straps to the two ends of the lap belt and lock the harness down with the pull of a latch attached to the lap buckle. I tighten the shoulder straps and yank on the harness. It's not budging. Good! I turn my attention back to the gauge, and as I do, hear a tap-tap on the porthole behind me.

I turn, sick with dread, to see Dix's head, lit from below by the cone of his own flashlight. There's no expression that I can read on his face, just eyes like stone-cold marbles behind large square glasses, a set mouth inside a scraggy beard. I check the screen: The red line has made progress, but slowly and not enough. I look again. But Dix is gone. It's just a black porthole.

It's come to this now. Waiting. The air in the pod becomes heavy, close, like a gloved hand over my mouth. Nothing more I can do.

The bar on the floor of the pod jerks. I know Dix can tear the port open in one go, and the feeling of being a trapped animal floods my mind, trapped between the whims of the invader and this machine.

A beep sounds from the monitor. "Configuration Complete," it reads. "Press ENTER." I do. Nothing happens. I press ENTER a couple of more times again. Nothing. The T-bar jolts again. "Shit!" I want to bring a fist down on the keyboard, but my thoughts are interrupted by a huge sound that overwhelms the pod. It's like a jet engine powering up and gathering force.

Now I feel pressure. A pressure like a huge invisible animal against my body. I don't even check the screen. I shut my eyes as the world fills with a blazing light. The force gets more intense until it's got me pinned against the seat back. I can't move. I try to lift my arm against it, and it drops like a dead thing onto the armrest. The whooshing, from wherever it's coming, overwhelms every other thought or sensation. There is shuddering, and I feel the pod roll backward. I'm upside-down, and the pod's rolling every which way for what feels like seconds—or it could be minutes—before a sensation of freefall overwhelms everything. Weightless. I chance taking a peek around and see my backpack pinwheeling gently in midair. I squeeze my eyes shut again because the light through the portholes is daggering my retinas like the sun is right outside the pod. Slowly, slowly, I find myself slipping into a dark pool deep in my mind. I dream of forever.

The air is stifling and still. But there's no noise, no one trying to break into the pod. I'm still in my seat, buckled in, but the pod is rolled onto its back side, and I'm facing upward. And another thing: the pod is pitching and rolling gently, fluidly. And each time it rolls, there's a dull thud beneath me as if the pod is brushing on a hard, gritty surface. Daylight streams in from the porthole above me. The messages on both monitors read: "All systems normal."

I'm achy, bleary, but not groggy. I go over my name, address, all the people and events that got me here and feel pretty sure I'm okay. At least my head's clear, whatever's happened.

How long was I out? Why is that daylight?

I lurch forward out of the seat, push against the seat mount with my legs so I can reach the handle of the hatch with my arms. I turn it counterclockwise. It clicks, and I push. The hatch swings open, letting in a rush of warm air that smells of the sea, and all I see is the lapping surface of water.

I start, seized by fear I'm about to drown. The pod sways, filled with sounds of water lapping against the sides, the silty texture of sand underneath. The pod isn't filling with water. I'm okay. I peer out again but can't see anything because the hatch is on the underside.

I push upward again and swing my legs over the lip of the hatch, my shoes dunking into water. *Shit.* I draw my leg back and take off my shoes, socks, and shove them into my backpack. I pull on my pack and roll up my jeans. Breathing, I pivot my body all the way around so that I'm leg-first through the hatch. Carefully, I lower myself out.

The water is warm. I think of a shallow Pacific tide pool at the end of a scorching California summer. It goes up to my knees. The curve of the pod keeps me from standing up. I take a few short steps so I can straighten up and get a look around.

The sun's over my right shoulder, and I shield my eyes from ripples of water winking at me like diamonds. My eyes adjust to the immense brightness. Keeping my eyes shielded, I scan where I am.

This is a cove. To my left, it opens out into a massive body of water, a lake, river, or sea—I have no clue. Lush vegetation towers up only yards away from the shore and hugs the shoreline all the way around the cove.

How the hell did I get here? This is not California. This is not where I was. Is this some kind of trick?

The trees are exotic, tropical; I don't know their names. Many have root systems that plumb the water like millions of fingers, others have pinwheels of fronds that fan out above thick, lattice-like trunks. Close to the water, there are spiky fronds and feathery fronds, stands of banana leaves as big as hammocks, and, behind these, there are strange, towering, flat-topped trees. Birds circle above them on the far shore.

I wade the three or four yards to shore and drop to the sand, exhausted, unslinging my backpack. A warm breeze carries the smell of flowers, vegetation, and mud. I lift my face to catch the direction of the wind, picking up odors of fish, when I notice two moons in the blue sky: a closer one, which looks like a worn ancient coin, its markings cryptic, and about five finger-widths to its left, a smaller, fainter one, which looks like a daub of blue-white paint.

I'm hallucinating. I have to be. There is no other known explanation.

I'm taking all this in, trying to understand what just happened to me, when a gentle, familiar voice calls out: "Hello?"

I turn, and he's there, standing about twenty feet away, in the trees. Thin, bearded, with a thatch of dark hair touched with gray. He's got on a checked shirt, the sleeves rolled up, jeans, hiking shoes—it's like seeing the person from the dream come to life. Could it be? Something in the eyes, kind, searching . . . I get to my feet and try to rub this mirage from my eyes.

But he's still there.

"Dad?"

"Who're you?" He steps onto the sand, and his hands go up to his face. "Is that . . .?" He walks toward me, a hand to his mouth. His eyes become watery, and he staggers and stops, a couple of yards away.

Grasping on to any figment of logic left, I say again, "Dad?"

He glances at the pod and back to me, and finally, under his breath, mutters, "No way."

"It's me," I tell him.

He takes one step back, and, in a whisper, asks, "How long? How long have I been gone?"

I swallow. "Ten years."

His eyes go wide, mouth opened to speak. He's like that for a moment, frozen. "Holy shit," he whispers. "Dev."

In two strides, he's got his arms around me. Now I know it's him. I hug him back. He's not as tall as I remember, but it's me who's grown up!

"But," I go on, "but how?"

He grasps my shoulder, touches my cheek, beams at me in wonder. "There are so many hows in your mind right now, son." He wipes his eyes. "And whys and wheres."

I'm aware of nodding dumbly in response.

"First of all," he says, "you're not seeing things. You're okay, do you understand?"

I take a deep breath. He goes on, "I know you're probably both terrified and relieved to hear that. I'm still trying to figure it all out myself, but, seeing you—and it is *you*, right, Dev?"

Again, I nod, more vigorously this time.

"You're seventeen."

"Yes."

"So . . . one thing is for sure. We have time dilation. My God." He backs up a few steps, never taking his eyes off me. As he's doing this, I can see that he hasn't aged from the pictures and memories of my childhood.

Words don't form. *Can't* form.

"Dad," I finally ask, "how long have you been here?"

He looks off to the pod again. "Seventy-three days." We stare at each other, astonished. "I just can't believe you made it. You made it."

He walks to the edge of the shore. "And you got my messages, didn't you?" He turns to me with this goofy grin of disbelief. "I wasn't sure if anyone would get them."

Messages.

"I got all of them, Dad, I dreamed them."

"*Dreamed* them. Then it *did* work." He begins to laugh, raking his fingers through his hair, walking to the waterline and back.

"And this—" I reach into my pack and pull out the book. "Check this out." Its cardboard-bound pages of thoughts, theorems, equations in ink and pencil are all here, faded and smudged but exactly as when Conner, Abby, and I found them on that cold-blasted morning on Eagle Peak, days, weeks, or was it eons ago?

I hold the book out to him, and as he takes it from me, it's like a circle has closed: secrets returned to their rightful owner. I try to bridge that morning on Eagle Peak to here, wherever *here* is, and know deep down that it's absurd to bridge *here* and *there* in space and time, that the gap is beyond reckoning.

Dad closes the book and looks up at me, his smile gone now. "But why you, Dev? Why not Bollinger or Anton or—?"

"Bollinger . . . No. Bollinger is dead. Triton killed him."

He doesn't reply, only sighs, the shock washing over him.

"They took everything. The servers. All the data. They took Megan and Anton too."

Now I tell him the whole story, starting with the airburst over LA, how the parasites in the rocks are also the cause of a terrible outbreak overrunning cities. I tell him about the journey to Tahoe, to the bunker, Bollinger's betrayal, the raid. About Dix, about Abby trying to get to her family. And how we lost Conner.

He lets out a long, tired breath. "I'm so sorry."

I hesitate then. "And there's something else." I feel tears welling up. "Mom."

He darts his eyes to me, puzzled. "Yes?"

After I tell him, he drops to the sand and bows his head to his knees. I crouch down beside him and put my hand on his shoulder. His eyes are closed, shaded by the book clutched in both hands. I see that he's quietly sobbing, shaking his head, fighting to contain his hurt. He hadn't seen her in seventy-odd days. But, for her, it had been ten years. She'd been grieving him all this time, and now he's grieving her for the first time. And again, it's like a circle has closed.

I gaze out at the cove, at the moons. "But it's all happening in another world." And the terror in me grows. "I don't know where we are, Dad."

He doesn't answer for a while, I don't press him. He sniffs and clears his throat, reaches down and takes off his shoes. After rolling up his jeans, he wades out to the pod, its hatch wide open. He crouches low and peeks in. Finally, he shimmies inside. I can hear him fiddling around with something for a minute before he emerges, his legs plopping back into the water. He shuts the latch and straightens up as he wades back. In the crook of one arm, I see a shiny tube—it's the steel cylinder I remember seeing attached to the wall of the pod.

He drops the cylinder into my backpack, along with the book. Collecting his breath, he nods at the pod. "Should be safe here for the time being." He doesn't speak, just puts his shoes on, lost in his own world of thoughts. I can't blame him.

As he stands, wipes the sand off the back of his jeans, I ask him, "What is this place?"

He slings my pack at his shoulder. "Maybe the best way to answer that, Dev, is to ask where *you* think you are."

I look around, breathe in the air. "Earth? But . . . not Earth, obviously."

"And you'd be right." He places a hand on my shoulder. "There's so much to tell you. But let's get to shelter. We can talk there, and you can rest. Come on." He leads the way up a low slope toward the trees. My first steps are unsteady, but soon we're walking side by side.

A buzzing rises, nearing, and I duck in time to avoid a dragonfly the size of my head whirr away against the sun. *Whoa!* I'm collecting my breath when there's a splash on the far shore and a crocodile shape lunging, then retreating into the water as a slender-necked *something* flaps on yellow-gold wings deeper into the brush.

"Did you . . . did you see?"

"You'll be seeing a lot of weird things here. We need to be careful."

Ripples settle across the water, and the cove is still again, shimmering. From the sandy slope, I follow him through a patch of flowering trees, their leaves as big as hands. Birdcalls fill the air, echoing off the canopy. At the edge of the trees, he picks up a walking stick—really just a long, stout branch—and taps at the ground and the trunks of trees as he walks. "Keeps the critters away," he informs me. He walks on, staying a couple of steps ahead.

"Where are we going?"

"It's not far. Up the ridge on the other side of these trees."

"Dad." And I stop in my tracks. He turns to me. There is so much I need to know. But only one question really matters right now. "Is there a way back?"

He arches his brows and looks at me inquisitively. "Well?"

I know he wants me to search within and find my own answer. It's his way. But my mind is numb from exhaustion. And the exhaustion is a balm, sealing me off from memories of all I've left behind, my fears of all that's to come. I'm only aware of one name and one face and the aching wish to be with her again. "If there's a way here," I answer, "there's a way back."

A Note from the Author

Thank you for spending quality time with this book. If you enjoyed *Edge of Light*, I hope you'll consider leaving a review on Amazon, Goodreads, or the online bookseller of your choice. Even a few lines could really help in attracting potential readers.

And if you'd like more *Edge of Light* news, updates, and info, please visit jayantani.com and sign up for my mailing list. Currently, I'm hard at work on the book's sequel, and my site is also where you'll find updates on that front. Thanks, again.

I appreciate your readership. Let's stay in touch!

Acknowledgments

As fascinating as it was to watch countless videos about particle physics and the multiverse and to read books about cosmology and time travel, I needed much more in bringing this book to life. I needed dedicated beta readers like Susan Antani, Sharon Coleman, Lonya Julin, Paul Morrissey, David Schreiber, Carol Stutz, and Claudia Zaniolo, all of whom provided essential and insightful feedback on successive drafts. I'm deeply grateful to them and to editors David Downing and Lynda Dietz, both world-class storycraft specialists. Many thanks also to Rafael Andres, for lending his superb design chops to creating such a beautiful book. And finally, I want to thank my family, friends, and my readers for helping to transform all this scribbling into a real and blessed vocation.

Made in the USA
Middletown, DE
20 November 2020

24470879R00195